MW01611033

WOODSIDE

Sisters of Woodside Mysteries

Book 5

A Regency Romance

by Mary Kingswood

Published by Sutors Publishing

Copyright © 2019 Mary Kingswood

ISBN: 978-1-912167-22-7 (paperback)

Cover design by: Shayne Rutherford of Darkmoon Graphics

All rights reserved. This is a work of fiction.

Author's note:

this book is written using historic British terminology, so *saloon* instead of *salon*, *chaperon* instead of *chaperone* and so on. I follow Jane Austen's example and refer to a group of sisters as the Miss Wintertons.

Woodside: Sisters of Woodside Mysteries Book 5

About the book: *The dramatic conclusion to the series!*

Ten years have passed since the sisters of Woodside found happiness. Their grief for their young brother, Jeremy, tragically drowned at the age of twelve, has faded. The sadness of losing their home, Woodside, to strangers is but a memory. They no longer wonder just what became of their mother's fabulous jewels, which should have guaranteed their dowries. They are looking forwards, not back into the past.

But the past is not always willing to be left behind. In the industrial north of England, a young man can only step into his own future if he revisits the past. And so he begins a journey that will change everything the sisters thought they knew, and reveal the darkest secrets of the Winterton family of Woodside.

The final book of the Sisters of Woodside Mysteries series. This is a complete story with a HEA, but is best read after the earlier books. A traditional Regency romance, drawing room rather than bedroom.

About the series: *When Mr Edmund Winterton of Woodside dies, his daughters find themselves penniless and homeless. What can they do? Unless they wish to live on charity, they will have to find genteel employment for themselves. This book is set in England during the Regency period of the early nineteenth century. Book 0 takes place 5 years before books 1-4, and book 5 ten years later.*

Book 0: The Betrothed (Rosamund) (a short novel, free to mailing list subscribers)

Book 1: The Governess (Annabelle)

Book 2: The Chaperon (Lucy)

Book 3: The Companion (Margaret)

Book 4: The Seamstress (Fanny)

Book 5: Woodside

Want to be the first to hear about new releases? Sign up for my mailing list at: http://marykingswood.co.uk.

Table of contents

The story so far...

Woodside, in the village of Frickham in the county of Brinshire, was home to the Winterton family — Mr Edmund Winterton, a gentleman, and his wife Anne, together with their six children, Rosamund, Annabelle, Lucy, Margaret, Fanny and Jeremy. They were an ordinary sort of family, contented enough with their lot, although with the usual little disagreements that befall any group of people living in close proximity to each other, without much variety to their lives. But the seasons passed pleasantly enough, there was sufficient money for their needs and the children grew up.

Mrs Winterton sickened and, in time, died, but the very same year an even greater tragedy befell the family. Twelve-year-old Jeremy was sent away to sea to be a midshipman and learn to be a man worthy to inherit the Woodside estate. Within a week of boarding, his ship had sunk with all hands to the bottom of the Irish Sea. Mr Winterton consoled his grief with brandy and dice, and when this did not answer, he gambled with ever greater recklessness and began to fall into severe debt. His wife's jewellery, worth a fortune that he now needed, was nowhere to be found. Rosamund, the eldest daughter, escaped the now comfortless house by marrying a neighbour, but for the remaining four daughters, left with their increasingly erratic father, their only comfort was each other.

Five years after Jeremy's death, Mr Winterton died, bequeathing to his daughters the house of Woodside and a mountain of debts. They were destitute. The four remaining daughters had to leave the only home they had ever known to find genteel employment as a governess, a chaperon, a companion and a seamstress. But Providence (and love) favoured them, and, despite great trials, each of them found a man to cherish them. Woodside was sold to settle the debts, and the sisters of Woodside married and moved on with their lives.

Ten years after these traumatic events, they are all well settled.

Rosamund is married to Mr Robin Dalton, now Baron Westerlea. They live at Westerlea Park in Frickham, just a mile away from Woodside, with their four children (two boys and two girls), and Robin's Aunt Mary.

Annabelle is married to Allan Skelton, the Earl of Brackenwood. They live at Charlsby, near Kenford in Cheshire, together with his three daughters from his first marriage, and their own three (a boy, a girl, then another boy), plus his mother.

Lucy is married to the very wealthy Leo Audley of Stoneleigh Hall, in Shropshire, and Bath. They have a son and a daughter.

Margaret is married to Mel Haymer, a clergyman, and heir to Viscount Delacrost. They live at Pendarreth in Shropshire with their two sons.

Fanny is married to Ferdy Makenham, Viscount Craston, heir to the Marquess of Dilborough. They live at Lennister Hall, in the West Riding of Yorkshire with their three sons and a daughter, and adopted orphan Eddy Smith.

Woodside is now the home of Mr Geoffrey Tyrrell, a widower, and his unmarried daughter Jane.

Of Jeremy's tragic death, a few small snippets of information had emerged. Captain Hunt had seen him to his ship in Liverpool, but reported that he was small of stature, and very keen on his new career — quite unlike Jeremy. It seemed possible that Jeremy had fallen victim to footpads, and been killed for his uniform and small purse of coins, with some other boy taking his place. But the Moreton family, with whom he had stayed in Liverpool before taking ship, had happy memories of him which relieved the sisters' minds of some of their concerns. They had tried to contact Johnny Moreton, who had befriended Jeremy in Liverpool, but to no avail, and with their busy married lives, they thought about their brother less and less.

Meanwhile, in the small mill town of Branton, in Lancashire, a young man turns his thoughts to Woodside and ponders his future...

The Winterton family

Hi-res versions of all family trees available at:
http://marykingswood.co.uk.

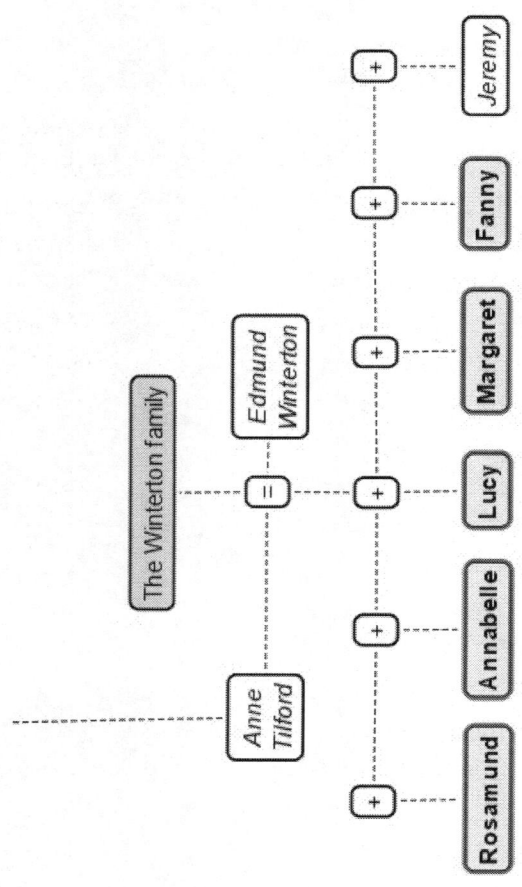

1: A Journey (March)

John Moreton stared unseeingly at the page of the book he held. The only sound in the room was the occasional shifting of the coals on the fire, and his uncle's rustling newspaper. He reached for his port glass, sipped, then replaced it on the small table beside him. Then, with a sigh, he closed the book.

His uncle's newspaper lowered, and he looked over the top of it at John, a wry smile on his face. "It is a big step, is it not? Takes a deal of thinking about. That was partly why I never married myself — never could wind myself up to do it."

John laughed and shook his head in resignation. "You always know what I'm thinking, you old rascal."

"You have the world's most expressive face, Johnny. I can read you like a book — better, at all events, than you are managing with yours. Have you turned a single page since we came through after dinner?"

"Not a one." He grinned ruefully. "It *is* a big step, but it is not the prospect of marriage that makes me thoughtful. I decided long ago on that head, and Ridwell has been tolerably encouraging."

"And the lady?"

"Ellen will follow her father's wishes. She is a dutiful daughter."

"She's a cold fish, that's what she is," his uncle said sharply. "You haven't asked for my advice, but I'll give it anyway. If it were me, I'd look for a cosier wife to bed, and never mind about the mill."

"Never mind the mill?" John said, shaking his head in bemusement. "Cragforth? Ridwell's most profitable? A fine dowry, indeed."

"If it's money you want, I'll increase your share of the profits from Hazlehead — fifty fifty, how does that sound? You do all the work anyway, so it's more than fair, and you'll get the lot when I'm gone. Don't make a wrong choice, Johnny. You're not the type to look for your fun elsewhere, and I'd hate to see you unhappy."

"I'd as soon have a mill of my own than any amount of money. Besides, Ellen's a rare beauty."

"Cold fish," his uncle muttered, but a smile softened the words.

"She will be warmer once we're wed and she's out from under that mother of hers."

"Ha! I wish you joy of *that*. But if it is not the prospect of being leg-shackled that has you ruminating, what is it?"

"Unfinished business," John said thoughtfully. "If I'm to be wed, I must needs settle all the loose threads of my former life. I may need to go on a journey. You will not mind that, I daresay? Hadley and Donwell will take good care of Hazlehead while I'm gone."

"How long?"

"A month, perhaps. Maybe a little more." A hesitation. "Will you manage without me for that long? I don't like to think of you all alone here of an evening, with no one to thrash at piquet."

His uncle chuckled. "I shall be fine. I have my friends for whist once a week, and Donwell plays a reasonable game of piquet. There's always the club if I need company. I'll miss you, of course, but it will do you good to see something of the world beyond this part of Lancashire. You've not left it since you came here fifteen years ago. Where are you off to — Liverpool?"

"No... Not Liverpool, although some day perhaps I must go back to see the family, I suppose. Not that they take any interest in me. The only time I ever hear from them is when there is a death or a wedding. I never knew I had so many female relations of marriageable age, but ever since I sent twenty guineas to Jenny, they have all come crawling out of the woodwork."

His uncle cackled with laughter. "Aye, when there's money to be had, they're all about. But where, then, if not Liverpool? You never mentioned interests elsewhere."

"Brinshire. Woodside, the home of Jeremy Winterton. Do you recall the tale? He stayed with the family in Liverpool before he went to sea. I have had in mind for some time now to go and see his people, to tell them... well, the truth. They deserve to know what really happened to their son."

His uncle lowered his paper fully, folded it neatly and put it aside. "Winterton, eh? Be careful with the truth, Johnny — it's a very sharp sword."

"I know it, but I believe it must be done before I marry."

"Hmm." His uncle watched him thoughtfully for a moment, then heaved himself to his feet. He was only twenty years older than John, and not yet fifty, but already his joints were showing the reluctance of age. "There is something you should see before you go." He went to his desk, the private one he kept for his personal papers, unlocked a drawer and withdrew a folded paper. "A man came looking for you... oh, it must be ten years ago now. Not a Winterton, but a friend of one of them, wanting to talk to you about this Jeremy Winterton fellow. Walked in here as bold as brass in all his London frippery. I never saw the like! Here... his card, and the letter he sent in with it. You were at the mill that day, but I thought you'd not want to be bothered with it, so I never mentioned it."

John turned the card over in his hands. *'Mr Ferdinand Makenham, 25 Harlington Terrace, Sagborough, West Riding'* "I do not recognise the name."

"Why should you, indeed? Who is he to us? I did not like it above half, I tell you. I gave him my aged imbecile impersonation and told him you were gone to America, and he seemed convinced. Never came back, anyway. But there, if you're going to the Wintertons, it's as well to know about it, in case the name comes up."

John read the letter, but it told him nothing that his uncle had not already said. It was high-handed of him, but it was true, he would not have wanted to deal with such a person, not then. Ten years ago, or even less, he would have been discomfited by anyone asking about Jeremy Winterton. How fortunate that Uncle Giles had got rid of him, and even more fortunate that Mr Ferdinand Makenham had never thought to return to Branton. John had not been ready to deal with the Wintertons before. But now... now he must. Yes, this was the right time to do it.

~~~~~

It would be an awkward interview, that much was certain. John toyed with the idea of wearing his newest coat, only just delivered from his tailor in Lancaster, but that would impart an unwarranted importance to the occasion. He chose his third best coat instead, and walked briskly out of the house, past the modest mill which brought his uncle's wealth. Almost without conscious thought, he assessed the constant thrum of the engine and the looms, his expert ears listening for the slightest untoward tremor. Lady Hazlehead, he called her, his precious engine, so anxiously tended and cosseted. But today all was well. The engine was alive and well and driving the many looms.

He made his way into town by way of the new bridge, then turned away from the line of mills lining the river and began the gentle climb to the hill. It had an official designation in the parish records, but to everyone in Branton it was merely *the hill* — the place where the wealthiest or grandest of the town's inhabitants lived, far from the bustle and noise and smoke that paid for their fine houses and secluded gardens.

The Ridwells lived in the finest house with the most secluded gardens. A matched pair of bewigged Negro footmen in dazzling gold-trimmed livery opened the front door to him before he knocked. He had never had to use the knocker, he reflected, nor the gilt bell-pull. Inside the marble-pillared hall, two Negro boys relieved him of hat and gloves, while a butler and two more footmen stood by. The pillars and statuary from Italy would have given the hall an air of cool, classical style, were it not decorated with a multitude of silver sconces and crystal chandeliers, gold-framed paintings covering every inch of wall, cherubs flying all across the ceiling, six full sized potted palm trees and a stuffed elephant. The hall was capacious, but it felt very crowded.

The butler bowed low.

"Good morning, Weald, and how are you today?" John said. "Recovered from that chill that laid you low?"

"Good morning, Mr Moreton, sir. How kind in you to enquire about my health. I am happy to assure you that I am quite recovered now. May I convey you to the ladies? They are in the gold saloon today."

"Thank you, Weald, but my business this morning is with Mr Ridwell."

The butler inclined his head. "Then pray follow me, sir."

Henry Ridwell's library was large, an over-sized room filled with over-sized furniture, and shelves of books bought by the yard, although at least there were no cherubs to be seen. Every room at Ridwell Court was large, designed to impress, although it was hard to know who might be impressed by it, for the Ridwells were too important to mingle much with the inhabitants of Branton, and not important enough to be acquainted with anyone of true rank in the county. A man who could see the smoke of his own weaving sheds from his house would never be acceptable company for a gentleman.

Their only daughter, Ellen, had been given two seasons in London in the hope that her beauty would attract a noble, or at least a respectable, husband. But it seemed that London society had no value for a dowry that came in the form of bricks and glass and a very large beam engine, for despite her beauty Ellen had returned unwed and the Ridwells had lowered their sights a trifle. That was when their eye had fallen on John.

"Well now, Moreton," Ridwell said affably, a companionable arm around John's shoulders. "What brings you to me rather than to the ladies, eh? Ellen is looking very lovely today."

"Miss Ridwell looks lovely every day." John said politely. "Regretfully, I am come to bid you farewell, for I have business that takes me away from Lancashire."

"Ah. But it will not keep you from Ellen's side for long, I'll wager."

"I shall be gone for a month or two," John said evenly.

That caused a raised eyebrow. "Serious business, Moreton, to detain you so long."

"It needs to be done. I have delayed it for too long, but can delay no longer. I must… settle my accounts, so to speak."

"Ah — yes, indeed. Clear away all the outstanding matters and start with a clean slate. An excellent notion. Are you away soon?"

"This very day. The chaise is ordered and my valet is packing as we speak, so…"

"Of course, of course, but you will not rush away without seeing the ladies?"

John allowed himself to be led out of the room, across the hall, through the newly refurbished Chinese saloon draped with overpowering red damask, and into the gold saloon, its white walls with narrow green panels cold and unwelcoming to John's eyes. He had preferred the blue that had prevailed last year. Next year, perhaps, it would be rose pink or lavender.

The two ladies sat at either end of a chaise longue, Ellen playing with the fringe of her shawl, while her mother waved her embroidery frame as she talked. She broke off at once as the two men entered.

"Mr Moreton! How delightful! What an unexpected pleasure! Look, Ellen, Mr Moreton is here to see us."

She held out her hand to be bowed over, simpering girlishly at him. But then she dressed like a girl, too. The two women wore gowns identically styled, with the same gold sash and shawl, their hair arranged in the same artfully disordered curls. Even their necklaces and bracelets were similar. Only the colours of their gowns — green for the mother, virginal white for the daughter, chosen to match the walls — and the wisp of lace on Mrs Ridwell's head distinguished them.

"Mrs Ridwell, how delightful you look today. And Miss Ridwell, as lovely as ever." He disliked such arrant flattery, but the Ridwells seemed to expect it.

"Thank you, sir. You are most kind," Ellen said with a polite smile, her voice carefully modulated. "How pleasant to see you again."

She was a beauty, there was no doubt, and every man would envy him when she was his wife. From her abundant golden hair and skin as luscious as a ripe peach, to her delicate, slippered feet, she was perfection, a vision to turn heads wherever she went. He could imagine himself entering a drawing room with Ellen on his arm — *'Mr and Mrs John Moreton'*, the butler would say, or perhaps, in time, it would be *'Sir John and Lady Moreton'*. Ellen. His Ellen, in a few weeks. A lovely creature, who moved with grace and smiled a great deal. There was no warmth in her eyes, but he did not ask for warmth in his wife, only compliance.

Perhaps if he had ever fallen in love or felt even the tiniest tremor of affection for a woman he would not view marriage so pragmatically, but in truth, he knew himself to be every bit as cold as Ellen. His heart was as frozen as hers — two creatures trapped in an icy carapace, all warmth leached out of them by circumstances, or, in Ellen's case, by her mother. But once they were married, they could thaw each other's hearts and be happy. Or contented, at least.

He did not stay long at the Ridwell's, and in truth he scarcely listened to their expressions of regret at his impending absence. He would be back — he knew it, and they did too. Soon, he would return and then... he would marry Ellen and be master of Cragforth

Mill, and he would have taken his first step on the road to being *somebody*. It was his destiny.

~~~~~

Brinshire was a shock. Hardly any towns, and the villages as poor as in Lancashire, with urchins running barefoot in the mud alongside the post-chaise. Each village consisted of a church, a shabby inn and a row or two of dilapidated cottages, that was all. Then farms and scrubby woodlands and scrawny sheep until the next pathetic village. Occasionally he would catch a glimpse of a substantial house tucked away behind high walls or at the bottom of a long drive. Once, he saw a shooting party crossing a distant field, dogs at their heels, and he had an unexpected yearning to be part of that way of life, to spend his days in drawing rooms or out on his own land, to dine with lords and dance with ladies. To be not just somebody, but a gentleman. One day, perhaps, he could make that claim.

Frickham was a little larger than most villages, boasting two inns, a well-kept church, a smithy, an apothecary and two properties of substance, Westerlea Park and Woodside. He left his valet to settle in at the Frickham Inn, and walked through the village until he came to a pair of stone gateposts, high and sturdy. 'Woodside', they said, in neatly engraved letters. There was no lodge, and none needed, for there were no gates to be opened or closed. Just the posts, and a short gravel drive, the house glimpsed through the trees lining it.

Taking a deep breath, he passed through the entrance and began the walk up the drive, his boots crunching on the gravel. There before him was the house, a plain frontage with mismatched wings on either side, one of earlier date, and one later. He rapped loudly with the door knocker, then stood back and waited.

After an age, the door opened. A stern-faced young woman stood on the threshold, dressed in neat grey poplin, a small cap on her head, hands clasped in front of her. The housekeeper, to judge by the chatelaine at her waist. "Yes?"

"Good day. Is Mr Winterton at home?"

An odd look crossed her face. "Mr *Winterton?* You will find him in the churchyard. He has been dead these ten years."

The world spun. John felt the blow as surely as if he had been punched in the stomach. *Dead?* How could he be dead? He sagged against the door frame, and would have fallen but for its support. Of all the outcomes he had considered for this journey, that was the one that had never occurred to him. How had he missed the notice in the newspaper? Surely the death of Edmund Winterton of Woodside would have been posted? But — ten years ago! He had not bothered to read the London papers then, so no wonder he had known nothing of it.

"Now, do not collapse like a balloon, for people die all the time," the housekeeper said gruffly. "Here, take my arm. Come inside and sit down for a minute, but whatever you do, do not fall down, for it will take four men to lift you again, a great tall fellow like you."

He breathed, pulled himself off the door frame to stand upright, breathed again. The odd, sick feeling passed and the world stopped spinning. Even so, he felt weak.

"Thank you, I will come in for a moment."

He walked — no, staggered — into the hall unaided, and collapsed into a chair beside the console, the housekeeper hovering nearby.

"Are you about to swoon again like a girl? If so, I have smelling salts to wave under your nose, but if you can manage to stay conscious, brandy might be a more apt remedy for a man as large as you."

"Thank you, yes, a little brandy would be helpful."

She bustled off down the passage to the kitchens, and he heard low voices, then the chink of glass. She came back with the brandy in a wine glass.

"Here, drink this. I never meant to give you such a shock. It never occurred to me, not after ten years. How did you not know? Were you in Australia or some such place?"

That made him splutter into his brandy. "Lancashire," he said indignantly. "There's some that might like to see me transported, I daresay, but it hasn't happened yet."

"Lancashire," she mused. "Yes, I can hear the accent now. For a moment I mistook you for a gentleman. Still, you have come a fair distance to see Mr Winterton, so I am sorry your journey has been wasted."

John pushed down rising exasperation. He had suffered worse insults before, after all, although it was a bit rich coming from the housekeeper. "Who lives here now?" he said.

"My father. Geoffrey Tyrrell."

"Oh... I took you for the housekeeper. My apologies, Mrs... er?"

"Miss. Miss Jane Tyrrell." Her eyes were a cool grey, looking at him with disfavour. Well, at least the insults were evenly balanced now.

"Miss? Then why the cap? You are not so old as to despair of ever finding a husband."

"I thank you for the *compliment*, sir," she said acidly, "but I am five and twenty, and unlikely now to meet a man of sense who is not already wed, or too old to want to be so."

"You astonish me, Miss Tyrrell. Brinshire must indeed be devoid of men of sense if there is not a single one to be found willing to lead you to the altar."

"It seems to me that Lancashire is equally devoid of men of sense, if you are typical of the county," she shot back.

He laughed at that. "*Touché*, Miss Tyrrell. I will allow my county to be every bit as wanting in sense as yours. Are you always this waspish, or only to men of Lancashire? It seems to me that we have got off on quite the wrong foot. Allow me to prove myself not entirely devoid of manners. I am John Moreton, manager of Hazlehead Mill in Branton in Lancashire, and, as you so aptly pointed out, not a gentleman." He swallowed the last of the brandy, and set the glass down on the console.

In housewifely fashion, she picked it up, with her handkerchief wiped away the small ring it had left and set it carefully on the cloth beneath the vase of dried stems that stood there.

"Are you *sure* you're not the housekeeper?" he said teasingly, and her lips quirked into the promise of a smile, instantly repressed.

"In a way, I am," she said, her tone softer now. "Havelock gets so muddled now that I cannot even trust her with the keys to the linen cupboard."

Havelock... He remembered that name.

"Thank you for the brandy," he said, rising unsteadily to his feet. "I should go and leave you in peace."

"Not until I am sure you are yourself again," she said firmly. "Let the brandy do its work. Mr Moreton, I do not know what your business was with Mr Winterton, and he left no son behind that you might deal with, nor any male relative that I ever heard, but he had five daughters who may be able to help you. They would know the name of his attorney, if it is a legal matter."

Before he could reply, the knocker sounded.

"And this might be one of them," she said. "I sent word to Rosamund."

She opened the door, and there stood a matron resplendent in velvet and fur, who swept into the hall in a cloud of exotic perfume.

"Whatever is going on, Jane? Someone asking for Papa?"

"Indeed. This is Mr John Moreton, from Branton in Lancashire. Mr Moreton, this is Lady Westerlea, eldest daughter of the late Mr Winterton. I am sure she will... Rosamund? Whatever is the matter?"

She had gone as white as a sheet. "*Moreton?* John Moreton? No, *that* you are not... Good God... is it possible? *Jeremy?*"

So there it was. There was no hiding now.

"Hello, Rosie. You're looking well."

2: *Woodside*

"How dare you? *How dare you?*" From the feathers trimming her very expensive hat to the dainty kid boots, dyed to match her pelisse, Rosamund quivered with righteous indignation. John bowed his head under the onslaught. "How dare you turn up here after all these years? How dared you let us think you were *dead?* We grieved for you for years — *years!*" She paced up and down the hall, and his only thought, incongruous as it might be, was that the familiar threadbare rug had gone, replaced by a neat strip of something richly coloured. But Rosamund's tirade rattled on. "Ha! Fanny was right, then. Whoever would have guessed it? She thought you were alive after some captain or other — Captain Hunt, that was it — he saw you just before you boarded your ship, but he said you were small, and very keen to be at sea, which sounded nothing like the Jeremy we knew."

"Rosie—"

"Do not call me that!" she cried, stopping right in front of him. "You have no right, not any more. Poor Fanny! Poor, poor Fanny. She was so excited — someone must have taken your place, she said, because it could not possibly have been you that Captain Hunt saw, so you must still be alive. And we had to explain to her gently that it could not conceivably be so, because how could you still be alive and *not let us know?* Any normal, feeling son would *tell* his family if he was believed drowned and yet lived. Any person with an *ounce* of kindness in his body would have done so, but you did not. Why, Jeremy, why?"

He ran his hands through his hair. How could he possibly explain it? "Rosie—" She stamped her foot. "Rosamund... Lady Westerlea..."

"Better." And then, as abruptly as it had started, the storm blew over, and the Rosamund he remembered reasserted herself. "Pfft. What are we doing, shouting at each other in Jane's hall? Come for dinner tonight, Jeremy. Robin will want to meet you, and we have no other guests invited today, so you can explain it all to us at your leisure, if you can. You remember where the Park is?"

"Of course." He made her an ironic bow before remembering that Rosamund was probably impervious to irony. Her question was genuine, as if somehow he might have forgotten everything from the first twelve years of his life.

"We dine at six, and we dress formally." Her eyes ran up and down him, the question left unsaid.

He answered it anyway. "I shall inform my valet." He saw the relief in her eyes. She too had feared he was not a gentleman, and he was not, it was true, but he had all the trappings of it — the valet, the silk evening breeches and stockings, the intricately tied neckcloth, and if his valet helped a little with the latter, it was a secret kept by the two of them.

Dinner at Westerlea Park. Well, that was unexpected.

~~~~~

Jane shut the door behind them with mixed feelings. Relief, primarily, but also disappointment. So little happened in Frickham! Day after day, week after week, month after dreary month — the seasons rolled round with little excitement to relieve the monotony. And now something dramatic had happened, the long-dead Winterton son was returned in the very bloom of manly good-health, and she was excluded from it all. Rosamund would tell her some of it, undoubtedly, but how she longed to hear it from the man himself. Mr Moreton. Mr Winterton. Whatever his name was.

Such a handsome man! Seeing the two of them side by side, Rosamund and Jeremy, sister and brother, she could see the family likeness — the same green eyes, the same well-sculpted nose and chin, the same regularity of features. Yes, he was as good-looking a man as she had ever seen, and so imposingly tall... tall *and* broad about the shoulders and chest. Not a man to be ignored, in any company. His speech was not all it might be, with that hint of a Lancashire accent, but that came and went, and he was quick enough of mind, that much was certain.

Betsy was loitering near the service stairs, but Jane dismissed her with a flick of her head. Then she walked through to the eastern wing and her father's study. He was hard at work with his day's collection, paintbrush in hand.

"More snowdrops, Papa?" she said, then bent to kiss the top of his head.

He patted her hand absently where it rested on his shoulder. "I like snowdrops. Who was that at the door?"

"Mr Jeremy Winterton."

Geoffrey Tyrrell laid down his paintbrush, removed his spectacles and turned to look at her fully. "Jeremy *Winterton*? A long-lost cousin?"

"A son. To be precise, a long-dead son. Drowned, I think. He looks quite well for a man who has spent a dozen years and more with the fishes."

Her father chuckled. "But... how? And why? Why now? Has he been abroad all these years? Lost his memory?"

"Who knows? I do not, for Rosamund came and shouted at him, then sent him away. He is to dine at the Park tonight, so we shall only hear what she cares to tell us."

"Hmm. But what is he like? Age? Disposition? Well-dressed?"

Jane smiled. "So many questions. Let me see... tolerably well-dressed. His clothes are serviceable rather than fashionable, but well made. In looks, he is much like Rosamund — a male version of her. He is about my age, or a little older. As to his disposition, I cannot tell you. His manners are acceptable, if not polished, although his accent needs improvement."

"Will he call again, do you suppose?" She lifted one shoulder in a shrug. "Well, if he does, or if you encounter him in the village, invite him to come and see me."

"You might encounter him yourself on your rambles about the countryside."

"And pass him by, unrecognised," he said with a gentle laugh.

"Oh, you will recognise him," she said. "He is as large as a giant."

"He intrigues me more with every moment," her father said. "I should very much like to meet this Jeremy Winterton."

~~~~~

John was always conscious of his appearance when he dressed for a formal evening engagement. During the day, he would select for practical reasons — buckskins and top boots for riding, pantaloons and hessians for visiting the town, practical dark moleskins for his days at the mill. Choosing a coat was the only difficult part of the operation. But for evening wear, he always felt trussed up like a bird ready for the spit. He was too large and ungainly for elegance, but nevertheless he was obliged to wear the conventional garb. Flimsy silks, lightweight shoes, a delicately embroidered waistcoat, a too-tight coat and finally the curse of the starched neckcloth, over which he and his valet laboured for upwards of half an hour, sometimes. And then he could barely turn his head.

There was no closed carriage for hire at the inn that day, so he was driven to Westerlea Park in a lowly gig, thankful that it was not raining. It was an imposing house, fit for the residence of a baron and his lady, and John envied them just a little — not the title particularly, but the gilded life of elegant rooms, manicured lawns and silent, efficient servants, far, far away from the noisome chimneys and eternal racket of a mill town.

As the gig pulled up, a footman emerged to assist him to alight, and at the entrance a butler awaited, his silhouette stark in the evening gloom as light spilled from the house behind him. In the entrance hall John was relieved of cloak, hat and gloves, then the butler led him in stately procession to the drawing room. Why was it that butlers always moved so slowly? They must once have been limber footmen, but as soon as they assumed the mantle of butler, they became pompous and superior, never moving anywhere at above the pace of a slug.

"Mr John Moreton, my lady." So they were keeping to the false name. Interesting.

The drawing room was plain compared with the Ridwells' overblown decorations, but there was an elegance about it — indeed, about the whole house — which John could recognise, even if it was not much to his taste. The colours were restrained, furniture was arranged in artful groupings and there were no cherubs on the ceiling. He hated cherubs on the ceiling.

Lord Westerlea rose to greet him, looking every inch the nobleman, young enough to be slim and healthy, old enough to have developed an air of gravitas. Rosamund's features had softened with the years, but she was not yet stout and would still be accounted a beauty. Both of them were fearsomely fashionable in the London manner, and everything about them reeked of old money, carelessly taken for granted.

How much were they worth? He found it difficult to judge these estates. Show him a mill or a manufactory, a shop or a warehouse, and he could estimate the owner's income to within fifty pounds. But these grand houses might conceal a world of debts, and who could say how much the tenancies would bring in? Still, if he had to guess, Westerlea Park must be worth three times the value of Woodside, so perhaps six thousand a year. No wonder Rosamund was growing fat on such riches. And a baroness — yes, she had done well.

There were greetings, smiles, some business with sherry, and then they made civil conversation until dinner was announced. His journey, the state of the roads and his accommodation at the inn took them through the first course, and then there was Branton to be discussed. They asked nothing about his mill.

Eventually, the butler and footmen withdrew, and as the gentlemen finished their claret and Rosamund ate a fruit pie with cream and then some syllabub, they came to the point.

"We have not told anyone who you are," Lord Westerlea said. "Your true identity is for you to reveal, as you choose."

"It hardly matters, since it will be known everywhere within a day," Rosamund said, her spoon suspended in mid-air. "Jane Tyrrell is a dreadful gossip."

"Still, a little discretion never goes amiss," Lord Westerlea said.

"I expected it to be known," John said easily. "I came here to reveal myself, after all. The only surprise is that Papa is dead and I had not the least idea of it."

"The notices were posted in the newspapers," Lord Westerlea said. "Did you not happen to see them? Letters were sent also to your father's few remaining relations. Had I known of your existence—"

"Of course," John said easily. "The blame is entirely mine, I quite accept that. I never read that section of the London newspapers, only the news items, although occasionally a line from the society reports catches my eye. Lady Craston dancing at the Marford House ball, for instance — *'the former Miss Frances Winterton'*. That was a delight to read — little Fanny a viscountess! You were mentioned once or twice, Rosie, and is Annabelle married to an earl? The print was smudged and I could not quite make it out."

"Yes, she is Lady Brackenwood now, and Margaret is married to Lord Delacrost's heir, a viscount. Only Lucy's husband has no title, but he is as rich as Croesus, so she does not repine."

"How well you have all married! So many changes to get used to."

"There must be much that is different, or has been forgotten after so long," Lord Westerlea said, with unexpected sympathy.

"Indeed. Like you, for example," John said with a wry grimace. "I thought I remembered the heir to the barony, but he was nothing like you. My memory must be faulty." He recalled a bluff, tall man, always active, sensibly dressed, not like this dandy.

The baron smiled, seeming abruptly younger and less austere. "That would be my older brother, Richard, who died. I am the younger brother, Robin. I doubt we ever met."

"Ah." John glanced at Rosamund, recalling the widespread expectation that she would marry Richard. Yet here she was married to Robin.

Rosamund sighed and set down her spoon. "I was betrothed to Richard, but then he was killed a few days before the wedding. Thrown from his horse while hunting. I married Robin instead."

She said it so plainly, as if it were the most normal thing in the world when one's betrothed died to transfer one's affections at once to the next brother in line. It seemed cold, almost heartless, but then Rosamund had always been practical. Besides, John's own marriage plans were every bit as calculating.

"You need not look so disapproving, brother," she went on. "Richard left me in difficulties, and Robin very gallantly offered to rescue me from my predicament. We have been, and continue to be, very happy together. Oh, but—! I never enquired — are you married, Jeremy?"

He laughed, hesitating, not quite used to the name. "Not yet. I am… considering matrimony, and I am not in the least disapproving of marriage for pragmatic reasons. The lady I have my eye on has two attractions — her great beauty and a fine cotton mill. When I marry her, she will make me a very wealthy man. *If* I marry her, I should say, for I have not yet spoken, although her father knows I intend to."

"So that is why you came — to obtain your father's blessing on the union?" Lord Westerlea said.

"Not exactly, no." He hesitated but there was no point in prevaricating. "I came to secure my inheritance — Woodside. To tell my father that his son and heir yet lives. Or his *eldest* son, perhaps?"

"There have been no more sons," Rosamund said sombrely. "Nor daughters either. Papa never remarried."

"Oh." That was a surprise. "I thought—"

"So did we all, but nothing came of it."

"Interesting," John said. "So part of my reason for staying away was without foundation. I did *not* want a step-mother. At least, not *that* step-mother."

"Nor did any of us," Rosamund said in a low voice. "Although in some ways it might have been better— However, it was all a long time ago. Jeremy, will you explain to me *all* your reasons to stay away, for I confess that it still seems a cruel undertaking to me. I imagine we can guess how it began. Since you are in Lancashire, pretending to be Johnny Moreton, we must presume that the real Johnny Moreton is at the bottom of the sea, pretending to be you."

"It is as you say," he said quietly. "Such a clever idea, it seemed to us. We were the same age, and both of us unwanted by our families. Both of us expected to do work for which we were entirely unsuited. He had little skill in reading or writing, and no interest in machinery. He had never wanted anything but to go to sea, but it would be humiliating for his father, it seemed, as the owner of a shipping line, to have his son as a humble sailor. He was to be sent to learn about weaving looms. Whereas I was the opposite. I loved machinery of all kinds, but the prospect of a life at sea terrified me. It took us but twenty four hours to conceive our scheme and make our plans. And it worked! I went to Branton to meet Giles Moreton, who had never met his nephew and had not the least notion what to expect. And Johnny took my place as a midshipman. But then…"

"His ship sank," Lord Westerlea said.

John nodded. "I had been at Branton two weeks when word came, and I know what you will say, Rosie, that I should have owned up at once. Of course I should. But I was twelve years old, I had left behind a home where I was unhappy and a father who despised me, and found myself for the first time in my life in a situation where I was truly valued."

"Papa did not despise you," Rosamund said, in surprised tones.

"Well, he gave an excellent impression of it," he said acidly. "Do you remember the clock in the morning room? No? It stopped working, so I took it apart. Papa railed at me — I was the most foolish boy in Christendom, I would never amount to anything, I had broken the clock beyond all repairing and why was he cursed with such an imbecile of a son? And so I put that clock back together, every tiny little cog and spring, and *it worked*, Rosie, it worked, and what did he say to that? Nothing! Not a word passed his lips on the subject. So, yes, I say to you that he despised me, and I had not the slightest wish to put myself back in his power. What do you think would have happened if I had told him I was still alive? Why, he would have sent me straight off to sea. And then there was the likelihood that he had remarried. So I said nothing and learnt about mills and beam engines and listened to my tutors and was happy. I told myself that I would write to Papa, of course I would — next week, or perhaps the week after. And somehow the weeks went by, and then the years, and the time was never right. Until now. Now I hope to marry and I need to secure my inheritance, so that I can promise my bride that one day I shall be not merely a mill manager, or even a mill owner, but a *gentleman*, as I was born to be."

"You relinquished any right to Woodside when you kept silent," Rosamund said coldly. "Papa believed you dead, and so he left Woodside to his daughters, along with all his debts, and we had to sell it to meet those obligations."

"Debts? Papa had debts?"

"Massive debts from too much gambling and too little prudent management," Rosamund said. "When I came to marry, he had to mortgage the house to pay the promised dowry."

"But what of Mama's jewels? That was your dowry, surely?"

"Gone. Papa searched everywhere for them, but they were nowhere to be found. Everything is gone, Jeremy — the jewels, Woodside, your inheritance, the family we once were. It is in the past, and nothing you can do will bring it back. Woodside will never be yours."

John twirled his wine glass thoughtfully. "Never... I wonder..."

Later that night, he walked home under clear moonlit skies, a shimmering canopy of stars far above, the frosted ground showing an answering sparkle. He came to the familiar gateposts — 'Woodside', they said proudly. He traced the etched letters with his fingers. Woodside. Five generations of Wintertons had lived there, and he had expected to be the sixth. He had hoped to watch his own sons grow up there and pass it on to his heir in his turn. Now it was gone.

If he had been here, could he have changed the course of events? Could he have paid off the debts and restored the estate to profitability again? Perhaps not, but he could have tried. The creditors might have pressed less closely, had there been a son to inherit. The bank might have been amenable to some arrangement. That was the way of it, with gentlemen. A mill manager must be beforehand with the world at all times, or there would be a stiff little note from the tailor or the linen-draper. *'It may have escaped your notice, sir... with the greatest respect... settled at your earliest convenience...'* On the other hand, a man of property could go to his bank and be given time to pay, time to recover. He could live in debt for years, and everyone treated him with respect. Yes, if he had been here, if he had been acknowledged as the heir, as a gentleman, he could have kept Woodside.

As he looked at the house, somewhere inside a light still gleamed. Not everyone was abed, then. Even at this hour, someone was still reading, or writing a letter, or merely pondering the day and wondering what the morrow would bring. Not the servants, that much was certain. They would be fast asleep at this hour, ready to rise again with the dawn. Mr Tyrrell, then, or his sharp-tongued daughter. Woodside was theirs now. They walked through its meandering passageways and sat in front of its carved fireplaces and gazed through the latticed windows at the neat gardens. Did they climb up into Margaret's tree house? Did one of them sleep in Mama's bed with the ugly carved headboard? Had they fixed the loose panel in the breakfast room and the dining room chimney that smoked when the wind was from the east?

With an angry fist, he pummelled the gatepost. *'Woodside'*, it said mockingly. Not his Woodside, not any more. But it would be. He would get Woodside back, no matter the price. And then he would be somebody. He would be a gentleman.

3: The Vicar's Room

"Master Jeremy? Master Jeremy?"

John opened one eye, then closed it again hurriedly to shut out the frightful sight of Tom, the ageing potboy, looming over the bed. Frickham Inn was not as uncivilised as many such small establishments, but Tom was not one of its more attractive features.

"'tis you! I'd know you anywhere, Master Jeremy."

John groaned. Was it morning already? How was that possible?

A woman's voice spoke up. "Come away, Tom. 'e don't want your ugly mug in 'is face, breathin' your mornin' ale all o'er 'im."

"But it's Master Jeremy, Dora."

"Don't matter nothin' to you if 'tis. Get that water jug to the gen'leman in number four, or Luke'll be in a right old pelt. Come on now, Tom."

Tom. The ostler, once, but now reduced to carrying water and coals for the chambermaid. Luke he vaguely remembered as the son of Carson, the previous innkeeper. Dora was unknown to him, but then she was not yet twenty. She would have been a grubby infant still clinging to her mother's skirts when John was last in Frickham.

He decided that, contrary to all reason, it truly must be morning. With another groan, he opened his eyes again, ignored the unshaven face just inches from his own, and hauled himself a little higher up the bed, using the lumpy pillow to prop his back against the wall.

"What is Hooper doing?" he growled. "This is his job."

It was Dora who answered. "Cussin' at the flat iron and gettin' in the way downstairs, sir. I'll send 'im straight up. *Tom!* Out!"

"'tis you, though, ain't it, Master Jeremy?"

"Yes, it is, but you are a horrid fellow, waking me at the Godforsaken hour of..." He pulled his pocket watch from under the pillow. "...oh. Ten o'clock. Good grief. Now get on with your work, and we will have a cosy chat later. Much later. And Dora, if you have any drinkable coffee in this place, I'll be your devoted slave for life."

She grinned. "I'll see what I can do, sir."

That had not taken long. Not twenty four hours since his arrival, and already the gossiping Jane Tyrrell had spread the word of his identity. Now there would be a deluge of unsavoury people like Tom claiming to remember him, and holding him hostage while they reminisced.

His valet arrived in a cloud of disapproval of the inadequate facilities prevailing below stairs, and how any person with standards was supposed to manage he could not conceive.

"Well, you will have to lower your standards for a while," John said briskly. "Try to remember that I am a salaried mill manager and not a duke. An unstarched neckcloth is not a tragedy of Shakespearean proportions."

After which, Hooper clamped his lips shut, and refused to say another word.

Coffee, a wash and a shave, dressing in clean, if slightly rumpled, clothes, and a solid breakfast restored John's good humour, if not his valet's. Tom was not allowed in the tiny cupboard the inn laughingly described as a private parlour, and by waiting until he heard him grumbling away to the kitchen, John was able to dash out of the inn's front door unaccosted. He would have to allow Tom his hour of memories, but not yet. Please, Lord, not yet.

He managed ten paces before a smiling matron stopped with a curtsy. "Mr Winterton! How wonderful to have you back. We had quite given up hope."

"Why, thank you, madam... erm, Mrs...?"

"Jackson. The physician's wife... widow, now. There's no physician in Frickham these days, only the apothecary, and as I was saying to Mrs Caddy only yesterday..."

John smiled and nodded, made some polite noises, escaped and moved on. Twenty more paces, and it was two men who hailed him from a wagon. Then an elderly widow he recognised — Mrs Petersham, who had been elderly and a widow ever since he could remember. By the time he reached the apothecary's shop, where the apothecary himself rushed out to shake his hand, he had had enough. He had walked barely a hundred yards, and at the present rate of progress would not make the other end of the village before nightfall. He bade the apothecary a hasty farewell, and ducked down the lane behind the smithy, and thence to the woods. Only when he was surrounded by trees, and not a single cottage or house was visible, did he breathe freely again.

It was not that he minded the villagers knowing who he was, for that was why he had come, after all, to show himself. But it was unexpectedly unnerving to be recognised and addressed as *'Master Jeremy'* or *'Mr Winterton'*. For fifteen years he had cloaked himself in secrecy, schooling his expression, watching his words carefully every time he spoke about his family. He had worn the carapace of John Moreton so thoroughly that he no longer even thought of himself as Jeremy Winterton. Yet now, here in this place, all the secrecy had fallen away and he felt exposed and vulnerable, like a snail whose shell has been ripped away.

He walked for some time, remembering parts of his route as vividly as if he had been there yesterday, while others seemed quite new to him. After a while, he realised that here and there a hedge or spinney had been grubbed out to enlarge a field, or a new one developed to provide cover for hunting and rough shooting. Beneath the surface changes, however, the land was as it had always been, and no doubt would continue unchanged for countless generations to come. Along places with wide rivers and near the coalfields there would be growing numbers of manufactories and mills and tall, belching chimneys, but here in the heartland of England agriculture was the predominant way of life.

He came by a roundabout route to a place at the edge of woodland. Years ago there had been a fallen tree to provide an informal seat, but it must have long since rotted away for there was no sign of it now. Someone had missed its utility, though, for there was a rough-carved bench in its place. He sat, gazing out at the view, one he knew intimately.

Only one field separated him from Woodside. Beyond the low wall he could see the orchard and glasshouses, the stand of ancient trees that hid Margaret's tree house and the beginnings of the pleasure grounds, with splashes of spring colour dotted about, yellow and white and palest pink. Behind stood the house in all its irregular glory, the windows dark without the setting sun to light them on fire. Some unseen maid was singing as she went about her work.

Edging the field was a small stream, and on the far side of it was the majesty of Westerlea Park, with its sloping lawns, its ha-ha and sheep, and its perfect symmetry. Two children were running across the lawn with a woman walking behind them — a nursemaid? Or was it Rosamund being maternal? He could not tell at such a distance, but the scene made him smile.

"It is a fine view, is it not?" said a voice nearby.

John jumped to his feet. A man of middle years smiled benignly at him, his face not yet lined, although his hair was silver. He looked and spoke like a gentleman, but he had no gun nor any dogs at his feet. He had a leather bag over one shoulder and carried fistful of twigs bearing catkins.

"It is indeed, sir," John said.

"You must be Mr Moreton," the man said. "Or is it Mr Winterton?" His smile widened, so that his eyes crinkled at the edges.

John smiled too. "There are no secrets in a village. I answer to either name."

"Do you? How fascinating it must be have two names. Almost like being two people. But how do you prefer to be addressed?"

"I think... around here it is easier for everyone if I am Jeremy Winterton."

"Delighted to meet you, Mr Winterton. I am Geoffrey Tyrrell. I am just going home for some tea. Would you like some? Or I have some Madeira, if you prefer. Do come, for I am sorely in need of male company."

John went, allowing Tyrrell to ramble on in his gentle manner. He explained that he took a walk every day no matter the weather, observing nature and collecting samples that presented themselves to his notice. Then he spent the rest of the morning recording his thoughts and painting the samples.

"Spring is late this year," he said. "I should have liked a primrose, but there were none to be had and I must make do with more catkins. But in another week, the woods will be carpeted with primroses."

It was the oddest feeling for John to walk into Woodside through the scullery door, just as he had always done, yet knowing that it was not his home any longer. Everywhere there were reminders — the unfamiliar cloaks on the pegs, the deep tub filled with walking sticks of every size and style, the walls repainted in a paler colour so that the passage seemed lighter. In the house itself, there were new paintings on the walls and rugs on the floor. But mingled with the new were some old pieces of furniture, so well known to him that he could almost imagine his father's hat on the console, or a forgotten glove on the floor beneath it. It would be Lucy's, of course. She was always in a great hurry, and talking so fast she never noticed. He was overwhelmed with grief, abruptly, for his father, for his sisters, for his home. Gone, all gone.

He must have made some sound, or perhaps it was simply that he stopped moving. Mr Tyrrell turned to him, with a gentle smile.

"It must be difficult for you to return here and find strangers in your home," he said, his voice heavy with sympathy. "I hope you will not stand on ceremony with us. Call whenever you wish, and look into the rooms. You will find it not much changed — fresh wallpaper here and there, a worn rug replaced, that sort of thing. Here we are. This is my sanctuary."

"Ah, the vicar's room," John murmured.

Mr Tyrrell turned to him with a gleeful expression. "The vicar's room? You entertained the vicar here, and not in the drawing room? How seditious of you!"

"Papa would not have let him cross the threshold at all, but he came to do his duty by Mama after she became too ill to attend church. He was always put in here to wait until Mama was ready to receive him. Havelock brought him tea and buns, so he went away quite happy whether he had seen Mama or not, especially if it were cold or wet outside. Poor man, the living was not a good one, and he had a numerous family. Well — this room has scarcely changed."

He gazed around, noting a new worktable under the window, spread with paper, brushes and paints. The pictures on the walls were different, seascapes or heathery moors replacing the stiffly posed portraits. But the books spread about, open, on every surface were much as he remembered, the worn leather chairs beside the fire were the same, and the rug still bore the hole where a spark had spat from the fire, causing the girls to run screaming from the room. Jeremy had stamped out the smouldering ember with the heel of his boot long before the servants had come in. Papa had not praised him for that, either.

Mr Tyrrell waved him to a chair. "Yes, we kept most of the downstairs furniture, since what we had before belonged to my wife's family. We brought a quantity of bedroom furniture with us, and our own linen and plate. Ah, Betsy, some tea, please. And some cake for my guest."

They talked about his painting for a while, and he brought out his notes to show John — delicate watercolours, with the description of each in an elegant, flowing hand. Some pages were just writing, describing the weather, or the harvest, or the lambing. Not that Mr Tyrrell was interested in sacks of grain or numbers of ewes producing or the values at market, for his descriptions were those of an observer, a man recording the natural cycle of the seasons, yet not a part of it.

"Do you hunt?" John said, seeing a painting of a ploughed field, and having an urge to gallop across it himself.

"I? No. I neither ride nor shoot, nor have the desire to do either. I am quite misplaced as a country gentleman." He gave a low chuckle. "Yes, quite misplaced. Whereas you... this is where you belong, I think. You cannot conceive, Mr Winterton, just how many of my worthy neighbours believe that. Oh, not that they say so to my face, naturally. They are far too well-bred for that. But if I send along a marrow to the church harvest festival, they say brightly, *'That's just what the late Mr Winterton would have done.'*" He managed a tolerable imitation of the local accent. "And if I should forget, they say, *'Ah, but you're new here, sir, just finding your feet. Now, the late Mr Winterton was so particular about his marrows.'* I do not know what it is about marrows, but the good people of Brinshire are obsessed with them. Such an insipid vegetable."

John laughed, and said, "I like a stuffed marrow, myself."

"There you are, you see," Mr Tyrrell said, in pleased tones. "You belong here amongst the marrow-eaters of the county. It is your destiny."

"Unfortunately, not so," John said. "I belong here no more, for Woodside is yours now, sir."

"Ah, but such matters are not irrevocable. I should not be averse to selling the place to you, if you were to make me a reasonable offer."

John could not breathe. He could buy Woodside! It would be his again, as it should be, and he would be a gentleman, as he should be. His destiny, Tyrrell had called it, and John could not disagree with him. He was born to be master of Woodside, and now it could be his. All he had to do was...

"What is a reasonable offer?" he said, his voice a mere croak.

"Ah, straight to the point. That is the mill manager speaking, I suspect. A gentleman would hedge and prevaricate and come at every question roundabout, but business is much better conducted with briskness, I feel. I was a wool merchant, once, before I came into a little money and married a little more, so we may come to terms as businessmen and then shake hands on it as gentlemen. Let me show you the numbers."

He opened a cupboard and pulled out a folder. Untying the laces, he passed papers to John — the bill of sale and titles to smaller pockets of land, plus a neat ledger with quarterly income and outgoings. John perused each document carefully.

"So the income from the estate was no more than... let me see, a little under three hundred a year when you bought the place, but you have added more land, and now it is worth... eight hundred and fifty? Do I have that right? My father always said it was worth two thousand."

"Perhaps it was, once," Mr Tyrrell said, smoothing a crease from his breeches. "Three hundred it was when I bought it, and I had someone from Martin's Bank on my doorstep before we had even unpacked, wanting to sell back to me all the tenant farms and so forth that had been acquired through defaulted loans over the years. *'The bank is not in the business of land management, Mr Tyrrell,'* he said with great indignation."

Jeremy laughed, hearing the strangulated tones of old Mr Martin very clearly.

Tyrrell went on, " *'Then why did you not sell it on?'* I asked him, not unreasonably, I thought. *'Because it belongs to Woodside, sir,'* he told me, greatly affronted by the idea of disposing of so much as a pebble of it. So I bought it all back from him, and some from Lord Westerlea, which he had bought as a favour to his friend. Mr Claremont has some he would sell, too, but I had spent all my capital by then. There is a deal of land that might be added to the estate by a man of means who has the ability to strike a good bargain. You might even see two thousand a year once more."

Two thousand a year... but he would first need to find enough capital to buy the land that would bring him such an income. Two thousand a year! He would be a gentleman indeed with such an income. He had a sudden vision of himself striding about his estate, gun in hand, pointers at his heels, and when he returned home, there would be Ellen, presiding gracefully over the teacups, smiling welcomingly. And perhaps, in such a situation, when he had made her a lady, she might smile with real warmth that reached her eyes.

But first to find the money. "I shall need to consider the matter carefully," he said.

"Of course, of course. Take your time," Mr Tyrrell said genially. "Come for dinner tonight, if you have no other engagement, and we may discuss the matter in greater depth."

"Thank you, I should like that, but... if you leave Woodside, where would you go? There are no other houses of substance in the neighbourhood."

"Something much smaller would suit me now. Nine years ago, when first I came to Brinshire after my wife died, I had my mother and four young daughters with me. Jane, the eldest, was just sixteen, and Charlotte, Helena and Ruth were still to be launched into society. For several years there were balls and dinners and card parties to attend, young men calling every day, cousins visiting... such a whirl of activity. But the younger girls married and Mama died, and now it is only Jane and me, and before too long, I hope, it will be only me, and I have no need of a barn of a place like Woodside. It is a family home, Mr Winterton. It needs children and life and someone who belongs here."

"I see. So Miss Tyrrell is soon to be married?"

Tyrrell frowned. "How I wish that could be so, but as soon as Ruth was married, Jane put on a cap and gave up dancing. She would not go out at all were it not for the kindness of Lady Westerlea and Mrs Claremont, who invite her to their houses. Even so, she only goes for the sake of politeness. She is more housekeeper than daughter already, and I would not have her waste her best years tending an old man, and giving up all chance of a family of her own. What will happen to her when I die? She cannot live here alone. I have fretted about her for some time, but it was not until your arrival that a way of resolving the problem presented itself. If the house is sold, then I shall take Jane to Bath and put up a good dowry for her, and I defy even her determined spinsterhood to resist the onslaught of charming young fortune-hunters who will pay court to her. And then I shall look for a cottage where I may dwindle into old age without the least trouble to anybody. So you see, you will be doing everyone a favour if you buy Woodside."

Jeremy laughed. "Even so, it is an uncommonly generous man who gives up his home to someone entirely unknown to him."

"Ah, but you see, you are not unknown to me at all. I have seen your initials engraved on the table where you studied your lessons. I have read the books with your name on the flyleaf. I have seen the wooden horse you carved at the age of eleven. I have seen the magnificent drawing by your hand of the workings of a clock."

"I gave that to Papa," Jeremy said.

"It had fallen behind one of the bookcases in the room that must have been his study once. I had it framed and hung upon the wall there. Then there were all the things from your bedroom, which had never been touched, I believe, since the day you left home. The door was locked, but when it was opened, the room was just as if you had stepped out for a moment."

"Good God," Jeremy said, appalled.

"Your sisters took one or two things, as mementos, and told us to dispose of the rest. We never have, however. We never needed the room, so there it stays. Would you like to see it?"

Jeremy was overwhelmed. He had wondered many times how his father would react to his return. His father had never liked him above half and might have turned against him completely, and who would blame him? Not Jeremy himself. He would have won his father round in the end, he was sure of that, but there would have been some sticky ground to be got over first.

But now, just as he was trying to come to terms with the loss of his father and his home and everything he had expected to find, this kindly stranger offered him everything he wanted. Behind the benign smile and twinkling eyes, however, was an astute businessman. John had dealt with enough mill owners and merchants to recognise a hard negotiator when he met one. This was a business deal, and he must not allow sentiment to cloud his judgement. He refused the invitation to view his old bedroom, therefore, and, after a very few more minutes, made his farewells.

He had barely reached the gateposts when an elegant carriage bowled past on the road, heading towards Westerlea Park. It drew to a halt, and Rosamund's fetchingly bonneted head peeped out of the window.

"There you are, Jeremy. I have been asking all over the village for you, and here you are poking about at Woodside. You must not disrupt the Tyrrells, you know."

With anyone else, Jeremy might have been annoyed, but somehow the familiar sharpness made him unexpectedly nostalgic. Rosie had always been brusque with him, and with her sisters, too. It was just her manner, he knew that. When Mama had grown ill, Rosie had taken on the role of mother to them all, and it had robbed her of some of her carefree youthfulness. She meant well, even when she hectored him.

"Mr Tyrrell invited me in to take tea with him," he said. "What was it you wanted with me?"

"We have decided that you should not be putting up at an inn like a common traveller. I have given orders for your things to be packed up and brought to the Park."

"Thank you, Rosie," he said meekly, and not even her highhandedness could dent his complaisance. A guest at the Park! That was better than the Frickham Inn, and even his grouchy valet could not be displeased at the change.

4: Dinner At Woodside

Jane was always amused by her father's efforts to match-make. Every young man who arrived in the neighbourhood was sure to be invited to dinner a few times, until the lack of interest on both sides became too obvious even for her father to ignore. He never berated her for her lack of enthusiasm for matrimony, but he could not help himself from hoping, she supposed. Perhaps he felt it was his paternal duty to marry off *all* his daughters, but she wished he would be satisfied with three good matches and three daughters reasonably contented with the wedded state, and leave his eldest daughter to spinsterhood.

On this occasion, she made no objection to the last-minute addition to the dinner table, for she very much wanted to know more of the interesting Mr Jeremy Winterton. She had enough time to order a couple of removes for dinner, and some extra vegetables and desserts. With the table at its smallest size, the food would stretch to two full courses, she thought. Mrs Locke was very good at making a meal go further, and although there was no fresh game or fish to be had, the still room was full of potted varieties. They would be able to put a reasonable spread in front of their guest.

What sort of dinner was he used to, she wondered? Bread and ham with his workers at the mill, or did he go home to turbot and the best cuts of beef and a claret of good quality? He dressed well enough, so perhaps a mill manager lived like a gentleman. Would he play whist? She should invite a fourth, just in case... There were several widows in the village who were grateful for a free meal, and also capable of taking their places at the card table without disgrace. She dashed off a hasty note to Mrs Plummer, the relict of the previous clergyman.

Then she went to her room to look out a gown. Her choices were limited, for she had not had a new evening gown for two years now. She had little interest in dressing up, but Papa expected it when they had guests. At least now that she was older, she could wear the vibrant colours that suited her complexion. Her years in pale muslins had been a great trial. She chose an amber silk with some decorative flounces around the bodice. It was not her newest, but it would do for a mill manager. She took it downstairs for Lottie to press.

Mr Winterton arrived early, in Lady Westerlea's carriage, and Jane had to admit that in his evening clothes he looked every inch the gentleman. He bowed and smiled and said everything that was proper, and after a few minutes' attention to Jane, he moved to Mrs Plummer and good-humouredly engaged her in conversation. The widow was delighted to find that he remembered her late husband, and they talked animatedly of his lengthy sermons in the summer, and briefer in the winter, according to the appointed hour for dinner.

"He so enjoyed his dinner on a Sunday," she said, heaving a nostalgic sigh. "It was the only day of the week when we could afford a decent joint of meat, and sometimes Mr Winterton was so kind as to send fish or game, too. Mr Richard Dalton was another one who was very generous with whatever was in season. So very kind to neighbours! Of course, his father was not such a keen sportsman, nor the present Lord Westerlea, so one does not expect the same little gifts. Mr Claremont, on the other hand— Oh dear me, is it time for dinner already? Might I trouble you for your arm, Mr Winterton? My knees are so troublesome these days, especially after sitting for a while. Oh goodness me, I do beg your pardon! Heavens, I almost fell upon you! There now, I am quite upright. Is my cap askew? Deary me, it is such a trial to be an old lady, but what a great comfort it is to have a strong young man to assist me. There we are, I do believe I am quite ready now."

Jane's father politely offered his arm to Mrs Plummer for the procession across the hall to the dining room, and Mr Winterton fell in beside Jane, although he offered no support, which rather pleased her. She had never quite understood the idea that a well-bred lady was incapable of moving from one room to another without leaning on a man's arm, as if she were a delicate, wilting creature who might fall down without a man's aid. In Mrs Plummer's case, the need was obvious, but Jane was fit enough to walk unaided.

In the dining room, she was disappointed but not surprised that her father managed the seating so that Mr Winterton was beside her. It mattered little, for with only four at table the conversation must necessarily be general, but still she would have preferred him anywhere else. He was not troublesome company, however, complimenting her on the new lighter wallpaper — *'It was always a little gloomy before'* — and praising every dish with apparent sincerity. When these routine topics had been exhausted, however, he ranged further afield. To her astonishment, Jane found herself discussing with great energy such disparate subjects as poetry, the situation on the continent, the uses of elephants, the King's health, the purpose of art and the orbits of the planets. Never had a dinner flown by so speedily or so pleasurably. It was only when she happened to catch Mrs Plummer's eye and that lady gave the slightest dip of her head towards the door that Jane realised she had been so engrossed that she had neglected to withdraw at the proper time.

"I do beg your pardon, madam," she said as they left the dining room. "I had no notion it was so late."

"Oh, I could see that, dear. Such a charming young man, and you were having such a lovely chat that I did not quite like to interrupt, but I am not as young as I was and one does get a little *uncomfortable* after a while."

When the two ladies were settled in the drawing room again, Jane bent her head towards Mrs Plummer and whispered, "So what have you discovered about him?"

Mrs Plummer needed no explanation of which *'him'* was under discussion. "My dear, his valet had *no idea!* Can you imagine? Mrs Clark had it directly from Dora at the inn. Mr Hooper was under footman at Mr Moreton's house — Mr *Giles* Moreton, that is — when Mr Winterton arrived there fifteen years ago at the age of twelve, and he has never heard him called anything but John Moreton. He is supposed to be old Mr Moreton's nephew from Liverpool, and that is what everyone knows of him. Mr Hooper says that even Mr Giles Moreton himself cannot have the least idea that his supposed nephew is an impostor."

"He is living with a man supposedly his uncle?" Jane said, astonished. "Giles Moreton was established at this town in Lancashire already — Branton? Yes, Branton — and a twelve-year-old boy turned up pretending to be his nephew? And he accepted him?"

"Oh yes. According to Mr Hooper, Mr Giles Moreton had never seen the boy, so he had no idea. He expected a boy to arrive, a boy *did* arrive, so that was that."

"But whatever can have happened to the real John Moreton?" Jane said.

"Clearly he is the one at the bottom of the Irish Sea."

"But how? Why? It makes no sense!" Jane cried.

Mrs Plummer laughed. "That is because all this happened before you ever came here. It was all old history, so I daresay not much talked about by then. It all came about after Mrs Winterton died. Ah, such a lovely lady, the gentlest creature imaginable, but when she died, her husband went to pieces rather. Some men do that, don't they? No idea how to go on without their wives. There was some talk he would marry Lady Elizabeth Drake, and that she persuaded Mr Winterton to get rid of Master Jeremy because he had taken her in dislike, but I daresay that was just hearsay. Anyway, Master Jeremy was sent away to be a midshipman, and he had to wait in Liverpool for his ship to arrive, so he stayed with the Moreton family. Friends of Lady Elizabeth's, they were. Or acquaintances, anyway."

"Ah, so that is how Jeremy Winterton met John Moreton."

"Exactly, and no doubt the two boys swapped places for a lark, as boys do. And then the ship sank and John Moreton was drowned and Master Jeremy never liked to own up to it, I suppose. And here he is."

"But why does he come here now, after all these years?" Jane said thoughtfully.

"Oh, there's a lady up in Lancashire, a Miss Ridwell, the most beautiful creature that ever lived, according to Mr Hooper," Mrs Plummer said. "A betrothal is imminent, although Mrs Clark did wonder whether *you* might—" She tugged at the sleeve of her gown, smoothing an infinitesimal crease, as Jane protested. "Well, you know what people are like, dear. A young man, a young lady, and Woodside... what could be more fitting than for the two of you to make a match of it? Everyone is saying so. But, sadly, he is to marry this Miss Ridwell instead, and that is that. I expect Master Jeremy wanted to tell his father about it. Well, *that* must have been a shock. And he knew nothing about his father's death?"

"Not a thing," Jane said. "He walked up to the door here and asked to see Mr Winterton. I directed him to the churchyard."

Mrs Plummer gasped, hand over mouth. "You did not! The poor man! Such a dreadful shock for him."

"He practically swooned on the spot, but how was I to know? The man died ten years ago, so anyone asking for him could hardly be a close friend, one would suppose." The clock struck the half hour, and she frowned. "They are lingering over the port rather. I wonder what that means? Papa is usually keen to get the card table out."

It was a full hour before the gentlemen came through, by which time the ladies had exhausted all the gossip and Mrs Plummer was half asleep over her needlework. Jane was glad to send for the tea things and then settle down for an hour or two of whist for farthing points. Her father had arranged them so that she was opposite Jeremy Winterton, giving her ample opportunity to examine him properly.

He was handsome, no question about that, with a hint of mischief in those green eyes. His hair was longer and less disorderly than many fashionable gentlemen affected, but she liked him the better for it. There was just one wayward strand that flopped across his forehead, making him look boyishly young. The Lancashire accent was almost undetectable in company, with only the occasional jarring vowel, and his manners were not such as would attract comment. He was quick, too, winning points very easily at first, but then moderating his play so that Mrs Plummer won a great many farthings, smiling broadly as she gathered them up. So there was a generous heart beneath that rough-hewn exterior.

Yet still she could not make him out. What kind of man would assume a false identity and leave his family to believe him dead for fifteen years? It was beyond belief. Even if the boy of twelve was terrified to admit to the scheme, surely the grown man must have appreciated the grief he had caused and the cowardice in remaining silent. And here he was, sipping Papa's expensive brandy, full of the best veal and mutton, playing whist after dinner as if nothing in the world untoward had happened, as if he had not deceived a hundred people or more for fifteen years. Worse than that, he acted as though all was now set right, for he had admitted his little deception so how could anyone be displeased with him? She remembered Rosamund's anger — Rosamund, who had never raised her voice in all the years Jane had known her — yelling fit to burst at her brother. *'How dare you?'* she had shrieked at him. *'How dare you turn up here after all these years?'* Jane could hardly blame her for it.

Mrs Plummer was the first to show signs of tiredness, and Mr Winterton gallantly offered her a ride home in the Westerlea carriage, to save the bother of putting the Woodside horses to. While her father saw Mrs Plummer safely stowed and listened to her effusions on the plushness of the appointments within the carriage, Mr Winterton stayed in the hall to make his thanks to Jane.

"Nay, do not thank *me*," she said. "It is I should be thanking you for keeping Papa so well entertained. There are few men who can hold his attention for a full hour over the one glass of port he permits himself. I cannot imagine what you talked about all that time."

"Oh, the question of Woodside, of course," he said absently, his gaze fixed on the carriage waiting outside. "Gentlemen are never so engrossed as when they are discussing business."

"Business? To do with Woodside?" She wondered what sort of estate business her father would share with a relative stranger.

"Yes, but it is no good, sadly. I cannot afford to buy it, and the alternative is out of the question."

Jane felt as if the ground had slid from under her feet, plummeting her into some strange underworld. Papa wanted to sell Woodside? He had given no sign of discontent. And then—

"What alternative?" she said sharply.

He must have caught her tone, for he turned to look at her. "Oh… you did not know. Then I beg your pardon, Miss Tyrrell. I should not have mentioned the subject." More gently, he added, "It was a wild idea of your father's, not such as I could contemplate, so you need not be anxious on that account. Thank you again for an excellent evening. Good night."

With a few words of farewell to her father, he was gone. Conscious of Timpson, their manservant, busily bolting the front door, she kept her tone even as she said, "Papa? Shall we have some tea before bed?"

His face brightened. "What a good idea. Tea, Timpson, in the drawing room."

As soon as the drawing room door was closed, Jane rounded on him. "When were you planning to tell me, Papa? About selling Woodside? Why would you do such a thing?"

"Oh, did Winterton tell you about that?" He flopped into his favourite chair, not in the least discomfited. "It is more his house than ours, you know, and I thought it would be amusing to take ourselves to Bath for a while, and—"

"Bath!"

"—find you a husband. But you need not worry, my dear, for he has not the readies for it, and he will not take out a loan for the purpose. I like him the better for that, for it shows a high degree of prudence. He wants the house, certainly, but he will not bankrupt himself to buy it back."

"And the alternative? Mr Winterton declared the alternative to be out of the question."

"Oh that." He hesitated, but then, with a long intake of breath, he plunged on, "I told him he could have Woodside as dowry if he would marry you."

"What!"

"Now do not fly up into the boughs, Jane. No one will force you into matrimony kicking and screaming, you know, and no rational man would want to. It would be your choice, but surely you can see the merits of the arrangement. In one move, I might restore Woodside to its rightful owner without the least inconvenience and also see you settled at last. The small annuity from your mother's family will be more than enough to support my modest wants. A little cottage somewhere, a manservant and a maid of all work — that will suit me perfectly, and you may stay on as mistress of Woodside. I have no one else to leave my money to, after all, and since you make not the least exertion to secure your own future, someone has to work on your behalf."

"No one has to work on my behalf," she cried. "Can you not accept that I am perfectly happy unwed? I have you to look after and the house to manage, I have my friends and some alms for the poor to keep me busy. I do *not* need a man to take care of me. Not every woman is happier married, Papa."

"My dear girl, it is not merely a question of your happiness. One must be prudent, too. What will you do when I die?"

"You are only fifty five, and perfectly fit. You could live for thirty years yet," she said, her chin raised defiantly.

He sighed. "And that would be worse, for you would then be five and fifty yourself, and an old maid, and who would take you in?"

"I would live here, of course. I could easily find a companion."

"Oh, Jane!" He picked up his spectacles, discarded on the card table, and polished them vigorously with his handkerchief.

Just then Timpson came in with the tea tray, and for a few minutes there was nothing said that did not relate to the important business of making and pouring and drinking the tea. Eventually Timpson withdrew again, and Jane's father laid aside his tea cup and saucer.

"Jane, dear, I fear that the ways of the world are against you. A woman can no more manage an estate like Woodside than fly to the moon. It has been difficult enough for me, Heaven knows. Even the gamekeeper tells me *"T were different in old Mr Winterton's day, sir'* whenever I make a suggestion. I am very tired of old Mr Winterton's day, I can tell you. With you, they would not listen at all, and you would get cross and then they would give notice and go to some obscure corner of England where old Mr Winterton's day still prevails. I cannot allow that to happen, and so I shall never leave Woodside to you, dearest of my daughters."

"So you would give it away to any half-civilised man prepared to marry a dried-up old spinster like me, is that it?"

"No, I would give it away to Jeremy Winterton, who has some right to it, at least, and is not only fully civilised, but a rather attractive and pleasant young man. You could do a lot worse."

She bit back an acid retort on the subject of Jeremy Winterton, not wanting to lose the focus of her argument. Setting down her cold tea, she knelt at her father's feet.

"Dear Papa, all I ask of life is to stay here and continue on exactly as we have done for the last nine years. I am *happy* here with you, and no other life could make me happier. When the dreaded day arrives that I must bid you farewell, then I shall go to live with one of my sisters and make myself useful to her and her family. But until that day comes, I need nothing else, I assure you, except you and Woodside."

"Then I fear you are doomed to disappointment, daughter," he said. "Jeremy Winterton has not the means to purchase Woodside, nor the inclination to marry for it, so he plans to take the matter to law. He intends to challenge his father's will, which left Woodside to his sisters."

"Can he do that, after all this time? And can he win such a case?"

"I am no expert on the law, but I believe we should be prepared for such an outcome. And if that happens, then we shall lose Woodside, whether we wish it or no."

5: Mr Plumphett Advises

Mr Plumphett had not grown any thinner in the fifteen years since Jeremy had last seen him. He imagined the lawyer ordering a new waistcoat every year, each one an inch or so wider than the one before. He wheezed slightly as he walked, his corsets creaking a little with every movement, as he slowly proceeded the short distance from the front door to the library at Westerlea Park. He had brought a junior with him to carry papers and boxes, of which he had a considerable number.

He made deep bows to Rosamund and Lord Westerlea, exclaimed over Jeremy — *'A miracle, sir! An indisputable miracle. Such a great pity your esteemed father did not live to see you restored to us, sir.'* — and smiled with an *'Ah!'* of satisfaction when Madeira was mentioned. Carefully he settled himself, still wheezing, onto the largest chair that could be found in the library, a glass of Madeira in readiness on a table beside him, as Rosamund, Jeremy and Lord Westerlea waited for him to compose himself. He took a sip of Madeira, reached to set the glass down again, then thought better of it, cradling the glass in his pudgy hands.

"Now my lord, my lady, Mr Winterton, let me see if I have the matter clear in my mind. In your letter, my good sir, you indicated a desire to inform yourself of your position in law as the only son of your late parent, missing for some years and sincerely believed to be no longer in the mortal realm, who is, in point of fact, and most happily for all of us who knew you as a boy, yet living. It is a fascinating situation, most intriguing from a legal perspective, for I do not recall any case of this precise nature, although there are a few which have some bearing here which I and my colleagues have been perusing on your behalf. I know of one, which, although not precisely relevant, may shed some light on—"

"Mr Plumphett," Jeremy said, with as much patience as he could manage. "I am sure this is most interesting, and perhaps we may wish to hear such details at a later date if matters proceed, but pray tell me at once — do I have the right to make a claim?"

"Oh yes, most assuredly," the lawyer said. He took a sip of Madeira, and sighed with satisfaction before continuing. "You are the heir at law, Mr Winterton, the clear and sole heir of your late and much lamented parent. Indeed, until two years before his sad death, you were the sole beneficiary in his will. You, and you alone, would have inherited everything, and your sisters would have depended on your goodwill for their dowries. That was your respected parent's manifest wish. Had he known, or even suspected, that you still lived, he would never have changed his will at all, that much I can assert with the greatest authority."

He paused for another sip of Madeira, and Jeremy took the opportunity to say, "And it does not matter that ten years have passed?"

Mr Plumphett sipped again before replying in measured tones, "I will not say that it does not matter, for you will appreciate that complications arise as a result of the delay, but the court will take into account that you raised the issue the instant your father's demise was made known to you. The delay is unfortunate, but it could not, I feel, have easily been avoided. One might say that greater efforts might have been made to trace a missing heir, but there was every reason in the world to believe in your decease. One might say that it is a pity that you saw no notice of your father's unhappy demise, but one cannot read every word of every newspaper. One might say that it is unfortunate that an indication of your continued existence was not brought to your father's attention earlier, but again, there was no reason to regard such a step as necessary. No, the lapse of ten years is regrettable but does not, in itself, invalidate your right to make a claim. That is my opinion, although of course it is solely for the courts to determine such matters."

"So I may challenge the will?"

Another pause ensued as Mr Plumphett drained his glass and then stared into its empty depths mournfully until Lord Westerlea refilled it for him. "Ah, most kind, my lord, most kind. Such generous hospitality! Most gracious of your lordship. As to the question at issue, there is no reason why the challenge should not be made, in my view, and indeed, my considered opinion is that you would have a strong likelihood of success, Mr Winterton. However..."

"There is always a *however*," Jeremy said, with a smile.

"Oh, indeed there is," Mr Plumphett said, his round face creasing into a smile in response. "In law there is always an alternate point of view. In this case, the situation regarding Woodside is unduly complicated. Firstly, it was not a property in good heart when your dearly loved parent met his Maker. It was, not to put too fine a point on it, sadly encumbered, to such an extent that your sisters were obliged to sell it to meet the obligations of debt. The property was bought by... let me see..." He flicked a finger towards his junior, a young man barely adult, who shuffled some papers about helplessly.

"Mr Tyrrell," Jeremy said.

"Ah, indeed. Mr Tyrrell, yes. The proceeds of that sale were then expended to fulfil all outstanding obligations incurred by your late and much missed father. Mr Tyrrell has, as I understand it, since employed a portion of his own fortune to improve the property by the acquisition — or perhaps I should say re-acquisition — of land. That is, he bought back some parcels of land previously belonging to the Woodside estate. So we have an inheritance much changed from its situation ten years ago, and now a most valuable property. If you were so fortunate as to be awarded the title to Woodside, you would be faced with an estate by no means the same as it was left by your well-respected parent all those years ago. There would be reparations to be made, compensations, any amount of difficulty. And perhaps in my profession I ought not to say such a thing, but pursuing such a course in law is an expensive business. Lawyers' fees are considerable, Mr Winterton. You might find yourself a great deal worse off than you began."

There was a silence in the room, as Mr Plumphett applied himself once more to the Madeira, and Rosamund and her husband watched Jeremy.

Lord Westerlea shifted on his chair. "It seems to me that the matter could be settled without recourse to the law. Mr Tyrrell is a reasonable man, and might perhaps be amenable to some arrangement."

Jeremy shook his head. "He would be a fool to take less than the current worth of the estate for it, and he is certainly no fool. Besides, why should I buy what is mine by right?"

"You need not, perhaps, but *someone* must compensate Tyrrell for the loss of Woodside."

"Regretfully, that is the case," Mr Plumphett said. "If you were to succeed in contesting your estimable parent's will, Mr Winterton, you would have possession of Woodside, but Mr Tyrrell would be obliged to sue your sisters for reparation, and not just the plain value of the estate. There is also the loss of amenity, the considerable inconvenience, a fair return for the time and effort expended on improving and maintaining the property."

"He could sue *us?*" Rosamund said in alarm. "But we sold him Woodside in good faith."

"Yet you did not, perhaps, have the right to do so," Mr Plumphett said gently. "It may be, if Mr Winterton wins his claim, that you did not own Woodside at all, and therefore sold it falsely to Mr Tyrrell. He would be perfectly entitled to sue for reparation."

There was a long silence after this depressing comment. Jeremy could see no way out of the impasse.

Mr Plumphett drained his glass once more, and set it down on the side table with a sigh of regret. Then he laced his fingers over his ample stomach and said, "There is, perhaps, an alternative approach, Mr Winterton."

Jeremy brightened. This was more like it! Some slightly circuitous method that would avoid unpleasantness and excessive lawyers' fees. "I am open to all suggestions, Mr Plumphett."

"There are your dear mother's jewels."

They stared at him. It was Rosamund who said coldly, "They were lost long since, Mr Plumphett. If we had had the jewels, then much would have been different."

"Not lost, my lady. Hidden, merely. Hidden so well that they could not be found, but they are still there, somewhere in that house."

"They are *not* there," Rosamund said. "They were in Mama's room, everyone knew that, yet when Papa looked for them, they were nowhere to be found. He took that room apart, Mr Plumphett. The wall panels, the bed hangings, the chimney, every single drawer and piece of furniture that could be dismantled *was* dismantled. He took the floorboards up, tore apart the mattress and even probed into the ceiling plaster. The jewels were not there."

"Hidden," Mr Plumphett said firmly. "Your dear mother kept them in her room, of that I am sure, but no one knew where. It was a pity that she had no faith in the banks, for that would have been a much better solution, as I many times tried to convince the dear lady, but she would not have it. Her husband would get hold of them, she said, or her brother, and then—"

"Her *brother?*" Rosamund said sharply. "Uncle Arthur?"

"Mr Arthur Tilford, yes," Mr Plumphett said, beaming genially at her. "Did you never hear about his visit to London? No? Well, perhaps your dear mama thought it best not spoken of. He was a man of great charm in his youth, seemingly, and when he was eighteen or so, he went to the bank where his father kept his money, wheedled twenty thousand pounds out of the manager, went straight up to London and contrived to gamble away the lot in under a week."

"Good grief!" Rosamund said faintly. "No wonder Mama would not leave her jewels in the bank."

"Quite so. Mr Arthur Tilford became an attorney thereafter, so one may surmise that his father considered that he had already received the inheritance due to him and cut him off, but your dear mother once told me that her brother regarded it as the most enjoyable week of his life. In any event, both he and, I regret to say, your sadly missed father, enjoyed the cards and the dice too much to be permitted access to the jewellery, so it was carefully hidden. All done while your respected parents were on their wedding tour, and the servants sent away, and so forth. Very secret. However, your dear mama made provision for the jewels to be located after her death in time of need. She left a sealed letter with me to be opened only if I deemed the cause sufficiently dire to necessitate the immediate release of funds."

"Then why did you not do so?" Rosamund said. "When Papa needed money for my dowry—"

"He came straight to me, my lady," Mr Plumphett said, "and naturally I agreed that it was a cause that your dear mama would have approved. Indeed, that was her whole intention, to provide for her daughters."

"So you opened the letter?"

"Three letters, by that time. Let me show you... Horace, if you please. No, the other box... yes, yes, in there. Ah, here we are."

He handed over three opened letters, which Rosamund read in silence, passing them to her husband who passed them to Jeremy. The first said *'William Tenterden'*, with an address in Birmingham. The second read *'Walter Tenterden'*, at the same address. The third said only, *'Jeremy knows how to find my jewels'*.

"But I do not!" he said, bewildered. "Mama never told me how to find them. I know no more than anyone else, which is nothing."

"Who are these other people?" Rosamund said. "William Tenterden and Walter Tenterden."

"The uncle and cousin of your dear mama," Mr Plumphett said. "Long dead now, sadly. We pursued enquiries, naturally, but all we could find was that they were clock-makers — the sort fitted on churches and other great buildings, where angels and demons pop out to do battle every hour, on the hour."

"Automaton clocks," Jeremy said, suddenly interested. "How curious! I never heard of such people in connection with the family."

"They made the clock for St Mark's in Brinchester, it seems," Mr Plumphett said. "But the name and the business died with them, so they are no help to us."

"I do not see how any of this helps us," Rosamund said. "If Papa could not find the jewels, I do not see how Jeremy can do so, and even if they can be found, they are part of the Woodside estate, and therefore the question of ownership must be settled by law. Is it not so, Mr Plumphett?"

Mr Plumphett rubbed his nose thoughtfully. "Not entirely, Lady Westerlea. It is true that the jewels were intended to be part of the estate, but your dear departed father added a note to his will giving rather different instructions. Horace, the codicil, if you please." This time the young man had the paper ready. Mr Plumphett went rather pink, and said, "Forgive me, my lady, if I do not put this into your hands for you to read yourself, but the language is... rather immoderate, shall we say. Pray allow me to read it aloud, so that I may... *paraphrase*. The note reads thus: *'To whom it may concern, Regarding my late wife's jewels, I have scoured the house looking for the... um, things, but they are nowhere to be found, and they are of no... no use to me now. If any man should find the... gems, he may keep them with my goodwill for they will not help me in the... um, in the grave.'* And it is signed and dated and witnessed by his valet and groom, all very correct. So you see, Mr Winterton, if you should find the jewels, they will be yours, beyond any dispute."

"They were supposed to be for my sisters' dowries," Jeremy said slowly. "There is a moral obligation—"

"Nonsense," Rosamund said. "We would have been glad of the jewels years ago, to be sure, but we are all of us very comfortably situated now. Besides, if Papa had had the jewels, he would never have mortgaged Woodside, and we should not have been obliged to sell it to settle his debts. No, if you can find the jewels, they are yours. They may perhaps enable you to settle matters with Mr Tyrrell directly, should you wish, without recourse to law."

"Which would be splendid, if I knew how to find them," Jeremy said in frustration. "But I have not the least idea."

"Then they are lost for ever," Rosamund said sombrely.

~~~~~

Mr Plumphett's gig had barely disappeared from view down the drive, and Jeremy and the Westerleas were still on the steps overseeing his departure, when there was another, and rather grander, arrival. A train of three carriages rolled up the drive, one very stylish and the other two somewhat plainer, of the type used for transporting servants and luggage. Jeremy was not left for long to wonder who the visitors might be, for almost before the first carriage had drawn to a halt, the door was hurled open and out flew his sister Lucy, beaming from ear to ear, and chattering non-stop. He laughed, and ran down the steps to sweep her into an affectionate embrace. Behind her, descending more decorously, was his next-to-youngest sister Margaret, who said nothing, but threw her arms around him and burst into tears.

Some things would never change. They were older, of course — Lucy older and thinner, and Margaret older and plumper — but they were his own sisters in essence, and their very presence wrapped him in the comfort of familiar affection, the unquestioning love of family.

Lucy talked non-stop the whole way into the house and through the introductions to their two husbands, who smiled with understanding eyes as they made their bows. She talked as she shed bonnet and gloves and pelisse, and she talked as the group moved forward into the library, there to hover round the fire. Even when tea and toast and cakes arrived, she carried on talking in an incessant flood, and it was not until her husband took hold of her hand and said in amused tones, "Might we perhaps hear what your brother has to say, my love?" that she finally subsided a little.

Jeremy told his tale, and then there was the situation with Woodside to be discussed, and Mr Plumphett's advice, and perhaps they would have talked the whole day, had not Rosamund stood up and said briskly, "There will be plenty of time for this over dinner, and I daresay Annabelle and Fanny will be joining us in a day or two, and it will all have to be gone over again. Let me show you to your rooms so that you may rest after your journey."

Before anyone could move, the door was thrown open and the butler intoned, "The Lady Elizabeth Drake, my lady."

Jeremy froze. The very name sent him back instantly to his twelve-year-old self, unsophisticated and inarticulate, fear and loathing squirming inside him in equal measure. She paused on the threshold, raking the room with stony eyes until they fell on him, and lingered there, the brows contracting.

"Well. So rumour has the truth of it for once. It *is* you."

She was old, and that was a surprise. To his youthful self, Lady Elizabeth had always seemed old, in the way of dowagers used to having their own imperious way, but now she had the sagging skin and greying hair to put the matter beyond question. He had never thought about her age before, but he supposed she must be drawing close to sixty. Her bearing was still queenly, though. The rigid back, the raised chin, the unsmiling countenance, the haughty demeanour — these had not changed at all.

But Jeremy had changed. He was not twelve any longer. Even though his heart pounded and fear roared through him like a whirlwind, he would not be cowed by her. Not any more.

"Lady Elizabeth," he murmured, and executed a modest bow, just restrained enough that she could take it as an insult if she pleased.

The others had all risen at her entrance. Now they made her their bows and curtsies, but she made no response. After a moment, she strode across the room to claim the central chair. Again her eyes swept the room, and even Lucy took a step backwards, while Margaret shrank into her tall husband's shadow.

"May I offer you some refreshments, Lady Elizabeth?" Rosamund said calmly. "Tea, perhaps?"

"Nothing," Lady Elizabeth said. "All I want is an explanation. What do you have to say for yourself, young man?" Her gaze rested on Jeremy again.

"Why, nothing at all," he said. "Whatever explanation I choose to offer is for my family alone."

Her eyes narrowed. "That is not good enough. I insist that —"

"No," he said quietly.

There was surprise on her face, and also puzzlement. He had caught her off guard, and he could almost see her considering her response. Would she let her temper fly, or would she choose a softer approach? He saw the moment she settled on softness. Years of dealing with astute businessmen had given him the ability to read faces far more guarded than hers.

"Jeremy, my dear boy," she said, with an attempt at an amused smile. "Why so hostile to an old friend? I have only your best interests at heart, after all."

This was so disingenuous that Jeremy could barely breathe for the anger welling up inside him. He controlled it — that, too, he had learnt over the years. He gave her back a smile just as artificially amused as her own.

"Your concern for me is perfectly well understood," he said with emphasis. "Forgive me, Lady Elizabeth, but I have some letters to write before the dressing bell."

With a neat bow, he left the room, crossing the hall in swift steps and taking the stairs two at a time in case anyone should attempt to drag him back. In the sanctuary of his room, he paced back and forth like a lion at a menagerie, too restless, too *angry* to sit.

As he passed in front of his dressing mirror, he caught sight of his face and stopped abruptly. Goodness, how fierce he looked! Abruptly, his anger died away and he smiled wryly at himself. Why was he upset? He had stood up to her, after all. He was not twelve years old any more, he was a grown man and the Lady Elizabeth Drake had no power over him.

He began to laugh.

6: *Shades Of The Past*

A timid scratching at the door interrupted his thoughts. A servant? Surely they would be busy preparing rooms for the new arrivals. He strode to the door and flung it open, looking down at the position where a maid's face would be. He encountered only waistcoat. Raising his eyes, he found he had to look up. There were few men taller than he was, but Margaret's husband was one of them.

"So sorry to disturb your letter-writing." he said softly, "but Margaret has vanished and since the others are still... entertaining, it occurred to me that you might know where she has gone."

Haymer, that was his name. The clergyman, and heir to... was it a viscountcy? He rather thought it was. Quiet little Margaret would be a viscountess one day. Astonishing thought.

How could Jeremy possibly know where she might have run off to...? But he did, he realised. "The tree house."

Haymer smiled. "Yes, of course. Might I prevail upon you to show me the way?"

They crept down the stairs and across the hall, Lady Elizabeth's haranguing tones still echoing from the library. Outside, Jeremy set off across Westerlea's immaculate lawn and into the shrubbery. Skirting the formal gardens, he led his companion down the steps to the park and thence to the boundary wall, where a wrought iron gate gave them access to a tree-sheltered glade with a rushing stream running through it. The bridge was still there, and on the far side, the place with steps set into the wall. Climbing over, they stood in the grounds of Woodside.

Several paths led in different directions through dense woodland, but Jeremy unhesitatingly selected one narrow track. In a very few minutes, it brought them to an ancient oak tree right on the edge of the woodland. From its high boughs one might look over the tops of the trees towards Westerlea Park or Frickham village, or over the informal gardens of Woodside. It was the perfect place for a tree house, and there it still was, the sturdy platform visible through the boughs.

"Margaret, dearest," Haymer called. "Are you there?" A long silence, then a small, white face peered over the platform rail far above. "May we come up?" She nodded, and the face disappeared again.

Haymer set one foot on the ladder.

"Let me go first," Jeremy said. "Those rungs look ancient, and might not bear your weight."

"Mr Winterton, if you imagine that I am going to allow you to risk plunging to your death only days after returning to the family fold, you are very much mistaken. I shall go first, and if the ladder bears my weight it will certainly bear yours."

Jeremy laughed and agreed to it. Haymer climbed ponderously, and when he had vanished over the edge onto the platform, Jeremy made his own ascent. The years dropped away as he rose through the branches, still leafless at this season. Except that the rungs of the ladder appeared to be closer together now, he might have been twelve again. When he reached the platform, it seemed smaller than he remembered. He had to duck low to enter the house, and already it felt crowded, with only Margaret and Haymer in it. Jeremy took the opposite bench, positioning his legs with care so as not to tangle with Haymer's even longer limbs.

For a while they sat in silence, Haymer holding Margaret tight while she rested her face on his coat, eyes closed. They seemed right for each other, this composed, self-effacing clergyman and quiet Margaret. Rosamund and her rather grand baron were a good match, too. Lucy and the handsome man with the roguish eyes? He would reserve judgement on that. Then there was Annabelle and her earl, and little Fanny, who was already a viscountess, and would be a marchioness one day. How well his sisters had married! They had made better matches, perhaps, than they could have expected had they stayed in the confined society of Brinshire.

"Tell me," Haymer said to Jeremy in his soft voice, "what is it about this Lady Elizabeth Drake that so distresses Margaret? And *you* dislike her, too, I could see that in your face when she was announced. All I know of her is that she is the daughter of an earl, and a widow."

"She was... very close to Papa," Jeremy said, thinking back. How best to describe her? "Too close, perhaps. She had too much influence over him. After Mama died, she... well, she stayed at Woodside several times. Helping, she said, but I know some of the neighbours thought it rather scandalous. There was an expectation that they would marry as soon as it was decent to do so. I am sure she was glad that Mama was dead. She always disliked me, and it was her doing that got me sent away."

"Jealous," Margaret said, looking up suddenly. "Mama."

"She was jealous of your mother?" Haymer said, understanding this cryptic utterance without difficulty. "Lady Elizabeth is a widow of long standing, I believe?"

Margaret nodded. "Copied Mama," she said. "Gowns, furniture, receipts. Dinners, balls. If Mama... held a dinner... she had one... grander."

"You remember all that?" her husband said, in affectionate amusement.

"Some. Mrs Claremont told me... more." She paused, took a deep breath, and then took her husband's hand firmly in her own. "She wanted to have everything Mama had. She had copies made of her gowns, her necklaces, even furniture — the hall console and chairs, and the dining room sideboard." To Jeremy, she said, "Mrs Claremont said that Lady Elizabeth hated the way you used to wander about the house at night."

"I never slept much," Jeremy said. "The house was lovely at night, creaky and *alive* in a way that it never was during the day, when it was filled with bustle. I used to imagine that it slept during the day, but woke up at night, watching over all the secret goings-on — the mice in the pantry, the groom slipping into the scullery maid's room... and me, wandering here and there, feeling its energy all around me."

Margaret nodded. "I used to, too. Wander about at night. But I expect you saw something, or she thought you did."

"Her leaving Papa's room? Yes, I saw her do so more than once in the dead of night. I disliked it, although I was not sure why, then. At twelve years old, one does not fully understand the adult world, but I knew it was wrong. She asked me once why I disliked her so, and I told her that I had seen her at night and that she was a bad woman. She told me I was a nasty, sneaking little boy, and not long after that Papa sent me away."

"That is very bad, to come between father and son," Haymer said.

"Papa was not himself after Mama died," Margaret said. "Too easily influenced. But they fell out after you died... I mean, after you were *believed* to have died." She smiled, then. "So happy you are not dead."

He laughed. "So am I, sister, so am I, although I missed a great deal while I was dead, seemingly."

"Are you going to try to find Mama's jewels?"

He exhaled, then said ruefully. "I suppose I must try, although I am not sure how to begin."

"Mama's room," she said. "That is the place to begin."

He rubbed his ear thoughtfully. "This may be a wild goose chase, you know."

Margaret shook her head firmly. "Mama believed you could find them, so you can."

~~~~~

That evening was a delight to Jeremy. With three of his sisters there, he began to feel as if he had found his family again, despite the splendour of the surroundings. He had seldom been inside Westerlea Park as a boy, for although the families were neighbours, there was no intimacy beyond polite morning calls and occasional invitations to dinner. The previous Lord Westerlea had been a distant, aristocratic figure, who had taken little notice of the young Wintertons, and the house had seemed unimaginably grand to Jeremy's boyhood self. Even Carrington Hall, Lady Elizabeth's house, had not seemed quite so imposing.

Yet here Rosamund was completely at home, with her jewels and elaborately arranged hair and London gowns. All three of his sisters had turned into ladies of fashion, and their husbands no less stylish. Jeremy felt oddly rustic, with his coat from the second-best tailor in Lancaster, and his plain waistcoat and simple neckcloth.

Before dinner, the others talked of their children, details of new teeth and scraped elbows so domesticated that he could almost forget that they occurred in mansions of scores of rooms on vast estates. But during dinner, the talk turned to the coming season in London, and the arrangements for hired houses and balls and the proper number of footmen required, and whether it was better to take one's barouche from home, or rent one in town, and he began to feel out of his depth. A mere mill manager could have nothing to contribute to the discussion.

So while they threw noble titles into the air like shuttlecocks — *'Lord Huntsmere's house may be available, or what about Lady Grassley's place? For I do not think we can squeeze in with the marquess again.'* — Jeremy let his mind drift back to Branton, and the mill, and Ellen Ridwell. What was he doing here, mingling with the aristocracy as if he belonged? He was no gentleman, that much was certain. He had no fortune, no great estate, not even a house of his own. He might one day inherit Giles Moreton's mill, and Ellen might bring him hers, but that was trade and therefore not respectable. It was neither land, nor wealth decently invested in the funds. That was his place, surely. He should go back to Branton, and settle down as John Moreton for the rest of his life.

And yet... this was his home, here in Brinshire. Woodside. This was where he belonged. His roots here ran as deep as any tree in the old woodland. This was his proper place in the world.

"What do you say, Winterton? Or may I, as a brother, call you Jeremy?"

It was Lucy's husband speaking, he of the handsome face and roguish eyes. Audley, that was his name. But it was a difficult question to answer. Was he Jeremy Winterton or was he John Moreton? He could not say. Tomorrow he might be John Moreton again, but for tonight he was Jeremy Winterton.

So he smiled and agreed to it, and they shared their names with him in return. Leo, with his amused eyes. Mel, the great, tall clergyman. And he was to call Lord Westerlea Robin. That would take some getting used to.

When the footmen and butler had withdrawn, the talk turned to Woodside, and the options open to Jeremy — to buy it from Tyrrell, to marry Jane Tyrrell, to claim it in law or to find the missing jewels. Jeremy explained the difficulties with each one.

"But there is yet another possibility," Leo said eagerly. "Allow me — or several of us — to purchase Woodside on your behalf. A loan, if you like, to be repaid whenever you can afford it. We wished to do so at the time, but there seemed little point then, when no one of the Winterton family would be able to live in it, and so the sisters all agreed to let it be sold."

"Even Fanny?" Jeremy said, to general laughter.

"Fanny has discovered that romantic sensibilities do not always answer," Rosamund said, with a smile. "But do you truly want Woodside, brother? You have been away from Brinshire and living a very different life for so many years. Would you be happy here as a man of leisure, with no work to keep you busy?"

"Woodside is mine by right," Jeremy said sharply. "Whether I wish it or not, it is my inheritance, and I will neither buy what is mine, nor borrow for the purpose. The law is uncertain, and if the risk were not sufficient deterrent, there is the upset and disruption for everyone else involved. Besides, it could drag on for years, while the lawyers grow fat at our expense. Nor, I regret to say, can I accept your charitable assistance, Leo, although you have my heartfelt gratitude for the offer, which is generous indeed. You may talk about loans and easy repayment terms, but I will not under any circumstances put myself into debt to obtain Woodside. If I am to leave my time in trade behind, I must at least begin my life as a gentleman with an unencumbered income, free of debt, or I shall be no gentleman at all. I would sooner give up all prospect of recovering Woodside than allow myself to be so beholden, even to family."

"Then your options are few," Robin said. "To find the jewels, if you can, and trade them for your inheritance, or to marry Jane Tyrrell."

"The jewels are gone," Rosamund said. "But Jane Tyrrell... you could do far worse, Jeremy. She has a prickly exterior, it is true, but she is an excellent manager and would make any man a good wife."

"I have a wife in mind already," he said. "It seems that all avenues are closed to me. I must consider carefully what I shall do next, but it may be that I will leave Mr Tyrrell in possession for now. If I return to Branton and marry Ellen, then in a few years I shall perhaps be rich enough to buy Woodside without incurring debt or employing all my capital."

"Ellen!" Lucy said excitedly. "Oh, *do* tell us about Ellen, brother."

And the rest of the evening passed in the pleasurable delineation of his future bride's manifold attractions, and his anticipation of many years of married bliss.

~~~~~

The following day saw the arrival of the rather battered travel coach of the Earl of Brackenwood and his wife. The earl was a surprise, for despite his exalted rank, he was dressed with more regard for comfort than style. He pumped Jeremy's hand genially and told him to call him Allan. Annabelle, however, eyed Jeremy up and down with great suspicion.

"Well, you *look* like my brother, that much is certain, but are you indeed Jeremy or a clever impostor?" Annabelle said.

"Test me," Jeremy said promptly. "Ask me something that only Jeremy would know."

"Who fell in the stream by the farm?" she said at once. "And who let the pig out?"

"Nurse fell in the stream, and it was *not* my fault, for once. Fanny let the pig out, because she was sure it was unhappy to be so confined. But *I* let the bull out, to see what would happen."

"And what did happen?"

"I got thrashed, mainly. The rest is of lesser significance in my mind, for some reason, but I was vaguely aware that there was a great deal of commotion, and cabbages came into it somehow. Mr Price's cabbages, I think."

She laughed. "Jeremy! How wonderful to see you again! Bewildering, of course, but wonderful."

And later that day, when they had already sat down to dinner, a post-chaise and four arrived, the horses sweating and exhausted, to disgorge an excited Fanny and her breathtakingly elegant husband.

"Jeremy! Oh Jeremy!" Fanny squealed, while crying all over him.

"Dearest?" said her imperturbable spouse, offering her an immaculately folded handkerchief. To Jeremy, he said, "Let her have her cry, Mr Winterton, and she will be quite composed by and by. I am Ferdy, by the way."

"Lord Craston," Jeremy said, bowing as best he could with Fanny weeping into his waistcoat and clutching his coat.

"No, no," he said. "Everyone in the family calls me Ferdy." He looked round at the faces gathered around the dining table. "Ah, I see we are the last to arrive. How cosy this is."

Jeremy had nothing to do that evening except listen to Lucy explaining every detail of the situation to the new arrivals, occasionally smiling and saying, "Yes, that is indeed so," and to tolerate Fanny clinging to one arm as if she could thereby prevent him ever leaving again. But with all the sisters now present, dressed in their evening finery and with husbands just as well-arrayed, Jeremy felt even more like an interloper. Far from being the wandering son returned to the fold, he more greatly resembled a cuckoo in the Winterton nest.

~~~~~

Jane fretted after her talk with her papa. Her whole future, which she had believed secure, was thrown into uncertainty by the return of Mr Jeremy Winterton to Frickham. Such an oddity as he was, to pretend to be someone he was not, to leave two families unaware of the truth — one believing their son to be thriving in a northern mill town when he was drowned in the sea, and the other grieving for a lost heir, when he yet lived. How wrong of him! And now he would extend the wrong to yet another family, to *her* family, by depriving them of their home.

She knew of her father's offer to him, she had heard through the servants that the fat solicitor had been summoned to the Park, and she had seen the many elegant carriages passing by. All five sisters were now present in Frickham, and since the Westerlea servants were close-lipped, she might not have an opportunity to find out anything before they all met at church on Sunday. So much was going on from which she was excluded, yet she and her father were directly affected by any decisions made.

Whatever might be said of Jane, she was not retiring. She needed to know how matters stood regarding Woodside, so after waiting two days for word which never came, she determined to go to Westerlea Park and ask directly. Knowing the family breakfasted late, she timed her visit to arrive just after they should have finished. It was a risk, for the gentlemen might well have gone out already, but even she dared not disrupt the family at breakfast.

She had only just turned out of the Woodside gates, however, when she encountered a large group walking towards her — the five Winterton sisters, and their brother. Amidst the deluge of greetings, it emerged that they had come in search of her, just as she had hoped to see them.

"Jeremy wishes to talk to you," Lucy said.

"We are come especially for the purpose," Fanny said.

Jeremy, choosing not to speak for himself with so many sisters to speak on his behalf, merely smiled and nodded.

"You wanted to see me?" Jane said, surprised.

"And your father, naturally," Mr Winterton said. "You must have many questions in your mind, and it would be reprehensible in me to keep you in the dark as to all that has been discovered about Woodside. It is your home, after all."

She was much mollified by this openness. "My father is gone to Brinchester for the day, but if I alone would make an acceptable recipient of your confidences, I will undertake to convey the whole of it to my father when he returns."

It was agreed, so they all proceeded up Woodside's short drive. Inside, Jane led them into the drawing room, and after the offer of refreshments had been refused, the ladies disposed themselves about the room, while Jane and Mr Winterton sat decorously on opposing sofas. Hushing his sisters as only a brother could do — "Do stow it, all of you, while I talk to Miss Tyrrell" — he told her everything that the lawyer had said, and how it seemed that all his options had closed up. She listened quietly, finding that his explanations were so lucid that she was left with no questions to ask. Except one.

"So what will you do?"

He smiled then, his eyes lighting up with amusement. "Ah, straight to the point — I like that. Yet how can I answer? It is an imponderable question. Every avenue is fraught with difficulties. If I had fewer scruples about indebtedness, I should allow my brother-in-law to fund me. Yet somehow I dislike the idea of being a gentleman without the income to support it. But unless I borrow, I cannot buy Woodside outright. The law is open to me, but it is both expensive and uncertain. The very idea of marrying to secure a home must be repugnant to both of us."

"You are already betrothed, are you not?" she said.

He hesitated. "Not betrothed, no. Nothing has been said on either side, but it is my hope, certainly. That is why I came here, to resolve unsettled matters before moving into matrimony. It seemed to me that my suit would be more acceptable with the prospect of a gentleman's estate in the future."

"You were uncertain of the outcome, then?" she said.

He raised an eyebrow at such a personal question, but answered readily, "No, for the lady's parents were amenable to the idea, but Ellen's dowry would be Ridwell's most productive mill, and my prospects were much less. It would have pleased me to bring a gentleman's estate to the marriage, to balance the scales somewhat."

She was struck by his business-like approach to the matter. "And what of the lady? Was she likewise amenable to the idea?"

He gave his wide smile — so like Rosamund, and yet different. "Ellen will do as her father bids her."

"What a feeble creature she must be, to have no opinions of her own."

He raised his eyebrows a shade more, but replied composedly, "She is a lady, Miss Tyrrell, and very well brought up. Naturally she will obey her parents."

"And how shall you like to have such a biddable wife, Mr Winterton? Every meal will consist of you declaiming about topics of interest while she says *'Yes, sir'* or *'No, sir'* in a timid voice. No doubt if you ask for veal for your dinner, she will send every servant out to find some for you, and spend the afternoon in tears if there is none to be had, instead of telling you robustly that you will have mutton and like it. And heaven help you if you praise one of her gowns, for she will wear pink sprig muslin every day thereafter. You will be bored of her within a twelvemonth."

He shifted restlessly, a flash of anger crossing his face but it vanished as quickly as it came. Instead, he laughed. "Rosamund said you were *prickly*, Miss Tyrrell, and I must agree. Talking to you is like tangling with a holly bush." Perhaps he caught the amusement in her face, for he sighed and said, "You are teasing me, I collect."

"A little, although I do think a timid wife would bore any rational man half to death. I am sure your Ellen will show more spirit once she is mistress of her own home. Little Rose Claremont was a perfect mouse until she became Mrs James Crewe, and then—"

"Rose Claremont and James Crewe?" he said in astonished tones. "But they were *babies* when I left."

"And now they are wed and have babies of their own," she said briskly. "Shall we sit here talking about all the changes that have occurred since you went away? We might be here until Michaelmas."

That made him smile, but he said only, "I do not know what else I may do here."

"Apart from enjoying my sparkling wit, you mean?" she said. He raised his hands in mock surrender. "There is one thing you *could* do while you are here — you could look at your Mama's room, and see if you may deduce where she kept her jewels."

"Yes!" Margaret said. "Jeremy can... find them. Mama said so."

"If Papa could not find them, I do not know what more I may do," he said. "Still, by all means, let us look at the room."

7: A Walk In The Garden

The room looked very different from Jeremy's memories. The walls were papered in pale colours, there were new rugs covering the dark wooden floor and flowery drapery hung from the windows. Once the holland covers were removed, the furniture was seen to be light and elegant, in the modern style. Only the bed remained the same, planted solidly in the middle of the floor as if rooted there, although with new hangings to match the curtains.

"What happened to the rest of the furniture?" Jeremy said.

"None of us wanted any of it," Lucy said before Miss Tyrrell could reply. "That is no surprise, for I never saw anything so ugly. Fanny took her own bedroom furniture, from sentiment, but we left everything else here for the Tyrrells to do with as they pleased."

"We kept most of the formal furniture downstairs," Miss Tyrrell said. "We had our own bedroom furniture, however, so what we could find no use for, we sold if we could, or gave away. No one wanted the washstand, which is in the housekeeper's room, and the dressing table stool is in my room."

"Yet you kept the bed?" he said, in amused tones. "That is the ugliest of the lot."

"No one could shift it," she said, pulling a face. "We tried, believe me, but even with the groom and coachman, the gamekeeper and his boy and the gardeners, it would not move so much as an inch. So we left it in place, but with enough drapery to cover up the worst of the carvings. Did your mother truly like it? For if so, I think poorly of her taste."

"It was supposedly a family heirloom," Jeremy said with a shrug. "Well, I have seen the room, and there is nowhere for the jewels to be hidden that has not already been investigated by Papa. Rosamund, you said he took the room apart, did you not?"

"He dismantled everything — the walls, the floor, the chimney, the ceiling, and every stick of furniture."

"What about a secret compartment?" Jane Tyrrell said. "A drawer with a false bottom would be large enough to conceal a necklace."

"It was more than just a necklace," Jeremy said. "There could not have been anywhere capacious enough to hide the jewels. They were in four boxes, each perhaps two feet by two feet."

"That is a lot of jewels," she said in surprise.

"Two were parures, of mostly emeralds and rubies. There was a necklace, the Tilford Sapphires, with one very large stone, a famous thing. Then there was a box of unset gems, mostly diamonds."

Her eyes widened. "Oh — I had no idea. But if you could find all of that, you would be rich indeed. Whatever would you do with such wealth?"

"Buy Woodside," he said at once.

"Yet you expressed your repugnance for buying what was yours by right," she said.

What an irritating woman she was, for she always cut straight to the heart of the matter, without prevarication. Yet such directness was refreshing. "Yes, Woodside is mine by right, but I will not impoverish myself to regain it, whether through the law or by outright debt. If, however, a fortune should fall into my lap, I could use that for the purpose and still be able to live as a gentleman. I must be able to live independently. I have never been in debt in my life, and have no intention of starting now. I am sure you can appreciate such a sentiment."

She nodded. "Yes, I see. But are you quite sure the jewels were in this room?"

"Oh yes. They could have been nowhere else. For the last year or two of her life, Mama was not well enough to leave her room — indeed, she was almost bedridden. Yet I saw the sapphire necklace only a month or two before she died. They were her great joy, those jewels, and not just for their value. She loved to take them out of their hiding place at night when all the candles were lit, just to watch them sparkle and dance. She would invite all of us in here to admire them. Then she would send everyone out of the room while she hid them away again. There was nowhere else she could have hidden them. They were in this room, beyond doubt."

"Then they must have been in the furniture," she said firmly. "*Not* the room itself, for if your father dismantled even the wall panels and chimney, he must have found any safe or other hiding place. What about the bed? The end panels are so large that any number of jewel boxes may be hidden in there, and the weight of it suggests there may be a small safe concealed within. Was it dismantled, too?"

"Papa stripped away all the hangings," Rosamund said, "and shredded the mattress and all the pillows and bolsters. The rest of it is solid wood, with no drawers or cupboards built in, despite the size of it."

"Was that tested?" Jeremy said. "Did anyone drill through the wood to probe for hidden spaces within?"

"I... do not think so," Rosamund said. "Do you really think—?"

A frisson of excitement swept through Jeremy. The bed — yes! He strode across the room, sweeping aside the hangings to examine it. The panel at the head of the bed was several inches thick, the outer side covered with a bizarre array of animals and birds, all bulbous noses and sharp ears. The inner side was smooth in the centre, with only the perimeter engraved with vines laden with grapes. The foot panel was perhaps four feet thick, and covered on both sides with relief carvings.

Rosamund pulled a face. "So ugly! But do you think the jewels may be inside?"

"It is possible. This part of the bed is certainly large enough, but there would need to be a secret door." Jeremy felt all over the outer side of the foot panel, running his hands over the protrusions, looking for any part that moved or twisted or showed any sign of such a possibility. Then he knelt on the bare mattress, and repeated the procedure for the inner side. "The light is poor in here. Do you have a lamp of some sort, Miss Tyrrell?"

"I will fetch one," Jane said. When she came back, she said, "What are you looking for, precisely?"

"A shiny surface," he said absently.

"A... what? Oh... shiny from use, you mean?"

He looked up at her as she held the lamp above him. "You are very quick, ma'am. Precisely so. If any part has been frequently used to open a concealed compartment, the handle will be— oh!" He practically fell back onto the bed as a door popped open. "Oh, it just needed to be pulled. No wonder these creatures have such large noses. And this must be the other door. Oh. It is only a clock."

With the two doors opened high in the centre of the foot board, a large and ornate clock face was revealed.

"No wonder the bed is so heavy," he said. "With all the workings of this thing, it is hardly a surprise that no one could move the bed. The foot board needs to be high to conceal the pendulum. But there is just the clock, a drawer for the key to wind it, and no more noses open any doors, that I can find. Well, that is a disappointment. No doubt Papa knew of the clock's existence, so he never attempted to dismantle the bed."

"Then the jewels must be in the other furniture," Jane said. "The stool in my bedroom is very heavy — shall we see if we can find another secret?"

He looked at her in amusement. "Do you enjoy secrets, Miss Tyrrell?"

"Of course! Who does not? Come on, this way."

They followed her down a passageway, and the sisters exclaimed in delight when she threw open a door.

"Oh, Rosamund's room!" Lucy cried.

"But how pretty you have made it," Rosamund said. "I love the wallpaper. Whatever kind of birds are these, with the long legs, like pink storks?"

"I have not the least idea," Jane said. "My sister Charlotte chose it. I should not have bothered for myself, but this was her room until she married, and she was always able to wheedle money from Papa for whatever she wanted. I moved in here after she left, for the view over the drive. Here is the dressing stool."

It was, like all his mother's furniture, a monstrous ugly piece, both large and heavy. It lacked the exotic birds and animals, but there was heavy decoration all about it, of the style popular a hundred years ago, and ill suited, Jeremy would have thought, to a lady's bedchamber. But Jane was right, for the legs were short and the large box that formed the seat was certainly roomy enough to conceal secrets. Jeremy knelt down and examined all sides of it, but it looked very solid.

"The lid conceals a storage space," Jane said helpfully, lifting the padded seat. "But I see no way to access a hidden compartment beneath."

Jeremy stared at it gloomily. It was true, for the inside of the empty box was smooth on all sides.

A small hand patted his shoulder as Margaret bent down to whisper in his ear. "Mama said... you could do it."

"You are so good with gadgets and devices," Annabelle said. "If anyone can find a way in, you can."

"Well..." Jeremy pondered the problem. Where would he hide a secret place, if he were making such a piece? The lid? But that was a solid piece of wood, with padding. Nothing there. The sides of the box were too thin to conceal anything, but the base... He measured the depth with his hand... yes! There was a hidden space at the bottom. But how to access it? He ran his hands carefully over the carved outer panels and the smooth insides of the box. Nothing. He pushed and pulled and twisted the carved shapes. Nothing. He tried the underneath. Nothing.

"Lamp," he said.

Jane fetched the lamp from the other bedroom, and held it close.

"Aha!" Two spots which were more polished than the rest of the carving. *Two* spots... so it needed both. He pushed and pulled and twisted the two places at the same time. Pop! A concealed door shot open from inside the box. The ladies all gasped excitedly.

"It is empty," Lucy said sorrowfully, peering in. The ladies all sighed their disappointment.

A shallow compartment was revealed, and indeed it was empty, but Jeremy was not disheartened. He knew at once that it was not large enough to account for the whole space available at the bottom of the box. His fingers probed again, something shifted and slid and opened, and there was the secret space revealed.

It was not empty.

Carefully Jeremy drew out the contents one by one. A sheet of paper. A large coin. A silk purse, heavy. And that was all.

The ladies fell on these treasures with cries of glee. The purse was found to contain a modest necklace of garnets.

"One of Mama's trumpery pieces," Annabelle said in disappointed tones. "These are not the valuable items."

Rosamund had the paper. "This is strange," she said. "A quotation, I think, but none that I recognise. *'Why, if you have a stomach, to't, monsieur: if you think your mystery in stratagem can bring this instrument of honour again into his native quarter, be magnanimous in the enterprise and go on; I will grace the attempt for a worthy exploit: if you speed well in it, the duke shall both speak of it, and extend to you what further becomes his greatness, even to the utmost syllable of your worthiness.'* What can it mean? Annabelle?"

"Shakespeare. I think it is from *All's Well That Ends Well*, but as to what it means or why it was hidden away, I cannot say."

Jeremy rolled the coin in his fingers. Was it even a coin? A smooth disc of polished metal, that was all that could be said of it, with the number '4' engraved on one side and the number '15' on the other. From a game? Yet he knew of no game with such pieces, and why only one such, and hidden so secretly? It was a puzzle.

Jane Tyrrell's voice cut through his ruminations. "Shall we look at the washstand next? It is in the housekeeper's room."

"Really, Jane," Rosamund said in her best dowager's voice, "we can hardly traipse through the servants quarters *en masse*, rummage around for secret compartments and perhaps produce more jewellery. It would be all over the county within the hour. A little subtlety is called for. Can you find an excuse to get the washstand out of Havelock's room without attracting attention?"

"I am sure I can fabricate some reason to remove it," Jane said.

"And can you keep all this to yourself?" Rosamund went on relentlessly. "These jewels are worth a king's ransom, and we do *not* want it shouted from the rooftops that they might still be in the house."

Jane Tyrrell flushed.

Jeremy felt his sister's rudeness exceedingly. "I am sure Miss Tyrrell understands the importance of secrecy."

"Naturally I do," she said in a low voice. "Whatever do you take me for? Shall we go downstairs and have some refreshments?"

The ladies agreed to it, but there being some agitation in the kitchen on account of the number of guests, Rosamund suggested that they should all take a turn about the grounds for half an hour. This was agreed to with alacrity by the other sisters, who had few opportunities to stroll around their former home, and Jeremy had no objection.

He soon found that his sisters were slow walkers. They stopped every ten paces to exclaim over some tree or bush or bench which they remembered, or, conversely, which had been placed there since they left. Either case, it seemed, required endless discussion. So it was that Jeremy and Jane Tyrrell soon outpaced the others and found themselves back at the house.

"There is a chill wind," she said. "I am not minded to stand outside and wait for your sisters. Shall we go inside?"

"By all means," he said. He wondered if he ought to apologise for Rosamund's rudeness, but Miss Tyrrell had not seemed upset by the exchange, talking composedly as they walked about the garden, and, after all, it was not his place to apologise for the behaviour of a baroness. So he said nothing, following Miss Tyrrell into the house.

The dining room had been prepared for their repast, but was deserted. She took a deep breath, then turned to him with a determined expression on her face. "Mr Winterton, I do not suppose you have given much thought to those affected by your efforts to recover Woodside, by whatever means. No—" She held up one hand, even as he opened his mouth to protest. "No, it is perfectly natural, and Papa is quite happy for you to have the place. But I am not." She glared at him in a manner he could only interpret as belligerent. At least he need not worry that she was offended by Rosamund. Clearly she had other issues on her mind.

"That I can appreciate," he said gently. "Woodside is your home, just as it was mine."

"It *is* my home," she said fiercely. "But it is also my independence, and I will not give it up without a fight. Do you understand?"

"I do, for that is just how I feel myself," he said at once. "But we cannot both have Woodside. If you and your father keep it, then

I must leave, and if I take charge of it, then *you* must leave. There is no avoiding that."

"Hmm. You would not, I suppose, consider employing me as your housekeeper?"

"I would not, and if you considered the matter rationally for five seconds, you would not wish for it. Can you imagine what the world would say if I were to live here with you as my housekeeper? Your reputation would be destroyed, and it would hardly be helpful to mine. I am trying to establish myself as a gentleman, not as a libertine. No, it will not do, Miss Tyrrell. There is only one way in which you may remain at Woodside if I own it, and that is as my wife, an outcome we neither of us wish for. There is no alternative — you must leave Woodside. Your father will establish himself elsewhere, and you will be mistress of his house, just as you are here."

"No, he means to marry me off. He will drag me to Bath and bestow a handsome dowry on me."

Jeremy laughed. "No one can force you to marry, Miss Tyrrell, and I pity the man who attempts such a feat. You would shred him with that sharp tongue of yours."

She made no response, chewing her lip thoughtfully. "It all comes back to money, does it not? If I had money of my own, I should not be subject to Papa's whims. Mr Winterton, if I aid you in recovering your mama's jewels, will you pay me something? A percentage of the proceeds, perhaps. Enough to give me a little independence. I should not mind moving, you see, even to Bath, if I knew I could escape to one of my sisters if the fortune hunters became too oppressive. A modest income of my own, enough to pay for a post-chaise now and then."

"And if I find the jewels through my own endeavours?"

"Oh, I am not afraid of that. How do you imagine you will find your mother's jewellery?"

"The secret is hidden in her furniture, that much is clear, so I shall track down all the pieces that were sold or given away and—"

"And how will you accomplish that? Tell the world that certain extremely valuable items of jewellery are hidden in secret compartments in her old furniture, and could you please have them back?"

"Oh. Well, I shall tell them that I plan to buy Woodside, and I wish to recover everything from Mama's room, for sentimental reasons."

"They would wonder why you were worrying about furniture from years ago, when you have not even bought the house yet. I have a better plan."

"Then by all means let me hear it," he said, feeling anger rising again. Never had anyone had quite such an uncanny ability to needle him. The dratted woman was so wordy! If only she would come to the point.

She smoothed her skirts, not quite locking him in the eye. "We should do what everyone has been expecting anyway, and announce our engagement."

8: *Dinner At Westerlea Park (April)*

Jane lifted her head to watch the bewilderment cross his face, before he carefully schooled his expression. He thought himself controlled, no doubt, but he was not yet experienced enough to show no emotion at all.

"Are you mad?" he said eventually. "Marriage is the last thing either of us wants."

"I did not say marriage," she said levelly. "An engagement only. Once you have the jewels and I have my share, I shall cry off, with no blame to you. Easy enough to say that we would not suit, for never was a form of words so true. We should not suit at all, and there is no intent whatsoever for the marriage to take place, that much is certain. But a betrothal — that would give us an excuse to find lost items of furniture. Naturally you want to restore Woodside to the way it was when you were a boy. What could be more plausible?"

"I do not need a false betrothal to do that," he said. "Once I own Woodside—"

"Yes, indeed," she said, smiling up at him. "So go ahead and borrow the funds to buy it outright, or challenge the will in law, or whatever other expensive and difficult option you can dream up. Or you can pretend to like me for a few weeks, and have everything you want without debt or inconvenience. And I get what I want, too."

The others came into the room just then, laughing and excited, and the servants behind them with the refreshments, so that all opportunity for private discussion was at an end, but Jane was pleased to have planted the idea in his head. He would probably not agree to it — he disliked her too much, she suspected — but she was rather proud of the scheme. It would be useless if he could not find the jewels, of course, but they must be in one or other of the furniture items from the mother's room, hidden away in some unsuspected concealed drawer. The secretary — that was the most likely, for it was huge. Or the armoire.

For an instant, she considered the straightforward option — simply going to each purchaser, and asking to examine the item. What could be simpler? Just as quickly, she dismissed the idea. As soon as one person had been approached, word would fly around the neighbourhood, and that would be the end of it. They would search for the jewels themselves, and give every excuse not to return the furniture. *So sorry, we burnt it years ago. Or sold it on, or chopped it up for firewood. No, there was nothing hidden in it.* And every sneak and rogue for miles around would be breaking into any likely house and looking for secret compartments. No, Rosamund was right, as usual. If it were to be done, it had to be subtly, through subterfuge. Honesty would not serve, in this case.

But Jane was good at subterfuge. When everyone had gone, she made an excuse to visit the housekeeper's room, where

Havelock's scanty possessions were distributed on Mrs Winterton's washstand.

"That is an ugly old thing," Jane said, with seeming casualness. "It is too big for this room, anyway. Should you like a lighter piece in here, Havelock?"

"Oh, don't you be worrying, madam," Havelock said. "I'm used to it now, and there's plenty of space in those drawers down the side."

"What about that nice set from the little bedroom at the back of the house? The washstand is plain, but the dressing table is very pretty and would give you just as many drawers."

"From the bedroom Miss Annabelle and Miss Lucy shared?" Havelock said, scandalised. "I can't use the *family's* furniture."

Jane only laughed. "There is no family here any more, Havelock, except for Papa and me, so I do not see why a senior servant of many years' standing should not have good quality furniture in her room. Empty the drawers on that thing, and when the gardeners are here tomorrow, I shall get them to move everything around."

"Very good, madam," Havelock said, bemused.

~~~~~

APRIL

Jane and her father were invited to dinner at Westerlea Park, in honour of the return of the Winterton son. The Claremonts were there, with their sons John and Rupert, and John's wife Cecily, as well as Lady Elizabeth Drake, with her nephew Percival and niece Cressida, and the Whites and the Sheridans. All the important families within visiting range.

Jeremy Winterton was much exclaimed over, although the older ones were inclined to be censorious of his long neglect of his family.

"Really, Jeremy!" Mrs Claremont said. "It is too bad of you to have stayed away for all these years, and not a word to your poor papa. You drove him into an early grave, as I hope you are aware by now. He blamed himself entirely for your death."

"Did he so?" Mr Winterton said, in the mildest of tones. "I wonder who else he could have blamed?"

Jane smiled to herself at this robust answer. He was no milksop, that much was certain.

They sat down thirty to dinner, and Jane had never felt so drably provincial. Her best evening gown and modest strand of garnets were no match for the array of terrifyingly fashionable silks and bejewelled heads of the ladies, and the snowy froths of linen at the gentlemen's throats. It was unfortunate that she found herself squeezed between two of the most elegant of gentlemen, Fanny's husband Lord Craston and Rupert Claremont. Ever since Rupert's poor wife Lydia had expired in the effort to provide him with a son, the Claremonts had eyed Jane speculatively, and never lost an opportunity to push them together. She imagined them conferring together and putting her name at the top of the list. *'So suitable,'* they would say, *'and such a good manager.'* Rupert's wife would certainly have to be a good manager to live on a second son's meagre income. If he would find himself a sensible profession and rein in his proclivities towards the gaming table and women of uncertain morals, he could live quite comfortably, although she was quite determined that he would have to do it without her.

Percival Drake was another name much associated with hers. The three Drake children were not Lady Elizabeth's own but the offspring of her sister. Or so she said, although sometimes it was a cousin, or *'not exactly a sister, but a close relation'*, so naturally rumours flew as to the truth. An illegitimate sister, some said, or even Lady Elizabeth's own illegitimate offspring. But the only facts that could be gleaned were that no sister was recorded in the august pages of Debrett's Peerage, and that when the youngest was a year old, the supposed sister had died and Lady Elizabeth had brought all three of them to live with her and declared them her heirs, having no children of her own. They had dutifully taken her name and settled down to a life of indolence with enthusiasm.

When Jane and her father had first arrived in Brinshire, Lady Elizabeth had paid them a great deal of attention and pushed Jane and Percival together whenever possible, for they were much of an age. But that interest had dwindled, although whether it was her dowry of only two thousand pounds that deterred them, or Percival's own inclinations, she never discovered. Perhaps if he had been offered Woodside as dowry, he might have persevered. Whatever the cause, it was a relief to her. Even had she been looking for a husband, she could never like Percival Drake, whose oily manner reminded her of the worst kind of social climber, always paying compliments, never saying an honest word. She neither respected nor trusted him.

And now there was Jeremy Winterton, and she saw the speculative glances being cast from one to the other and then back again. Her father had no male heirs, so what more natural than that he should miraculously increase her dowry to encompass the entire Woodside estate? The returning heir and the daughter of the present owner — what could be more fitting? The only small rub in the way was the beautiful Miss Ridwell waiting patiently for her suitor up in Lancashire. And then there was the trivial hindrance that Jane and Jeremy disliked each other cordially.

With so many dining, there were several conversations ongoing, and Jane was kept busy listening to as many as she could. Not that anyone would say anything interesting in such mixed company, but one never knew. The only snatch of talk that intrigued her came from Lord Craston. He was near to Jeremy Winterton, and over the transfer of a dish of braised cabbage, Lord Craston said, "And how did you enjoy your stay in America, Mr Winterton?"

Whereupon Jeremy looked bemused for an instant, and then guilty. "Oh... that was you, of course. Well... I never was in America, in point of fact."

"I rather thought not," Lord Craston said cheerfully, and then the two men laughed, the dish was passed on and nothing further was said.

Jane had never accounted shyness amongst her attributes, so when Lord Craston politely turned to her, she boldly said, "How came you to think that Mr Winterton had been to America, my lord?"

He smiled at her, and she felt uncomfortably as if he were laughing at her, and expected him to fob her off with a bland answer. She could hardly blame him, for it was none of her business. To her surprise, he answered her seriously. "Some years ago, my wife and her sisters heard conflicting reports of Mr Winterton's last known activities. I set myself the task of visiting one of the last people to see him, Mr John Moreton in Branton. I saw Mr Giles Moreton, his uncle, who told me that his nephew was in America. If I had but known it, I was closer than I had realised to discovering information about Mr Winterton, but at the time it seemed as if all trails were cold."

"He did not want you to see Mr Winterton, then?" she said. "But why?"

"Oh, I never try to guess *why* anyone does anything, Miss Tyrrell. Such an exercise usually makes my head ache dreadfully. Should you like a little more of the goose? It is very tasty, is it not?"

And that, she supposed, was all he was prepared to say on the subject.

~~~~~

Jeremy felt that the evening went off tolerably well. He was berated by the Claremonts, of course, but he had expected that. There was much talk amongst the gentlemen over the port about legal proceedings regarding the will, and he received some astute estimates of his likelihood of success. The general consensus was that he would probably win, but the affair would quite likely bankrupt him. Tyrrell, who was honest to a fault, told the assembly that he would be quite happy to sell Woodside to Jeremy, if a reasonable offer were to be received. He even mentioned the possibility of making the estate Jane's dowry. Jeremy chose not to reply. No one was so crass as to ask him if he could afford to buy, or whether his wealthy brothers-in-law would fund him, or whether he wanted the place badly enough to marry Jane Tyrrell for it. The jewels were mentioned once or twice — *'Such a pity your dear mama's jewellery was never found'* — but if anyone had asked directly, he would have been able to answer truthfully that he had not the least idea what had become of them.

Lady Elizabeth disliked travelling after dark, so she and her nephew and niece expected accommodation to be found for them. Rosamund offered them the use of Holly Lodge, which had been her own home for some years, and was a very snug little property. However, it would not do for Lady Elizabeth and she had to be squeezed into the main house, already uncomfortably full with Jeremy and his sisters.

In the end, Lord Westerlea's elderly aunt gave up her room to Lady Elizabeth and Cressida, while Jeremy was forced to share his own room with Percival Drake. He had seldom been required to share sleeping quarters with anyone else, and Percival was a particular trial. Having imbibed freely of Lord Westerlea's hospitality, he was in garrulous mood, disposed to share with Jeremy every detail of the acquisition of his new hunter, his proposed visit to London after Easter and his recent conquests in the female line.

"Expect you'll be cosying up to bony little Jane, hur hur hur," he said, stretched out on the bed so that he commandeered two thirds of it. "Not much to my taste, but I daresay you'll think it worthwhile when that tight-fisted father of hers makes the house over to you. He has no heir, so whoever can stomach the daughter will get it. I did think about it myself, but she's too shrewish for me, hur hur. Expect you're less fussy, with your northern ways. Women are different in the north, so I've heard, hur hur hur." He yawned capaciously. "Lord, I'm tired. Westerlea keeps a good table, I must say. I like a man who is open-handed. We thought of brokering a deal for Julianna with one of his boys when they are all old enough, but not sure it would come off. Hate to say it of m'own sister, but she's dreadfully boot-faced, hur hur. And freckles, too. No hope for her. You were luckier with your sisters, Winterton. Expect they have a high old time in town, now that they've done their duty with the heirs and so forth, hur hur hur." Another enormous yawn.

Jeremy lay rigidly, turned away from his unwanted bedfellow, eyes closed. Eventually, Drake lapsed into silence for a while before the bed was shaken by stentorian snores. Jeremy sighed. It was going to be a long night.

~~~~~

Morning was never Jeremy's best time. He could go to bed drunk or sober, early or late, but whatever the case, he would wake late, convinced he had time for just one more hour of blissful sleep. His valet routinely had to shake him awake in time for breakfast.

The ladies were still abed, and most of the men had gone off to the Claremonts' estate some miles away for some rough shooting, so only Lord Westerlea and Percival Drake were left in the breakfast room.

"There is still time for you to catch up with the party, Jeremy," Lord Westerlea said. Robin, Jeremy reminded himself. "Or you, Drake," he added politely. "Lady Elizabeth will understand the appeal of guns and muddy fields and dogs, I am sure. You know where the gun room is, and you may borrow one of Lady Westerlea's hunters and ride on to Carrington Hall later."

"Thank you, but I am not minded for any sport today," Drake said, sullenly. "I shall knock a few balls about the billiard table."

"For myself, I should relish some time alone," Jeremy said. "I shall walk around the whole perimeter of Woodside, I think, and familiarise myself with its ditches and hedges once more."

"Ah yes, beating the bounds," Robin said sagely. "I try to do the same at the Park once a year, although I confess that my wife has greater enthusiasm for the enterprise than I do. My antipathy towards mud has not diminished with the years. I shall think of you and your ditches and hedges while I am ensconced beside the fire in my library."

Jeremy laughed. "The Park boundary is rather greater than that of Woodside, I fear, so your aversion is understandable. I wonder you do not construct a road around the margins of your land so that you might be conveyed in the comfort of a carriage."

"Perhaps one day I shall," he replied. "And now, gentlemen, my estate manager awaits me, I fear, so I shall leave you to your breakfast."

"I shall go too," Drake said. "Good day to you, Winterton. Enjoy your walk." And he smirked in a manner that made Jeremy wonder why he should look so pleased with himself.

He was in no rush to leave the comfort of the house, for it was one of those damp days of early April which looked pleasant enough when viewed from within, but a man might easily be chilled to the bone when venturing out. He reread his last letter from Branton, wrote a brief response, listing the many nobles and gentlemen attending the dinner last night, although without mentioning his own connection to many of them, and then donned his thickest greatcoat for his walk.

The sheep beyond the ha-ha grazed stolidly, impervious to the weather. Jeremy wished that he, too, had such a thick woollen coat to ward off the late winter cold, but his greatcoat and scarf would have to do. He quickened his pace a little as he passed beyond the Westerlea Park boundary, crossed the small stream and entered the grounds of Woodside. This time, he turned aside and began to follow the boundary wall in its ponderous loop through the countryside.

He had traversed the ground enough over the last few days that he no longer needed to pay attention to his surroundings. He knew where the woodland pressed close to the perimeter wall, and where it drew back, leaving him passing through open fields. He was aware of each small stream that meandered across his path, and the small wooden bridges or stepping stones that were conveniently placed for crossing them. He remembered the gamekeeper's small cottage, smoke rising gently from the chimney, its small patch of garden neatly laid out in squares of vegetables.

He recognised the denser woodland that indicated that his path was circling back to Woodside's pleasure gardens again.

The air was cool but crisp and he breathed deeply, his mind floating free for once. Out here in the clear English air, no problem was intractable, no worry so great that it could diminish his pleasure in the day. His long legs covered the ground without effort, his lungs were filled with invigorating air — he was young, he was full of life, he had a successful future ahead of him. Nothing could destroy his exhilaration in the day.

Nothing but the sharp crack of a gun, and the ping of a ball slamming into a tree not two feet from his head.

9: A Puzzle

Jeremy stormed into Woodside through the scullery door, startling the kitchen maid emerging from the cellar with a bucket of carrots. He went directly to Tyrrell's room, and after a perfunctory knock, walked straight in.

"What the devil is your gamekeeper doing shooting so carelessly in Hardby Wood, Tyrrell? Damned near took my head off. Oh... I beg your pardon, Miss Tyrrell. I didn't see you there."

"No one is shooting in Hardby Wood," she said calmly.

"I beg to disagree," he said sharply. "Someone is out there with a gun at this very moment. I am lucky to be alive. You need to tell your gamekeeper to take more care."

"Dingwell is at the market in Brinchester today," she said. "More likely someone from the Park is out with a gun."

"No, that cannot be," her father said. "They arranged to go to Claremont Hall today. Besides, no one shoots on Woodside land without my permission. Lord Westerlea is most punctilious about such niceties."

"A poacher?" Jeremy said, but even as he spoke, he knew it could not be so, not in broad daylight and almost within sight of the house.

"I will tell Dingwell to be on the lookout for signs of poachers," Jane said. "You are not injured, Mr Winterton?"

"No, although it was a close thing. Another foot or two to the left, and I'd have had my head blown off." He huffed a breath, but his anger could not be sustained in the face of her composed good sense. The thought flashed through his mind that she would be a useful person to have around in a crisis, for she would never panic.

"You have sustained a shock, Mr Winterton." Mr Tyrrell said, smiling benignly at him. "Will you have a glass of something? Or tea? We are just having some ourselves, and would be happy if you would join us. I should like to talk to you, if you can spare me the time."

Jeremy accepted a glass of Canary, pulling up a chair to join the others where they sat around the fire. Jane picked up her half-drunk tea, but Mr Tyrrell steepled his fingers and looked consideringly at Jeremy.

"It seems that you have set a hare running, Mr Winterton," he said in his soft voice. "Now that I have begun to contemplate the prospect of selling Woodside, I am reluctant to set the idea aside. Jane and I have been speaking openly of our hopes for the future, and I now understand that hauling her off to Bath and dangling a dowry over her head would not materially improve her happiness. That scheme has been set aside, and I confess, I have no great enthusiasm for town life. I enjoy the beauties of nature too much to be satisfied with walking in Sydney Gardens. The idea of selling Woodside, however, is an appealing one. Both the house and the estate are too large for our small household, and — I speak frankly to you now — too expensive without considerable improvement, for which I have neither the skill nor the enthusiasm. Jane manages very well on what we have, and our wants are few, but I shall feel more comfortable as I decline into old age to live somewhere smaller. Lord Westerlea confirmed last night that there is a cottage in the village which would suit us admirably, and may be had for a peppercorn rent. Lilac Cottage — do you know it?"

Jeremy dredged through memories to find a name. "The Millbrooks' house — I know it."

"Mr Millbrook died some years ago, and his widow last year. It is church property and in need of some repairs, but it will be ready for occupation by the summer. So you see, this would be an ideal time for Woodside to change hands. Naturally, it would please the entire neighbourhood if it were to be *you* who purchases the property, but... I cannot wait indefinitely."

"I see." That put paid to any plan to return to Branton and buy Woodside later, when he had made his fortune.

Tyrrell coughed delicately. "Forgive me if this is impertinent, but there was some talk last night that your brothers-in-law might fund you for a while, until you have got the estate running smoothly again. However, I have no desire to pry into family matters."

"They *would* undertake to buy Woodside on my behalf, it is true," Jeremy said slowly. "However, I cannot do it. It is a firm precept of mine never to borrow and it has stood me in good stead. It would be so large a debt that it would weigh upon me, leaving me in the utmost anxiety. No matter the temptation, I will not do it."

"I honour you for such sound principles," Tyrrell said. "You are wise not to incur even so gentle a debt as your family would impose upon you. But there is still the option to marry Jane, you know, if you can convince her of the benefits of such a scheme."

"I should dislike it extremely, of course," Jane said. "Still, taking all the advantages of Woodside into account, I might be prepared to overcome my antipathy towards you and make the sacrifice."

Jeremy was about to exclaim in surprise when he saw a hint of a twinkle in her eyes, and realised that she was perhaps laying the foundations for her scheme of a pretended betrothal. It would look very odd to protest violently against the very idea, and then seemingly accept it with complacence.

Tyrrell laughed, not at all discomfited by his daughter's words. "It is not such a bad scheme, though, is it? There is no need to give up your present occupation if it pleases you, Mr Winterton. Then, when you are ready to settle down to life as a gentleman, here would be your home waiting for you. Why, you and Jane might even be on friendly terms by then, who knows?" He laughed heartily at his own joke, and then, rising, he went on, "Now leave me to my painting, the two of you. I have a sweet violet to capture before it wilts beyond recognition."

Out in the hall, Jane turned to him with the glimmerings of a smile. "You are quick, Mr Winterton. I was afraid you would repudiate any desire to marry me, and so sink any chance of pulling off our little scheme at the outset."

"It is still an absurd idea," he said. "Nor do you need it now, it seems to me. If you are not to be dragged off to Bath and—"

"Papa still plans to marry me off, however, and once he has set his mind to an idea, he is always most reluctant to relinquish it. He looks like the mildest of men, but he always gets what he wants, one way or another. Only by securing my own independence can I thwart him. It is the best way, you may be sure."

Jeremy rubbed his nose thoughtfully, not entirely convinced. "Well... I have few options open to me, so perhaps I too shall talk about the sacrifice necessary to obtain Woodside."

She nodded her head. "Good. You are considering it. Have you time to look at the washstand now? It is in your mother's room awaiting your examination."

"I am quite at leisure," he said. "Besides, I feel a great deal safer indoors than out, this morning."

She threw him a sideways glance, and he had the feeling that she did not quite believe his story of a wayward bullet.

When he started up the stairs, she made to follow him. At once he stopped. "Miss Tyrrell, you do not have a chaperon. Should we wait until one of my sisters is here, or shall I go on alone? I know the way to Mama's room, after all."

She threw him a wry glance. "Really, Mr Winterton! I am beyond the age of needing a chaperon in my own house."

"You are a gentlewoman of marriageable age," he said seriously. "Your reputation is a precious and irreplaceable asset, easily damaged by a single thoughtless moment. You would hardly wish to be put into the position of marrying for such a reason."

"Nor would I be," she said robustly. Then, more softly, she said, "Your consideration does you credit, sir, but I am known and respected here. My reputation is not at risk merely because I choose to show a friend a disused bedroom."

"Oh, am I a friend now?" he said, teasingly. "This is progress indeed, Miss Tyrrell. I am encouraged. Perhaps I ought to seek your hand in earnest."

She laughed, but shook her head. "Oh, pray do not! I should be disappointed in you were your antipathy so easily dispersed."

"Far be it from me to disappoint a lady, but I have never reciprocated your antipathy. If I am not partial to your sharp tongue, it is only because it is so often right. But you need not be alarmed that I may press my suit, for I have already chosen my future wife."

"Ah, yes, the boring Miss Whatever-her-name-is. *She* does not have a sharp tongue."

That made him laugh. Jane Tyrrell would not suit him as a wife, but he liked her quick mind, and he was even growing accustomed to her caustic remarks.

"You have the better of me, Miss Tyrrell," he said mildly. "Lead the way, then, and I will allow you to be the best judge of what is proper for you."

She made him a little bow of acknowledgement, and turned to the stairs.

The washstand had never made much impression on his boyhood self. The bed, with its profusion of carvings, and the massive secretary, reaching almost to the ceiling, had been more memorable. The washstand had simply sat in a corner, half hidden by the basin, ewer and towels. Now he gazed in awe at its exposed ugliness. Three or four kinds of wood had been used in its construction, with no attempt at harmonisation, there was some undistinguished marquetry on the top, and the whole was edged with the same heavy ornamentation as the stool. The legs were shaped like those of a lion, except with bird's feet.

"It is so peculiar," he said, half to himself.

"No more so than the other pieces," Jane said.

When he looked around the room, he could only agree. The bed, the washstand and the stool, now brought through from Jane's room, were all different, yet there was a strange kind of conformity amongst them. They would never be pleasing to the eye, but as a set they were less grotesque. It was the other pieces in the room, modern and elegant, which now looked out of place.

Jeremy began his examination of the washstand, working methodically from top to bottom, feeling, prodding and measuring with his hands to determine the possibility of hidden spaces. He removed all the drawers and felt all over each one. Eventually, with only the empty shell left, he began to explore inside the spaces left by the removed drawers. Almost at once, he was successful. A small spring-loaded section of an inner wall popped out a hidden drawer, and inside that, as with the stool, was another compartment. Tucked inside was a paper, a box and a coin. Further exploration uncovered another secret place with another paper, box and coin. The washstand had provided them with two more quotations from Shakespeare, two more sets of jewellery and two more coins.

"These are still not the good pieces, I assume?" Jane said, opening the jewellery boxes and setting them on top of the washstand. "Pearls and topaz. Very pretty, but not the fortune you are looking for."

"No, but it is encouraging," Jeremy said.

"I do not understand the purpose of these writings," Jane said. "What does this mean? *'Here's a voucher, Stronger than ever law could make: this secret Will force him think I have pick'd the lock and ta'en The treasure of her honour. No more. To what end? Why should I write this down, that's riveted, Screw'd to my memory? She hath been reading late The tale of Tereus; here the leaf's turn'd down Where Philomel gave up. I have enough: To the trunk again, and shut the spring of it. Swift, swift, you dragons of the night, that dawning May bare the raven's eye! I lodge in fear; Though this a heavenly angel, hell is here. [Clock strikes] One, two, three: time, time!'* Good grief. At least this second one is shorter. *'Madman, thou errest: I say, there is no darkness but ignorance; in which thou art more puzzled than the Egyptians in their fog.'"*

Jeremy laughed. "Well that one is true enough! We are indeed more puzzled than the Egyptians in their fog. I wonder if Mama was intentionally setting us a puzzle? She loved such games — acrostics and number juggling and so forth. And here is another such." He held out the two coins. One was engraved with a *'1'* on one side and *'10'* on the other, while the second coin held the numbers *'8'* and *'13'*. "Shall we eventually have a full set of numbers, do you suppose? And to what end? What does it *mean?"*

"I think you are right," she said slowly. "It *is* a puzzle. The first quotation you found in the stool was about a *'mystery in stratagem'*, do you remember? And here we have *'this secret will force him think'* and *'thou art more puzzled'*. Of course it is a puzzle! How exciting! But look! *'To the trunk again'*? Is there a trunk anywhere? Perhaps the jewels are inside it."

He had to smile at her enthusiasm. "I cannot remember one. It would have been in the attics if there ever was such a thing, and Mama kept the jewels here in this room, that much is certain."

"Oh." She was instantly deflated. "I had forgotten that. But there must be some clue in these words."

"I think the puzzle is in the coins, and the numbers upon them," he said. "The writing is merely to point out that it *is* a puzzle, in case we had missed the significance. What we must do is to find all the remaining items of furniture, and locate the secret compartments. I have the way of it now, so there should be no difficulty in recovering the rest of the coins. Then we may determine what they mean."

"We?" she said, so softly that he almost missed it.

He caught his breath. That was the heart of his dilemma, was it not? He could not easily find the rest of the furniture without her aid, and yet every feeling abhorred the idea of a false betrothal, even for so worthy an end. If they could succeed in finding the jewels, he would be rich enough to buy Woodside outright, Jane would have the independence she craved and they would both be free to marry where they pleased after, or not marry at all, in Jane's case. That would be something to be proud of, would it not? Was not a little deception justified for such a cause? There had been so much deception in his life, so what was a little more?

There was another consideration, too. Without a betrothal, Tyrrell would want to sell the house to allow him to move to Lilac Cottage. Jeremy would be forced to turn to his rich brothers-in-law for funding or else give up all hope of ever winning Woodside. A betrothal, however, would ensure that the house could not be sold elsewhere. Even if the jewels could not be found, it would give him a little time to plan, to determine on a different strategy.

He sat down on the stool, gazing at her. She was perched on the edge of the bed on the bare mattress, her feet side by side on the steps. He had thought her stern-faced when they had first met, a no-nonsense housekeeper with her neat cap and plain gown. He knew her a little better now, aware that her acid tongue and cool grey eyes hid a sharp intelligence. She was not pretty — even her best friend would not describe her as such — but as she watched him now, the eagerness in her face not quite hidden, he thought there was enough mettle in her nature to keep a man intrigued for a lifetime, if he could but find a way past the thorny thickets of her animosity. So different from Ellen, who was all polished exterior and no inner fire at all. She would be a placid, conformable wife, her life revolving around her husband's comfort. Jane's husband, if ever there should be a man brave enough to wed her, need expect nothing but argument and strife and little consideration given to his wishes. Jeremy could hardly imagine a wife who would suit him less.

Still… a betrothal for a short time, until he had secured Woodside… that would be bearable, would it not?

"How precisely would it work — this fake betrothal?"

Her face lit up. "We would need to be subtle, and not rush at it. A few weeks, perhaps—"

"A few *weeks!*"

"Everyone knows my feelings on the subject of marriage," she said tartly. "I cannot be seen to surrender my principles in a matter of days. However, it is widely known that Papa would give you Woodside if you marry me, so you must pay court to me and in time I will yield to your entreaties. Then I shall begin to recover the furniture."

"*You* will? Why should not I do so?"

"Men never care about household matters. It would be thought very odd in you to be chasing around after dressing tables and the like. I shall tell people that you are sad that so much of the furniture you loved as a child has been dispersed, and that I am buying back as much as I can as a surprise wedding gift for you. Everyone will think it very romantic."

"That will be terribly convincing," he said caustically. "You are, after all, noted for your romantic sensibilities."

She laughed. "Oh, no one will believe it. They will account for it by supposing that you have ordered me to do it. But we must not be selective and look only for your mama's pieces, or it will be guessed that they are particularly wanted. It must be everything that was sold off or given away. And so, slowly, piece by piece, we will find all the secrets of your mama's room, and thus we will find the jewels."

"And then?" he said.

"Then I shall realise that we are not suited, and call the whole thing off. Papa and I will move to Lilac Cottage, and you will go back to Lancashire to court the lovely Miss Something-or-other."

"Ridwell," he said, smiling at the thought. "Ellen Ridwell."

"Is it likely that anyone in Brinshire would have acquaintances in Miss Ridwell's circle? It would be fatal to your chances if word of your betrothal to me reached her ears."

A horrifying thought. He quickly considered the matter, but could not recall any mention of Brinshire from anyone in Branton. "No, it will be quite safe."

"Then you will do it?" she said, and there was just a hint of anxiety in those expressive eyes. She almost looked vulnerable.

"Let me consider the matter carefully," he said. "What I need to do is to review *all* the options available to me. There are still questions to be put to the lawyer, for example. And perhaps after reflection I may come to the opinion, as my sisters have already done, that Woodside is part of my history and has no place in my future."

"Then you would go back to your mill and the dull Miss Ridwell? You would be content not to be a gentleman?"

Lord, but she was perceptive! Straight to the heart of the issue.

"Perhaps I would," he said crisply, rising to his feet. "Perhaps that is my destiny after all, to manage the mill and tend the precious engine. Machinery and devices of all kinds have always fascinated me. It may be that God never intended me to be a gentleman at all."

10: The Clock Tower

When Jeremy had first decided to visit Brinshire, he had settled in his mind that the business would take no more than a month or two. He would reconcile with his father, stay for a week or two to reacquaint himself with Woodside and the neighbourhood, perhaps visit some of his sisters and then he could go back to Branton with a clear conscience to offer for Ellen.

It had not worked out as he envisaged. The shattering news that his father was long dead had changed everything. Whether he entered upon a battle in the courts to recover his inheritance, or else the delicate process of recovering the jewels with Jane's help, the matter could not be concluded swiftly and he would be obliged to stay longer than he had intended. He would need to make arrangements at the bank to ensure he had enough money to pay his way, for the Westerleas would soon be departing for the London season and Jeremy would be obliged to return to the inn. He amused himself occasionally by imagining Hooper's reaction to this change in circumstances, for the valet had taken to life in a baron's house as to the manner born.

When there was a break in the tempestuous spring weather, Jeremy borrowed a horse from Lord Westerlea and rode to Brinchester. The ostlers at the Royal Oak recognised the horse instantly — "That be Lady Westerlea's best 'unter, sir. We'll be sure to take good care on 'im." So that accounted for the well-filled stable and the surprising number of hunters at the Park, for Lord Westerlea was a man who liked his own fireside too well to be a sporting enthusiast. Yes, Rosamund had always been a keen horsewoman, he remembered now.

The head ostler directed him to Martin's Bank, where he was received with great courtesy by one of the owners. Mr Henry Martin, a man thinner than a lamp post, said it was the greatest pleasure to have him back, he looked just like Lady Westerlea and he would have known him anywhere. He then read the letter of introduction from Jeremy's banker in Lancaster, and assured him that there would be not the least difficulty in the world in accommodating his monetary requirements during his stay.

"Indeed, sir," the banker went on, "if sir should require a larger sum for any purpose, that could certainly be arranged. It would delight the entire county, I make no doubt, to see a Mr Winterton settled once more at Woodside. We had the pleasure of doing business with sir's father, and his father before him, and even his father before him, you see, so if there is anything we can do to facilitate such an outcome, sir has only to ask."

"That is most obliging of you, Mr Martin. However, I am disinclined to undertake a large loan for the purpose. The interest payments would consume most, perhaps all, of the estate's income."

Martin raised one delicate eyebrow. "You would not find us avaricious, Mr Winterton. For such a valued client, our terms would be most reasonable, and would be well within the means of the estate. It is not, of course, in such good heart as it was some years ago, but the combined income of sixteen, or perhaps seventeen, hundred a year would be more than ample to cover the costs of the loan without the least inconvenience to yourself."

That gave Jeremy pause. Sixteen or seventeen hundred? That was not what the books showed. Eight hundred and fifty was the present income, according to the ledgers Tyrrell had shown him.

Carefully, Jeremy said, "Your numbers are precise. Do you have the management of the estate's finances?"

Martin waved his hands airily. "Not as such, you understand, but the value of land and the transfer of it are matters of interest to a number of professional men in the town — solicitors, land agents and so on. We know the exact amount of land held by Woodside, and the estimated value of each portion. We can be tolerably precise in such matters." He grinned smugly.

Jeremy was tempted to tell him the truth — that the estate was worth only half the amount postulated. But then a horrible thought occurred to him — perhaps the estate was truly worth seventeen hundred a year, but Tyrrell had, for some reason of his own, lied about it, and given a lower value? And if so, the next obvious question was — why would he do such a thing? The true value would be bound to emerge if Jeremy were to buy it from him. Then an even more horrible thought — what if Tyrrell's manager were embezzling funds from him?

The banker had moved on to other matters — some portions of land once held by Woodside might be available for purchase. Would sir like discreet enquiries to be made?

"Thank you, but not at present. Such purchases would deplete my resources considerably."

"The letter from Lancaster intimates that sir's account is in excellent order, with a good capital sum accumulated. Sir lives well within his income, and could easily afford some judicious expenditure."

"True but I hope to marry soon," Jeremy said, rather irritated by this intrusive interest in his finances. It was the fellow's job, he supposed, but how he spent his money was his own affair.

"Ah, the capable Miss Tyrrell, I suppose," Martin said, chortling. "An excellent choice, sir."

That was too much for Jeremy. He jumped to his feet, and it was as much as he could do to make his departure with the usual pleasantries. He was still fuming as he left the bank, and finding that his next objective, Mr Plumphett, was not available did nothing for his temper. Jeremy had one other mission in the town, and after asking for directions, set off with long strides, taking little notice of his surroundings. He was so engrossed in his own thoughts that he failed to hear himself hailed.

"Winterton? Hoy, Jeremy! Dash it — John Moreton!"

He stopped, turned, found himself looking into the grinning face of Leo Audley.

"How amusing!" Audley said. "You still answer to the name of Moreton. But then you have spent more of your life with that label than the real one. How are you, Winterton? You were out early this morning. Your absence at breakfast was noticed." The smile widened. "The ladies are very proprietorial, you know."

Jeremy's disgruntlement could not withstand Audley's cheerful bonhomie. He could feel his spirits lifting with every word. "Westerlea made an excellent horse available to me, so it seemed a waste merely to ride to Brinchester and back. I came by way of High Frickham and then round by Brinwater Heath. Most enjoyable. But what brings you to Brinchester?"

"Ferdy and I brought the ladies in for a little shopping, but I do not myself see the attraction in ribbons and lace and decorated combs, so I have left them to it."

"Even Craston? Um, Ferdy?"

Audley laughed. "Ferdy has exquisite taste, and is much called upon for such expeditions. Robin too, but he is busy with his agent today. Oh, the demands upon a man of property, as you will find out when you have Woodside back. Are you bound on private business, or may a forlorn fellow male impose upon your good nature for company?"

Jeremy laughed at his brother-in-law. "Tell me, how do you like clocks?"

"If they keep good time, I like them well enough," Audley said. "Whatever can you have in mind?"

"Ah, you will see."

The church of St Mark's was tucked away down a side street as if hiding. It was not an easy building to hide, its impressive Gothic facade taking up the whole of one side of a large square, the massive clock face sitting in its tower above the great wooden doors and the arched window with its intricate coloured glass picture of the last supper. The rest of the square was occupied by houses of a shabby nature, where ill-dressed and unsavoury characters came and went with furtive glances. No doubt the square had once been home to the wealthy and fashionable, but the tide of Brinchester had swept over it and washed the fashionable to some other quarter, leaving St Mark's stranded like a starfish on a beach.

A little investigation uncovered the rectory behind the church, where they found the clergyman, a Mr Everton. He was a plump man, with a perpetual smile, as if life were a constant joy. He responded to their request as if nothing could afford him greater pleasure than to abandon his accounts and take them up the tower to look at the back of the clock. He took a large wrought iron key from a hook and led them to a small door at one side of the church, which opened to reveal a tight and gloomy spiral staircase.

"Mind the steps, gentlemen," he said, adding cheerfully, "Don't want you breaking your necks, now do we?" He chuckled, as though the prospect amused him.

Above them sounded the rhythmic deep clunk of the clock ticking, and enough light penetrated from the narrow slits in the walls that Jeremy could just make out the steady motion of the pendulum.

"It is very dusty," Audley muttered. "Look! There are cobwebs."

Jeremy only laughed. On such occasions he was glad his clothes were of sensible dark colours, and plain enough that a tear here and there was easily repaired.

"So sorry, sir," the clergyman said. "The housemaid doesn't get up here very often." Then he chortled at his own wit.

As they passed the bell-ringing level, the clock's tick was loud enough to echo off the stone walls. Then they emerged into the semi-gloom of the clock room. The clergyman rushed forward to open the door of the clock housing, and there were the huge cogs and wheels and rods and pulleys, a little rusty in places, but still functioning. On the facing was the inscription '*W & W Tenterden, Clockmakers, Birmingham*'. In a slot in the floor, the great pendulum swung slowly back and forth, each movement punctuated by the clunk of a cog shifting one notch further on, and moving the unseen hands on the outer dial by a minute degree.

Jeremy sighed with satisfaction. "Wonderful!" he breathed. "Have you ever seen anything so fascinating, Audley?"

"Many things," Audley said faintly.

His look of horror made Jeremy laugh again. "No, no! Clocks are marvellous devices. Look, here is the going train, and here the striking chain, and that over there must be the quarter striking train. This is the setting dial and— You truly do not find this interesting?"

Audley pulled a face. "All I ask of a clock is that it shows the correct time, and so long as— Oh Lord, now what is happening?"

"Oh, famous! The clock is about to strike."

"No, no, no!" Audley cried. "Tell me it is not noon, for we shall certainly be deafened if the bells strike twelve times."

"No, it is only half past eleven, unfortunately," Jeremy said. "We shall hear the half-hour chimes, however, so that is something."

"Indeed," Audley said in a thread of a voice. "Should we—? Oh, there they go!"

Above them, the hammers hit the great brass bells in sequence, creating the chimes. The whole building reverberated to the sound, and Audley covered his ears with his hands. It was soon over, just a faint humming left in the air, but Jeremy laughed in sheer exuberance. This was more like it! How he had missed his machinery, and his precious engine — no one could care for it as well as he could. For an instant, he was tempted to throw up the whole Woodside endeavour, and simply go back to Branton to be a mill manager again. That was where he belonged, after all.

But he could not leave Brinshire now, not when there was a clock of such magnificence to be examined.

"It is an automaton clock, is it not?" Jeremy said eagerly.

Mr Everton beamed at him. "Oh, yes, or rather, it *was*. It has not worked for... oh, close to thirty years, perhaps. My predecessor thought it frivolous, so when it became jammed one day, he had it all disconnected. The townspeople were very disappointed, seemingly, for they still speak of it with regret. It was quite an attraction in its day, and perfectly suitable for a church clock, I should have thought. Our Lord and the Holy Apostles arriving for the last supper, attended by the faithful bearing gifts of food and wine, while angels flew overhead. Nothing *frivolous* or *debauched*, oh no, no, no. Nothing like that. But my predecessor thought it distracted the lower classes from their work, and was therefore to be deplored."

"Might I take a look at the automata?" Jeremy said. "It would be a most enjoyable exercise for me to attempt to restore the moving parts to full working order. If you would like me to, naturally."

"Oh! Would you really? How kind... how very kind."

"And your bishop would not disapprove?"

"Oh, dear me, no. There was some talk of getting it fixed a few years ago, but it involved a man coming down from London and somehow it all fell through. No, there would be not the least objection. The angels reside in that box near the ceiling there, and the other figures are accessed from the floor below us. Come, let me show you, gentlemen."

"Not me," Audley said firmly. "My tolerance for scrabbling about in bat-infested towers is limited, I regret to say. I shall leave you to it, my friend."

Jeremy barely noticed his departure. The rector showed him where everything was located, and then, seeing that he was quite prepared to crawl into small, dusty spaces in pursuit of parts that might yet be repaired, sighed.

"You will not mind if I return to my accounts now? Just lock up as you leave, Mr Winterton."

Taking the key absent-mindedly, Jeremy began his explorations.

In no time at all Mr Everton returned.

"Still here, Mr Winterton?" he said mildly. "We are just about to sit down to our dinner. Will you join us?"

"Dinner? So early? It is— oh!" He spotted the setting dial, which showed that it was almost five o'clock. "Have I been here all day?" he said sheepishly.

Mr Everton beamed at him. "So it would appear. To tell truth, sir, I imagined you gone long since, with the key in your pocket. But there, you must find these old cogs and gears of some interest."

"Oh yes, it is fascinating, and I do think the automata can be repaired, although it will require some work. I shall have to dismantle the entire mechanism and clean everything, and the figures are in need of repainting also, and then—"

"My dear sir! You are welcome to do so, of course, but not today, I beg you. Look at the state you are in! Do come into the rectory and let me assist you to remove some of these cobwebs. Oh dear, this sleeve is quite torn."

"It will be easy enough to mend," Jeremy said with a shrug. "I do not regard such things when there is so much pleasure to be had. Regretfully, I must decline your very kind offer of dinner, for I am expected in Frickham. I must ride home now as quick as may be or I shall be late for dinner, but may I come again tomorrow? Please? I am enjoying myself so much."

"How could I possibly refuse?" the rector said with a laugh.

Jeremy was there the next morning before eight o'clock, hammering on the rectory door until the bemused clergyman, still in his nightcap, opened a window and threw the belfry key out to him. He had brought paper and pencil with him, to make a list of tools he might need, and when the rector invited him in for breakfast, spent the entire time enumerating his requirements while Mr Everton explained where he might obtain them. An hour in town provided most of his needs, after which he set to work in earnest in the tower, sketching the arrangement of rods and gears that drove the moving figures and marking areas of concern.

He was thus absorbed when a head appeared round the entrance from the spiral staircase. "Good morning," the head said, as its accompanying body emerged into the room sideways in little lurches, like a crab. He was a young man of much Jeremy's own age, but not a gentleman, a labourer of some sort, with his simple kerchief knotted at his throat and an old-fashioned coat with full skirts. His eyes were averted, and he rubbed his palms nervously against his trousers.

"Good morning," Jeremy said cheerfully. He was perched at the top of a ladder investigating the last supper characters high up in the bell-ringing room, so he looked down onto the newcomer's bushy head of hair, which looked as if it had not seen the use of a comb for some time. "May I help you?"

"No."

"Oh." A long pause, while the young man hovered uneasily near the door, his eyes fixed on the floor. Jeremy tried another tack. "Are you looking for the rector? He may be in—"

"No." Then, in a rush, he said, "Dudley sent me to help you. Said you could do with another hand. I've got two hands." He held them up to show Jeremy.

"Well now, that is very kind." He skipped down the ladder, then said, "I am much obliged to Dudley. Who exactly *is* Dudley?"

"My brother. Sent me to help you. Said you could do with another hand. I've got two hands, see?"

"I do see, yes. How do you do? I am Jeremy Winterton." He held out his hand and the man grasped it firmly, shaking it so vigorously that Jeremy was afraid his arm might be pulled off altogether.

"Christopher Everton."

"Oh, *Everton*. So Dudley is the rector?"

"Yes. My brother. Sent me to help you. Said you could—"

"That was very kind of him. So what can you do to help, Christopher?"

"Kit."

"Um... I beg your pardon?"

"Christopher for how d'ye dos, Kit for everything else."

"Oh, I see. How very sensible of you, to have two names — a long one for formal occasions, and a short, practical one for everyday use. My name is unchanging, and has to serve for all purposes. How I wish I had a short name too."

"Jerry," Kit said. "You can be Jeremy for how d'ye dos, and Jerry for everything else."

"Jerry," Jeremy said thoughtfully. "Yes, why not? But tell me, Kit, in what way did your brother consider you might be able to help me? What are you good at?"

"Paint. I can paint. Wooden soldiers. Horses. A carriage, sometimes. A little house, once, with furniture. Bill made the pans for the kitchen, Tilda sewed the curtains, and I made the people and the furniture."

"Bill is...?"

"Smith. Bill made the pans, Tilda sewed the curtains and I made—"

"—the people and the furniture," Jeremy said, smiling. "How clever you must be, Kit! I expect you could repaint these figures, could not you?" He ran back up the ladder and came down with two of the figures. "Saint Andrew and Saint Bartholomew, I believe. The colours are almost gone. Can you repaint them? Make them colourful again?"

"Yes. Make them colourful again. Yes." He held them in his hands, turning them slowly. "Saint Andrew. Saint Bartholomew. Make them colourful again. Yes."

"Excellent. You will be the greatest help to me, Kit. Thank you."

"Greatest help to you. Yes. Make them colourful again. Yes." And he looked Jeremy straight in the eye, and smiled. "Yes."

~~~~~

Jeremy's days settled into a pattern. Apart from Sundays, he spent almost every hour of every day in the clock tower, crawling about in the small spaces allotted to the automaton workings, slowly dismantling every piece and then cleaning, mending, straightening. He had breakfast with Dudley Everton in the faded splendour of the rectory breakfast room, and then returned at once to his self-appointed task. He had set up a small workshop in a corner of the clock room where he kept his tools and worked on the current rusted piece of metal. Everton came in from time to time, shook his head at such energy and went away again.

Kit worked at the local dairy until noon, carrying buckets and butter churns about, and helping to keep the place clean. In the afternoons he worked on his painting projects, and was much in demand to make wooden toys and models. His large hands were remarkably dexterous at fashioning the most delicate items. He added the various saints, the faithful and the angels from the clock to his rather large collection of assignments, and one by one restored them to vibrant life.

Jeremy set out for home late in the afternoon, usually much later than he intended for he was inclined not to notice the time when he was absorbed in his work, even with the great bells chiming the quarter hours only a few feet above his head. Then he would set his horse to a fast pace across the fields to Frickham by the most direct route, fringing the Woodside orchard in the end to shave a few precious minutes from his journey. He generally arrived at Westerlea Park just as the dressing bell was sounding.

But his time at Westerlea Park was drawing to a close. Most of his sisters had already left, and Rosamund and Robin would themselves be leaving soon for London, the duties of Parliament and the pleasures of the season. The house would be closed up for several months, but Jeremy would not be forced back to the inn, for Dudley Everton had offered him accommodation for as long as he needed it.

As Jeremy made his way back to Westerlea Park for the last time, his head was full of the necessary chore of moving and the farewell dinner for the leaders of local society to be held that evening. The horse was used to the route now, so he had no need to concentrate and his mind was elsewhere.

So it came about that he had no warning, no inkling of trouble as he rode at an easy pace around the Woodside orchard. Just a loud noise nearby, his horse rearing and, before he even had time to be surprised, he was falling, falling, falling.

The ground rushed up and hit him hard, there was an explosion of pain and then darkness.

11: Recovery

Measles. That must be it. He had never had the measles, so that must be why he was confined to his bed. Although why was he in so much pain from measles? Fever... it should be fever, not pain. He was ill, that much was certain, but he was safe, for Mama was there... No, not Mama, for she was ill too. Rosie, then. Yes, it must be Rosie. There was nothing like an older sister to comfort a small boy who was suffering.

He was thirsty, but his attempt to ask for water came out as a strangulated groan. A face peered at him.

"Awake?" A solemn face, concerned, the voice soft spoken. Someone who looked a lot like Margaret, but older, wearing a matron's cap. He was more feverish than he had suspected, his mind muddling Margaret with Mama. How foolish! Margaret was only four years older than he was, not even out yet. She could hardly be married.

Another face, one he could not recognise. This was confusing. "Jeremy?" Some low talk between the two women, then the strange face lifted his head and pushed something into his mouth. A spout... ah, blessed water. A small sip, then the spout was withdrawn. "More?" He nodded, and she smiled. "Ah, good. Here...

slowly, mind." The spout again, and more cool, soothing water. He drank, then closed his eyes.

~~~~~

He woke in near-darkness, pain crushing both arms. He must have made a noise, for there was the strange face again.

"Jeremy?"

He groaned.

"Can you drink this if I lift you up a little?"

She raised his head, and set a small cup at his lips. Something sickly-sweet. Laudanum. Willingly he drank and then lay in the gloom waiting for the pain to subside. A couple of lamps were shaded to avoid dazzling his eyes, and there was a more distant glow from the fire. Low voices murmured somewhere out of sight, then Margaret's face appeared again and pressed a cloth to his forehead. Ah, lavender water. It *was* Mama, then, and not Margaret after all. He must be very poorly if Mama had left her own sickbed to tend him.

The pain began to recede and he closed his eyes again, drifting into sleep.

~~~~~

Someone humming.

The pain was back, but bearable this time. Different in each arm. One was a dull throbbing, the other was sharper, stabbing. When he tried to move that one, it felt heavy and cumbersome. Bandaged. Not a splint, though, so perhaps he had not broken anything. His ribs hurt, too, so he must have suffered some kind of accident. Wait... he remembered! He had fallen out of the tree-house, that was it. He had been doing something foolish no doubt... leaning over the rail... no, climbing on it, that was it. He had—

The humming stopped, and someone prodded him on one cheek. "Jerry? Wake up, Jerry." Another prod, this time on his nose. "Wake up!"

Jeremy opened his eyes.

"He's awake, Mistress! Jerry's awake!"

The world shifted back into alignment. "Kit?" He was not a boy back at Woodside, he was a grown man and—

"*Mistress!* He's awake. Jerry's awake."

"So he is." A face, hardly recognisable with a smile across it.

"Jane?" Jeremy said. "Wait… why am I in my old bed at Woodside?"

"Your horse threw you. Kit, run and fetch Mrs Haymer, will you?"

"Mistress Haymer. Yes."

"My horse?" He struggled to remember. He was not a reckless, neck-or-nothing rider so how…? "A rabbit hole, perhaps? Or did something spook him?"

She laughed, and lifted his head to allow him some water before she answered. "I should say that something spooked him, yes. Something very loud, to judge by the bullet hole in your arm."

"What?" He lay back on the pillows, trying to make sense of it, staring at the bed canopy above him. He had not slept in this bed for fifteen years, but every crack in the wood, every knot and imperfection was as familiar to him as his own face. No wonder he had thought himself a boy again.

A bullet hole in his arm… that was the second time someone had shot at him. Once might be ascribed to accident, but twice? No, this was someone trying to kill him. Yet why? Who could possibly want him dead?

Margaret was there, bending over him with the lavender water again — so like Mama! He smiled at her, and she smiled back and for an instant the years rolled back again, and he was twelve... But then Kit appeared and the illusion shattered.

"See?" Kit said. "Jerry's awake. Yes. He's awake now."

"Yes, he is," Jane said briskly. "Kit, would you be very kind, and go and help Annie with the vegetables? She is rather overwhelmed with so many extra mouths to feed."

"Help Annie with the vegetables. Yes." He disappeared, still repeating the words as he went.

"What on earth is he doing here?" Jeremy said. "He is the rector's younger brother, and should be in the rectory with his paints."

"Well, that is all your foolish fault, Mr Winterton. If you had not inconsiderately decided to get yourself shot, Kit would not have been anxious about you and would not have walked out from Brinchester—"

"Walked!"

"—to find you. Yes, he walked almost the whole way, except that the peddler gave him a ride on his wagon the last two miles or so. Very agitated, he was, by the time he arrived on our doorstep, and it was lucky that Margaret was here and knew who he was, for *I* should have sent for the constable."

"He is a little unusual," Jeremy said, smiling. "Did he give you a fright? I am sorry for it, if so, but he is perfectly harmless."

"So I have discovered, and he has been making himself useful about the house. We sent word to Mr Everton who came at once to fetch him away, but he will not be shifted from your side, so you will just have to put up with him. And with being called Jerry," she added, laughing. "You are *not* a Jerry, I feel. Jeremy has a certain dignity, but Jerry sounds like a ditch-digger."

Jeremy laughed, and then winced as pain lanced through him. He had to take a couple of long, slow breaths before he could answer. "Everyone has two names, Miss Tyrrell — one for how d'ye dos and one for everyday use. Kit is Christopher for how d'ye dos, and Kit otherwise. You are Miss Tyrrell for how d'ye dos and—" He stopped, as her face darkened suspiciously. "—and Miss Tyrrell for all other occasions, too," he went on blandly.

She laughed. "And you are Mr Fustian all the time." But there was no heat in her words. She was remarkably friendly, for a change. "How is the pain? You cannot have more laudanum for another hour or so."

"It is not so bad. The bullet wound... is there much damage?"

"The merest scratch, and perfectly clean. Mr Caddy, the apothecary, has been here several times to attend to it, and a physician is to come out from Brinchester today, so you see, you are receiving the best of attention and need not depend upon my deplorable sickroom skills. Apart from that, you have a lot of bruising but nothing important is broken. It was fortunate that you landed mostly on your head."

"Fortunate?"

"Nothing in there to damage," she said tartly. "We are agreed that men of Lancashire have no sense, if you recall."

"Oh, that is better," he said.

"Better?"

"I was beginning to wonder what you had done with Jane Tyrrell. You *look* like her, to be sure, but a friendly, cheerful form of her. But no, the old Jane is still present. What a relief. I should not know how to respond if you were to be civil to me all the time."

She blushed, for some reason, but said robustly, "Careful, or I might shoot you in the other arm myself. I would shoot you in the head, of course, but we have already established that it would cause no damage."

That made him laugh again, although with a start of pain, but he was insensibly cheered by her badinage and was able to give a good account of himself to the physician when he arrived, and describe himself as tolerably comfortable. As the day wore on, he ate a little, slept a little, ate a little more and began very gradually to feel more like himself again. Parts of him hurt abominably, but he was alive and safe and on the mend, if a little battered.

He slept well that night, although vaguely aware when he half woke that he was never alone. There was always a shaded lamp lit, glowing in the darkness, and, since the bed curtains were drawn back, he could see a still figure sitting in the chair beside the fire. But he was comfortable enough to drift back to sleep, and before he knew it, the room was bright again.

The sleep had so refreshed him that he was well enough to get up, be washed and shaved by his valet, and eat his breakfast sitting at the round table in the window. It had been his place for making things when he was a boy, the surface constantly spread with clock workings or bits of wood and tools. Now it bore an embroidered tablecloth and blue-painted china, a pot of porridge and baskets of buns and toast. Margaret, Jane and Kit joined him, and Jane spread his toast with butter and preserves, since he had not the full use of his arms yet.

"Shall I feed pieces into your mouth?" she said. "I can spoon porridge into you as well, if you wish. Or perhaps Margaret should do that, since she is skilled with small children. Never having had any myself, I should pour it into your ear, as like as not. Oh, did I just liken you to a small child? I beg your pardon. No insult was intended." And she went into peals of laughter.

Jeremy laughed too, not in the least affronted. "You may employ your wit at my expense as much as you choose, Miss Tyrrell. Since you are taking such good care of me otherwise, I shall not complain even if you fill both ears with porridge. You have all my gratitude for your hospitality, which must be the greatest inconvenience to you."

She was taken aback, her cheeks rather pink at his unexpected gallantry, and for once was lost for words.

"I take it I was dumped on my head somewhere on Woodside land," he said, "and that is why you have been obliged to offer shelter to a most unwanted patient."

"Oh... well... it was none of my doing. Your horse was seen wandering about on our lawn, so Timpson went out to look for you. We brought you here because it was the nearest house. We should have done the same for anyone, so you may spare your gratitude."

He smiled, seeing that her gruff manner was due more to embarrassment than any resentment, but to spare her blushes he turned to Margaret.

"Should you not be in London, sister?"

She shook her head. "Mel..." she said, them lapsed into silence again.

"Mel has gone?" A nod. "But not you. I hope you did not stay on my account?"

Another nod, accompanied by a smile. "Happy..." Again she stopped. She had always been shy, a girl of very few words, but he could not remember her being quite so inarticulate. With an "Oh!" of frustration, she reached for a box that lay on a side table. It opened like a writing box, with a sloping surface, but with a slate to write on instead of paper. Margaret produced a chalk from inside the box and began to tap away on the slate.

'Mel has gone to London because his father expects it of him. I hate London, so I am very glad of an excuse not to go. Thank you for falling on your head, brother.'

Jeremy laughed, but said, "How is it that you cannot talk at all, Margaret? You never had much to say for yourself, but this is different, I think."

She scratched away again. *'The words get stuck. It started when I was sixteen, but my sisters helped me make myself understood. When I met Mel I got better. Much better. But this house brings it all back and now the words are getting stuck again.'*

"Poor Margaret! And here you are, constrained to stay in this place which brings back bad memories. I am very sorry, sister." He took her hand, and she smiled, tears trembling on her lashes.

With quick strokes, she wrote, *'Happy to help you. I shall be better when Mel comes for me.'*

Kit had been eyeing the box with fascination while they were talking, but now the temptation was too great. He stretched out a hesitant finger to touch it, his eyes averted from Margaret's. Quickly he snatched the finger away, then, slowly, it crept nearer again. Margaret pulled out a cloth, wiped the slate clean and then pushed the box and chalk towards him. He looked at her in wonder, then ran his hands all over the box. He lifted first one side, then the other, before carefully placing the chalk in one side. He closed the lid, closed up the box, opened it again, lifted one side and then the other...

"That will keep him occupied for hours now," Jane said. "No hope of getting any potatoes dug today." She sighed. "I wish we could keep him, in truth, but I expect his brother will want him back eventually."

After breakfast, the ladies hustled Jeremy back to bed, dosed him with laudanum again and left him to sleep. Mr Caddy, the apothecary, came, a round man with a genial face who told him he would be in plump currant in no time, and later a whey-faced physician tutted over him, prodded him with painful enthusiasm and told him not to think of moving from the house for at least a week.

"So you are saddled with me for a while longer, Miss Tyrrell," Jeremy said to her after the physician had left.

"Think nothing of it," she said. "If you are troublesome, there is plenty of straw above the stable where you may make a tolerably comfortable bed, and I am told that bread and water is a nourishing diet for invalids."

"Only bread and water? May I hope for a little thin gruel now and again?"

"Possibly, if you are very well-behaved," she said, in severe tones, but he thought there was a twinkle in her eyes. She could be abrupt and even downright rude sometimes, but there was a gentle heart inside the gruff exterior.

He was tired, so he closed his eyes and slept again.

~~~~~

Jane woke abruptly, her neck sore from sleeping at an odd angle in the chair, and one leg numb from being tucked underneath her. The room was dark apart from the slight glow remaining in the ashes of the fire.

A movement near the window caught her attention. Jeremy was sitting on the window seat, gazing out into the garden. Jane was up at once, wincing at her stiffened limbs.

"Are you all right? Do you need anything?" Anxiety made her voice sharp.

He turned then, his face a featureless shape in the gloom. "Did I wake you? I am sorry for it, if so. I was trying to be quiet."

"Are you in pain?" she said, crossing the room to sit on the other end of the window seat.

"No. Well... nothing to speak of. I feel remarkably well, considering the situation. I have felt worse with the grippe, and look — I can move both arms perfectly well now." He waggled them to prove it, but then his expression darkened. "Miss Tyrrell, you really should not be here, alone with a man at night, and in my bedchamber, too. It is wildly improper. My valet would watch over me, if indeed you still feel that I need to be watched at all hours."

"Dr Frank gave us very strict instructions to observe you most carefully for any manifestations of putrid fever or infection, and not to relinquish our vigilance for several days. Since your valet is an idiot who would not know a fever from a macaroon, the duty falls to your sister and to me. Besides, I think I am safe from you, given that you have two injured arms and some cracked ribs. It would not be a difficult matter to fend off any misplaced amorous intentions. There is a good-sized poker in the hearth that would do admirably for the purpose."

He laughed, and she was pleased to see no sign of pain. "You know you have nothing to fear from me, because—"

"—because you would be incapable of overcoming your revulsion sufficiently to ravish me," she said, trying not to smile.

That made him laugh even more, and this time he did wince. "Ouch! You had much better not make me laugh, Miss Tyrrell, or else you will delay my recovery by days, and I know how you long to be rid of me. I am too polite to comment on your bad manners in interrupting me, but I was just about to say that you have nothing to fear from me because I am from Lancashire, and therefore have not the sense to take advantage of your unprotected state."

She laughed, too, and said, "You remind me of my sisters. They talk like this, chaffing each other mercilessly."

"Mine are like that, too," he said, his face softening at the thought. "They are all older than me, so they were always very protective — of me, and of each other. Not that I appreciated it at the time. I would have traded them all for a brother. Another brother, I should say, for there was Andrew, but he died."

"Was it horrible, when he died?" she said softly, her throat suddenly tight. Lord, how easily the memories returned at the least little thing.

"Probably, but it was before I was born, so I knew nothing of it. He came between Rosamund and Annabelle."

"How old was he?"

"Four... five... something like that. I am not sure, because no one ever spoke of it. It was old history by the time I was of an age to understand, and long forgotten."

"It is never forgotten," she said, the words barely audible. "If it is not spoken of, it is because it is a grief too raw and painful to be expressed. One never forgets."

He stretched out one hand to touch hers, the merest touch, but it brought the foolish tears to the surface.

"Forgive me," he said. "It was not my intention to cause you pain or awaken unhappy memories. I am so very sorry."

She shook her head, as if to dispel the grief-stricken thoughts that hopped about in her mind like so many ravens, black and dolorous.

He lifted her hand and stroked it gently. "Perhaps such sorrows *should* be spoken of, and often, so that those left behind may learn to live without the deceased, and those who never met them may know of their lives. If the dead are never spoken of, it is as if they never lived at all."

"Yes!" she said with sudden fierceness. "They should never be forgotten — not your Andrew, and not Angela. No, she must never be forgotten. Such a golden child! The palest blonde hair in soft curls around her sweet face, and the happiest disposition. Never was a child so contented! Mama called her a little angel, and so she was. Papa perhaps would have liked a son after four daughters, but he never complained. He loved her too. It was impossible not to love her, so good and affectionate as she was. Of course, everyone indulged her, for she was so much younger than the rest of us. Three years we had her, before God wanted her back. Three years and three days... It was not enough."

She fell silent, her mind filled with memories. Angela running, smiling, chasing butterflies, laughing — happy, always so happy. Papa lifting her up or swinging her round. Jane and her sisters making daisy chains and winding them around Angela's head. Angela bending down to look the farm chickens in the eye, Angela reaching over the pool to touch the fish...

Perhaps she made some sound, for he said quietly, "What happened to her?"

She stood up, smoothing her crumpled skirts, then crossing her arms over her waist. When she spoke, her voice was harsh, like the croak of the raven. "She fell into the waterlily pool and drowned. Papa had the pool drained and filled in, and erected a temple there in her memory, with sweet-smelling roses all around. Angela's house, we called it. A summer house, for she was a child of summer, all sunshine and gentleness. I used to go and sit there, to weep and remember and tell her my troubles, and somehow I always felt better afterwards, as if being in my sister's house gave me strength and hope. Sometimes I even slept out there on the warmest nights, and it was as though she were there with me." She took a deep breath, forcing herself to keep her tone flat and emotionless. There had been enough emotion spilt for one night. "But then Mama died and we had to leave the house and Angela. We moved here and that was the end of it. And now, Mr Winterton, I have wearied you sufficiently with my maunderings that you should be able to sleep again. Shoo! Back to bed with you."

12: *Courtship (May)*

MAY

It was ten days before Dr Frank would consider allowing the patient to return home. Ten days during which Jane could not decide which she wanted most — for him to leave or for him to stay. Never had a man confused her so thoroughly. It was not as if she had never seen a handsome man before, or a charming one, or a man so tall and imposing. It was the combination of all these attributes in one person, as well as quickness of mind and a delightful smile and strong, capable hands, that so undermined her resistance. And his green eyes — ah, those eyes. Rosamund had them too, but hers were humourless and staid, whereas in her brother they conveyed so much amused enjoyment of life, and something more, something that made Jane as weak inside as a schoolroom miss whenever he looked at her in that teasing way he had.

As each day passed and he recovered his strength, he was able to do a little more — to dress, to sit downstairs for an hour or two, to take short walks in the garden, to help Kit mend chairs in the carpenter's workshop and finally to join them for dinner, where her father had smiled benignly at him and encouraged him to treat Woodside as his home.

"For after all, it was your home once and may yet be so again," he had said, beaming at his guest.

Jeremy had said all that was proper, expressing his gratitude for Jane's care, and her father had said only, "Jane is very good. I am happy that she has been of service to you."

Not a word was said about the impropriety of her tending a single gentleman, which a father might be supposed to care about. But then Margaret was still there, since her husband could not yet leave London to rescue her, and it would be supposed by everyone that she would be attending her brother's sickroom. Who more proper to care for him than his own sister?

No one realised how many excuses Jane found for entering his room each day. "I am just making some tea, would you like some?" Or it might be a plate of fresh cakes or a jug of lemonade or a sachet of lavender to tuck under his pillow to help him sleep. Nor did anyone know, she hoped, how often she crept into his room at night while he lay sleeping, just for the pleasure of watching his peaceful face. He slept on his side, arms sprawled out in front of him, and she could see from the way the covers lay that he had one leg stretched out and the other bent at the knee. When she returned to her own bed, she could imagine him lying next to her in sleep. Even though such thoughts shocked her, she could not shake them away.

He had not mentioned her proposal for a false betrothal, nor his mother's jewels, but she thought about it constantly. She still had no intention to marry him, for why would she surrender the sweet freedom of spinsterhood for the slavery of matrimony, even for a man as attractive as Jeremy Winterton? Nevertheless, a betrothal would be something to remember, long after he had wed the boring beauty from his smoky northern town. She shivered with anticipation at the thought. For a little while, she could walk beside him, enjoy his full attention, perhaps even kiss him. She had never kissed anyone, had never wanted to, but for Jeremy she might make an exception.

Eventually Dr Frank agreed that his patient was well enough to move to Brinchester.

"No riding, mind," he said in his gruff way. "You must travel in a well-sprung carriage. And no crawling about on the floor of your clock tower or climbing ladders or any such nonsense. Rest, moderate your consumption of rich foods and strong wines, and take a walk every day unless the wind be in the east or the rain drenching. Occupy yourself with sedentary pursuits, like reading. Come to see me twice a week so that I may keep an eye on you, for I know what you young fellows are like — too energetic to be sensible, and then you will have a putrid infection in that arm and it will have to come off."

"Since I am fond of both my arms, I shall follow your advice," Jeremy said.

No one mentioned the possibility that someone had tried to kill him. The parish constable, one of the farmers, had come to see him, laboriously made notes of everything Jeremy could remember and then gone away again, muttering about poachers. Morning callers who came to enquire solicitously after the invalid murmured about Romanies and tinkers. Mrs Claremont talked about their elderly gamekeeper, now retired, but who still went out with a gun and was confused about where Claremont land ended. No one talked of attempted murder.

Jane could not believe it. If there had not been the earlier shot, she could perhaps have accepted the theory, but two shots on Woodside land was no coincidence. However, Jeremy was insouciant about it, and assured her that there was no one in the world with any reason to want him dead, so she contented herself with warning him to be careful. She could do no more.

The day was fixed when Jeremy was to leave with Kit to make his temporary home with Mr Everton while the clock underwent repairs. Jane could not quite understand his enthusiasm for the clock but she enjoyed listening to him describing its workings, his expressive hands waving and his eyes alight with excitement.

The day before his departure, he came to find Jane in the kitchen where she was supervising the making of jellies.

"I beg your pardon for disrupting the work," he said with his charming smile, as the cook and kitchen maid dropped into curtsies. "I could not find you above stairs, Miss Tyrrell, and there was no servant about that I might send to find you. But I see that you are busy." The disappointment in his voice was unmistakable. "I had hoped to tempt you to a walk in the garden now that the rain has stopped."

"Annie can finish these," she said quickly, untying her apron. "Let me just fetch my bonnet."

Almost as soon as they had left the house and begun walking along the gravel drive towards the shrubbery, he turned to her and said in a low voice, "I have been considering the proposition you put to me... the betrothal idea. Are you still minded in that same direction?"

"Why, yes, but you surprise me, Mr Winterton. I had thought you to be adamantly opposed to the scheme."

He gave her a look of amusement. "It remains an absurd scheme, as I have always maintained. But if I wish to own Woodside without encumbrance and live as a gentleman, then I have very few options. I have had many hours lately to ponder my situation and it seems to me that the idea has merit. If I can recover all Mama's furniture, then the principal jewels must be hidden within one or other of the pieces. I know the way of finding the hidden places now, so a very little effort will put them in my hands and then… then I should be able to do all that I want."

"And I too," she said, suddenly finding it hard to breathe. Heavens, the effect this man had on her! It was fortunate that he would soon be removed from Woodside and, in time, from her life altogether, for otherwise she might have been in danger of falling into the honey-trap of love. "But what of Miss Ridwell? She will be distressed to hear of your betrothal."

"Why should she hear of it?" he said airily. "Besides, she knows me only as John Moreton, so the engagement of Mr Jeremy Winterton in a different county will not trouble her in the slightest."

She said nothing, not quite liking such deception. But then, the whole enterprise was built around deception, so she could hardly criticise him on that score, and to him, who had lived half his life in a lie, it might seem a trivial matter.

"There is another circumstance which renders the scheme particularly apt," he went on. "My injury has thrown us together rather, thus rendering a betrothal between us rather more credible. You have nursed me back to health and grown to appreciate my manifold charms. My gratitude for your tender care has blossomed into love. What could possibly be more plausible?"

She laughed. "Almost anything, to those who know us well, but it may well convince the credulous. Indeed, if we are careful, and do not rush into it too quickly, and display a little less antipathy towards each other, we may even persuade the sceptical that there is a genuine affection between us. Can you play such a part with conviction, do you think, sir?"

He smiled down at her, his green eyes gleaming with amusement. "Miss Tyrrell, I have been playing a part for fifteen years. I am a consummate actor, I assure you. Besides, my antipathy towards you is non-existent, as I have more than once pointed out to you. It is *your* antipathy towards *me* which may cause us the greatest difficulty, I fear."

"Do not worry about that," she said, flushing a little. "You are not the only one skilled in playing a part." He looked at her searchingly, and she hoped desperately that he would ask nothing more. Quickly she went on, "Besides, if anyone disbelieves our sudden burst of affection, he or she may instead consider that my reputation has been compromised by the hours I have spent in your sickroom. But let us not worry overmuch what others may say. There are those who have expected our engagement long since, as the most natural way to settle the ownership of Woodside. It may be that their views will prevail."

He said only, "Well, I am prepared to try this, if you are also. You understand, of course, that once we are betrothed, I cannot honourably withdraw? The only means of breaking the engagement is for you to cry off."

She heard the implication there, that she might be planning to trap him into matrimony. Surely he knew her better than that? But there was no point in taking offence, for she was getting what she wanted, and an insult or two along the way was a small price to pay. She tried to make light of his remarks. "Oh, you are claiming to be a gentleman now, are you? Too honcurable to withdraw, indeed, and you nought but a mill manager." He smiled at the sally, and she went on, "Do not suppose for one moment that I should not do it. Surely you must recognise that jilting you will be the most enjoyable aspect of this whole endeavour. That alone would be sufficient inducement to me to agree to it. "

That made him laugh. "Very well. We are agreed, and agreed also that we must do nothing precipitate. I shall move to Brinchester tomorrow, as planned, but I shall find some excuse to call upon you rather frequently thereafter. Once the neighbours begin to comment upon this and cast knowing looks at you, then I shall talk to your father. When we are safely betrothed, then I shall leave you to use your feminine wiles to recover the missing furniture."

"It could take several weeks," she said, suddenly anxious. "Can you stay away from Lancashire for so long?"

"Oh, that is no problem," he said airily. "My uncle — who is not my uncle at all, of course, but I cannot escape the habit of calling him so. My uncle, then, has already informed me that the mill is running along famously without me, and I am authorised to stay as long as I need to. As for Ellen, she is gone to London with her aunt."

"London?" Jane said, stopping dead, so that he was obliged to stop too, and turn to face her. "Is she casting you off, then?"

"No, no! Nothing of the sort. It was not planned, but a cousin who was to have gone came down with the grippe, and Ellen was invited to take her place. She will be gone for weeks — months, perhaps, if they go on to Brighton after. So you see, I am not at all wanted in the north, and we may implement our scheme at leisure."

"I wonder you are not afraid of one of the smart London bloods stealing her away from you," she said, watching his face curiously.

There was no hint of concern there. "It is agreed with her father," he said, with the slightest lift of one shoulder. "She will not marry to disoblige her family."

"But if a man of rank should fall for her beauty—"

"Her father lives within sight of his own mills," Jeremy said, with a hint of impatience. "Her dowry is not tucked away in the funds or in land, it consists of Ridwell's most prestigious mill. No good family will want anything to do with Ellen, despite her great beauty. She is tainted by her association with trade. This is not her first season in London, but it will be no more successful than the previous two, believe me."

Jane was not convinced. She had seen from her sisters' experiences just how determined a young man could become when he fell in love, and Ellen Ridwell sounded like a diamond of the first water, despite her father's mills. A young man of independent fortune could afford to marry to please himself. For her own part, Jane considered that Ellen's docility would be a greater hindrance to a good match, but the right husband could perhaps draw her out of her cocoon and turn her into a lively butterfly.

They wandered through the shrubbery, discussing the details of their plan, and had turned towards the house again when Jeremy reached into a pocket and produced a small box.

"A farewell gift for you," he said with a smile. "Something to show my gratitude for all those hours you spent in my bedroom watching over me."

She blushed as she took it. Did he know her secret? Had he seen her enter or leave his room when she should have been fast asleep in her own bed? But when she thanked him and dared to look at his face, she could see no sign of awareness. It was a more general compliment.

The box was small, not much larger than a pill box, and when she shook it, something heavy moved inside it. But it would not open. Try as she might, despite pulling, pushing and twisting, she could not shift the lid. Mutely, she held it out to him, bewildered.

He laughed, and folded her fingers around it. "This is a puzzle box, Miss Tyrrell. The means of opening it is concealed, but you are clever enough to work it out. If not, I shall show you the secret when next I visit here."

For the rest of the day, she wrestled with the box but it would not yield. She woke early the next day to try again. When the time came to bid farewell to Jeremy Winterton, she had still not succeeded in opening the box.

He grinned at her knowingly from the carriage window. "At least you will be glad to see me again," he said.

"Oh, I shall have worked it out by then," she said, with more assurance than she felt.

He laughed. "Then you will be able to tell me of your triumph." But his smile was smugly confident. "Until then, farewell, Miss Tyrrell."

She almost stamped her foot in annoyance. Irritating man!

~~~~~

Jeremy was not sorry to leave Woodside. He wanted to get back to his clock, and although he had been forbidden from strenuous exertion, he could continue his work with Kit's help. And then there was Jane Tyrrell. Being forced into intimacy with her, he had to admit to a certain admiration for the lady. Her mind was quick, and he enjoyed their verbal battles. He had never had the felicity of such dialogue before, even with friends in Branton, for he had always had to take care and watch his words. Here, where all his secrets were known, there was no need for caution. As she spoke her mind, so could he.

Her warning about Ellen had rattled him, though. Ellen... as the carriage rolled slowly along the road to Brinchester, he brought Ellen's image to mind, her blonde hair curled around that perfect face, her lips slightly apart as she gazed at him with limpid blue eyes... No, her eyes were brown, were they not? Hazel? No, they were blue, he was sure of it... almost sure. How strange that he could not remember. But the thought of Ellen in London bothered him not at all. Let her enjoy herself before she settled down to become Mrs John Moreton... no, Mrs Jeremy Winterton... Hmm, that was confusing. What name would he use from now on? He had no idea.

Of the future, however, there was no doubt. He would secure Woodside — that was the first step, before anything else. Then he would return to Branton as a man of property, and inform Ridwell of his situation. After that, he would marry Ellen and settle down... where? In Branton, of course, for he would be a mill owner after his marriage. But what about Woodside? He had assumed that his father would be still alive, and would keep Woodside safe for him, but now...?

Very well, then, he would install Ellen at Woodside, as the lady she deserved to be, put a manager in the mill and go there once a month himself to check that all was as it should be. But it was not very satisfactory. His success at Hazlehead Mill had been due to his constant vigilance. He had checked on his engine almost every day, overseeing the engineer and the loom master, talking to some of the workers employed to tend the machinery. One could not watch over a mill from a distance of a hundred miles. It was impossible. What on earth was he to do?

He did what he always did with an intractable problem — he set it aside, to be dealt with when he had more leisure to address the question. A way would be found! No matter how difficult the question, a way was always found, or else the problem quietly disappeared of its own accord. Yes, sometimes it was better just to do nothing and hope that the difficulty went away.

For now, he would concentrate on the immediate issues — his betrothal to Jane, the jewels and his clock. His clock! He smiled as he thought of it, and settled down in his corner of the carriage to plan the next stage of his restoration.

Three days later, he decided it would be time to visit Jane again. Any sooner would look too particular, but an interval of three days was sufficient for him to return and express his thanks more personally than the brief letter he had sent. He took a posy of flowers, and, mindful of the doctor's instructions not to ride, he decorously hired a post chaise. The thought was also in the back of his mind that he had now been shot at twice. He could not conceive why anyone should want him dead, but whether the shots were bad luck or deadly serious, he was safer in a carriage than riding.

He was pleased to find the Claremont carriage outside when he arrived. A morning call from Mrs Claremont and her last unmarried daughter would be perfect for reporting to the neighbourhood that Mr Winterton had arrived bearing flowers for Miss Tyrrell. Timpson the groom, in livery but still smelling of the stables, showed him into the drawing room.

He made his greetings to the Claremont ladies and Margaret before turning to Jane. As soon as he saw the small brooch pinning her fichu, he burst out, "You solved it then!"

She smiled happily. "Yes! As soon as I began to think about it logically, I realised what needed to be done. Thank you for my brooch, Mr Winterton." She blushed so prettily that he almost wished he were courting her in earnest. How attractive she was when she was behaving like a lady, instead of snapping his head off.

"Most ingenious, Mr Winterton," Mrs Claremont said. "Jane has been showing us. Where did you come by such a device?"

"I made it myself, ma'am. I love puzzles, and these are as much fun to make as to solve. Are you minded for a harder one?" he said to Jane. "This one is a little more challenging."

She almost bounced with excitement as he pulled the new box from his pocket. They sat together, heads bent over the box while she struggled happily with it, chattering enthusiastically. They could not have presented a more perfect picture of two people in the process of falling in love. Mrs Claremont smiled knowingly at them as she left.

Two days later Jeremy called again, and the following week he called three times. At the third visit, Jane said, blushing slightly, "Papa wishes you to come to dinner. Would Tuesday suit you?"

He agreed that it would suit him very well. So it came about that, when the ladies had withdrawn after dinner, he had his discussion with Mr Tyrrell, who smiled in his benevolent fashion and said he would be "...delighted, my dear fellow, quite delighted..." to allow him to pay his addresses to Jane. She was called in, they were left alone for just two minutes and in that short time Jeremy found himself engaged to be married.

As the carriage conveyed him back to Brinchester, he reflected with some satisfaction on the smoothness with which he had achieved his aim. Jane had fulfilled her role admirably so far, and he felt confident that he could now depend upon her to recover all the missing furniture. The plan was working remarkably well.

13: An Announcement

Jane soon discovered the disagreeable aspects of a false betrothal. She had to smile as congratulations poured in from their acquaintances, who were uniformly thrilled at the news. Those who had predicted it were delighted to be proved right, and those who were taken by surprise were, it seemed, equally delighted to be wrong. It was universally understood that ownership of Woodside would now be transferred to Jeremy, and that Mr Tyrrell would move to Lilac Cottage, within convenient walking distance of the house, and what could be more comfortable or more fitting? And if anyone thought it a hasty and rather opportune betrothal, allowing Jeremy to recover his family home without the least inconvenience or expense, no one expressed such thoughts in Jane's presence.

"There now, I always knew there would be a young man somewhere in the world who would appreciate your many good qualities," Mrs Claremont said to Jane, beaming. "Now you will be valued as you ought to be."

"So romantic," whispered her daughter, Sarah, with a sigh of satisfaction. "Shall you be married soon, Jane? Shall you get a special licence? For there is no need to wait, is there?"

"They will not marry before Rosamund and Lord Westerlea return from London," her mother said repressively. "One does not rush these things, Sarah. There will be wedding clothes to be thought of first, and Jeremy will want to order the carriage. I hope you will come to me for advice about warehouses, Jane, since you have no mother to guide you. My mantua maker will be happy to accommodate you. She will give you a little more... well, style. You need not dress so plain when you are married, you know. You will want to take on a few more servants, I daresay. I wonder if Maria Bowen's under footman would come to you? She was only saying the other day that she cannot see the need for three, for the grooms and valets double up, you know. Yes, you will need a footman, and a housekeeper, for you cannot go on as you have been, not as a married woman. And a lady's maid... you will need a proper lady's maid. My Anna might do for you. Shall you make any changes to the house?"

Jane seized the opportunity gratefully. "Perhaps. Mr Winterton was a little upset to find so many alterations here since his childhood, and so many favourite items of furniture missing. I thought it would please him if the house is restored somewhat to its former state."

It was enough, she felt, to put the idea into circulation. Then, when she asked for specific pieces, it would occasion no surprise.

"Excellent idea," Mrs Claremont said. "You are thinking of your husband's comfort already, and that is exactly as it should be. Now as to linens—"

"Never mind about that, Mama," Sarah said. "I want to know what he said when he proposed. Did he kneel? Did he... did he kiss you? Were you quite overcome? I should be overcome, if ever a man should offer for me. Did he talk about love? Was it all terribly romantic?"

Jane had a struggle to suppress her laughter. "I cannot tell you, for it all happened so fast. I was not overcome, but then I was expecting it, you see."

"Oooh, did he hint? Did he say, *'Miss Tyrrell, there is something very particular that I wish to say to you'?* Or was there just... a certain look in his eye?"

She tried very hard to answer patiently, and honestly, too, where she could, without puncturing all the poor girl's idealistic notions. And after the Claremonts, it was the Bowens, and the Sheridans, and even old Mrs Wilkes, who never left her house nowadays except for church, but would have been mortified not to honour a betrothal by paying a congratulatory call on the future bride.

The worst moments of all were when Jeremy was there. Jane squirmed in terror that he would say the wrong thing, some little detail that contradicted her version of events, and might expose them both to ridicule and censure. But he did not. He was utterly composed, answering every question readily, although as often as not his answer was a mysterious, "I could not possibly say." And then he would look at her with that heart-stopping, stomach-churning smile, which reduced her to blushing incoherence and a very tolerable impression of a love-struck maid. Which was very much what she was, of course.

The worst visitors were her sisters. All three of them came to stay, although happily not all at once, and with them she could not prevaricate. They would not be fobbed off with vague remarks like, "It all happened so fast."

"Nonsense," said Ruth robustly. "I remember every word that Malcolm said to me, even though I was not expecting it in the least. Quite took me by surprise, he did. But every word is seared into my mind, as fresh as if it was yesterday. *'My dearest Ruth,'* he said, and

I guessed then what was coming, for never had he used my name before, and so my heart was going pit-a-pat, I can tell you! *'My dearest Ruth, I cannot imagine my life without you by my side. Will you make me the happiest of men?'* Those were his exact words, and you have always had a good memory, Jane, so do not pretend that you cannot remember. What did he say?"

"It is private," Jane said resolutely. "Words spoken on such occasions are... are private. I do not wish to share them."

She blushed as she spoke, as much from embarrassment as anything else, but this had the desired effect. "Why, Jane, you really are in love, the two of you! How sweet! I never thought you would ever meet the man you could hold in respect, never mind admiration, but it delights me to be wrong."

Helena, on the other hand, wanted to know all about Jeremy's financial situation and the details of Jane's settlement, which was easier to deal with since she could be referred to Papa, who told her firmly that money affairs were a matter for men, and such questions were unbecoming in a woman.

Last came Charlotte — dear, affectionate Charlotte, increasing again already and just as thrilled as the first time. "Yes, we are so blessed," she said simply, when Jane offered congratulations.

"But so soon after little Roland," Jane said.

"Ronald, dear," Charlotte said, then laughed merrily. "Not that I blame you for muddling the names, for their father does so, too. Foolish man!" she added, in loving tones. "But dear, dear Jane, just think — perhaps a year from now, you will have a sweet little baby of your own, and then how happy you will be!"

There was nothing at all Jane could say to such heartfelt wishes, so she merely blushed and looked away, but guilt swept over her at such moments, when she thought how disappointed

Charlotte would be when the engagement was called off. But not as disappointed as Jane. She was beginning to fear for her own peace of mind, and wonder if, when the time came, she could let Jeremy go with any degree of composure.

~~~~~

Jeremy rather enjoyed his betrothal. He had not expected quite so much fuss, but he supposed that Jane was well liked in the parish. As for himself, as Mr Winterton of Woodside he would have to accustom himself to a certain amount of attention. Nor was it difficult to deflect awkward questions. Jane might be the recipient of some probing from her female acquaintances, but a gentleman was not expected to approach the matter in a romantic light. His hand was pumped, his back was slapped, he was offered endless congratulations but mostly the engagement was viewed pragmatically — he would get his hands on Woodside without the bother of going to court, and if Jane was no beauty, she was widely acknowledged as a sensible woman who would make him an excellent wife. Tyrrell had been pressing him rather hard to set a wedding date and discuss settlements with the lawyers, but so far he had managed to fob him off.

It was all very satisfactory, and he began to estimate how many weeks it might be before he could go north again to claim his real bride.

Such an idyll could not last, of course. It all came crashing to earth one morning at the breakfast table. Jeremy and Dudley Everton were quite comfortable in their friendship now, so little was said beyond the conventional greetings of the day and the occasional request for the marmalade. Everton was reading the latest newspapers from London, while Jeremy had a book propped open in front of his plate.

"Ah, here is something to interest you," Everton said, folding the newspaper and sliding it across the table. "There!"

Jeremy scanned the page, saw nothing of note. "What is it you wish me to see?"

"The forthcoming marriages."

"Oh…"

And there it was. *'Mr Jeremy Winterton of Brinshire, also known as Mr John Moreton of Branton in Lancashire, only son of the late Mr Edmund Winterton of Woodside, Brinshire, to Miss Jane Tyrrell, eldest daughter of Mr Geoffrey Tyrrell of Woodside in Brinshire. A date for the marriage has not yet been set.'*

He opened the paper out. The Gazette. One of the London newspapers. One read by Giles Moreton, and probably also by Henry Ridwell. Would Ellen read it? Possibly not, but undoubtedly one of her friends would take pleasure in revealing to her that the man she had expected to marry was betrothed to another.

Jeremy swore under his breath.

"Whatever is the matter?" Everton said. "Is there a mistake in it?"

"He has put *both* names," Jeremy said helplessly. "It is bad enough to post such a notice without asking, but to put both names…!"

"Tyrrell? He sent the notice? But why—?" Everton stopped, some inkling of the truth having occurred to him. "You did not want them to know, is that it? Your acquaintances in Branton — it was meant to be kept secret from them? But why?"

"I wished to tell them myself," Jeremy said fiercely. "There was no intent to deceive… not for long, only until… until…" He could not finish the sentence. *Only until I have the jewels and Jane has jilted me. Only until I am free again.* But he was not free, and now Ridwell would know it and all hope of marriage to Ellen was at an end. Ridwell would see it as a betrayal of the worst kind. And how could Jeremy possibly explain it? *'Nothing to worry about, it is only a false betrothal, it means nothing.'*

Fortunately, Everton leapt to the kindest interpretation. "Of course you did not wish to deceive, my dear boy. That is understood. You did not wish them to hear of it except from your own lips. I have heard a rumour that there was a lady in the north who might have had certain... hopes, perhaps. Naturally you would not wish her to read of your betrothal in the newspaper, like any common acquaintance. Your feelings do you credit."

Such praise was too much for Jeremy. "I am not so worthy as all that, Everton," he said, with a wry smile.

Everton nodded in sympathy. "Well, well, perhaps you wished to keep all avenues open until the last moment. Jane Tyrrell was not known to be looking for a husband, and may yet change her mind, eh? And if so, and all hope is lost here, why then it would be convenient to have another possibility waiting for you in Lancashire. That is nothing but common prudence. But be not afraid that I shall tease you about it, for your affairs are no concern of mine. If anyone raises the issue with me, I shall say only that you wished the news of such an important matter as your marriage to be conveyed personally."

"You are a good friend to me, Everton."

Jeremy was too angry to wait for a carriage to be hired from one of the inns, so he had his own horse saddled and rode across the fields to Frickham village, despite the physician's orders. The man was a gloomy soul, who would have all his patients keep to their beds at all times for fear of accident or illness. Jeremy felt himself to be fully healed by now.

His rage had carried him half way to Frickham before he remembered that he had twice been shot at in the Woodside grounds. He was still a shade disbelieving of any deliberate attempt to kill him, but there was no point in taking undue risks, so he turned away from the fields and instead rode the rather longer distance to the village by road.

Tyrrell was in his study, as usual, bent over his painting table. "I cannot spare you more than a few minutes, I fear, Winterton," he said, wiping his hands on a cloth. "The blossom of the crab apple is such a delicate shade that one must capture its essence at the earliest possible moment, before it loses its bloom. What is on your mind?"

"You put a notice in *The Gazette* of my engagement to your daughter, sir."

Tyrrell gazed at him, his expression unchanging. "It is usual in such cases," he said in mild tones.

"But you did not consult me on the matter. I would not have worded it so."

"Was there a mistake? Was any point in error?"

"Not in error, no, but—"

"Then what is the problem, Winterton?"

Jeremy heaved a breath to curb his annoyance. No blame could attach to Tyrrell, after all. How could he have known the disaster he was invoking? "It is unfortunate that you chose to include both the names by which I am known, so that my acquaintances in Branton will hear of my betrothal through the newspaper rather than directly from me."

"Then you have been dilatory in your letter-writing, have you not? There has been time enough to inform them. No, no, let me speak," he said, holding up a hand to forestall Jeremy's next objection. "Consider my position, Winterton. You pay court to my daughter, yet you also have a lady waiting for you at home in Branton. It is so, is it not? So when you betroth yourself to Jane, yet show no sign of wanting to get on with the business, I wonder about you. *'Plenty of time for that,'* you say, whenever I ask about settlements or dates or whether you have ordered your carriage. Meanwhile, Jane is happily scouring the countryside for furnishings to please your taste. You see my concern, I am sure. I wish to assure myself that you are not planning to jilt my daughter and run back to the beautiful Miss Ridwell."

For a moment, Jeremy was almost too angry to speak. "So you did this deliberately!" he hissed.

Tyrrell said nothing, his smile undiminished and his good humour unimpaired.

Jeremy took a deep breath, and then another, forcing himself to composure. "I am betrothed to marry your daughter," he said stiffly. "I cannot cry off, as you know perfectly well. No gentleman can honourably break off an engagement."

"Which is the nub of the matter," Tyrrell said amiably. "*Are* you a gentleman, sir? You are a mill manager, a salaried employee, at your northern town, yet you would be Winterton of Woodside here. You were born to be a gentleman, but raised to be something lower. You are Jeremy Winterton and you are also John Moreton. But I put it to you, sir, that you cannot be both. You can only be one or the other, and this is the point at which you must decide. Marry my daughter and be a gentleman, or return to your mill and be a part of the manufacturing class."

~~~~~

Jane heard the story without alarm. Poor Jeremy! He stood to lose the beautiful Miss Ridwell because of this precipitate announcement, so no wonder he was upset. A pang of envy assailed Jane towards the unknown lady who held his hopes for the future in her hand. But it was necessary to calm him, to ensure he did not panic and repudiate the betrothal, for then there would be no hope of finding the missing jewels.

"This is just my father's way of pushing me into matrimony," she said calmly. "He thinks your Miss Ridwell will turn tail and run when she hears of it, so you will have no option but to marry me, but have no fear — I shall cry off as arranged."

Her throat was unexpectedly tight as she spoke. In her more fanciful moments, she imagined him turning a shocked face to her at such words. *'No! You cannot truly mean it. Dearest Jane, now that I have come to know you, I want nothing more than to make our betrothal a real one. I love you—'*

Such foolish nonsense!

They were walking in the garden, with Margaret a little way ahead of them, to give them privacy without sacrificing propriety. Despite the season, a chill wind whipped the ribbons of Jane's bonnet about her face, and the long stems of early roses swayed about, trying to grab her skirts.

"Ellen will not turn tail, but her father will," Jeremy said grimly. "He holds his consequence as high as any duke, and he will not stand for any man who deals dishonourably with his daughter. No father would."

"You have *not* dealt dishonourably with her — have you?" she said. "I thought there was no engagement."

"No, no, but there was an understanding of sorts, and a widespread expectation. It will cause him embarrassment."

"But what of the lady?" Jane persisted. "It seems to me that your concern is all for the father, when it is the daughter who will be seen as the injured party. If she is sincerely attached to you—"

"There is nothing of that sort," he said scornfully. "She has no feelings to be hurt by my seeming defection, I assure you. She is a cold fish."

"Then I wonder you want to marry her," Jane said in astonishment. "And even if you did not, you should not talk so of any lady."

He exhaled sharply, and stopped abruptly, hands on hips. "You are right to chastise me," he said slowly. "You speak your mind, Jane, and sometimes I dislike such honesty, but that is because more often than not you penetrate to the heart of the matter. I must go back to Branton for a while, I think."

"To mend your bridges?"

"No, to apologise. Ellen is in London, and I cannot see her or write to her, not without her father's permission, but I shall talk to him and abide by his wishes. And if all is at an end with Ellen — well then, so be it."

"Well, if you ever get truly desperate, you will just have to marry me after all," Jane said, with as light a tone as she could manage.

To her astonishment, he lifted her gloved hand to his lips and said, "There are far worse fates, Miss Tyrrell."

He smiled and her foolish heart turned over and over.

14: Apologies (June)

It was the chimneys that Jeremy noticed first, as his post-chaise drew into Branton. The smoke he was used to — every town was smoky, after all — but the chimneys struck him for the first time as ominous, thin fingers pointing at the sky as if in defiance of God. And then the clothes were different, too — darker, looser, less fashionable. He had been mingling with the gentlefolk of Brinshire, who were not exemplars of style, in the main, but they showed a little more elegance than the people of Branton.

He went first to his own house and his uncle. Not truly his uncle, of course, but the habit was hard to drop.

The footman who opened the door showed no surprise, although Jeremy had not written to announce his arrival.

"Good day, William," Jeremy said, as he handed over his hat and gloves. "Is my uncle at home?"

"The master is in his study, I believe. Was your journey tolerable, sir?"

"About as tolerable as a hundred miles on dusty roads can be."

"Indeed, sir. Shall I have a bath sent up to your room, sir?"

"Not yet. I shall see my uncle first. He will not mind my dirt."

"Very good, sir."

The footman bowed, and disappeared briskly to the nether regions. Well, he had never announced Jeremy before, so he would not expect to do so on this occasion, either, but Jeremy felt that there should be some observance of the change in circumstances. Perhaps he should send in his card first, but there was the difficulty of knowing which one to use. After a moment of agonised indecision, he realised there was nothing for it but to face his uncle's wrath. Even if, by some miracle, he had missed the notice in the paper, Jeremy would have to tell him of it, so there was no escape. He took a deep breath and knocked on the door.

"Enter!"

He went in.

"Johnny!" His uncle beamed at him, leaping from his chair to grab him by the hand and shake it vigorously. "What a delightful surprise. How dare you give me no warning of your return, you little rascal. So how are you, Johnny? Or should I call you Jeremy now?"

Jeremy inhaled sharply. This was not what he had expected. "Aren't you angry?" he burst out.

"Angry? About what?"

"That I deceived you? *Lied* to you? I've let you believe I was Johnny Moreton for years."

To his astonishment, his uncle laughed. "Deceived me? Not for a moment. Come and sit down, Johnny, and let's have a celebratory brandy, eh? Let's drink to your impending marriage, shall we, even if it's not quite the one I was expecting." He chuckled as he turned to the sideboard where the tantalus stood.

Jeremy sat before his legs humiliated him by giving way. "You knew?" he croaked.

His uncle poured two measures of brandy and then, after a moment's thought, doubled them. "Here," he said, pushing a glass into Jeremy's hand. "Drink that. Of course I knew. I realised as soon as I clapped eyes on you. My brother had told me that Johnny was *'the runt of the family, too small and chuckle-headed to be of the least use to us, for he has trouble reading and writing and cannot cipher at all. But he's a good worker, so I'm sure you'll find something to keep him occupied.'* And then you appeared, not in the least runtish or chuckle-headed, and with no difficulty with your words, or numbers either. Obviously you were not Johnny Moreton. It took me a while to work out exactly who you were, mind you, but when the ship went down you became so quiet that I was able to work it out. But honestly, Johnny, if you think it matters to me, you are very far out."

"You astonish me," Jeremy said. "Yet you never said a word."

"The secret was yours to reveal or not, as you chose," his uncle said easily. "I always hoped you would confide in me, but I understood your reasons not to do so, and I was happy enough with your progress not to rock the boat, shall we say. Johnny would have been just as exasperating to me as he was to his father, but you — you have always been a delight, as a boy and as a man. No, if silence kept you here and working my mill so effectively, then I would not be the one to speak. Naturally, once you began to think of matrimony, it was only fitting that you should disclose your true identity. I know little of the Wintertons of Woodside. Will you tell me about them, and how you came to be Johnny Moreton?"

So they talked and sipped brandy and talked again. Jeremy described Woodside and his family, his exile to become a midshipman, and how he had escaped that fate. He then explained that Jane was the last daughter still unmarried and her father wished to see her settled.

"A pragmatic arrangement, to transfer Woodside back to its rightful owner with the minimum of disruption," he said airily. He said nothing about jewels or furniture or false betrothals. "It is unfortunate that Tyrrell sent the notice to *The Gazette* before I had had a chance to explain the position to Ridwell."

His uncle laughed. "He came here, you know. Ridwell, that is. Waving the newspaper, spluttering fit to burst his waistcoat buttons, striding up and down with his head bobbing, like a demented wood pigeon. Very irate, he was, when I told him that you had not confided in me. Do not expect to be received in that quarter."

"I harbour no such expectations, I assure you. He must be offered an explanation, but if he will not see me, then I shall depend upon you to spread word of my situation."

To Jeremy's surprise, however, when he sent a note to Ridwell asking for the favour of an interview, the footman brought an immediate response — Ridwell would see him at his office at eight o'clock the next morning. Eight o'clock. That was typical of the man — he always rose early to see to the details of his various businesses, spending two or three hours before breakfast with his managers, agents and advisers. Jeremy was not and never had been an early riser, but on this occasion he would simply have to make the effort.

Ridwell's office was situated in an unobtrusive terraced house just off the main street. It had once been the Ridwell family home, and Ellen had been born there, and played Bilbo catch and quoits in its small garden as a girl. When the new house on the hill had been built, the old house had remained the offices for Ridwell's many ventures, while the lowest floors had become a sedate gentlemen's club where, for a modest annual subscription, a man of means might dine and meet his friends and enjoy some gentle play with cards or dice. Jeremy was not yet a man of means, but Ridwell had sponsored his entry anyway.

Jeremy was shown up to Ridwell's office at once. Although it was an upper room, and not one of the principal rooms with high ceilings and ornate cornices, it was fitted up with light, elegant furniture and boasted a pleasant view of gardens and trees. It was not at all like the ornate and over decorated residence on the hill.

"Ah, Moreton! Come in. Come in." Ridwell rose to usher him into the room. Although he smiled and his manner was welcoming, Jeremy felt there was some restraint there, some consciousness that had never been present before. Natural enough, under the circumstances, but there was no hint of anger or coldness in him at all, and that *was* surprising.

By the time Jeremy had been seated and a glass of Canary poured and the general enquiries as to health and travel and the weather got out of the way, Ridwell seemed almost at a loss for words, and that was most unlike him. He was not brought up to the high manners found in the best society, but he generally had an easy way with him in company. But now he sat chewing his lip like someone unused to the world.

It was for Jeremy, then, to attack the awkwardness of the encounter head on. "I am grateful to you for giving me the chance to apologise for what must appear as unconscionable behaviour," he began, "and perhaps to explain, if you will hear me."

"Oh, no need to explain," Ridwell said, with an airy wave of one hand. "I am no greenhorn, and I'll not blame you for doing whatever is best for you. Your father once owned this Woodside that was named in the newspaper, and now you are to marry the daughter of the fellow who presently owns it. I see how it is, Moreton... or do you prefer Winterton, now?"

"I answer to either," Jeremy said, too startled to consider his reply. "But I should be sorry to have caused any distress to Miss Ridwell."

"Ellen will be fine," Ridwell said. "Her mother, now... Ha! Yes, her mother is another matter. Had plans for the wedding which are quite overset now, but that is her own foolishness for advancing too rapidly. *'Wait until it's official,'* I told her, but women never listen, do they? As for Ellen... you know she is in London with her aunt? They have few acquaintances there, but they are enjoying themselves — the theatre, the shops, the parks, the great buildings. I gave Ellen plenty of money to spend, and she is jaunting about to this and that great wonder. London is full of wonders, seemingly. Have you ever been there?"

Jeremy shook his head. "My family never went there when I was a boy, and I have been too occupied with looms and engines in recent years to consider the possibility."

"But you will go now, I daresay. Your wife will wish to enter into the best society, no doubt. As a gentleman with your own estate, you'll want to mingle with your own kind. Besides, your sisters all go there, don't they?"

His sisters? What did Ridwell know of his sisters? He was remarkably well-informed for a man who had only seen one small announcement in a newspaper.

Ridwell laughed, and went on, "You look surprised, Moreton, but you know what folk are like. Winterton... Woodside, in Brinshire... not hard to look these things up. And then Dillinge's wife is friendly with Lady Masters over at Wrayforth, and her brother is married to a Winterton, so—"

"Is he?" He thought back over his brothers-in-law, trying to remember if any of them had mentioned a sister called Lady Masters. "Oh... Fanny! My youngest sister. Lady Craston."

"Exactly," Ridwell said, eyes gleaming. "A viscountess, I believe. And one of them is a countess and another a baroness, as I understand it? I expect they will all be in London just now, for the season."

Jeremy began to have an inkling of why Ridwell was not hostile towards him. "Indeed they are. I wonder, sir... would you like me to write and ask them to call upon Miss Ridwell? I cannot guarantee that—"

"My dear sir, this is generosity indeed!" Ridwell exclaimed, his face breaking into a beaming smile. "Such graciousness! My Ellen would be so thrilled to have a card from a titled lady to put upon the mantelpiece. So thrilled! Your kindness is beyond anything, sir. Do come for dinner this evening. Mrs Ridwell would be most happy... pot luck, you know. We do not stand upon ceremony with you, such a good friend as you are."

So Jeremy went to dinner and talked, as he knew he was expected to do, of his five sisters and their rich and noble husbands, their houses and estates, their carriages and jewels. The Ridwells smiled and listened avidly to it all, committing the details to memory to be related afterwards to all of their acquaintances, with the magical words, "He is to ask his sisters to call upon Ellen, you know. Just think — dear Ellen receiving a call from a countess, perhaps, or a viscountess, or a baroness."

~~~~~

Jeremy stayed three days in Branton, which was just enough time to meet a few friends, to acquaint himself with all the latest news and to reassure himself regarding the health of his precious engine,

Lady Hazlehead. This done, he went on to Liverpool, where he made his abject apologies to John Moreton's father, his mother having died some years before. He, too, had seen the notice in the newspapers, or rather, had had it pointed out to him by shocked friends, but he himself had not been at all shocked.

"We realised at an early stage that something was amiss," Mr Moreton said, regarding Jeremy ruefully with eyes milky with age. "Johnny was our youngest child, and not in the least clever. Amiable enough, certainly, but not quick enough to play any part in the family business. Shipping is just such an industry where accuracy in recording and a facility in ciphering are absolute requirements, and Johnny would only have been a liability. So, we arranged something we thought would suit him better."

"His real yearning was to go to sea," Jeremy said sadly. "He was so enthusiastic about the idea of sailing the world's oceans. He could hardly credit the unfairness of life, that I was to be sent aboard ship who hated the prospect, whereas he could conceive of no greater delight."

"Aye, but his mother wouldn't have it. Too dangerous, she said, and look how right she was." He was overtaken by a fit of coughing and a young woman, granddaughter or niece, perhaps, rushed forward to help him drink a little water, and to adjust his shawl and cushions. When he had recovered, he went on, "It was your letters that gave you away, Mr Winterton. The first few — well, typical Johnny, all blots and ill-formed letters. Then there was a dramatic improvement, and they started to show signs of good sense, so we did wonder. And the reports from Giles were positively glowing which seemed a miraculous improvement, even given the expensive tutors he hired. So we had a suspicion all along."

"The letters were my idea, to convince our respective parents that we had done what was expected of us," Jeremy said ruefully. "We each wrote three. Mine were full of details of the sailor's life, which Johnny described to me, for him to send to my father. I suppose he never had the chance to send any of them. His were about his new life in Branton, which involved much guessing, for neither of us knew anything about mills or engines or manufactories. Did you find them convincing?"

Mr Moreton laughed and nodded. "They were convincingly Johnny's work, that much is certain. Even when we wondered about the later letters, so well crafted and literate, my wife would not entertain the idea that it was *not* Johnny up there in Lancashire. *'He wrote to us,'* she would say. *'Those letters could not have been written by any other hand.'* She was right, as usual, but I am glad to know the truth, Mr Winterton, and have that little mystery solved. And I forgive you the deception, for now I know that Johnny achieved his ambition — he went to sea and was happy, for the short time he was given. His mother would not have seen it that way, nor would she have forgiven you, so perhaps it is as well she never lived to see this day. For myself I have no quarrel with you. It was not your fault the ship sank, and I cannot blame you for keeping quiet. If you had confessed, then you would have been sent off to sea in your turn, and perhaps you would be sleeping with the fishes now, too. So it is a good ending for you, and for that I am glad."

~~~~~

JUNE

Jane's hints about recovering the Woodside furniture to please her future husband had borne more fruit than she had dared to hope. The ladies of the county had entered enthusiastically into such a romantic notion, and day after day had seen a wagon or cart crunching up the drive bearing a bed or a table or, in one case, a very large and ugly pianoforte which Jane had never seen before.

"Shall I be obliged to construct a new wing to house all this?" her father said in his mild way one day, when the hall was completely blocked by the vast canopy of a bed. "Did we sell so much when we arrived here?"

"I suspect the neighbours are taking the opportunity to unload all their unwanted items," Jane said with a rueful smile. "I do not recognise this at all. We can store it all for now, and in a few months we will be able to quietly dispose of anything we do not want."

"You mean anything that your *husband* does not want," her father said, with a gentle smile.

She flushed a little at the rebuke. How many times had she forgotten that she was supposed to marry Jeremy? No, not quite that. She had not forgotten the *idea* of marriage to Jeremy, for it haunted her mind and kept her awake at night. What she tended to forget was the deception — that others saw her as a happily engaged woman, busily planning life with her future husband, while in reality she was planning only for her freedom. Just a small independence, that was all she asked. Enough to keep her out of abject poverty when her father died. She had no illusions about living on her own, for no respectable spinster could do so. No, she would have to make a home with one or other of her sisters, or a cousin, perhaps, but at least she would not be dependent on charity, and if one home became uncomfortable for her, she could move on. And in the meantime, she would live contentedly with her father at Lilac Cottage, knowing that her future was secure.

They had already gone to look at Lilac Cottage, stepping around the painters who were still at work and the carpenter hammering away at the shutters. Jane had rather liked it, although it was very small, having no more than four bedrooms, but the principal rooms were spacious and high-ceilinged.

"We should be able to seat twelve or fourteen here," she mused, gazing around the dining room. "And the drawing room is large enough for my pianoforte."

"That would be useful if you were to be living here," her father murmured, making her curse her foolish tongue once more. Her slips seemed to amuse him, however, for when they were examining the bedrooms, he said, "Now, this one would suit you very well. What a pity you will not be able to take advantage of it." And he smiled at her in that way he had that made her imagine he could read her mind. It was almost as if he knew perfectly well that she would not marry Jeremy, and was teasing her.

They were agreed, however, that Lilac Cottage would suit her father perfectly.

One day, they had an unexpected visitor at Woodside. Jane had only just time to recognise the elaborately decorated carriage as that of Lady Elizabeth Drake when the lady herself stepped down from it. Jane rushed downstairs from her bedroom, where she had been dusting, to open the front door, for it would not do to keep so haughty a visitor standing on the doorstep like one of the village widows.

"Good heavens, girl, have you no manservant to open the door?" Lady Elizabeth said, looking disparagingly at Jane's apron and the threadbare old gown she wore for morning work.

"He is more useful in the stables and chopping wood," Jane said, forgetting to curtsy in her annoyance at this abrupt greeting. "I have never seen the point of paying a man to sit about in the hall just in case a caller may arrive."

"Nonsense!" Lady Elizabeth said. "Have you no sense at all? He may chop wood as much as he likes, but it is his duty to answer the door. The scullery maid will fetch him, when needed."

"And by the time he has been fetched and removed his apron and rolled down his sleeves and put on his coat and got to the front door, the visitor will be half way home. Pray give me leave to manage my own house in my own way, Lady Elizabeth. Will you come in, so that you may berate me in the greater comfort of the drawing room?"

Lady Elizabeth's eyes narrowed dangerously, but she condescended to cross the threshold and enter the drawing room, where she perched on the edge of a chair, gazing around with disapproval, while Jane removed her apron, ordered tea and sent word to her father of their distinguished visitor. She knew it was no use telling Margaret of it, for she had such an antipathy towards Lady Elizabeth that she was probably already half way to her refuge in the tree house. Jane sat and waited politely for her visitor to begin the civilities.

Lady Elizabeth was not, however, a lady with much time for civilities. "What is the purpose of gathering all this furniture?" she said.

Jane raised an eyebrow at this forthrightness, but she preferred a straightforward question to the various none-too-subtle stratagems employed by some of the other ladies of the county to determine her motives. "Mr Winterton expressed some regret at finding so many of the familiar furnishings from his childhood dispersed. I thought it would please him to recover some of them, if I can."

"Hmpf. Sounds like poppycock, to me. Nobody cares that much about furniture. If one has not enough of it, or one gets tired of it, one buys more. Besides, I never in my life heard of a *man* who cared tuppence for one chair above another, so long as it does not tip him onto the floor and it is near enough to his glass of Madeira. There is some subterfuge going on. Ha! You look conscious, so I am right, and I might even hazard a guess as to what that subterfuge might be. Given that Anne Winterton's jewels were never found, it may be that Jeremy hopes to find some clue to their whereabouts left behind in the furniture."

She cackled with laughter, so that Jane's blood ran cold. Their secret was not so hard to guess after all. To her surprise, Lady Elizabeth smiled, which chilled her even more.

"Far be it from me to hinder so worthy an enterprise, my dear. I have a secretary that you sold me, and a great ugly thing it is too. Useful, of course, but I shall be glad to buy myself a prettier one. If you will undertake to repay the amount I gave for it, plus a little something for the inconvenience, then I shall arrange for the carter to bring it over when next he has a day to spare for the task. Ah, Mr Tyrrell! How pleasant to see you again."

"Lady Elizabeth," Jane's father murmured as he entered, executing a perfunctory bow. "You are well, I hope? I trust my daughter has been keeping you entertained."

"Oh, indeed. We have been having a most comfortable conversation."

"Excellent. And there is tea on the way?" he added hopefully.

Jane laughed. "Just as soon as Betsy can manage it."

"I shall not stay to take tea," Lady Elizabeth said, rising to her feet with the aid of her cane. Jane and her father sprang up, too. "I came only to tell you, Mr Tyrrell, that Lilac Cottage is not available to you. My nephew Percival will be moving in as soon as the repairs are concluded. I have arranged it with the bishop, so it is all settled. Good day to you both."

So saying, she swept regally out of the room, leaving Jane and her father staring at each other in bemusement.

15: Remonstrations And Reputations

When she saw Jeremy riding up the drive, Jane was struck by unexpected nerves. She was all too aware that thoughts of her handsome fiancé had filled her mind to a deplorable degree of late, but she knew, too, that he was not hers at all. His journey north had been prompted by the hope of salvaging his chances with Miss Ridwell, if he could.

But when she went outside to greet him, his smile lit a fire inside her that no rational thought could quench.

"My dear Jane!" he cried, sweeping her hand to his lips as he bowed. "How delightful to see you again. You are well? You did not write to me, so I began to imagine you afflicted with all manner of ailments."

She could not stop herself from blushing, but she answered robustly, "What nonsense! I doubt you thought of me at all. Shall I send for Timpson to take your horse round to the stables?"

"No, no. I shall take him round myself. Will you walk with me? I do not scruple to ask it of you, for I think you are not one of those women who dare not venture outdoors without hat, gloves and parasol, and probably a change of gown and shoes as well."

She laughed and agreed to it. As they walked, he told her of his business in the north and she told him of Lady Elizabeth's visit.

"So she suspects that we are looking for the jewels? And yet will not hinder us? That sounds suspiciously unlike her. No doubt she will thoroughly examine the secretary before sending it back."

"Then she will find the jewels," Jane said sadly.

"Perhaps," he said. "Although everything we have found so far was concealed with great ingenuity. Let us hope that she is not clever enough to find it out. But what is this about Lilac Cottage? Is your papa terribly upset at the loss?"

"Very little upsets Papa, as you must be aware," she said. "It is awkward, however. While the world thinks us betrothed, you need only smile and pretend you do not mind the prospect of your father-in-law remaining in residence, but once you have sole possession of the house you will want us out."

"Oh, there is no great urgency," he said easily. "Woodside is big enough for all three of us."

She turned and looked at him in astonishment. "What, share a house with the woman who jilted you and her father? And when you marry Miss Ridwell—"

"Let us not look too far ahead," he said. "One day at a time... that is my philosophy, and generally things work out for the best. But it is inexplicable about Lilac Cottage. I thought Grantley had as good as promised it to your father, too, but I suppose the bishop takes precedence over the parish clergyman. Lady Elizabeth is a hard woman to refuse when she sets her mind to a thing. Yet I cannot see why Percival Drake should want it. What on earth need has he for an establishment of his own, and in Frickham, too?"

"I cannot imagine," Jane said. "Papa and I have fretted over the point for hours, and can think of no good reason for it."

"Clearly, he is jealous of me, and hopes that he may yet win you for himself," Jeremy said, which made her laugh.

"Do not tease me with such thoughts. I cannot imagine a fate more dreadful than to be the object of the attentions of such a man. His very touch would make me shudder, and if he kissed me, I should curl up and die on the spot, I swear it."

He laughed a little, his voice low and warm. "As your betrothed, I should perhaps make delicate enquiries as to whether my kisses would also have such a dramatic effect on you. It would be most unfortunate if I should think to avail myself of the privilege of our engagement, only to find you curled up like a hedgehog."

She blushed crimson at such talk, and his laughing eyes as he threw her surreptitious glances made her blush even more, but she was not going to let him get away with such outrageous flirtation. "Impossible to say, but I should advise you not to make the attempt, sir, just in case."

In seconds, he had dropped his horse's rein and scooped Jane towards him, one arm firmly around her waist. "Are you daring me to do it, you little termagant? I assure you, there is nothing I like better than a challenge, and I should not mind your hedgehog state, for it cannot be any more prickly than you are as yourself."

Jane blushed and blushed again, held tight against him and hardly knowing where to look when his face was so close that she could feel his warm breath on her cheeks. She was so shocked that she could not say a word. Her greatest relief was that they were out of sight, screened from the house by trees and from the stables by dense shrubs.

Jeremy chuckled, his voice a low rumble in her ear. "Have you any idea how pretty you are when you blush so?" he murmured. He still held her firmly against him with one strong arm, but the other hand crept up to stroke the back of her neck in a way that made her shiver inside in the most exquisite manner. "Pretty and quick-witted and fun and very, very kissable."

Very gently, he raised her chin so that she could not avoid looking into his face — ah, those laughing eyes, and the mouth that was curved into an irresistible smile. The mouth that was already half way to hers, and moving nearer.

Her hands, somehow, were on his chest — how fortunate, for a single hard push stopped him in his tracks.

"Enough! What a dreadful flirt you are, Jeremy Winterton," she said, her voice wavering slightly. "Let go of me."

And to her intense disappointment, he did exactly that, with another low chuckle. "Termagant," he whispered again, still smiling, and her treacherous heart turned over. If only he were less handsome or less charming or less kissable... no, that was quite the wrong line of thought. A distraction was urgently needed.

"Did you have word of Miss Ridwell?" she said, and if *that* did not remind him of the true nature of their betrothal, nothing would.

"She is well and enjoying herself in London," he said, smiling broadly and not in the least abashed. "My sisters are to take her about a bit and introduce her into rather better society." He gathered his horse's reins and they began to walk on. "I do not suppose they can get her vouchers to Almack's, but they can show her off a little — drives in the park, musical evenings, that sort of thing."

"And you are still not concerned that she might forget you in London?" Jane said, astonished at his tolerance.

"In many ways, I hope she will," he said seriously. "She could do far better for herself than me, you know. And I am beginning to think that I could do much better for myself, too." And he smiled so warmly at Jane that she blushed all over again. Could he mean—? No, surely not. He was teasing her again, dreadful man.

To cover her confusion, she said quickly, "There are two more pieces of furniture for you to examine. The vicar sent back the armoire, although I had to ask him outright for it, and Mrs Claremont sent the dressing table, without prompting, and insisting that she wants no money for it, as it is such a romantic notion. An early wedding present, she says."

"A romantic notion..." he mused. "How sweet. Everyone is persuaded that we are truly betrothed, then?"

"Oh, yes," she said, coolly. "The convenience is acknowledged, but your attachment to me is *so* convincingly portrayed. Why, you even attempt to kiss me, even though there is no one here but me."

He smiled at her, and said, "I could hardly do so in front of an audience, now could I? Do be reasonable, my little hedgehog. If I am to kiss you, it must necessarily be done in private."

"It need not be done at all," she snapped back. "Do not waste your charm on *me*, sir." At once she cursed herself for any suggestion that she found him charming.

"Oh, but it is such fun to tease you," he said, in plaintive tones. "Do not forbid me the attempt, I beg you, for you blush so delightfully, and, who knows, perhaps one day I may succeed and think how rewarding that will be. Ah, here we are. Timpson? Where are you hiding?"

Their arrival at the stables robbed her of the chance to retaliate, but inside she seethed. She was determined to pay him back for his temerity, just as soon as her heart had settled to a steadier pace and her insides had stopped flip-flopping about in the most alarming manner. He was very, very charming, but he was not for her — she must keep reminding herself of that fact.

~~~~~

Jeremy had no opportunity to examine the new items of furniture for some days, on account of the pretence that it was to be a pre-wedding surprise. He had to wait, therefore, until there was a day when almost everyone was out of the house, and that took some contrivance on Jane's part. Eventually, she had everything organised. Mr Tyrrell, Margaret and the two lady's maids were to go into Brinchester for the day, Betsy, the housemaid, had her half day off, and Havelock would be snoozing in her room.

"So long as you avoid the stables and come in from the terrace into the drawing room, no one will see you," Jane said brightly, as they walked in the gardens one afternoon.

"How can I avoid the stables?" Jeremy said, bewildered. "I can hardly leave my horse tethered to a bush for hours, and if I bring my groom he will want to know why he is not allowed to enjoy a gossip with Timpson."

"Well, leave the horse at the inn."

"But then the ostler will want to know why I do not bring him here."

"Good heavens, Jeremy, must you quibble over every little thing?" she said crossly. "I have arranged to get everyone out of the way, now you must find some way to deal with the horse."

In the end, he left the animal at the smithy to have his shoes attended to, but even this contrivance almost failed.

"I'll have the boy bring him up to the house when I've done," the smith said genially.

"Oh… no need for that. He will not like to be moved once he is settled. You can find him a bucket of oats, I daresay."

The flash of silver in the smith's beefy hand brought a smile and an assurance of the best quality oats. Jeremy walked the short distance to Woodside, through the shrubbery and in by way of the terrace doors. Jane was waiting for him in the drawing room, apron on and pretending to dust.

"Do you not have servants enough to do that for you?" he said, frowning. "You are the mistress here, not a housemaid."

"We are not as wealthy as your sisters' husbands," she said tartly. "Not everyone can afford hordes of matched footmen."

Jeremy watched her carefully as she spoke. Was there a degree of consciousness in her manner? That could be a natural reticence on the vulgar subject of money, but it could also be something more interesting. He said with studied casualness, "Woodside supported us in affluence despite Papa's fondness for cards and dice and expensive brandy. With the debts gone, it would certainly keep two frugal adults in the greatest comfort. You could afford another housemaid, I fancy."

"Oh, are you telling me how to run my house now, Mr Winterton?" Her voice rose in pitch as she spoke, and her eyes narrowed. "You know nothing of our finances, so do not presume to lecture me about housemaids."

He made her an ironic little bow. "Your pardon, Miss Tyrrell. I had no idea that your father's circumstances were so reduced that the extra ten or fifteen pounds a year would be beyond his means. Your housewifely skills must be considerable to contrive to put meat on the table as often as you do."

To his surprise, she laughed and her tone softened. "We are not so desperate as all that, but we must be careful. Besides, I like to be busy, and Betsy is a little heavy-handed with the ornaments. Papa would be mortified if any of Mama's precious porcelain were to be damaged. Shall we look at the armoire and dressing table?"

He accepted the change of subject without demur, but said, "I shall look at them, but it would be best if you continue your dusting."

"No, no, no! You cannot deprive me of so much fun. In any event, I have to watch over you in case you gull me, Mr Winterton. You must know that I do not trust you an inch. You Lancashire men are devious schemers."

"I must protest!" he cried, holding his hands up. "We Lancashire men have little sense, we are agreed upon that, but we are honest to the bone. Brainless, but *virtuously* so."

She laughed and allowed it to be so.

"But still," he said more seriously, "I think it best if you stay here. You may be assured that I will show you whatever I find."

She tipped her head on one side, gazing at him. Those grey eyes were penetrating as she assessed him, but she said only, "Are you being nonsensical about my reputation again?"

"Someone has to have a care for such matters, and if you will not then the duty falls to me."

"You have no right to tell me what to do!" she said hotly.

"Now there you are quite wrong," he said, but he kept his tone level so as not to antagonise her even further. "We are betrothed, so indeed I have the right. I shall not exercise it, however. You may do as you think fit, but bear in mind that if a betrothed couple is found to be lingering alone in a bedroom, then certain inferences will be drawn and the marriage will be expected sooner rather than later. To cry off at that point is to invite certain censure. You may find that your circle of acquaintances shrinks a great deal."

"And do you think I care tuppence for anyone who would treat me so shabbily?" she cried. "My true friends know my worth, Jeremy. Besides, there is no one here to see what we do. I do not fear for my reputation."

"Well, I fear for mine," he said. Seeing her mulish expression, however, he shrugged and allowed himself to be shepherded upstairs to his mama's bedroom.

He began to remove the drawers of the dressing table, methodically feeling each one to determine if it hid any secret places. The drawers yielding nothing, he began to move around the shell of the dressing table itself, touching, prodding, feeling for any small imperfection or crack that might suggest a spring loaded door or a part of the decoration that could be moved.

Jane perched on the bare mattress of the bed with her knees drawn up to her chest, ankles neatly crossed. Very shapely ankles, he noted with approval. Ankles such as any man would be pleased to run his fingers over, feeling the warmth beneath the stockings. For an instant, he had an urge to gently roll those stockings down and slip those shapely ankles out of them, so that his hands could—

No, that way led only to madness. Jane was not a woman he could desire, for she was not a great beauty like Ellen. Did Ellen have shapely ankles? He had never noticed. She had smooth shoulders, which were admirable, and a short neck, which was less so. That was her only feature that fell below perfection. That and her cold eyes, of course. She was a little plumper than he liked, now that he thought about it. Was Ellen *too* plump? He rather thought she was. Now Jane was just the shape he liked — thin, but not *too* thin. And those ankles...

"Is there a hole in one of my stockings?" she said.

"Um... what?"

"You keep looking at my legs, so I wondered if—"

"They are very attractive legs," he said, unable to resist teasing her. She blushed so prettily that he laughed and jumped up to sit beside her on the bed. "You know, Miss Tyrrell, when you display such delightfully trim ankles to a man, you make him quite forget what he is supposed to be doing and instead make him want to kiss you."

He slid one arm around her waist, and to his surprise she did not move. "What nonsense you do talk," she said, but she neither pushed him away nor tried to evade him. Instead there was a look in her eye that he had never seen before, not in Jane. In other women, sometimes, but not in his prickly Jane. Was it possible that—?

The sound of a carriage made them both jump up.

"Papa and Margaret!" she said. "They are early. What are we to do? Papa cannot find you here!"

"So *now* you worry about your reputation," he said with a sigh.

"I care nothing for that, but Papa must not know anything about the jewels or our arrangement. If he finds you here in this secretive way, he is astute enough to draw conclusions. Can you sneak down the back stairs? You will have to be very careful creeping past the kitchen. Oh Lord, how unlucky that they should return so early. I must go down to let them in."

"Go, then. I will tidy up here and escape through my old bedroom window, which drops me directly into the shrubbery."

"But when will we get another chance to investigate?" she said, hands on hips.

"Invite me to dinner and to stay overnight," he said, with a grin. "Much easier at night. More fun, too. Go, now!"

She went, and Jeremy had a last, delicious glimpse of her trim ankles as she dashed out of the room. As silently as he could, he replaced all the drawers, then crept along the landing to his own room, even as voices drifted up from the hall below. He slipped into his old room, climbed out through the window onto the projecting roof of Papa's study, then jumped down to the ground before disappearing into the shrubbery.

Collecting his horse from the smith, he rode slowly back to Brinchester, his head full of ankles and legs and stockings and the unexpected light in Jane's eye. He had very nearly kissed her, and she had very nearly let him. What could it mean?

16: *Saturday Evening*

Jane raced downstairs to admit her father and Margaret, although they were obliged to knock three times before she opened the door. She could only hope they would not notice how flushed and out of breath she was.

"Still hard at work, my dear?" her father said in his affable way. "Surely it is time to set aside your apron for the day. Shall we have some tea?"

"Of course, Papa. Was your day successful?"

"Very. Whittaker's had the perfect blue that I need for the Demoiselle Dragonfly. I shall be able to attempt its likeness tomorrow, I hope. There are so many of them in the water meadows just now. Tea in my room?"

"As soon as I can find Betsy, Papa. Margaret, did you enjoy your day?"

In answer, Margaret waved the numerous packages with which she was laden, and laughed. And by the time the purchases had been duly admired, news of acquaintances met in town had been conveyed and the tea had been drunk, it was time to dress for dinner. There were guests that evening, so it was not until the Claremonts had left and Jane, her father and Margaret were sitting down to a final cup of tea that Jane was able to raise the issue of inviting Jeremy for a night.

"It is such a long way back to Brinchester in the middle of the night, and I am sure it would be more comfortable for him to stay here," she explained hurriedly, her cheeks growing hot at the subterfuge.

"Excellent idea," her father said, smiling benignly. "You will have the pleasure of your betrothed's company at breakfast, too. How charmingly romantic you are becoming, Jane."

That made her flush even more.

"Why not invite him to dinner on Saturday?" her father said, in innocent tones. "He will not be able to travel on Sunday, so you will have him here until Monday morning. He may care to attend church with us and speak to Mr Grantley about the banns. After all, the summer is getting on and you must be keen to set a date now that you have filled the house with furniture."

His smile widened, but Jane was too dismayed to answer him. Now she was caught in a web of her own devising! The last thing she wanted was to talk to the vicar about calling the banns.

Surprisingly, it was Margaret who came to her rescue. She flipped open her slate and wrote, *'Pray do not rush Jane towards the altar. Marriage is a tremendous change for a woman, however welcome, and she needs time to become accustomed to the idea.'*

"Is it not also a tremendous change for a man?" he said gently.

Her chalk tap-tapped rapidly on the slate. *'Of course, but he has been slowly growing towards the estate of manhood for many years. By the time he marries, he is settled in his ways, his mind is fully formed and he understands his place in the world. A wife is only an enhancement to his life. But a woman'* She rubbed out her writing and tapped away again. *'must relinquish her former life entirely. She owes her duty now to a man she hardly knows, with responsibilities and cares she can barely imagine. It is not easy, even with mutual affection and respect.'*

"One might suppose that a woman spends her entire life training for the role of wife," he said, in his mild way.

'But it is still a shock when it happens,' Margaret wrote firmly, and he ceded the point to her.

Later that night, when Jane was preparing for bed, a scratching at the door heralded the arrival of Margaret.

"May I?" she said.

"Oh yes!" Jane said. "I wanted so much to thank you for slowing Papa a little. He is in such a hurry to see me wed, for some reason."

Margaret looked about the room. After appraising its furnishings, she chose a small table and brought over a chair and the dressing table stool. Then she lit more candles and sat down on the stool, her slate box on the table before her. Jane took the chair, and watched as Margaret wrote with swift strokes of the chalk.

'Your father worries about you. He wants you to marry and be happy."

"Perhaps those two states are not compatible for someone like me."

Margaret smiled, and bent her head to her slate. *'Not even with Jeremy? Your future husband?'* Jane blushed, but before she could compose a reply, Margaret wrote, *'Your father thinks you have doubts and wishes to rush you into matrimony before you have time to change your mind, but that is the wrong way.'* With a quick wipe of the cloth, she cleared the slate, then went on, *'The longer the engagement continues, the greater the chance that you* will both realise how well suited you are and it will become a real betrothal.'

Jane exhaled slowly. "You know."

'Of course. It is an excuse to collect all Mama's furniture and try to find the jewels.'

"Does anyone else know?" Jane said.

Margaret laughed. *'Probably not. You are very convincing when you are together. If I did not know what Jeremy found in the dressing table stool I would not suspect either, although Jeremy was uncommonly upset about the announcement in the newspaper.'*

"Poor Jeremy!" Jane said, with a sigh. "That ruined his chances with the beautiful Miss Ridwell, I fear."

'The boring Miss Ridwell. Jeremy would be tired of her within a month. He needs a clever wife who challenges him.' With a mischievous glance at Jane, she added, *'Do you know anyone like that?'*

Jane laughed, blushing again despite herself.

Without waiting for an answer, Margaret wrote, *'The boring Miss Ridwell is causing something of a stir in London, according to Mel."*

"Good," Jane said. "I warned Jeremy how it would be, but would he listen to me? Not a bit of it! He thinks she will have a pleasant time and then go back to Branton to wait for him, but it would serve him right if she were to find herself a fine husband in London. Is she as beautiful as he described?"

'Oh yes. A diamond of the first water. Fanny and Ferdy have had the dressing of her, and she is turning heads wherever she goes. She is admitted everywhere, despite her trade connections. Rosamund has even got her vouchers for Almack's.'

Jane was aware of a twinge of envy. It was not that she had ever aspired to a London season or Almack's or to be an acknowledged diamond, for she was content with her quiet life in Frickham, but even she had to admit that her life was dull and uneventful. The highlight of her week was gossiping after church about why Mrs Plummer's maid had been turned off, and whether Mr Caddy's apprentice had been gulling the old man to the benefit of his own purse, and it was not terribly edifying or even interesting. Dancing at Almack's was not especially interesting either, she supposed, but it would be something of note in her life. When she was old and grey and a wizened spinster, it would be pleasant to look back on a time in her life when she had walked amongst the nobility for a short time. A few memories to warm her old maid's heart, that was all she asked. To be admired, to be loved just a little, perhaps. Or, if that was asking too much, at least to be kissed.

Margaret's chalk tap-tapped again. *'I almost forgot what I came for. Tell Jeremy not to use the track through the woods from High Frickham when he comes here. There was a thin rope stretched across it this morning, tight enough to bring down a fast horse. Tell him to keep to the roads, even if it is longer. Best to come in a chaise as well.'*

Jane's heart ran cold. "Someone is truly trying to kill him, then. I had hoped... that shot was just a mistake. Who on earth would want to kill him?"

Margaret shrugged. *'I cannot imagine, but someone does, and he is very determined.'*

~~~~~

Jeremy followed Jane's instructions to the letter, hiring a post-chaise and four to get him to Woodside on Saturday afternoon. Despite the summer warmth and Hooper's dismay, he drew up the blinds as they passed at speed through Frickham, so that no one lurking with a gun could get a clear sight of him.

There were no shots, only Jane's smiling face to greet him as he opened the door and stepped down from the chaise.

"Miss Tyrrell... how delightful!" he murmured, sweeping her hand to his lips and holding it a moment or two longer than propriety dictated. She blushed quite charmingly, and dipped into a curtsy.

"Mr Winterton. Goodness, so many horses and postilions just for you and your portmanteau. Are you trying to impress me?"

"Not at all, Miss Tyrrell. I should have arrived in a high-perch phaeton, if so, and swept you away for a long drive."

"I should be more impressed by a barouche," she said severely, although he thought her eyes twinkled. "It is just the weather for a drive in a barouche, and not so unstable as a phaeton. I should dislike extremely being so high above the ground."

Hooper emerged at that moment looking exceedingly green, dashing behind a convenient bush to dispose of his breakfast.

"Poor man," Jane said. "Whatever were you about, to have all the windows closed up on such a warm day?"

"Trying to avoid being shot," he whispered in her ear. "Ah, Margaret! How are you, sister?"

By the time all the greetings were out of the way and Mr Tyrrell, the indefatigable tea drinker, had forced Jeremy to imbibe two cups of the dreadful liquid, it was time to dress for dinner. Hooper was less green, but not at all pleased with the conditions prevailing below stairs. There was no butler and no footman either, the groom being the only manservant, since the coachman was not fit for indoor work, and while Hooper was quite happy to wait at table, he felt it to be rather beneath his dignity to do so alongside a groom.

"I am sure it is very distressing, Hooper," Jeremy said. "However, it is only for two nights, so there is no need to fall into flat despair over it."

"Oh, I'm not one to complain, sir, as you know," Hooper said, having complained steadily for half an hour at least. "You'll set all to rights once you're married, sir. Two footmen, at least, for a gentleman in your position, and perhaps a butler as well."

Jeremy had no answer to that, and wisely concentrated on tying his cravat. He had made a study of his brothers-in-law's methods, and although a Mathematical or an Oriental might be somewhat ambitious, he felt that he might contrive a tolerable Mailcoach. He had learnt, also, that a true gentleman must tie his own cravat unaided, and would never let his valet do more than hold a pile of starched neckcloths. On both counts, however, his efforts fell short, and in the end he allowed Hooper to manage the business.

"I shall get the hang of it in time, I daresay," he said gloomily.

"Of course you will, sir," Hooper said cheerfully, perhaps heartened by the discovery that he was, after all, indispensable.

"And not a word to a soul, Hooper, or I shall personally throw you from the clock tower."

"My lips are sealed, sir." But Jeremy thought he looked far too gleeful at his failure.

Dinner was enlivened by the company of Percival Drake, newly arrived to take up residence at Lilac Cottage, the clergyman and his wife, Mr and Mrs Grantley, their rather stout and unprepossessing daughter Alice, and Mrs Plummer, to boost the number of ladies. They sat down nine to the table, and Jeremy found himself between Jane and the vicar, with Percival Drake's smug face across the table. Drake was just the sort of man that Jeremy disliked, having both a belief in his own superiority and the indolence that gave no foundation for it. All gentlemen enjoyed leisured lives with no need to earn their bread, but most found some occupation to fill the empty hours, whether by reading for the improvement of the mind or by some worthwhile interest such as Mr Tyrrell's delight in nature. Drake, however, seemed to fill his empty hours with drinking, gaming and wenching. Jeremy consoled himself with the thought that in a few years Drake would be a red-nosed, fat drunkard, with a pinch-faced wife whose sole object in life was to avoid his temper.

The vicar was excellent company, asking Jeremy with seeming interest about his mill and engine in Branton, and his endeavours with the clock at St Mark's in Brinchester. Jeremy was distracted, however, by Jane's conversation with Drake. At first he bored her with a long account of pair of sisters he was interested in as possible marriage prospects, who were both, seemingly, desperately in love with him. Then he talked of a horse he had been offered for sale recently, which was a great hoax, for reasons which he described in extensive detail. He, of course, was far too sharp to be taken in by such a scheme, but he had bought the horse anyway at a knock-down price, and then sold it at a great profit to a friend.

"Hur, hur, hur. A neat piece of work, would you agree, Miss Tyrrell? No one can gull me."

"I wonder you should speak of it with pride," Jane said with asperity. "It does you no credit to boast of such a scheme, and to play such a trick on a friend is abominable."

"Pft, he would do as much to me if he could," Drake said, with a languid shrug. "You do not understand gentlemanly behaviour, but I assure you that friends employ such ruses against each other all the time. It is a game, like cards. One always plays to win, even against friends. Especially against friends, I might even say."

"There is no similarity, Mr Drake," Jane said coldly. "You deceived your friend by persuading him that the horse was a good one, and he bought it because he trusted you. He had no idea that it was merely a game to you. Yet in a card game, every participant knows that a game is being played and understands the rules which must be obeyed, and cheating is very much frowned upon, even by gentlemen. *Especially* by gentlemen. A sense of honour is still regarded with favour in gentlemanly circles, is it not?"

Drake's eyes flashed with anger. "And who are you to lecture me about honour?"

"I am your neighbour," she said at once. "I do not know why you choose to live in Frickham, Mr Drake, but let me assure you that here people can and do comment on the behaviour of their neighbours. And now that the subject has arisen, why *did* you choose to live here? I should have thought Brinchester would have been better suited to a gentleman of your sociable nature. Or even London. Did you not have plans to enjoy the season this year?"

Jeremy did not hear Drake's answer, for the vicar drew his attention again, and shortly thereafter Hooper and Timpson came in to remove the first course, so all conversation lapsed for a while. During this interlude, he reflected with some pleasure on Jane's robust responses to Drake. She was no shy miss, that much was certain. For all he chaffed her about her waspishness, he rather admired it, too. There was something glorious in a woman who could speak her mind and puncture the pomposity of the likes of Percival Drake. Jeremy had thought her shrewish at first, but he had seen her gentle side when she had nursed him to health and he had to admit that he enjoyed their badinage. And her ankles, he remembered. Then he began to wonder about that moment when they had almost kissed...

"Mr Winterton? Will you pass me the asparagus, if you please?"

Jane's voice cut through his reminiscences.

"I beg your pardon," he said, reaching for the dish. "I was lost in my own thoughts."

"They seemed to be pleasant thoughts, to judge by the smile," she said quizzically.

He laughed. "So they were, Miss Tyrrell, but I shall not tell any more just now, for I should not like to make you blush in company."

Naturally that brought colour to her cheeks. "You are abominable, sir. As if I cared to know your secret thoughts."

"Ah, that is better, Miss Hedgehog."

She blushed even more strongly, although with laughter on her lips, throwing him a quick glance that in any other woman he would interpret as flirtatious.

Across the table, Drake watched them with a sour expression on his face. He had Alice Grantley on his other side, but at first he made no effort to speak to her, applying himself with enthusiasm to the claret and with less enthusiasm to his plate. However, eventually boredom or politeness drove him to turn to Miss Grantley, and they conversed in some ease for the rest of the meal.

When the ladies left and the gentlemen regrouped around Mr Tyrrell, Jeremy was annoyed to find Drake following him around the table, and settling in the chair next to him. It was rude, for it meant that all the guests were on one side of the table, making general conversation impossible and leaving Tyrrell with only the vicar to talk to.

"Well, Winterton, you seem to be getting on very well with Miss Tyrrell, hur, hur," Drake said, with a leer.

"Not a great surprise, since we are affianced," Jeremy said coolly.

"Would have thought the house was the principal attraction," Drake said. "I might have married her myself if I'd known the deal would be sweetened, but she is too prickly for my taste. I like a more... *compliant* wife, if you know what I mean, hur, hur."

"How fortunate, then, that Miss Tyrrell is to marry me and not you. Are you settled in at Lilac Cottage? Are you pleased with Frickham?"

Drake was happy to enumerate all the deficiencies of the village and the house at great length, although he never grew so interested in the conversation as to miss the port decanter when it came his way. He poured and drank and poured again, and only a certain increase in loquacity signified the effects on him. He was a large man, rangy rather than muscular, and he lounged at his ease, leaning against the chair with one arm casually thrown over the back of it, while the other hand was engaged in the important business of raising port to his mouth.

Eventually, the decanter came to a stop beside Drake's glass. Jeremy was not a great drinker himself, having found that his best business deals were made at times when he was more sober than the other party, and neither Mr Tyrrell nor the vicar drank more than a single glass after a meal, but Drake drank on, and talked on, endlessly.

Jeremy was on the point of making some excuse to leave, when Drake said abruptly, "Been shot at lately, Winterton?"

"Happily, no."

"Good, for I should not like to think I cannot leave my own house without the risk of someone taking a pop at me, hur, hur."

The vicar caught this exchange. "We must all hope for no recurrence of such an event, Mr Winterton. Dreadful thing to happen. Was the person responsible ever apprehended?"

"No one ever admitted to being in the vicinity at the time," Jeremy said. "Not that that is any great surprise. No poacher who accidentally shot a passer-by would ever admit to it, and if it were deliberate, the need for secrecy is even greater."

"Deliberate?" the vicar said, flustered. "Surely not? It could not be— You cannot think that someone actually tried to kill you? Can you? It is hard to believe, here in peaceful Frickham. Why, the worst that ever happens here is that Mrs Caddy's pig escapes."

Jeremy laughed, as he knew he was meant to, for the anxiety on the fellow's face was clear. "I am sure it was not so," he said. "Why, who on earth would want to kill me? I have not an enemy in the world."

But the smirk on Percival Drake's face suggested that he knew otherwise.

17: Saturday Night

"Why would Percival Drake care what becomes of you?" Jane said, when Jeremy told her of the discussion later. "Lady Elizabeth holds you in dislike, that much is clear, but the nephew has no reason for any antipathy."

"Nor has she, if it comes to that," Jeremy said. "Your throw."

They were engaged in a game of backgammon, chosen so that they could sit apart from the others. Mr Tyrrell, the vicar, Drake and Mrs Plummer were playing whist, and Margaret was at the pianoforte with Mrs Grantley and Miss Grantley, so Jane and Jeremy were able to conduct a conversation in some privacy.

"There must be something behind it," Jane said. "It is rumoured that she persuaded your father to send you away to sea."

"I never understood that," Jeremy said. "Why would she care? She planned to marry Papa, that much is clear, and she was already his—" He stopped, remembering belatedly that Jane, however easy their dealings now, was still a single woman.

"Oh, his mistress, was she? I wondered about that. Margaret said once that she was close to your papa, and then she looked conscious, so I wondered. What is it? Why do you look at me so?"

"Jane, you should know nothing of... such matters."

"You mean mistresses? Good heavens, Jeremy, I live in a small village, where everyone knows everything about everyone. Luke Carson has been keeping Tom Miller's daughter for years, and Mrs Jackson— Well, never mind. I can see I have shocked you. What a sheltered life you must have led in your Lancastrian fastness."

"I do not, but ladies do. Or at least, if they do not, they have the delicacy not to mention it in mixed company. But then your forthright tongue is one of your most admirable qualities, my dear hedgehog. Well then, let it be said openly — Lady Elizabeth Drake was my father's mistress, and it is just possible that she dislikes me because I once told her she was a bad woman on that account. Shortly after that Papa sent me away."

Jane's mouth made a circle of surprise. "Truly? How brave of you to speak out against such a dragon of a woman, and when you were so young, too. Were you not terrified?"

"Oddly enough, I was not. I should have been, because she had so much influence over Papa and I *was* terrified of him, but I was too angry to be sensible. She had always stayed overnight at the house whenever she was invited for dinner, since she hates travelling at night, but after Mama's death she practically moved into Woodside, taking Mama's place at table and ordering meals and such like. It was insensitive of her, to say nothing worse. Even the servants felt it strongly. And of course she was creeping about the house at night."

"To visit your father?"

He nodded, and for a moment all the misery of those days rose up to choke him. His own grief, his father's apparent disdain for his only son and the encroaching Lady Elizabeth had made those months after his mother's death a nightmarish experience. And yet, looking back with adult eyes, he could see that his father was just as grief-stricken as his children, yet quite unable to express it or to offer comfort. Perhaps Lady Elizabeth brought him some welcome solace in his own misery.

Jane threw the dice and made her move swiftly, then said, "I do not know why she wished to send you away, but the consequence was that your father believed you dead, and blamed her. They quarrelled over it, and were not even friends afterwards. So I have been told."

Jeremy moved in his turn, then sat back, arms folded. "So perhaps she hates me now because she never married my father after all. Even so, why should the nephew care about it? And why move here, to one of Brinshire's smallest villages? It makes no sense." He shrugged, mystified.

"Perhaps he has harboured a secret passion for me all these years, and now hopes to steal me away from you," Jane said.

"Then I shall just have to challenge him to a duel for your hand," Jeremy said equably. "Ah, the whist table is breaking up. Have you left some candles in Mama's room for my investigations?"

She nodded, and there was no opportunity for further confidences as the guests began to depart.

~~~~~

Jeremy prepared for bed and sent Hooper away. Then he sat and waited, quietly reading in a chair as the hands on his pocket watch moved to midnight, and then one o'clock and finally two o'clock. That was always the best time to explore, when even the most wakeful of night owls was abed and deeply asleep, and no early risers yet abroad. Jane had thoughtfully placed him in his old room not far from his mama's, so he had only to open his door a crack, the hinges carefully oiled to avoid squeaks, and creep along the passage, his bare feet soundless. There had been no opportunity to oil the hinges of the door to Mama's room, and he winced at the creaking it made as he opened it, as loud as gunfire in the silence of the night. He had brought oil with him, so at least he could leave noiselessly when his work was done.

Hastily he drew all the curtains at the windows. It was unlikely that anyone was walking about the grounds at this hour, but there was no point in taking chances. Then he lit more candles, and set to work. He had barely begun removing the drawers when another candle appeared at the silently-opened door, with Jane's excited face behind it. She wore only a nightgown and wrap, her feet were bare and her hair hung in a long, thick plait far down her back.

"I stayed awake listening for you," she said, grinning at him, for all the world as if this were a pleasant excursion instead of a project of the night.

"Jane! Whatever are you doing here?" he whispered. "Go back to bed at once. You know what will happen if we are caught here, alone in a bedroom at night, wearing only nightgowns. There will be no escaping this marriage then, so if you want your freedom—"

"Oh, hush," she said. "No one else is about at this hour, you may be sure. Stop talking and get back to work."

"No, it will not do," he said, in rising anxiety. "It will be quite damaging enough to cry off an engagement, but this—"

"You worry too much. It is *my* reputation at stake, so— Wait, what was that?"

To Jeremy's horror, the door opened again and the silent movement stretched his nerves almost more than the creaks would have done. Another candle, another face...

"Margaret!" he said, his legs weak with relief.

She looked at the two them, then said with a smile, "Chaperon."

"Well, at least *someone* has some sense," Jeremy said. "Can you persuade her to go to bed? There will be the Devil to pay if she is found here with me."

"I am not going anywhere," Jane said. "I am going to light the candelabra and hold it for you to see to work, and Margaret is going to defend my honour if you should happen to catch sight of my ankles and be overcome with lust. Now get working, Jeremy Winterton."

Jeremy looked helplessly at Margaret. "Can *you* instil any ladylike behaviour into my betrothed?"

But Margaret was giggling too much to do more than shake her head. Jeremy gave it up, and he had to admit that the greater light was useful for his investigations. For some time he worked steadily, saying nothing and only giving a low yelp when Jane dripped hot wax onto his hand. Within an hour, the armoire and the dressing table had yielded up their secrets — two concealed compartments in each, cleverly hidden within other secret places, and in each one a coin, a piece of jewellery and a paper with writing.

It was too dark, and the hour too late, to examine them closely. Jeremy saw the ladies safely to their rooms, then crept back to his own room, locking his treasures safely away in the secret compartment in the bottom of his portmanteau. He should have been tired, but the exhilaration of the night's excursion made him too lively for sleep. For a while he sat by the open window as the night air cooled him, his thoughts not with the puzzle his mother had set him. Instead, he was pondering trim ankles and dainty little feet, and trying not to think about lust, and wondering why a woman who defied him at every turn was so much fun to be with. He had chosen Ellen Ridwell for her meekness... well, for her mill, mainly, if he were truthful, but he had found her demure manner appealing. Jane was the very opposite of demure. She infuriated and inspired him in equal measure, and he would be very sorry when their engagement came to an end.

Only when the sun was well above the horizon did he finally climb into his bed and sink into sleep.

~~~~~

Almost immediately, or so it seemed, Hooper shook him awake.

"Beg pardon, sir, but the ladies is wishful for you to rise and join them in the morning room."

Jeremy groaned. "It is barely morning. Can it not wait?"

"Seemingly not, sir. There is chocolate there for you to drink while I sort out some clothes for you. The blue coat for church, sir?"

"Church? Is it Sunday already? Please tell me I am not expected to attend an early service."

"Morning Service is *after* breakfast, sir."

"Thank heavens!" Some faint remembrance of the night's enterprise had by this time filtered into Jeremy's brain, so he had some inkling of why the ladies were so impatient. He hauled himself into a more upright position. "You do not suppose I could snatch another hour's sleep, do you?"

Hooper paused, a clean shirt over one arm. "The ladies did suggest, sir, that I might apply a bucket of cold water to your head if you was tardy."

"Ha! You had better not try it, Hooper, I warn you—!"

"I told the ladies that I was wishful to keep my position, sir," Hooper responded with dignity. "I take my orders from you, sir, not from a lady, not even one so forthright in expressing her opinions as Miss Tyrrell."

Jeremy laughed at that. "She is never one to hold back her thoughts on any subject, is she?"

"As you say, sir. If I might advise, sir, you never enjoy your chocolate so much when it is cold."

"You are a dreadful nag, Hooper," Jeremy said, but he reached for the chocolate and sipped. After a few mouthfuls, its spicy flavour and bracing warmth began to have the desired effect and brought him fully awake.

Jeremy was no dandy, regarding dressing as a pragmatic matter of removing one set of clothing and donning a different set. The only part of the business he took trouble over was shaving. If it were left to him, he would have dispensed with Hooper's services altogether and sent his laundry to a washerwoman, but Uncle Giles had insisted on a valet, and the fellow had his uses, after all. He had a deft hand with the neckcloth, and it was convenient to have someone to pack and unpack, and put a stitch in a torn sleeve. He was not needed to dress him, however, so Jeremy dismissed him and was nevertheless dressed and downstairs in no more than half an hour.

"Good heavens, Jeremy, whatever style of neckcloth do you call that?" Jane said, as soon as he appeared in the morning room.

"I call it... a knot," he said, smiling at her. "You are mistaking me for one of my brothers-in-law if you think I have names for that kind of thing."

"Well, I call it a travesty," she said. "An abomination. A disaster. Why do you not get Hooper to use a bit of starch on them?"

"I do for evening wear, but— Lord, Jane, what are you about?"

She unbuttoned the top of his waistcoat and flicked out the ends of the neckcloth, before nimbly retying them. "There!" she said, rebuttoning the waistcoat. "Much better. Do you not think so, Margaret?"

But Margaret was laughing too hard to answer. When she was more composed, she opened her slate box and wrote, *'Very wifely.'*

Jeremy chose not to dignify this with a reply, torn between amusement at the two ladies joining forces against him and surprise that Jane cared anything for how he looked. She had little regard for her own appearance, after all.

For an instant, he wondered just how much improvement might be achieved were she to dress in the style of one of his sisters, with their fine silks and jewels and furs and the London elegance they all displayed. Or Jeremy himself, if he dressed as fine as his brothers-in-law. He could see the two of them in London, mingling with his grander relations, perhaps dancing at Almack's. Would Jane like that when they were married—?

That train of thought came to an abrupt halt, as he reminded himself that she would never be his wife. To his surprise, he felt a pang of regret. Jane was so much fun to be with, and he enjoyed her outspoken ways. It would not be any great disaster to find himself married to her. His world shifted slightly as he adjusted to this realisation. It was lucky for his peace of mind, perhaps, that she disliked him so much. Despite her convincing performance as a loving wife-to-be, he knew her heart spoke differently and her only desire was for spinsterhood.

To cover his confusion, he emptied the bag he carried onto the table. There were his spoils of the night — four papers with quotations, four coins and four items of modest jewellery. There was a necklace with earrings, two bracelet sets and a brooch. Jeremy had no interest in the quotations, having already determined that each contained some reference to a puzzle or mystery or secret to be uncovered. They were, he was sure, no more than pointers for him, to tell him that this was a puzzle set by his mama. Nor did the jewels have anything to say, except to suggest what he would find if he solved the puzzle.

No, the secret was in the coins and the numbers they held. A '3' and a '6'. Another '6' and a '43'. A '10' and a '30'. A '57' and a '12'. What could they possibly mean? He pulled the previous three coins from his waistcoat pocket and turned them over and over in his hands. Then he borrowed Margaret's slate box and wrote out all the numbers in sequence:

'1, 3, 4, 6, 6, 8, 10, 10, 12, 13, 15, 30, 43, 57'

"If there were no duplicates, I would think it a numerical sequence. Mama used to make them for us when the governess left and she was teaching us our numbers. So '1, 2, 4, 7, 11' adds one more each time, so the next in the sequence is—"

"Sixteen," Jane said.

"Yes! You are very quick," he said, in genuine admiration. "Annabelle understood them, too, but Fanny could never see what it would be, and guessed wildly. Lucy could never be bothered. And Margaret—" He stopped, with a quick smile at his sister. "You never spoke, but when I said the answer, you always nodded. You understood them, too, I think, sister."

She nodded, then pointed at the numbers written on the slate. "Not those."

"Exactly so," he said. "I see no pattern to them, and it is odd how high these new ones are. Thirty, forty three and fifty seven. But with duplicates — that is hard to decipher."

"We are still missing a few," Jane said, peering over his shoulder at the slate. "The secretary will have a couple more, at least. But how will we know when we have found them all? Perhaps you missed one or two secret drawers."

He sighed. "It seems unlikely. I was rather thorough. Still, if we have made nothing of it when we have the secretary, then I shall go over everything again, just to be sure. What is this?" He picked up one of the necklaces. "Is it quartz? It is a very pretty blue, so pale it is almost grey. It would go well with your eyes, Jane."

She blushed scarlet. "What nonsense you do talk! Better get these put away. Papa will be back from his walk soon."

"Ah, Jane! My blushing bride," he said teasingly, sweeping her hand to his lips for a kiss. And there it was again, that fleeting expression of something in her eyes that was not antagonism, not in the *least* like antagonism. For an instant they stood thus, her hand in his, unmoving, and in the end he was the one who released her and looked away.

All through breakfast and the walk to church and the interminable service, unrelieved by so much as a single hymn, Jeremy tried to concentrate. He read his Prayer Book conscientiously, but his mind kept wandering to a pair of grey eyes regarding him unwaveringly. What did she mean by it? Jeremy was accomplished at reading the tiny gestures and subtle expressions in the faces of men, whether at cards or while discussing business. Ladies, however, were like a closed book to him — he saw only the outside, be it pretty or sternly practical, and could not guess what lay within. Jane was of the practical kind, strong and enduring, but unadorned. A book of sermons, perhaps. No, nothing so dry. Shakespeare or some other playwright, with depth of character and an entertaining scene on every page. Whereas Ellen bore an exquisitely worked exterior, but within was— fine poetry? A bawdy novel? Or nothing but blank pages, perhaps.

Then he chided himself for such comparisons, always so unfavourable to Ellen, and turned his thoughts resolutely back to the service.

Outside, there was the usual mingling, with greetings exchanged and news conveyed to those from further afield. Jane had a multitude of friends and was soon swept into a conclave of bonneted heads, smiling and chattering together like a flock of gaily coloured birds. Mr Tyrrell, too, had acquaintances to talk to, so Jeremy was left to stand a little apart. With the Westerlea Park family in London, there was no one else of consequence in Frickham. The apothecary and the miller exchanged a few words with him, but most of the villagers merely bowed or curtsied respectfully. That suited him very well, for it avoided any awkward questions about wedding dates, banns or honeymoon plans.

He was not alone, however, for Margaret clung to his arm. She was never comfortable in any situation where she might have to talk, but he understood. She would stay at his side, and he would deflect any conversation aimed in her direction. Her grip was tight, and he patted her hand absentmindedly, but he did not realised the extent of her fear until he saw Percival Drake bearing down on them. He had forgotten Drake, and as if the man himself was not enough of an irritant, he had brought his aunt and his sisters with him. They must have driven out from Carrington Hall for the sole purpose of spending Sunday with him. With anyone else, such a visit would be a touching display of family affinity, but with the Drakes he suspected some less affecting cause.

"Well, Jeremy, you are getting yourself very settled at Woodside, so I hear," Lady Elizabeth said, after the most cursory of greetings. "Staying overnight, I understand."

"Mr and Miss Tyrrell were so kind as to invite me so that I might attend church without driving out from Brinchester. One would not wish to travel on a Sunday, after all." He smiled, knowing perfectly well that she must have done exactly that.

Lady Elizabeth was impervious to insult, however subtle, so she ploughed straight on with what she no doubt had approached Jeremy to say. "Found your mother's jewels yet, Jeremy? You must have most of her furniture by now." And to his intense annoyance, she sniggered.

Again, Margaret's hand gripped his arm with painful strength. "Mama's jewels are lost, and no one knows where they may be," Jeremy shot back, and it was true enough, after all. "Did she ever hint to you where they may be? You were such a good friend to her, after all."

That barb hit home, and she had the grace to look slightly conscious. "Oh... well... Anne and I were never *friends*, exactly. Besides, if she never told your father where they were, she would hardly confide in me." Another snigger.

"No, I did not suppose she would," Jeremy said coolly. Again Margaret tugged at his arm, and when he looked at her, she was gazing fixedly at Lady Elizabeth's throat. A brooch sat there, a brooch that looked just like the one he had found during his overnight exploration. The stone was identical, and even the setting was the same. "Pretty brooch," Jeremy said recklessly. "Mama had one just like it."

"Did she?" This time she definitely coloured under his unblinking scrutiny. "I wonder why, when she had real jewels at her disposal. All those diamonds and emeralds and rubies and sapphires. What did she want with trumpery stuff like chalcedony?"

Margaret gave a small squeak, and clutched his arm again, but when he turned to her, she had lowered her gaze and was staring fixedly at the ground. Jeremy had had enough of Lady Elizabeth by then, so he made his farewells. It was not until they had walked most of the way back to Woodside that Margaret turned to him with shining eyes.

"Twelve," she said happily.

"Um... twelve?"

"Twelve coins... to find." And she smiled at him with glee.

18: *Peridot And Chalcedony*

Jane could barely contain her impatience. With her father lagging behind to examine some wild guelder roses in the hedgerow, and the servants almost out of sight, she had been able to walk alongside Jeremy, and thus heard Margaret's words. Twelve coins — Margaret knew the number! But how? How had she guessed? And did she now understand the numbers? It was too exciting for words.

Jeremy was as calm as usual, and only said to Margaret in a low voice, "Wait until Mr Tyrrell has had his tea. There will be time then to explain it to us all."

It was some time before they could discuss Margaret's idea. Tea with Mr Tyrrell was not a matter for haste. It was a Sunday tradition to retreat to his study, ostensibly to discuss Mr Grantley's sermon, but in reality to gossip about the neighbours. In general Jane enjoyed the hour greatly, and would not rush it, so she curbed her restlessness and tried to be as chatty as usual.

Having discussed the more pressing scandals of the day, her father said, "Well, Jane, I confess I was surprised to see Lady Elizabeth at church today."

Jane set her cup down with a clatter. "As if it is not trying enough having young Drake always about the village, but are we to have the rest of the family as well? What can she mean by it? I suppose she is keeping an eye on Jeremy. She is a meddlesome woman who takes a great interest in the Winterton family, and would love to winkle out all our secrets, I daresay."

"A meddlesome woman," her father said thoughtfully. "Yet Mr Winterton has been here for three months now. Long enough even for Lady Elizabeth to grow accustomed to his return from the dead. Nor should your betrothal occasion any great surprise. Perhaps it is no more than family interest in her nephew's new home."

"And that is what I do not understand at all. Why should Percival Drake settle himself here? It is most inconvenient, when he takes the very house you had fixed upon to move into."

Her father smiled in his benign way. Nothing ever ruffled him. "He may live where he chooses, I am sure. He seems to like it here, for I have encountered him several times as I take my morning walks. He is exploring the countryside in a very proper way, on foot, observing the minutiae of the flora. Why, he was absorbed by the prospect of a mossy stone yesterday, kneeling beside it to examine something that Miss Grantley was pointing out to him."

"Miss Grantley!" Jane exclaimed.

"Oh, yes," her father said blandly. "Their paths often seem to cross. She seems to enjoy exploring the countryside, too, and often carries a small bunch of flowers, just as I do. Why, perhaps they too are artists, gathering inspiration."

Jeremy snorted. "If Percival Drake is an artist, then I am a Chinaman. He has not a sensible thought in his head. *And* he snores, which I cannot forgive," he added. "I beg your pardon, Miss

Tyrrell, I did not mean to make you choke on your tea. A pat on the back is efficacious in such cases. Margaret?"

When Jane had been restored to a semblance of normality, Jeremy went on, "Drake may indeed live where he chooses, as you say, sir, but the question arises as to why he chooses Frickham, the sleepiest village in England."

"He has acquaintances here, at Woodside and Westerlea Park," Mr Tyrrell said. "That must weigh with him."

"Acquaintances, but no friends," Jeremy said. "Those he has mentioned in my hearing have all been based in Brinchester. As to acquaintances, he would do better at High Frickham, where he has the Claremonts, the Bowens, the Sheridans and the Whites, that I know of. No, he is an unpleasant man and he has some devious scheme in mind, and I do not like to hear of the vicar's daughter keeping company with him. Nothing good can come of that. Miss Tyrrell, you should not walk alone in the woods or fields while he is about."

"You truly despise him," Jane said, surprised.

"I do. There is something... underhand about him. Do you not feel so yourself? Do you not also dislike him?"

"Oh, I dislike everyone," she said easily. "Except you, of course, and Papa and Margaret." She smiled at him in what she hoped was a guileless manner, and to her dismay he smiled back, his eyes crinkling at the edges in the most attractive manner. If only he were a shade less charming, and not so utterly irresistible.

After an hour, her father finally chased them out of his study. "I shall read a sermon or two before the dressing bell," he said grandly, although Jane knew perfectly well that he would be snoozing in his chair.

They crept away to the morning room, and Margaret at once brought out her slate box and chalks.

'I think the necklaces and brooches are all in Mama's trumpery stones — do you remember? Chalcedony was one of them, and there were twelve altogether.'

"Oh, the twelve trumpery stones — I *do* remember," Jeremy said. "I have to confess, I never took much notice of the jewels we found. I always felt the coins were the significant part. What else have we found? Garnets — I remember those. Jane, do you remember?"

"Pearls," Jane said, frowning, struggling to remember. "Do you have them all here?"

"Only last night's haul. One black, one yellow, one almost the colour of your eyes." His smile set her stomach somersaulting.

Fortunately, Margaret's chalk was in motion again. *'Black ~ onyx. Yellow ~ topaz perhaps. The chalcedony. What was the fourth?'*

"Green," Jane managed, although it was hard to breathe with Jeremy still smiling at her.

'Peridot,' Margaret wrote. *'We should make a proper list. But I am sure it is the trumpery stones, so there will be twelve in total.'*

"Twelve," Jeremy said, looking smug. "So now we know that we still have five coins to find. That is a huge help. Thank you, Margaret. It will be easy now."

He seemed so certain that Jane had not the heart to voice her own doubts, that even when all the coins were found, they had still to solve the puzzle of the numbers and work out from that how to find the jewels. And that assumed they were even following the right path at all. It would be very far from easy.

~~~~~

Tuesday brought Margaret's husband, Mel Haymer, back from London. He was hot, tired and dishevelled, having travelled overnight by the mail coach in great discomfort, being such a large man, but he had not wanted to take the extra time to make the journey more comfortably. Margaret hurled herself at him and for fully ten minutes they stood in the middle of the hall, eyes closed, wrapped in each other's arms, quite oblivious, as Mel's valet and Timpson and Betsy carted boxes and packages around them. Jane watched them, swamped with some emotion that she could only ascribe to envy. Oh, to be so much missed, so longed for, so loved! She imagined herself resting against Jeremy's greatcoat in that way, her head almost reaching his shoulder, his cheek against her cap, his arms holding her tight... but such thoughts would drive her mad. She turned away, and occupied herself in checking that Timpson knew where to take Mr Haymer's things, and sending Betsy to the kitchen with orders for one extra for dinner, and was there any fish in the house?

Mr Haymer was as restful a guest as Margaret, quiet and easy to please. He ate his way stolidly through two or three helpings of almost every dish at dinner, and said little unless asked directly.

"Do you like London, Mr Haymer?" Jane said, as they lingered over the nuts and fruit. "It must be an exciting place to visit."

"Exciting... that is true. There is so much of interest in the great buildings and monuments. But the society— I do not enjoy London society. There are too many people who live only for pleasure, and do little of worth, despite the duties of rank and wealth. For those of us who cannot dance and choose not to gamble or pursue hedonism, there is not much of interest. I go to London from family duty, and to meet friends from far afield, but that is all the satisfaction such visits afford. For ladies, I understand there are other sources of enjoyment." He smiled affectionately at Margaret.

"Shopping!" she said, with a quick laugh.

"Mrs Haymer tells me she hates the place," Mr Haymer said, "yet somehow we always leave laden with purchases. It is most odd to leave London unburdened by bales of cloth and boxes of books and who knows what else — a harp, last year, so that Mrs Haymer might learn to play. But this year, I bear only letters. I have several for Mr Winterton. Do you expect him here soon, or shall I take them to Brinchester for him?"

"I do not know when he will be here again," she said, a little wistfully.

"Shall we take the carriage tomorrow and surprise him?" Mr Haymer said. "I should very much like to see this clock of his."

Margaret nodded her agreement, and Jane, with a jolt of happiness at the prospect of seeing Jeremy again so soon, agreed also.

~~~~~

Jeremy was humming quietly to himself, the ticking of the great clock keeping the time for his tune. He loved to be immersed in machinery like this, the cogs and wheels and rods all moving in well-oiled synchrony — clunk... clunk... clunk... once every second. Below him, the giant pendulum moved back and forth, and above him the giant bells hung motionless, awaiting their moment of glory four times an hour. He no longer consciously heard any of it, but, just as with his steam-powered beam engine at Branton, he would know the instant anything shifted even slightly out of alignment.

He was perched on a ladder, putting the finishing touches to the array of angels which would one day fly over the Lord Jesus and his Holy Apostles and the faithful who carried meat and bread and wine. Every day at noon they would fly, and only another day or two of work would see them ready to unfurl their wings. Kit had repaired and painted the angels first, insisting on approaching the matter with hierarchical rigour. Angels, he said, existed in the heavenly sphere, and thus took priority over all those in the mortal plane, even Jesus. Jeremy felt himself unqualified for such a theological debate, leaving such questions to Kit's brother who was, after all, a clergyman and might be expected to provide a definitive ruling on the status of angels. Still, he was happy to have some of the automaton figures restored, and minded not which ones were returned to him first.

The clock struck the first quarter after eleven, and Jeremy stopped work and stood respectfully still, as he always did. The chime was too magnificent to be ignored. But as the last note died away, he became aware of... something, he could not even say what. All his senses now alert, he stood still, listening, but there was nothing amiss with the clock. It ticked away as robustly as ever, unmarred by squeaks or grinding noises or anything untoward. But there was *something...*

It was on the stair outside the clock room. Someone was stealthily making his way up to the clock room. Jeremy quickly reviewed who it might be. Kit? No, he knew his tread, likewise Everton, and the verger who wound the clock each day, and the manservant who was sometimes sent with messages. It was none of those, nor would they creep up so quietly. Mindful of the two gunshots which had come so close to ending his life, Jeremy silently lifted the winding handle from its hooks on the wall. It was not an ideal weapon, and would be useless against a gun, but at that moment he felt the need for something heavy in his hand.

He slowly crept to a position where the opening door would hide him, and waited. The almost-inaudible sounds ceased. Then the latch lifted and the door slowly opened. It stopped. The interloper stood unmoving, his breath too quiet to be heard above the loud ticks of the machinery. Then he stepped forward, peering round the room, behind the door...

Jeremy raised the winding handle.

There was a squeak of alarm. "Great heavens, Winterton, what are you about?"

Percival Drake.

Jeremy breathed again, and lowered the winding handle. "Why are you creeping about like a thief, Drake?" he said, too annoyed to be polite. "I thought you were bent on mischief."

Drake sniggered. "Are you expecting mischief? Good Lord, I had no idea you were so jumpy or I should have called up the stairs. Is that imbecile about? I was taking care not to startle him. One never knows how a person like that will react."

"Imbecile? Are you talking about Kit? He would never hurt a flea." He huffed a breath, trying to calm his jangled nerves. Drake was not a person he was particularly pleased to see. "What is it you want with me? We can go into the rectory if this is a social call."

"I wanted to see this clock of yours," Drake said.

"Well, here it is," Jeremy said. Then, realising how rude he sounded, he added more gently, "Do you want me to explain all the workings? I have tried that with one or two people, but they merely look dazed, so I have given up hope of finding a fellow enthusiast. However, I am happy to describe how everything is managed if you find the subject of interest."

"Don't put yourself out on my account," Drake said with a laugh. "I can see that it is just like a long-case clock, only larger. My aunt has one with the pendulum visible, so I understand the principle." Jeremy tried not be offended by any comparison of his tower clock to a domestic type. "No, I wanted to see what you are doing here. What is up that ladder?"

Before Jeremy could answer, voices were heard on the stair, and one of them very familiar to him. With a rush of pleasure, he shot to the top of the stair and called down.

"Miss Tyrrell? I am up here. Take care on the steps — some of them are uneven."

And there she was, smiling up at him. He stretched out his hand to help her up the last few steps, and without the slightest hesitation she placed her gloved hand in his.

"How delightful to see you — oh, and Margaret, too. And Mr Haymer. Do come in to my workshop, all of you. I have so many visitors today — Careful, Drake!" he called out in some alarm. "That ladder is most unsteady unless one is accustomed to it. Pray come down."

"Just wanted to see what you are doing up here," Drake said. "Fascinating! What are these things with wings? Oh, I see it now, angels. How charming."

"Do not touch anything, I beg you! Everything is most precisely aligned."

With a snigger, Drake finally descended to the ground, and Jeremy breathed again. He was still holding Jane's hand, and she was watching him in some amusement.

"You are very proprietorial, Mr Winterton," she said, her eyes twinkling.

"So I am," he said. "About engines and clocks... and other things." He tucked her hand around his arm, and was unaccountably pleased when she made no protest, merely lowering her eyes demurely. It was an odd thing — he liked her prickliness, but there was something intriguing about this new compliant Jane, something that made his heart beat a little faster. He had long since realised that marriage to Jane would not be any great trial, but for the first time he began to consider whether it might not be positively desirable. Was she, abrupt and downright uncivil as she so often was, actually creeping into his heart? Strange thought.

But there was no time for reflection, not with four extra persons crammed into the clock room. He showed them all there was to see on both the upper floors, and then, with an excuse to Drake about *'family matters to discuss'*, he locked up the tower and took Jane, Margaret and Haymer back to the rectory for tea, Madeira and one of the plum cakes for which Everton's cook was renowned.

"I have letters for you from your sisters," Haymer said, once they were settled in the rectory's rather splendid drawing room.

Jeremy read through them rather quickly, for descriptions of grand balls and outings to Richmond and evenings at the theatre were of little interest to him. Only one or two sentences in each were noteworthy. *'Miss Ridwell is so much admired, nothing could be like it…'*, Fanny said. *'Your Ellen is enjoying herself now that we have got her away from the starchy aunt…'*, Lucy said. *'I do not know why you said she was quiet, for she is a lively girl, and very popular'*, Annabelle said. Only Rosamund sounded a slightly worried note, *'She is courted quite persistently by several suitors, some very eligible, although I cannot tell that she prefers one above another, and although she encourages them rather, she insists that she will not marry any of them. I do not quite know what she is about.'*

"There is one from Ferdy, too," Haymer said apologetically.

"Really?" Jeremy said, startled. "I wonder why he writes to me."

But as soon as he unfolded the page, he understood. *'Forgive my impertinence in concerning myself in your affairs, for it may be that you have the whole situation well in hand and will laugh at my foolish fears, but I am a trifle alarmed by Miss Ridwell's progress. Her situation is well known, and we all felt that she would attract no serious suitors because of her father's position in society. It is also understood within the family that, despite your current situation with Miss T, Miss R's future is already secured. There seemed no harm, therefore, in introducing her to better society and allowing her to enjoy a modest season. She has taken to* ton *life with great enthusiasm, and has a court of admirers, among them at least two with serious intentions. Fortescue's father will not accept her, certainly, but Dallen has an independent fortune, and the odds at the clubs are shortening by the day. If you still harbour hopes in that direction, I would respectfully suggest that you act to secure the lady sooner rather than later. However, if I have misread the situation, accept my sincere apologies. Yours with every wish for your future happiness, wherever it lies, Ferdy.'*

19: The Secretary

The ladies being anxious to visit certain purveyors of items of feminine apparel, Jeremy escorted Jane and the Haymers to the nearest such establishment, whereupon he and Haymer repaired to the inn where the carriage waited, to while away the hours until the two ladies had acquired sufficient parcels. Haymer had secured a private parlour, so they ordered Madeira and settled down to wait.

Haymer was a restful sort of man, Jeremy decided. He asked no questions, and filled the room with no useless chatter, but took a small book from his pocket and began to read, leaving Jeremy to his own thoughts. Jeremy pulled a chair across to the window, which overlooked a quiet side street, and tried to assess his own emotions.

Was he angry? Jealous, perhaps? He could not in all honesty say that he was. He was not unhappy at the prospect of losing Ellen and her mill— Oh, the mill. Yes, there was certainly a pang of regret there, for it was a fine mill and he had coveted it for a long time, or at least he had coveted what it represented. The mill would have made him *somebody*, a man of consequence in Branton. A mill *owner* was respected as no mere mill *manager* could ever be.

But for Ellen herself, he felt nothing except, somewhere in the swirl of his own selfishness, a sense of goodwill towards her. He hoped that she would find a man who would care for her as she deserved, and wished her nothing but happiness. The idea of Ellen Ridwell as his wife floated away and popped like a soap bubble, and he felt only pleasure in her London success.

He pulled out the various letters and read them again, more carefully. '...*enjoying herself... a lively girl... she encourages them rather...*' That did not sound like the Ellen he knew. He went back to the table, and sat down opposite Haymer.

"May I ask you a question?" Jeremy said.

Haymer marked his place in the book and set it aside. "Of course."

"What is your opinion of Ellen Ridwell?"

Haymer rubbed his chin. "She is a rare beauty, but not one who takes advantage of that, or even seems aware of it. When we first met her, with her aunt present, she was just as you described her, very polished but so repressed that one hardly knew if she was a woman or a doll."

"Repressed... yes," Jeremy said. "Her mother was an odd creature, always dressing the same as her daughter. It was my great hope that Ellen would blossom once she was away from her mother's influence."

"Oh, she has certainly blossomed," Haymer said, with a wry smile. "At first your sisters invited her to rather modest events — Vauxhall Gardens, the theatre, a musical evening, a card party, and very often the aunt went along too. But people started to enquire who the new beauty was, and ask if she could be brought to balls and routs. She had been fitted out with some more stylish gowns by then, so along she went with your sisters, and the aunt stayed at home. And she…" He paused, as if struggling to find the word. "Yes, let us say that she has blossomed."

"You sound almost disapproving," Jeremy said, amused. "Is that the clergyman in you, preferring the more modest chit to the lively prime article?"

Haymer rubbed his nose this time. "I *do* think modest ways would serve her better, it is true," he said soberly. "A quiet demeanour and the patronage of influential ladies, as your sisters now are, would see her comfortably settled with a man who would care nothing for the smell of trade about her. But when a girl is lively and flirtatious, then—"

"Flirtatious!" Jeremy exclaimed. "Ellen? Truly?"

"It is not easy to find a kinder description," Haymer said. "Indeed I would say she was flirtatious, and such a manner attracts a different kind of man."

"These two that Lord Craston mentions…"

"Ferdy," Haymer said with a smile. "All these titles are such a mouthful. You are family, so you may call him Ferdy, as we all do."

"It seems disrespectful to such a fashionable man, and one moreover who will be a marquess one day," Jeremy said, but then shrugged. "Well, he is my brother-in-law, after all. Ferdy mentions two names, Fortescue and Dallen."

"Mr Fortescue I liked very much," Haymer said. "He is very young, very dazzled by Miss Ridwell's beauty, very much in love, but his family will discourage his suit. Dallen, on the other hand…"

"Yes? Dallen?"

"I will not conceal from you that I do not like him, but that may, of course, be the clergyman in me," Haymer said with a slight smile. "He has a certain reputation as a rake who spends a great deal on his mistresses but has never yet been tempted into marriage. However, he is very attentive to Miss Ridwell, he has a taste for great beauties and he has no family to gainsay him. Ferdy thinks he will very likely offer for her. He knows all the talk in the clubs, and there are bets placed, seemingly. We were all concerned that... this might not please you."

"Diplomatically put," Jeremy said. He took a sip of Madeira, then set the glass down. "It was my intent to marry Ellen, but I find myself remarkably unmoved by the prospect of her marriage to another. I wish her joy of this Mr Dallen, and hope that he may bring her great happiness."

"Ah, your sisters will be very glad to hear that. Fanny, in particular, imagines you broken-hearted. But if you manage to find your mama's jewels, you will have no need of Miss Ridwell's mill."

And in that one casual sentence, Jeremy's life shifted from one track to another. With Ellen gone, and the prospect of her mill no longer his for the taking, there was nothing to keep him in Branton apart from affection for Giles Moreton, who had raised him, and the Hazlehead Mill, which had given his life purpose. Now he could live as his birth ordained, as a gentleman.

He would be Mr Winterton of Woodside, as his father had been, and take up a quiet life as a country gentleman. And if he was not, after all, to marry Ellen Ridwell, then he was free to seek another wife for himself, a wife who might, perhaps, suit him rather better.

~~~~~

A few days later, the secretary arrived, sent by Lady Elizabeth on the carter's wagon, so precariously balanced as it lumbered down the main street of Frickham that a group of children followed it all the way in the hope of seeing it fall and smash to pieces in the road. As the carter and his two hefty sons, aided by Timpson, the old coachman and the two gardeners, struggled to unload the monstrous piece and manoeuvre it up the stairs, Jane thought ruefully that any last shreds of secrecy over her little scheme must now be blown away. There could not be a single resident of Frickham unaware that all Woodside's former furniture was returning home. How many of them, she wondered, guessed at the reason? The missing jewels must be known about, and it was no great leap of deduction to draw conclusions about the furniture.

Lady Elizabeth had neglected to pay the carter in advance, so Jane was obliged to haggle with him for the transportation, and then add another two shillings for helping to shift the secretary up the stairs.

"I do not know why I am to pay you so much when my own men did most of the work," she said to the carter as he stood wiping his brow. "You stood about giving contradictory orders, and your men merely steadied the top as it was lifted. My men did all the heavy lifting."

"We'd have helped out, right enough, if the stair'd bin wider, Mistress. Too narrow for all of us, that's what it was. We did what we could, and we got it onto the wagon at the 'all, so it's a fair price."

"I daresay Lady Elizabeth's footmen did most of the work at the Hall," Jane said. "Two shillings extra, not a penny more, but if you go round to the kitchen door, Mrs Locke will find you something to eat, and then on your way home you may deliver a letter to Brinchester for me, to St Mark's rectory."

She was pleased that Jeremy was very swift to respond to her note, riding over the next morning. Mr Tyrrell was attending a parish meeting at High Frickham, so they were able to examine the secretary straight away. Margaret and her husband were spending the day with friends at Lower Brinford, but for once Jeremy made no foolish protest about Jane being alone in the bedroom with him. She was glad not to begin the day with a tedious argument, but she could not help wondering whether his lack of protest was a demonstration that he trusted her judgement, or evidence that he no longer cared about her reputation. But perhaps he was preoccupied with the news from London, and Ellen Ridwell's success there. He showed no emotion, but surely he must be anxious at the prospect of losing her. However, she did not want to think about Ellen, not when Jeremy was with her and she had many hours to enjoy his company. She sat on the edge of the bed and watched as he set to work on the secretary.

It was huge, reaching almost to the ceiling and dominating one wall of the bedroom. The external carvings were more restrained than on some of the other pieces, but even so, no person of taste would ever describe it as anything but ugly. The lower half had cupboards with shelves and large drawers, but the upper half, once the writing desk was unfolded, was filled with a myriad of tiny drawers and compartments.

"I imagine Lady Elizabeth has examined it thoroughly," Jane said.

"Certainly, but she will be clever indeed if she finds every concealed place in so complicated a construction," Jeremy said. "Is it not glorious? So much detail. Look, these drawers swivel — see? And this pops up, like so."

"Do you expect to find the actual jewels in this?" Jane said. "It is large enough to conceal them, but we are still missing five coins."

He stopped opening and closing little doors, and turned to face her, his expression thoughtful. "I do not see the point in the coins if the jewels are here to be found in the same way as everything else. The coins are some kind of code, of that much I can be certain. That suggests that they are the key to finding where the jewels are hidden, but if they are not here, I cannot guess where they might be. This is the last item of furniture, is it not?"

"It is."

His shoulders sagged for a moment, but then he took a breath and went on, "Well, let us not despair. Once we have all the coins, we will be able to decipher the code. Then we will know where the jewels are. You will not object if I remove my coat? It is easier to work so."

Jane had no objection at all, glorying in the intimacy of being alone with him when he was so informally dressed, almost as if they were married. She watched him eagerly, his long fingers deftly opening and closing, sliding and twisting, measuring depths with a folding ruler to uncover the location of hidden compartments. He found one, then another, then a third and finally one last one. Then he went over the whole secretary again, before sitting beside Jane on the bed, his face such a picture of chagrin that she wanted to take him in her arms and hug him like a child.

There were no secrets within the secretary. Every drawer and shelf and cupboard was empty, with not so much as a single sheet of paper to be found. Nor were there any secret compartments hidden within other secret compartments. There was nothing to be found.

"That is the end of it," he said, despairingly. "We have all the furniture and there is nothing left to discover. If there ever was anything hidden in the secretary, it has gone now."

"Then she has them," Jane said. "Lady Elizabeth has the jewels."

"No," he said, sitting up a little straighter. "That is impossible. There was no secret compartment large enough to conceal the boxes they were in, and they must have been in a secret compartment or Papa would have found them. If Lady Elizabeth has found anything at all, it is the last five coins, which will mean nothing to her. No, the jewels are not in the secretary, although..."

"Although?" she said.

"It is an odd thing," he said slowly. "In every other piece of furniture, the coins were hidden inside a second compartment, concealed within an already hidden compartment. Two layers of protection. A casual searcher, even knowing there to be secret compartments, would not look further when one is found. So the first compartment is empty, the searcher moves on, and fails to find the treasure still hidden within. But the secretary had no second layer of protection. No compartment concealed within an already concealed compartment. I wonder why?"

"These things are very common," Jane said. "Many houses have a secretary like this, complete with secret compartments. We had one at Hallow End, our old house, although not so large as this. Perhaps this is a standard piece of furniture, and all the others were specially made, and so were made more secure."

"Perhaps," he said, but he sounded unconvinced. "We were always told, as children, that the whole suite was specially made for Mama, as a wedding gift."

"We still have seven coins," she said. "It may be that we can yet learn something from those."

"Perhaps," he said again. Then, with a sigh, he pulled a small bag from a pocket and tossed it onto her lap. "There they are, and I have written the numbers out in sequence. See if anything jumps out at you."

She pulled out the coins one by one, laying them out on the mattress between them, but they were just as she remembered. Then she unfolded the paper that was also within the bag.

'1, 3, 4, 6, 6, 8, 10, 10, 12, 13, 15, 30, 43, 57'

"Nothing higher than fifty seven," she said. "Mostly low numbers, just a few high."

He looked up with sudden interest. "That means something to you?"

"No, but…" She flipped a few coins quickly. "The high numbers all have a low number on the back."

"That is natural," he said at once. "If there are mostly low numbers, it is very probable that a high number will be paired with a low one. There are several coins with two low numbers. What else?"

"It could be directions," she said. "One pace to the north, three to the east, and so on."

"Not paces," he said, his face alive with excitement. "Too big for this room, but inches, perhaps, or floorboards, counted from— Oh. But where would one start? And how would one know which way to turn? That does not work, but it is an ingenious idea. Anything measured would need more information."

"Pages in a book," she said, catching his enthusiasm. "Words on a page — no, the psalms. Your mama would have had a book of psalms, no doubt. Come on!"

They went downstairs to find a book that listed all the psalms, and then spent a futile hour trying to compose anything meaningful by connecting the numbers on the coins.

"This is useless," Jeremy said, throwing down his pencil in disgust and crumpling the paper where he had been scribbling words. "It cannot be psalms, and we must be running out of time. When will your father return?"

"We have another half hour yet," Jane said, glancing at the clock on the sideboard. "It is only three minutes to— Oh. Three minutes."

Jeremy's head shot up. "What is it?"

"Three minutes to the hour is *fifty seven* minutes *past* the hour. Nothing higher than sixty, and mostly low — it is clock times."

"Oh, but of *course* it is," he said, eyes wide. "How clever you are, Jane." He picked up a coin. "Forty three minutes after six o'clock. This one is thirty minutes past ten. And this could be three minutes after six or six minutes after three. It is to do with the clock in the bed."

Without a word, they headed for the stairs. Jeremy took them two at a time, racing ahead of her, so Jane gathered up her skirts and galloped after him. They arrived at the door, breathless and laughing, at the same moment, bursting into the room side by side. Jeremy leapt onto the bed without aid, but Jane more decorously climbed the steps. With the covering doors wide open, they beheld the clock, its hands permanently stopped at five minutes past twelve.

"How foolish of me not to examine the clock more closely," Jeremy said. "Yet it looks... very ordinary. It is an odd place for a clock, but the clock itself looks perfectly normal."

"Why should it not be normal?" Jane said. "Except that it is presumably an automaton clock like the one at—"

Jeremy yelped. "I am so *stupid!* It must be, of course. See here, these spandrels must—"

"The what?"

"Spandrels... these spaces between the square corners of the foot board and the rounded shape of the clock. I wonder if... oh, there is only one way to find out." He opened the shallow drawer below the clock, and withdrew the winding key. "Now, let me see… ah, here we are. The hands are disconnected so… and now it is easy to reset." He deftly wound the hands back to point to five minutes to twelve. "Now all we need to do is to get the thing going," he muttered, winding with the key. "Hmm. But how do we restart the pendulum?"

"How would you usually do that?" Jane said.

"The pendulum is normally visible, so… ah, here we are. This lever slides back and forth so… there!"

A gentle ticking sound began to fill the air, and the hands began to move an infinitesimal amount with each tick. They settled themselves to watch, as the hands gently shifted towards the hour.

"How do you know anything will happen?" Jane said, as the final minute ticked away.

"Well… there is no certainty, but if there is an automaton mechanism and it is connected and it still works, then it will activate at twelve o'clock. Some go off every hour, but if not, it will be noon. Listen… something is happening."

There was no musical sound, no chimes or bells or melody, but as the two hands drew towards twelve o'clock, the machinery gently clanked and ground and whirred. Then, in the space just above and to the left of the clock, a door opened and figures appeared. A woman, in the clothes of several decades ago, followed by a man similarly attired. Then another woman and another man, and another pair and yet a fourth. They moved across the open space revealed by the door and disappeared. Then the door slowly closed.

"Well, that was disappointing," Jane said. "I thought that— Oh." Another door opened, this time above and to the right of the clock. "Oh, there are four things to watch. That is more like it… but these are the same people... oh! Why is she in her undergarments?"

Jeremy shifted restlessly. "Bedroom stuff. I think you should not be watching this, Jane."

"Now, do not get priggish with me," she said. "They are only dolls, after all."

"Yes, but—"

"Oh!" The third door opened, and this time the little people wore no clothes at all. "Oh! Is that—? Oh! Good heavens, I had no idea!"

"Nor should you have," Jeremy said with some urgency, moving so that he blocked her view. "Look away, Jane, I beg you! You should not—! It is not seemly!"

"But fascinating," she said, peering round him. "I have never— I mean, I always wondered—Oh, do get out of the way, Jeremy!" And then the final door opened. "OH! So that is how it is!"

"Jane, you must not... do not look... close your eyes at once!"

She should have been shocked, but instead she was fascinated and quite unable to look away. So this was what happened between men and women! It was thrilling to uncover the secret at last, but she could not see the whole of it. Jeremy was annoyingly in the way. She pushed at him to get him to move aside, but he was far stronger than she was. He grabbed hold of her arms and they fell down onto the mattress, his hands pinning her down so that she could not move. The astonishing dolls were gone, her vision filled by Jeremy above her. For a moment they were motionless, she held fast by his strong arms, mesmerised by his face, he gazing down at her, his eyes shimmering.

Then he leaned forward and kissed her.

The world melted away. She was awash with the need for him, for something that her rational mind knew quite well was not love but at that moment she did not care. He *wanted* her, he found her desirable and kissable, and in return she gave him all the love that had been welling up inside her for weeks... no, months. Ever since she had seen him sagging against the door frame that first day, in fact. She had been aware of him for all that time, as she had never been aware of any other man. He cared nothing for her, that much she knew, but if he would kiss her like this sometimes, with urgency and warmth and longing, she could pretend to herself that he was hers and that he loved her, if only for a few moments.

By the time they broke apart, the clock was quiescent again, with only the gentle tick to show that it was active.

Jeremy laughed, and released her. "Jane, Jane — you are so much fun!"

20: A Summer Ball (July)

St Mark's rectory in Brinchester was fusty, Jeremy decided. It was a vast, echoing pile of a house, designed to accommodate the clergyman's wife and large troop of offspring. With only Dudley and Kit Everton and Jeremy in it, together with their handful of servants, half the rooms were dusty and silent, the furniture ghostly under holland covers. Even the few rooms they used were shabby from neglect. Jeremy was used to such conditions, for the house he had shared with Giles Moreton in Branton was much the same.

Even so, he saw the difference in other houses. The Ridwells' house, with its army of servants, was immaculate. The elegant environs of Westerlea Park suffered no speck of dust to settle. Wood was polished, glass sparkled and rugs were taken outdoors for vigorous beatings on a regular basis. Even at Woodside, where Jane herself was obliged to don an apron and wield a feather duster, the rooms smelled of beeswax and lavender, and were not in the least fusty.

That, he supposed, was the beneficial effect of a woman's management. Perhaps when he was settled at Woodside, he would see about getting a housekeeper. As the thought flicked into his mind, it ignited a little flame of regret, for if there was a housekeeper at Woodside, there would be no Jane.

So his thoughts ran as he crept around the empty rooms of the rectory at night. There was a bedroom on an upper floor which had a clear view towards the church, although not the face of the clock. In his nocturnal wanderings, he often ended up there, sitting on the window-seat with its moth-eaten cushion, peering through the window, listening to the house creaking and shifting around him, coming alive in the darkness. He could pass a whole hour there, sometimes, his thoughts meandering wherever they would. Although Jane featured rather prominently, he was aware, and especially since he had kissed her.

How he cursed himself for giving in to temptation like that! Now it would be twenty times as difficult to bid her farewell when their engagement came to an end. If it should come to an end. She had made it clear that she despised him thoroughly, yet once or twice he had seen something in her eyes which suggested otherwise. So perhaps he should put it to the test. Once he had the jewels, he would ask her what she truly wished for and then... then he would know. If she wanted it, he would marry her, naturally. That was what a gentleman did, and if he had the jewels and Woodside, then he would be a gentleman at last and his wife would be *somebody* and would never have to wear an apron again.

But that was only if he could recover the jewels... he was beginning to despair of it. He had a code that made no sense and nowhere else to look. He had all the furniture now, and no more secret places to discover. If there had ever been twelve coins, then five of them were missing and not the cleverest mind could deduce a meaning with only seven twelfths of the clues.

At least he had got the clock working. He always laughed out loud when he remembered it, even when he was sitting alone in the dark. That clock was amazing, and yet what else could be expected of a clock designed to fit into a bed? He imagined his father and mother in that bed, watching the automaton figures going through their little routine, and ending with— So ingenious! And salacious, naturally, putting the watchers into the mood for that sort of thing themselves. And Jane so curious, so unshocked! What an amazing woman she was, dreaming up one idea after another for the numbers on the coins, and then thinking nothing of the oddity of the clock hidden away. *'Why should it not be normal?'* she had asked. And that was—

He sat bolt upright. But it was *not* normal, it was hidden behind doors that were hard to find unless one looked carefully. Whatever was the point of a clock that was not on display? The bawdy automaton? But that did not need a clock, only a means to wind it up and set it working. So why would anyone hide a clock away? One would need *another* clock to tell the time.

And then he remembered. His mother's secretary had had a small clock set into its upper face. The one Lady Elizabeth had sent had none. It was not his mother's at all.

No wonder he had found no additional hidden compartments. There were none to find.

~~~~~

JULY

Jane moved through each day in a dream. He had kissed her! After all his teasing, he had finally done it, and it had been everything she had hoped. She could not stop thinking about it, and even though she reminded herself sternly that it meant nothing to him, and their betrothal was just a sham, she was still exultant and could hardly stop herself from smiling all day long.

With the London season drawing to a close and many local families returning, there was the ordeal of Lady Elizabeth Drake's summer ball to endure. These had been a regular feature when Jane and her father had first moved to Woodside, but had fallen into abeyance more recently as Lady Elizabeth had despaired of finding a husband for her niece Cressida. But with her younger sister Julianna now fifteen and on the verge of coming out, and Percival of an age to consider marriage, Carrington Hall was once again to be the scene for the most spectacular event of the summer. Everyone of consequence in Brinshire was invited, and those who lived some distance away were to stay at the Hall itself.

Jane had a particular reason for looking forward to the event this year, which had nothing to do with dancing or the others attending. No, she had a plan. As soon as Jeremy had told her that the secretary Lady Elizabeth had sent was not the one Mrs Winterton had owned, she suspected that Lady Elizabeth must still have the original secretary somewhere at Carrington Hall. It was hard to fathom that she would have possessed two near-identical secretaries, but she had certainly bought the one from Woodside, and had also owned the second one. Perhaps she had envied Jeremy's mother her furniture and bought a near-copy of the secretary years ago, and later bought the original to have a pair. Whatever the reason for the duplication, Jane was determined that she would find the Woodside secretary.

The Westerlea Park visitors, which again included Jeremy, would reach Carrington Hall in the afternoon, but Jane decided to be there early enough to make a thorough survey of the principal rooms.

"Must we leave so soon?" her father said plaintively, as she hustled him out of his study just after breakfast. "These orchids will fade so quickly. Let me at least sketch the outlines."

"I want to be sure we get the best rooms," Jane said, inventing ruthlessly.

"Lady Elizabeth will have assigned the rooms already," her father said. "We always get those little upper rooms."

"Perhaps we will be luckier this time," she said. "I have ordered the carriage for eleven."

With one last wistful glance at his little bunch of orchids, already wilting, he did as he was bid.

Lady Elizabeth was not pleased at their early arrival, but with a snap of her fingers, two footmen appeared to carry their bags upstairs.

"You may use the Blue Saloon when you come down," Lady Elizabeth said. "Ring for whatever you want. You will find books and so on there. Forgive me if I have no time to entertain you just yet."

Jane's father was right about the rooms, but he was too gentlemanly to say so, and, to judge from his twinkling eyes, he may have guessed that she had some plan in mind. Jane lost no time in beginning her exploration. After seeing her father ensconced in the saloon with a pot of tea and the newspaper, she said gaily, "I am going to find the gallery. There are one or two portraits I should like another look at."

"Very well, dear," her father said, smiling genially at her.

Jane set off determinedly. Carrington Hall was built on the usual plan of such houses, where the ground floor rooms were expansively high-ceilinged, stiff with marble and gilt and silk hangings and sparkling crystal, their gleaming splendour intended to impress. The floor above, with its state bedrooms, was only marginally less showy, but above that were the more ordinary rooms.

The secretary was too large to fit into any of those rooms, so Jane started with the downstairs rooms. She suspected the library, for that was the logical home for what was a grandiose writing desk, but it could be in a morning room, or even in Lady Elizabeth's bedroom, if she were to emulate Mrs Winterton in every way. Jane could only hope that was not the case, for while she could wander at will through the public rooms and explain it away as being lost, it would be awkward indeed to be caught in her ladyship's bedroom.

From the Blue Saloon, Jane progressed systematically from room to room around the house. Now that she was looking closely at the furniture, she noticed several pieces that were identical to those at Woodside. A sideboard, a gilt-framed mirror, a set of chairs and even a fireplace were all strangely familiar. Lady Elizabeth, it seemed, had copied much from Mrs Winterton.

The dining room and another saloon adjoining it were as busy as a disturbed anthill, with maids and footmen tearing about with plate and covers and candles and chairs. Each one stopped, bowed or curtsied as Jane sailed by, then scurried off again. A butler, or perhaps a very superior footman, asked if he might help her.

"Not in the least," Jane replied cheerfully. "I am admiring the plasterwork."

She had to scratch about for a suitable excuse, for Lady Elizabeth's taste ran to the heavy and overly ornate, with every inch of space on walls or ceiling put to use with a fresco or elaborate carving or flying nymph. There was, however, some plasterwork that was slightly less hideous that she could bear to look at for more than three seconds. It was a odd thing, but the rooms at Westerlea Park, despite being a shade smaller, had a light elegance that made them seem more spacious.

Jane entered a room where the shutters were closed and the furniture was shrouded in holland covers, with several ladders propped against the walls, and a bucket full of paint brushes.

Jane was not fooled. The furniture had not been moved away from the walls, nor had the rugs been rolled up. A fine crystal chandelier was still suspended, uncovered, from the centre of the ceiling. This was not a room in the throes of redecoration. She closed the door behind her, then waited a moment for her eyes to adjust to the darkness. There was enough light for her to make her way across the room and fold away a pair of shutters. Then she looked slowly around the room.

There it was! The secretary's distinctive shape was obvious when one knew what to look for. Swiftly she crossed the room and lifted the holland cover which hid it. It looked in every way identical to the one now sitting at Woodside, except for one small detail — in the centre of the pediment was a clock face.

Triumphantly she let the cover drop. She had found it, despite Lady Elizabeth's attempt to conceal it. Now all that remained was for Jeremy to find all the secret places hidden within, and the remaining five coins. Then they could begin to decipher the code.

~~~~~

Jeremy had arrived in time for a hasty walk in the garden, away from prying eyes or listening ears, so she had been able to tell him of her findings. His eyes gleamed with excitement.

"You are the cleverest woman I ever met," he said, with a smile that made her insides flutter about happily. "It will be awkward, though, at a ball. We cannot wait until everyone is abed. We will have to find an opportunity to sneak away."

We. She glowed with pride at the simple word. *We.* Yes, they were united in the enterprise now.

"Was there a lock to the door?" he went on.

She deflated at once. "Oh. I did not notice," she said in a small voice.

"No matter. I can put a chair under the handle. When the ball is well underway, or perhaps at supper... we will have to snatch a moment. No one will wonder if they see us creep away together. Jane, what a girl you are! Tonight we shall have all the pieces we need to understand Mama's little puzzle."

He squeezed her hand, which was resting on his arm. She turned her face hopefully towards him, but to her disappointment he made no attempt to kiss her.

Dressing for the evening was awkward, for she had no maid with her, and had to wait for Margaret's maid to attend her. The delay meant that the saloon was already crowded when Jane arrived. After greeting Lady Elizabeth, she looked about for Jeremy. He was not hard to find, being almost the tallest man in the room. Only Margaret's husband was taller, but Jeremy was the more imposing, having broad shoulders to match his height.

Perhaps he had been looking out for her, for as soon as she caught sight of him, he smiled, causing her insides to melt. It was disconcerting, this effect he had on her, and the novelty of actually liking a man was most unsettling. But for tonight he was her betrothed, and she could stand by his side and enjoy his company without the least guilt. She resolutely pushed away all thought of the future time, now dangerously close, when he would find the jewels and she would be obliged to release him.

"Are you much of a dancer, Miss Tyrrell?" he said, as soon as she had reached her. "For I must warn you that I am not, so you should be prepared for a great many squashed toes if you insist upon torturing me in the cotillion."

"I do not dance if I can help it," she said.

"Oh, thank goodness," he said, and his relief seemed so genuine and heartfelt that she could not help teasing him just a little.

"Even if you do not dance with me, you will naturally want to do your duty by the young ladies of the neighbourhood. I fear that gentlemen are in short supply."

His face dropped comically. "Oh no! Do not say so, I implore you! Truly, it would be the greatest disservice to the cheerful young ladies I see about me to inflict upon them the pain of a dance with a clodhopping fellow like me. If you do not mean to dance, then I shall cling, limpet-like, to your side, and no one will think the worse of me for displaying such devotion to my betrothed."

"How lily-livered of you, Mr Winterton. But if you are truly such a heavy-footed dancer, you are tempting me to wreak vengeance on every young lady who has ever slighted me, even in the smallest way. I shall insist that you dance with all of them, and bruise their toes as much as you can. That would be a most just and fair punishment, would it not?"

He tucked her arm into his and patted her hand in the most lover-like manner, saying plaintively, "But that would punish *me* even more than your victims, and I am sure you love me too well to be so uncharitable, my very *dear* Miss Tyrrell."

"If you loved *me* half so well as you love yourself, Mr Cowardly Winterton," she retorted, "you would gallantly spring to my defence and positively *want* to step upon their toes. That is how any gentleman would behave."

"Ah, but we established long ago that I am no gentleman," he said at once, breaking into broad northern vernacular. "Nobbut a plain mill manager, me."

She was laughing too much to reply to such nonsense. As they went into dinner arm in arm, she was perfectly aware of the knowing glances cast their way, and the smiles bestowed upon a couple seemingly so much in love. For her part, it was true enough, and he played the lover admirably. If she did not know better, she herself might even be fooled into thinking him well in love with her. Even as she understood the falsity of his actions, she gloried in the touch of his hand on hers, the warmth in his eyes and his light-hearted mood. Dared she call it flirtatious? No one had ever flirted with her before, but this must be what it was like. Whatever it was, it was wonderful, and she knew from these very first moments that the evening would be unforgettable.

Lady Elizabeth was directing the procession to the dining room, but when she ordered Jeremy to escort her niece Julianna, he said cheerfully, "Oh no, Lady Elizabeth, you cannot be so cruel as to separate me from my betrothed."

So it was that Jane had his company all through dinner, and although Lady Elizabeth seated Julianna on his other side, he spoke barely a dozen words to her. All his attention was fixed on Jane, with every consideration for her wants, and keeping her well entertained with his wit. The hour passed with the ladies was as dull as any Jane had ever spent, and she could not wait for the gentlemen to join them, to bask once more in the sunshine of Jeremy's smiles. How hard it would be to let him go! But she pushed that thought away resolutely.

But Lady Elizabeth had her revenge for Jeremy's earlier slight. As soon as the musicians began warming up for the first dance, she came to him and said, "Mr Winterton, you will oblige me by opening the dancing with Julianna."

"I?" he said, unconcealed horror on his face. "Surely there are those of higher rank who—"

"Married," she said succinctly.

And nothing he said could change her mind. Jane had the amusement of discovering that his own description of himself as a clodhopper was not so far short of the mark. Yet she thought his lack of skill was not so much innate as deriving from a lack of proper instruction. He was too large a man ever to be as graceful as some of his brothers-in-law, and perhaps he would never appear to advantage in so testing an arena as Almack's, but he could be taught to acquit himself tolerably. She would give him a few lessons when they were married—

No. How foolish she was getting, to forget. A wave of sorrow swept over her, but she allowed it no more than a moment's existence before she straightened her spine and increased the brightness of her smile. She would *not* repine, like some feeble debutante ruled by her emotions, in alt one minute and full of misery the next. Tonight she would smile and be happy, and worry about tomorrow when it arrived.

Jeremy's humiliation on the dance floor was not repeated. Julianna was returned to her aunt's side to be found a better partner, and no young ladies looked longingly at Jeremy. What was the point in it when his dancing gave his partner nothing but embarrassment? Besides, he was already betrothed, and therefore all interest in Mr Jeremy Winterton as an eligible bachelor had trickled away to nothing. He reclaimed Jane with obvious relief.

"Let us find a quieter spot," he murmured, leading her out of the gallery that served as a ballroom. In moments they had passed around a corner and into a silent corridor. He grabbed a candelabra from a console and turned to Jane with sparkling eyes.

"Now... let us do some exploring. Lead on, Miss Tyrrell."

Another turn took them into a darker passageway, lit only by night lamps. At the far end was the door they sought. With a quick look behind them to be sure they had not been followed, he opened the door, pulled Jane in and hastily shut it behind them.

A bubble of laughter rose in Jane's throat.

An answering laugh met hers. "Is this not fun?" he murmured. "But we must be quick, before we are missed. How long do we have on those candles, do you suppose? Two hours? Let us hope we do not need so long. Where is the secretary?"

She led the way, and flicked up the cover to reveal the monstrous piece of furniture, with the clock at the top. For the first time, she was struck by the oddness of the clock. "Why is there a clock in it?" she said. "There is a clock in the bed, after all, so—"

"A hidden one. This one was always visible," he said. "Clearly visible from the bed, too."

"But—"

"No time," he said. "Talk about it later."

Without another word he set to work, while Jane held the candelabra to light his nimble fingers. The secretary was full of papers and writing materials and ledgers and all sorts of odd objects to be moved aside, but the secret drawers were all in exactly the same place as in the one at Woodside. The only difference was that in this secretary, each concealed drawer hid another drawer deeper inside, and when these were opened, there were the expected three items — a paper, a coin and an item of jewellery in a bag or box. They had extracted the contents of three compartments, and Jeremy had just begun work on the fourth, when there was a soft click from the door.

Jane spun round with a gasp, remembering belatedly that they had intended to jam a chair under the door handle to prevent entry.

Too late now. There in the doorway, her face lit by a large lamp, was Lady Elizabeth. In her other hand she held a pistol.

"Ha! Thieves! I knew it! Prepare to die, you miserable peasants!"

21: *Explanations*

Jane's heart raced, but her mind was clear, every other consideration set aside to focus on this one problem, the elderly woman in full evening dress, diamonds threaded through her grey hair, yet implacably holding a pistol with a terrifyingly steady hand. For a moment, they stood motionless, the three of them, Jane with the candelabra in one hand, Jeremy holding a jewel bag and Lady Elizabeth with the lamp and gun.

Jeremy was the first to move, setting down the jewel bag and placing himself between Jane and the gun. "We are not thieves, Lady Elizabeth. We are your guests."

"Guests? Vipers, more like. Dishonourable scoundrels. Thieves and rogues and reprobates. Is that Jane Tyrrell behind you? I might have guessed as much. I would be justified in shooting you, coming upon you stealing from me like this."

Jane moved out from behind Jeremy. "You cannot shoot someone who holds no weapon," she said, her voice cold with scorn.

"I can do whatever I like," Lady Elizabeth said disdainfully, moving towards them.

"That is murder!" Jane cried, more angry than afraid. Surely this could not be happening? Lady Elizabeth would not truly shoot at them in cold blood — would she?

Lady Elizabeth laughed, a harsh sound in the stillness of the room. Far away, a thread of music could be heard, but here they were a long way from the ballroom and aid. "Who would gainsay me?" Lady Elizabeth said. "I heard a noise here in an unused room, I retrieved a pistol from the library and came here to investigate. Finding burglars on the premises and threatening me, I took action to defend myself. No magistrate would be anything but sympathetic. And then I would be rid of you once and for all, Jeremy."

Jeremy inhaled sharply, but it was Jane who recovered her wits first, anger and shock making her voice harsh. "It was you, then! You tried to kill Jeremy!"

"No," Jeremy said slowly. "That was Percival, I'll wager, but done at your bidding, Lady Elizabeth. That was why you installed him at Lilac Cottage, so he could take pot shots at me every time I rode to Woodside."

"Or strings across the track," Jane said, remembering. "But why? What has Jeremy ever done to hurt you?"

There was a long silence. Lady Elizabeth licked her lips, and the pistol began to droop slightly, as she realised her mistake. Her triumphant gloating had made her careless.

"It was because of what I saw," Jeremy said eventually, taking a step sideways away from Jane. "That was it, wasn't it? Because of that, you persuaded my father to send me away. How pleased you must have been to hear that I was dead. And how disappointed when I returned from the grave. Yet here I am, still alive."

"But not for much longer," she said, then, in agitation, "Stay where you are!"

"Or what? You will shoot me?" Jeremy said, moving again to circle around Lady Elizabeth, and, to Jane's astonishment, he actually laughed. "You do not have the nerve."

Jane saw at once what he was doing. Without any light near him, he was falling further and further into gloom. If Lady Elizabeth tried to shoot him, she could not get a clear shot, and might very well miss. But Jane herself was vulnerable...

Slowly she set the candelabra down on the secretary and took a step away.

"Stop moving!" Lady Elizabeth yelled, swinging the gun round to point directly at Jane. "Stop or I will shoot you."

"Oh, very good, shooting an unarmed female!" Jeremy jeered. "How cowardly. But if you shoot Jane, then I escape and you will hang for murder."

Lady Elizabeth swung round in his direction, cackling with glee. "I am an earl's daughter, you fool. No one will hang me. Everyone will believe me."

"But I will not," said a soft voice from the door.

It was Margaret, a single candle in her hand lighting her face with a delicate glow. Looming behind her was her giant of a husband. Jane heaved a breath of relief, exhaling slowly. Now there were four of them, and the odds were immeasurably improved.

"You!" Lady Elizabeth cried, changing direction again. "Who cares about *you?* Who will take your word against mine?"

"Everyone," her husband said.

"Especially when I tell them all about you," Jeremy said, "and what I saw you do... before."

Margaret gasped, and reached for her husband's hand. "You saw her too?" she said. "You saw her come out of Mama's room the night she died?"

There was an abrupt silence in the room.

"Mama's room?" Jeremy whispered. "She murdered Mama?"

Jane realised then that he had only been guessing when he had talked about seeing Lady Elizabeth. Or perhaps he had seen *something*, but not this dreadful thing that Margaret had seen.

Margaret nodded. "I could never— It was too— I never—"

"It was too horrible to talk about?" Mr Haymer said, squeezing her hand. She nodded. "So you became silent?" Another nod. "I always suspected that something dreadful had befallen you to cause your silence, but I never dreamt... How old were you?"

But she could not speak. It was Jeremy who said, "Sixteen. She was sixteen, and there was no one to tell. Papa would not have listened, and the rest of us... what could we have done? So she kept it all inside her for all these years. Oh, Margaret!"

Lady Elizabeth hissed in anger. Jane jumped, so shocked that she had almost forgotten her. A murderer. Lady Elizabeth was indeed a murderer, had murdered Mrs Winterton in order to marry her lover. And when she thought Jeremy had seen her, she had coldly had him sent away to sea.

"You killed my mother," Jeremy said, his tone dangerously soft. "What was it, an extra dose of laudanum? Something stronger? Or just a pillow over her face?"

The lamp swayed dangerously in Lady Elizabeth's hand, and now the gun was pointing straight at Jeremy. "She was going to die anyway, but I could not wait! Not any longer, not with Julianna—" Even in the shadowy light of the lamp, Jane could see her eyes narrow speculatively. "But it was *not* you. You knew nothing, saw nothing… not that night. It was *you!*"

She spun round to face Margaret, and Jane gasped, seeing the pistol aiming, seeing the fingers poised to fire. But the men were ready. Mr Haymer pushed Margaret sharply aside, so that she stumbled and, with a cry, fell into a pool of darkness. And Jeremy, brave Jeremy, careless of his own safety, jumped forward to grab the pistol.

There was a brief struggle, some gasps, a grunt and then — terrifyingly — a loud bang, and an acrid smell in the air. For one heart-stopping moment, Jane waited in the certainty that Jeremy would fall, blood spilling out of him, his life draining onto Lady Elizabeth's carpet. Then, with a great crack, the chandelier in the centre of the ceiling shivered and shook and fell to the ground, with a tremendous crashing and tinkling and sparkling. Shards of glass from the shattered crystal drops arced through the air and showered to the ground.

And there, in the midst of the debris, pistol in one hand and a sobbing Lady Elizabeth held fast in the other, was the magnificent Jeremy.

"Now we shall find out whether an earl's daughter will hang or not," he said grimly.

~~~~~

Jeremy hurt. He could feel the cuts from a hundred tiny shards of glass on his face and bare hands, like little pinpricks. The hand that grasped Lady Elizabeth's arm burned like fire. He handed the pistol to Haymer, but he did not loosen his grip on Lady Elizabeth. He shook his head, and a shower of glass shards flew about. Lady Elizabeth's face was scored in a dozen places, blood oozing slowly.

She set up a low wail, like a wounded animal, pulling against him, but he would not let go, despite the pain in his hands.

The noise soon drew the curious to the room. A few faces appeared in the door, then footmen bearing candles and lamps, so that the shadows were gradually driven back. More people arrived, amongst them two of the local magistrates, shocked but nodding quickly when Jeremy explained. Lady Elizabeth was led away, still wailing, still bleeding. Jane produced a handkerchief and wiped blood from Jeremy's face. His hand was worse, with deep gouges where slivers of glass had ground into the skin as he held the murderess fast. It was fortunate that the solid part of the chandelier had missed them, otherwise they would both have been dead, no doubt.

Chairs were found for Margaret and Jane, and Jeremy's sisters arrived, all a-twitter. Rosamund for once deferred to her husband, who took charge, barking orders with aristocratic assurance and sending footmen scurrying here and there. In no time, a troop of maids were on their knees with dustpans and brushes, scooping up shattered fragments of the chandelier.

Surreptitiously, Jeremy returned to the secretary and emptied the final compartment of its treasures. They had not been hard to find, once one understood the ingenious mind of the furniture maker. Four secret places, that was all. Perhaps there was a fifth still to be found, but he could not expect it. This secretary was the twin of the one Lady Elizabeth had sent to Woodside, with just two differences — the clock on the front, and the secondary compartments hidden beneath or behind or within the known ones. Now they had eleven coins, that was all, and no jewels, for they were hidden elsewhere. Carefully he tucked the coins and letters into his waistcoat pockets, and concealed the jewels in one bag which he handed discreetly to Jane.

Somewhere, far away, music still played and presumably dancers tripped on, unaware of or uncaring of events in this wing of the house. More people came, gazed wide-eyed into the room, exclaimed at the remnants of the chandelier then went away again.

"If you have found all that is to be found, let us escape from this place," Haymer murmured in Jeremy's ear.

He was happy to agree to it. He and Jane, his sisters and their husbands all slipped quietly away from the room and up back stairs to the bedroom allocated to the Earl of Brackenwood and Annabelle. As the highest ranked of the guests, this was a rather grander affair than the dingy little closet Jeremy had been assigned. He gazed around at the ornate bed with its elaborate curtains, the expensive carpet and gold-framed mirrors and smiled.

"I suppose *you* did not have to wait for your bath water to arrive," he said to Annabelle.

She laughed. "The privileges of rank. Sit, Jeremy. I have some tweezers, so let me clean up that hand of yours. Lucy, if you look in that second drawer down over there, you will find a pot of salve and a handkerchief to bind these cuts."

Jeremy sat, and realised with a shock that he was sitting on a copy of the dressing table stool from Woodside. How much of Woodside had Lady Elizabeth replicated in her jealousy?

Annabelle dabbed at his cuts, making him wince. "But is it true? Lady Elizabeth murdered Mama? And Margaret saw it?"

Margaret said nothing, sitting pale as a wraith on the edge of the bed with her husband's arm protectively around her.

"She saw... something," Jeremy said. "Lady Elizabeth creeping out of Mama's room in the middle of the night, and the next morning Mama was found dead in her bed. It is suggestive, perhaps, but—"

"I always wondered," Rosamund said abruptly. "Not about Lady Elizabeth, I had not the least idea that she was involved, but whether Mama perhaps grew so weary with her illness that she took her own life. She had laudanum that Mr Jackson had prescribed, although she rarely took it. I noticed that the bottle was almost empty, but I could not be sure how much was in it before."

Margaret leaned forward, tried to speak and failed. With a little cry of frustration, she ripped off her glove and grasped her husband's hand. "It was... more than half full. I used to... notice. If Mama... had a bad day, the bottle would be a little emptier. But when she died, it was almost empty and she would never have killed herself, never! I knew it was all Lady Elizabeth's doing."

"But why did you never tell anyone, dearest?" Rosamund said gently, dabbing soothing lotion into Jeremy's hand.

"What could anyone do?" Margaret said. "No one would believe me, not against Lady Elizabeth. Papa would not, certainly, and I was so afraid— I heard them talking once, Papa and Lady Elizabeth, and she said... she said she knew of an asylum, very discreet, that asked no questions. And Papa laughed and said, 'Let us hope it does not come to that.' I knew she would do it, too, if ever any of us crossed her, so I decided to say nothing. That was the only way for us to be safe. And after Jeremy was sent away, I... I could not speak at all. I was... so afraid. For *all* of us."

"But dearest," Haymer said, "could you not have told me?"

Fiercely she shook her head. "Not safe!"

"But you are safe now," Haymer said, holding her close. "No one can hurt you now, or your sisters, for I will not let them."

She closed her eyes, and rested her head on his shoulder with a sigh.

"Oh!" Jeremy said, realising a truth that had long puzzled him. "She thought *I* had seen what she did. That was why... Oh, it makes sense now. I told her that she was a bad woman — that I had seen her at night — so she thought... I meant only that I had seen her leaving Papa's room at night, but she must have supposed that I had seen her leaving Mama's room. *That* was why she wanted me sent away."

"What an evil woman!" Annabelle said. "I hope she *does* hang, frankly. I have never liked her. Such ruthlessness!"

"It is hard to believe," Fanny whispered. "I suppose she must have loved Papa greatly, to have been driven to do such a thing."

"Now, do not make it out to be romantic, Fanny," Rosamund said sharply. "Killing a man's wife so you can have him yourself is not love."

"Oh, no, no, of course not. But she could not have done it for practical reasons, for Papa had no money or title or anything of that nature."

"But I think it *was* practical, in a way," Jeremy said. "She said that she could not wait, because of Julianna, and the timing is right, is it not? She may have been with child and wanted to marry on that account. She would have been... what? A little above forty, then."

"Oh... so Julianna is *Papa's* child!" Rosamund said, eyes widening, looking up from the bandage she was wrapping around Jeremy's hand. "And perhaps Percival and Cressida also. There was always speculation about them. That makes a great deal of sense. She found herself increasing, and wanted to make it legal. And if it had worked and it had been a boy and Jeremy had indeed drowned—"

"Everything would have been different," Lucy said, with a shiver. "Poor Margaret, with such a terrible secret locked up inside you! You could not tell a soul — especially not me, for I would have been sure to blurt it out sooner or later. But the secret was kept, and none of us were dragged away to an asylum, and Jeremy did not die. For myself, I do not care whether Lady Elizabeth hangs or not, for I am glad that all has worked out well and we now know just what happened to Mama. But Jeremy, do you know where the jewels are?"

"Sadly not," he said ruefully. "What is worse, I only have eleven of the twelve coins, so I cannot decipher the code. There is another item of furniture still to be found, I suspect."

"What do you have already?" Rosamund said.

"The washstand, dressing table and stool, armoire and secretary."

Rosamund stared into the distance, remembering. "Ah!" she said at last. "The chair for the secretary."

"Of course!" Jeremy said. "Jane, was the chair sent to Lady Elizabeth with the secretary?"

She sucked in a breath, considering. "Only the secretary, I believe. Yes, I am sure. But I cannot for the life of me remember what happened to the chair. Was it carved the same way as the rest of the suite?"

"It was," said several voices.

"I do not *think* it was sent away," Jane said slowly.

"Then it must be still at Woodside," Jeremy said briskly, gently flexing his bound hand. "In one of the servants' rooms, perhaps. We will look tomorrow... today, I suppose. It must be past midnight. Has the band stopped playing yet, do you suppose? I wonder if there is anything left in the supper room. I am starving."

"What an excellent idea," Haymer said. "Some ham would set me up nicely, I do believe."

Margaret laughed suddenly, her face lightening as if the sun had emerged from a cloud. "You are always hungry, husband."

"There is a lot of him to fill with food," Rosamund said, her severe expression softening. "And Jeremy, too. For myself, I could not eat a thing, but a glass of brandy would not go amiss."

"I will bring something," her husband said, "but I do not think the ladies should go downstairs again tonight. Nor should Jeremy be seen in public, for the carriages will not be called for until dawn and he will not wish to be exposed to the speculation of the curious. Not with blood on his neckcloth, at least."

"Is there so?" Jeremy said, turning to a tall glass to check. An array of small cuts to his face, which had bled copiously onto his neckcloth despite Jane's efforts with the handkerchief. "Oh, Lord, look at the state of me. My valet will be so cross."

"Whatever does that matter?" Jane said impatiently.

"My dear Miss Tyrrell, you know not what you say," said Ferdy in shocked tones. "A disgruntled valet can make one's life utterly miserable. Tell your man to talk to mine, Jeremy. Wrackham has a wonderful way with stains, positively inspired. I once had a mark on a waistcoat, and not the least idea what it was or how I had come by it, and none of the usual methods worked, but Wrackham—"

"Really, Ferdy!" Rosamund cried. "Here we are in the midst of a crisis and all you care about is the removal of stains."

Ferdy raised one carefully shaped eyebrow, although his eyes twinkled. "What can possibly be of more importance than one's appearance? Even if one is embroiled in a crisis, one must look one's best, surely? For think how dreadful it would have been if

Jeremy had been shot at with his neckcloth askew. The shame, Rosamund, the shame!"

"Oh, for Heaven's sake!" she said laughing. "Such nonsense you do talk, Ferdy. Go away and fill Mel with ham, if such a thing is possible. Go on, now, and leave the rest of us in peace."

But there was to be no peace for Jeremy that night, for almost as soon as his brothers-in-law had left in search of food and drink, a footman arrived with a terse message. *'Mr Claremont's compliments, but he would be greatly obliged if Mr Winterton could attend him in the library.'*

Jeremy sighed. Claremont was one of the local magistrates, so the summons was not a huge surprise, although Jeremy had hoped it could have waited until the following day. The high excitement of the night's adventures was wearing off, leaving him exhausted and anxious for his bed. But such a summons could not be ignored.

The library was so immaculately tidy that Jeremy suspected it was little used. No book dared to disrupt the perfect symmetry of the cabinets, and not a single volume was cast carelessly on a table. No newspapers were casually abandoned on chairs, and every table was precisely aligned.

From one corner lit by candelabras, a beacon of light in the dimly-lit room, Claremont rose to greet him, his manner courteous but not affable. Behind him sat Tyrrell, who was not a magistrate, but might be supposed to have an interest in matters, the elder Mr Martin from the bank who was another magistrate presumably, and Dr Frank, the lugubrious physician. All of them had been guests, and still wore full evening dress. Jeremy was very conscious of his dishevelled and blood-spattered appearance.

And they were hostile, there was no doubt about it. These were people who had known Lady Elizabeth for a great many years, and even if they did not particularly like her, that was a long way from accepting her as a murderess. Her concocted story about hearing a burglar might seem all too plausible to these men, and there was no proof of anything. Whereas he was a relative newcomer to Brinshire, born to the life of a gentleman but raised very differently. Jeremy was aware of a prickle of unease. It would be so easy for these men to make assumptions, and then perhaps Jeremy would be the one behind bars. He would have to be very careful.

"Ah, Winterton," Claremont said. "Good of you to join us. Please sit. You will appreciate that it would be helpful to us if you could explain a few matters. You are not severely injured? The gun did not—?"

"No, no. Merely the effects of broken glass from the chandelier dislodged by Lady Elizabeth's shot. What do you wish to know?" He hesitated, but this was not the time to be timid or to hide behind the screen of civility. Nothing had ever been achieved by being submissive. He took a deep breath, then plunged on. "Shall we start with how Lady Elizabeth tried to kill me tonight? Or shall we look further back, to the several attempts on my life she has instigated since my return to Brinshire? Or do you wish to go right back to the beginning, and how she killed my mother?"

For an instant their eyes widened in unconcealed shock. He had surprised them, then. But almost instantaneously the mask of politeness descended.

"We are listening," Claremont said neutrally, and Jeremy knew that he had lost them.

There was one more throw of the dice. "You may ask Percival Drake, if you do not believe me. Ask him about the two occasions when he shot at me, and hit me, once."

"He will deny any such thing," Claremont said tersely.

"Of course he will. But you are all of you capable of judging a man, not by his words, but by how he behaves. Drake will deny it, certainly, but he will not look you in the eye when he does it."

There was a long, long silence. The others exchanged glances, and Jeremy held his breath.

It was Tyrrell who spoke. "I should like to hear what Mr Drake has to say," he said in his gentle way.

Claremont nodded, and went off to find a footman. Jeremy was left wondering at the oddity of the situation. His future hung in the balance, and the only man who could save him, it seemed, was the man who had already tried to kill him.

22: Honesty

They waited. The walls were so thick that no sound penetrated from outside the library, or perhaps the indefatigable orchestra had finally ground to a halt. Claremont sat with arms folded, face impenetrable. Mr Martin, the elderly banker, tapped his fingers restlessly on his plump knees, a sheen of sweat betraying his discomfort with the situation. Dr Frank stood beside the fireplace, for all the world as if he were admiring the fire screen there. Tyrrell leaned back in his chair, legs neatly crossed at the ankles. His face was as benign as ever, watching Jeremy with a slight smile on his face, as if he were reading Jeremy's innermost thoughts and finding them amusing.

Jeremy himself was calm. He had been in difficult confrontations before, although previously the matter at issue had involved a beam engine or a shipment of cotton. He knew how to read the atmosphere in the room, and how to judge the men he was dealing with. Claremont was the one he would have to convince, he knew. Martin would follow his lead, and the doctor would restrict himself to medical advice. Tyrrell — he was perhaps the only one Jeremy could not read at all. He seemed completely at his ease, as if this were just another of the unending series of jests life provided to divert him, yet there was surely a more serious man inside? He was a mystery.

The door opened and Percival Drake crept into the room, such a picture of abject misery that Jeremy almost pitied him. Beside him, the surprising sight of Miss Alice Grantley, the vicar's daughter. Jeremy had not noticed her at dinner or at the ball, but then she was not the type to attract notice. She was a dab of a female, short and rather stout, with the sort of homely face that was destined for a lifetime of spinsterhood, doing good works about the parish and caring for her parents in genteel poverty as they declined in years. Yet there was a determined set to her mouth now, and she held Drake firmly by the hand. It was hard to say, as they walked into the room, which of them was leading the other.

"Miss Grantley?" Claremont said. "I do not think—"

"Mr Drake wishes me to be here," she said composedly.

"I do, yes," Drake said, licking his lips. "I should like her to be here."

"Very well. Frank, bring a chair for Miss Grantley, will you. Drake, you may sit— Oh, very well. That will do, I suppose. Now, Drake, Winterton has made some very serious accusations against Lady Elizabeth and yourself, and has suggested we apply to you for verification. He has said that you shot at him and—"

"It is all true!" Drake blurted, with a quick look at Miss Grantley, who nodded her head, as if in approval. "I *did* shoot him... twice, and hit him once, and tied a rope across the track he often rode down, and looked at the ladders in the tower at St Mark's to see if— But I never did anything about that, Winterton, I swear! I have not tampered with them at all. Aunt Elizabeth asked me to go there, and I went because... because she does *harass* a fellow, but I did nothing, I swear, because I had met Alice by then — Miss Grantley, I mean — and she made me realise... You see... I want to do the *right* thing and be a good person and be worthy and... and so on. Did I do it right, Alice?"

"You have done well, Percival," she said. "But you must beg Mr Winterton's forgiveness also."

"Oh yes! I forgot that part! I am so very sorry, Winterton. Pray forgive me."

Jeremy saw his own astonishment reflected in the others. That Percival Drake, of all people, could be brought to redemption by the love of a good woman was not a possibility that had for one moment occurred to him. That Alice Grantley had seen something worth redeeming was even more remarkable. For a moment he was speechless.

Tyrrell, however, was not. Without stirring from his relaxed posture, he said amiably, "I am quite certain you had a reason for what you did, Mr Drake. We should be interested to hear it."

"My aunt made me do it," he said at once.

"No, dear," Miss Grantley said firmly. "She gave you reasons why she wished you to do such things, but you yourself chose to do them."

"That is so," he said, disconsolately. "I was very wicked. Aunt Lizzie gave me her reasons for wanting Jeremy dead, and I... I did what she wanted, and I wish I had not, now!" he cried in sudden passion. "I wish she had never told me anything about it. If only I had been resolute and told her... told her to make her peace with Winterton and—"

"With God," Miss Grantley said. "She should make her peace with God first, and with Mr Winterton after."

"And her reasons?" Tyrrell persisted. "What were Lady Elizabeth's reasons for wanting Jeremy dead?"

Drake licked his lips again, and looked at Miss Grantley for inspiration. She nodded again and squeezed his hand. He took a deep breath and then it all came out in a rush "Aunt Lizzie told me that she had killed Winterton's mother and Winterton knew of it and could get her hanged and so he had to die."

The silence in the room was so profound that Jeremy wondered if they had all stopped breathing. Into that silence, Miss Grantley leaned from her chair and patted Drake on the shoulder.

"Well done, Percival," she said. "That is the worst over."

"Have I done the right thing, Alice?" he said in plaintive tones.

"Honesty is always the right thing," she said, with absolute certainty.

If Jeremy had hoped that would be the end of the matter, he was to be disappointed. There were hours of talk before every last detail had been winkled out of Drake. After that, Jeremy had told what had happened that evening, with Haymer to support his version of events. No one liked to involve the ladies, but Haymer was the son of a viscount and a clergyman, and known as an honest man. His calm description of all that he had witnessed was accepted by all those present. Jeremy said nothing of missing jewels, only that Lady Elizabeth had sent the wrong secretary and that he and Jane were looking for the correct one. Tyrrell was the only one who commented on that, saying in his gently amused way, "How careless of her to muddle the secretaries."

Then there were a couple of hours of fitful sleep before Jeremy was required to drag himself from his bed to observe as Claremont questioned Lady Elizabeth. By that time, the Brinchester constables had arrived and the whole day was consumed by questions and explanations. She denied everything, of course. The heat of confrontation had given way to the cold calculation of odds. Deny it, and it became her word against Percival's and Margaret's, and with no clear evidence. She was an earl's daughter, her bearing regally haughty — who would dare to accuse her?

In the end, it was the taciturn Dr Frank who set the seal on Lady Elizabeth's fate. The constables had gone off to inspect the music room and the twisted remains of the chandelier, and Claremont, Tyrrell, Martin, Frank and Jeremy were having a much-needed restorative brandy when Tyrrell said, "What doctor attended Mrs Winterton? Was it you, Frank?"

"Not I. Jackson was alive then. He lived in Frickham, so he attended at Woodside, although I was called to Westerlea Park sometimes. He came to see me after Anne Winterton's death, to discuss his concerns. A quantity of laudanum gone, and should he mention it? The lady had been ill for some time, but her death was not imminent, he had thought. We agreed that any suggestion of self-immolation could only add to the distress of the family. However, he left his notes to me in his will, so I have his records in his own hand, should this case come before a judge."

"Ah," was all Claremont said.

~~~~~

Jane did not like leaving Jeremy and her father at Carrington Hall, not until Lady Elizabeth was safely behind bars and could do no more harm, but the two were, for once, united against her.

"You can do nothing useful here," Jeremy said.

"I should like it very much if you ensure we have a good dinner on the table tonight," her father said, which made her smile. "If you look in at Greenford's as you pass, you may pick up something tasty for me to carve."

"Will you dine with us?" she asked Jeremy, and was rewarded with one of his heart-twisting smiles.

"I should like that very much."

She diverted her eyes, hoping that her pleasure in his words was not too obvious. "Then I shall go to the poulterer instead, and see if I can get a turkey for you," she said.

"How charming," her father said. "You are paying attention to your future husband's preferences."

That made her blush, naturally, but Jeremy only smiled the more and raised her hand to his lips, not relinquishing his hold until she was obliged to move away from him. She loved such moments, but there was grief below the happiness, too. One day soon, she would buy a turkey and there would be no Jeremy to share it with.

She travelled back to Frickham with Margaret, Fanny and Ferdy, with the turkey at her feet, wrapped in brown paper and string. Margaret's husband and several of the others had stayed behind to offer what help they could, and there was an air of solemnity in the carriage. Fanny cried a little, and Margaret was still pale and silent, but Ferdy, bless him, kept up a little patter of meaningless conversation as they drove along, which did more to lift Jane's spirits than she might have expected. Ferdy might look like a coxcomb, but he had a kind heart and when he said, "Jeremy will be home soon, you will see," she believed him absolutely.

And so it was. By the time she had unpacked and changed into a fresh gown and given her orders in the kitchen and talked to the gardeners about some hedges to be trimmed, the day was almost gone. She had just settled down with her account books when the carriage was heard on the drive, and both her father and Jeremy descended.

"I thought it would be pleasant if Mr Winterton were to stay here for tonight," her father said. "No point going to and from between here and Westerlea Park. That will not inconvenience you, Jane, I imagine?"

A burst of pleasure assailed her — not just a whole evening in his company, but breakfast, too! And perhaps he would not rush away tomorrow... Another memory to warm the lonely years to come. "Oh... not in the least."

As her father hastened away inside, Jeremy tucked her arm in his and whispered, "What, no acid response, Miss Hedgehog? I can usually rely on your sharp tongue."

She was too happy to do more than laugh and say equably, "Not today, Mr Nonsense."

"How disappointing. When I am so elated at surviving my brush with death, too. I can usually depend upon my prickly Jane to bring me down to earth with a bump."

My prickly Jane. His Jane. Oh, if only she were! "I should like to do it, to be sure, but I find myself somewhat elated at your survival, too, and have not the heart to chide you. But this respite is likely to be brief, so enjoy it while you can."

They were half way up the steps to the front door, but he paused and gazed at her with such intensity that her heart turned somersaults.

"Jane—" he began, in such a serious manner that she grew hot and cold, and the thought flew into her mind that he was about to make a declaration of some sort. They were so close that he might almost kiss her—

Her father's voice made them both jump. "What are you about, Winterton, to keep Jane standing outside like that? There will be tea in my room."

With a sigh, she called back, "Coming, Papa."

It was, as she had anticipated, a wonderful evening, just the three of them. The turkey was cooked to perfection, the conversation at table was sparkling and the gentlemen did not linger over the port. After their tea, they played Speculation with great enjoyment for an hour or more.

"You young people will forgive an old man, I am sure," her father said at length, "but the last two days have quite worn me out. I shall have some tea in my room and then go early to my bed. I shall lock the front door, but do not forget to douse the candles before you go up, Jane."

Jane waited until they were alone, then whispered, "What coins did the secretary provide?"

He laughed. "Ah, straight to the point. That is what I like about you, Jane. Any other young lady, finding herself alone with her betrothed, would take advantage of the opportunity to steal a kiss or two, but Miss Practical would like to get on with finding the jewels, thank you very much."

Oh, to steal kisses from him! She coloured, but answered composedly. "And Mr Flirt would allow himself to be distracted. We have little enough opportunity to consider the puzzle your mama has set, and until we can solve it, we are both trapped in this fake betrothal, and you cannot marry your Miss Ridwell."

"She is my Miss Ridwell no longer," he said casually, emptying his waistcoat pockets of coins and laying them out on the table. "Now, these are the newest ones, so—"

"What do you mean?" Jane blurted out. "Has something happened in London?"

He looked up quickly. "Oh — you do not know. It seems that the beautiful Miss Ridwell has admirers."

"Other admirers, you mean? Apart from you?"

He looked almost bewildered for a moment, as if he had forgotten that he had an understanding with the lady. "Other admirers, yes. Serious admirers, with marriage in mind and far more eligible than me."

"And you do not mind?" It was bewildering, his casual acceptance of the loss of his future wife.

"Odd as it may seem, I do not. It was never a love match, you know."

"You only wanted her mill, was that it? The lady herself was of no account, and now that you will have your own house, her mill is of no importance. How... how *despicable* to use people so, as you are using me, to your own ends." She could feel anger rising, and had to breathe deeply to compose herself.

"Who is using whom?" he said, and she could not but admit that she was using him just as much as he was using her.

But then he smiled. Ah, that smile, that made her feel as shy and uncertain as a schoolroom miss... the smile that could melt away every drop of anger against him. She could drown in that smile. No matter how much he ruffled her sensibilities, he could always dissolve her irritation in a moment, with that teasing smile. She could not be cross with him when he made her feel... what did he make her feel? Like a woman, a beautiful, desirable woman. He was a natural flirt, she knew that, but no matter how often she reminded herself of it, still she could not help herself from responding to him. She could not resist him.

So she smiled back at him, and pointed to the coins laid out on the table. "Which are the newest ones... these?"

"Mmm. Twenty past two — that one is easy. But the rest... is this five minutes past four, or four minutes past five? What about seven and eight? Or eleven and five? There is no system to it."

"Of course there is," Jane said. "Your mama created this puzzle for you to solve, therefore you *can* solve it."

"Now you sound like Margaret," he said, with another little smile. "Dear Margaret! Such confidence in me."

"Why should she not have confidence in you?" Jane said. "The man who can make those intricate puzzle boxes can hardly be stumped by a few numbers. Have you written them all out in sequence, as you did before?"

"I have." He rummaged in another pocket and pulled out a folded slip of paper.

"Ah, how pleasant to have proper pockets," Jane murmured. "A reticule is nothing like as useful."

"But you have your chatelaine to carry your keys and watch and... well, whatever else ladies need to carry," he said.

"Where they are constantly in view, and get in the way whenever one walks," she said at once. "Believe me, pockets are better. In fact, men's clothing is much more sensible all round. You may stride about unimpeded by skirts, and need not ride side-saddle or wear silly feathers on your hats. I wish I had been born male."

"You must be alone in that wish," he said.

She looked up at him sharply, but there was no trace of levity in his manner. There was that intensity again, that made her wonder... but no, she must be mistaken. "Not... not alone," she said, her voice not quite level. "Papa wished I had been male too."

"Fathers always say they want sons, but when they have them, they despise them thoroughly," he said. "Whereas they love their daughters unquestioningly."

She could not mistake the bitterness in his tone. "Perhaps fathers have greater expectations for their sons," she said gently. "They must hope for an heir who will grow to be just like his papa, so that any deviation from that standard is seen as a failure."

"And nothing is expected of daughters, is that it?" he said, tipping his head on one side, assessingly.

"Except that they marry, and will be no longer a burden."

"Your father does not see you as a burden," he said gently.

"But he wants me to marry. That is the only proper path for a woman to follow, you see. Anything else is a failure."

Jeremy reached across the table and put his hand over hers. The warmth of it, the touch of him, burned through her as hot as fire. "Your father has talked to me of his own happy marriage. He wants you to experience that too, that is all."

"He has told you this?"

"More than once, when we sat over the port without your presence. He will be very lonely without you, but he truly feels you would be better off married. As do I, Jane. Beneath those sharp prickles of yours is a warm-hearted woman with more than enough love inside to share with a husband. Do not be afraid to let love grow."

She could scarcely breathe. Her hands trembled, so she detached them from his hold, and tucked them out of sight in her lap. "And what about you?" she said unsteadily. "You hide behind all that teasing and joking, but perhaps there is more to you beneath the foolery."

He laughed, and leaned back in his chair, breaking the mood as abruptly as a snuffed candle. "Ah, that is my Jane, always ready to turn my words against me."

The moment of intimacy was gone, and she could not say whether she was sorry or not.

23: *True Accounts*

Jane gazed unseeingly at the numbers.

'1, 2, 3, 4, 4, 5, 5, 6, 6, 7, 8, 8, 10, 10, 11, 12, 13, 15, 20, 30, 43, 57'

There ought to be a pattern to them, but her tired brain refused to focus on the problem. Long after she should have been fast asleep, she sat in bed, squinting at the paper by the light of a single wavering candle, and thought of *him*. His laughing eyes, his teasing voice, the way his hair flopped over his forehead and his smile... especially his smile.

Yet how foolish to be reduced to jelly by such superficialities. If she were truly to weigh Jeremy as a potential husband, she should consider his income, his respectability and his standing in society. Those were matters of relevance to the case, not the way his eyes crinkled at the corners or the way her stomach flip-flopped about when he looked at her with that intense gaze she had seen several times now. Or the way he kissed her...

She closed her eyes, and gave a little groan. Oh, that kiss! The desire to experience it once more was ever-present, gnawing at her insides like a living creature. She cared nothing for income or respectability if Jeremy would only kiss her again — just once more and then she would be happy. Except that she would never be happy again. Some time soon, whether he found the jewels or not, this false hope of an engagement would be at an end and she would fall into the torment of living the rest of her life without him.

The poets talked of the pain of unrequited love, but she had always laughed at such idiocy. Who could be so silly as to weep and wail in such a cause? Well, she hoped she would not weep and wail, but the pain was real enough, and the only cure for it was Jeremy, and his gentle teasing. And his kisses.

With a sigh, she leaned across to blow out the candle, and the list of numbers fell under her eye again.

"Oh... how odd..."

~~~~~

Jeremy was dragged from the depths of sleep by Hooper.

"Urgh. Go away." He put a pillow over his head, but Hooper firmly removed it.

"Miss Tyrrell told me to wake you. Said to tell you it's about the numbers, sir."

Jeremy sat up abruptly. "Is it, by Jove! Well, then, tell her I shall be down directly."

"Very good, sir. Shall you require my assistance in dressing?"

"I am perfectly capable of shaving myself, you know. Begone."

"Very well, sir, if you insist. You will find Miss Tyrrell in her office."

Jeremy dressed with indecent speed, and then positively flew down the stairs. Jane's office was the room he had known as the parlour, the place where Papa had dealt with his business visitors, people too grand to use the servants' entrance and not grand enough to be entertained in the drawing room. Then, it had been strewn with the account books and papers relating to the estate, with dark wood panelling and an array of paintings too dull to be wanted elsewhere. Now, it was a neat but very feminine boudoir, with pale walls and curtains, and vases of roses everywhere.

"How pretty you have made this room," he said, the numbers momentarily forgotten.

She coloured charmingly. "Why, thank you! I like it, too. It cheers me up when I have to do the accounts. But look…" She held out the list of numbers. "What is missing? Oh, never mind, I will tell you — there is no number nine."

"What do you mean, there is no number nine? Oh." He looked again at the numbers. *'1, 2, 3, 4, 4, 5, 5, 6, 6, 7, 8, 8, 10, 10, 11, 12, 13, 15, 20, 30, 43, 57'* "I understand you. There is no number nine, but I do not see the significance of that."

"There are so many low numbers," she said. "We know there are twelve coins, so I think they are numbered from one to twelve. The nine is the missing one, the one we think must be in the chair. So all we have to do is to sort them into the right order, and then the numbers on the *other* sides of the coins will be the code to be solved."

"But there are duplicates," he said. "There are two fours, two fives… six, eight, ten… I do not see how we can work it out. Besides, until we find the chair, we do not have the complete code."

"True," she said, "but I have made some progress there too. I have been looking through the records from years ago to see if the chair was ever sold, but I cannot find that it was. That means it must still be here at Woodside, somewhere. Probably in one of the maid's rooms."

"It would be just our luck if it has been chopped up for firewood," he said.

"Oh no, for all those pieces were in excellent condition, too good to be turned into firewood."

"And you are quite sure it has not been given away?" he said.

"Oh, certainly, for I record everything coming into the estate or leaving it."

"You keep all the detailed records, then?" he said, suddenly interested. "Your father showed me his account book once, but it was just a quarterly summary. I should be interested to see the true accounts."

She grew still, looking at him with oddly wide eyes. "What makes you think Papa's are not true accounts?"

All his senses suddenly twitched into alertness. What an odd question to ask! He had never suspected that they were not, in fact, true, but now he wondered. However, there was no advantage to pressing the point at this moment. "Why, nothing at all," he said, with what he hoped was an air of innocence. "It was an infelicitous form of words. I beg your pardon. I meant only that I should be interested to see the detailed accounts, but it was an idle whim. No doubt your records of linen sent to the laundry woman and shutters mended by the carpenter would be too tedious for words."

She looked at him thoughtfully, and he had the feeling that she was wavering between two courses of action. But Jane was never indecisive, so after a moment she rose, and shook out her skirts. "You may judge for yourself, if you wish. The ledgers are all in order on this shelf here. Woodside will be yours soon enough, so you have the right to examine the books. Here—" She pulled a handful seemingly at random, and deposited them on the desk in front of him. "Enjoy my laundry lists. I am going to talk to Havelock, to see if she remembers the chair. If it has gone into the servants' quarters, she will know of it."

And with a whisk of her skirts, she was gone. How strange! It was almost as if she did not want to watch him looking through the ledgers. Or perhaps she thought that he would be too polite to avail himself of the opportunity. But his curiosity was aroused now, so he waited until she had left the room and then flicked through one of the books. It was, as she had said, filled with laundry lists and orders to the coal merchant or chandler or grocer. No detail was too small. But on quarter days, there were details of the rents paid to the estate by the tenants, and these he read with interest. And then, because he had a suspicious mind, he pulled some of the more recent ledgers from the shelf, books that, he noted, she had not offered him. And as he read, he smiled.

By the time she returned, he had tidied the ledgers away neatly on their shelf and was standing gazing out at the shrubs that bordered the drive.

"Havelock remembers the chair, but is sure that it is not in the basement or any of the servants' rooms. She thinks it may be in the attic with the other unwanted items. Shall we go and look?"

"Certainly," he replied, turning to face her. "But first you can tell me what you have done with the rents from Wood End, Whitehill and Charford Minor."

She paled. "What... what do you mean?"

"Exactly what I say," he said, keeping his tone mild. In truth, he rather enjoyed her discomfiture. It was not often he had the better of her, and he could not suppress a twinge of triumph. "I intend no censure, for I am sure there is a very good reason why those properties do not appear on the accounts your father sees, but it would interest me to know what that reason is."

She exhaled sharply. "Well! There is no hiding anything from you, is there?"

"You gave me your permission to look at the books."

With a quick laugh, she said, "True enough, but I expected you to flick through one or two and get bored. How on earth did you find out my secret so quickly?"

"I mentioned to you that I have seen your father's summarised accounts, which showed an income of eight hundred and fifty pounds a year, entirely consistent with your style of living. Yet Mr Henry Martin of Martin's bank estimated the estate's income as twice that, based on his knowledge of land values and transactions. Mr Plumphett, the Winterton solicitor, said much the same — *a valuable property'*, he called it. That made me wonder greatly. Was your father's agent pocketing a fortune in undeclared rents? But the matter had slipped my mind until you looked so conscious just now. Since the opportunity presented itself, I compared the earlier books with one or two of the later ones, and of course there is a huge difference in the rents received, which your father knows nothing about."

"I meant no harm," she said, flopping down onto a chair. "In the early days, Papa bought several parcels of land that had previously belonged to Woodside, and that improved our income beyond our immediate needs. Unfortunately, all the decisions and shifting about of money made him excessively anxious. He has no head for business matters, and it was making him very unhappy. So I suggested that he leave all such matters to me, and give the solicitor the authority to act on his behalf according to my instructions. Papa agreed to it, and so it was done. An account was set up where the excess income could be placed each quarter, the solicitor continued to buy this or that property or patch of woodland, the rents increased and we are now very comfortably off. We do not need much to live on, so the account continues to grow. And to prevent Papa from fretting, I told him nothing about the new additions and the increased rents. So long as he has his flowers to paint and enough tea to drink and someone to play cribbage or piquet or whist with of an evening, he is perfectly content."

"But why do you live like paupers, when you are so well off?" Jeremy said. "You could afford to keep a full staff and live like a lady, instead of running around in an apron all day."

"Because Papa will leave that account to me when he dies," she said, with ferocious intensity. "That is all I will have to live on, other than the charity of my sisters' husbands. If you do not acquire it, Woodside will be left to a distant cousin we have never seen. Property is for men, not women."

Jeremy could not miss the note of bitterness in her voice. "What would you have done with Woodside if it were left to you?" he said gently. "You could hardly live here all alone, or even with a companion. I can understand your father's reasoning, and why he is so keen for us to marry. That way, you get to keep Woodside after all, and yet are respectably settled, with your own establishment and a position in society. Marriage is a far, far better option for a woman than spinsterhood."

He expected her to argue with him, but she did not, merely nodding sorrowfully. It was dreadful to see her so cowed. To distract her, he said cheerfully, "Well, you must have a tidy sum squirrelled away in that account by now, so even if we cannot find the jewels, you will not be destitute."

"It is not enough, however," she said sadly. "Better than nothing — a *great* deal better than nothing, but not enough. Well, shall we make a start on the attics?"

Much of the morning drifted away rootling around amongst the forgotten detritus of generations, most of it older than Jeremy. They were called downstairs several times, first for breakfast, and thereafter to receive several of Jeremy's sisters, who were making a final round of calls before departing for their own homes in a few days. Jeremy admitted he would be sorry to see them all go, especially Margaret, who had nursed him after his injury and then stayed on waiting for Mel to return from London.

"You will be glad to get home after all this time," Jeremy said to her. "It has been months."

"Three months," Margaret said. "I cannot wait to see the boys again. Fortunately, Mel's father and brother write constantly with every detail of what they are up to, so we have not been anxious about them."

"You are talking properly, Margaret," Jeremy said with a smile. "And Mel is all the way across the room."

She laughed. "The dreadful secret I kept is secret no longer, and Lady Elizabeth's wickedness is known to the world. I am not afraid any more, brother. Is it not wonderful? Even here at Woodside the words behave themselves and emerge from my mouth in an orderly fashion."

"That makes me very happy," Jeremy said. "But what of Percival Drake? We have heard nothing about him."

"The vicar sent word that he is not at all pleased about an alliance with Drake, but if he proves himself truly reformed for a year at least, then he will not stand in the way of his daughter's happiness. I very much fear that you will have to accustom yourself to having him as a neighbour. He seems settled at Lilac Cottage."

Margaret threw a glance at Mr Tyrrell, chatting to Mel, but said nothing more. She knew perfectly well that Jeremy's betrothal to Jane was a sham and might not last very much longer. And if Jeremy were to succeed in his hunt for the jewels, what then would become of the Tyrrells? But there was no point in worrying about such matters. First he had to find the jewels, and then the dice would fall where they may. But a little spike of sorrow reminded Jeremy that he was not as indifferent towards Jane as he had once been, and would miss her greatly when she was no longer around.

Last of all, Rosamund and Robin arrived with news from Brinchester. Lady Elizabeth was locked up in the courthouse there until the next quarter session, although in very commodious accommodation, after which she would be sent to Stafford to await the arrival of the assizes judges.

"But I doubt they will hang her," Robin said. "Not an earl's daughter."

"It should not matter who she is," Jane said with passion. "Whether she is the daughter of an earl or of a ditch-digger, she should receive the same impartial hearing of the case, and a punishment appropriate to the crime committed. Let us not forget that it is not only Mrs Winterton who was the object of her wickedness, but she also tried to have Jeremy killed, and almost succeeded. She should not be spared the noose merely because of an accident of birth."

"Well said," Jeremy murmured, although Robin looked a little affronted at so robust an attitude.

Rosamund laughed, however, glancing from Jane to Jeremy and back again. "You two are *so* well suited. Have you fixed a date yet?" Then she laughed again.

Jeremy laughed too, quite unperturbed by her gentle teasing, but Jane coloured up at once. To cover her confusion, he asked about one of the children, who had been unwell, and the moment passed. Before long, Rosamund and Robin rose to leave.

"Are you staying at Woodside tonight, Jeremy?" she said, with amusement in her eyes.

"I have no idea — am I invited, Jane?"

"Of course, if you can spare him to us, Rosamund. Papa does so like having a piquet player of his own ability."

"I am sure he does," Rosamund said, laughing again. "Enjoy your piquet, Jeremy. Your room is ready for you at the Hall whenever you are released from card duties."

And chuckling gently, she and her husband made their farewells. Jeremy could not quite share her amusement. She anticipated that the fake betrothal would soon become a real one, but Jeremy could not be so sanguine. If he could dare to hope—! And those flashes he had seen in Jane's eyes when he had almost believed— No, it was impossible. She had softened towards him, certainly, but beneath the apparent friendliness he knew that she still despised him thoroughly. Nor was he entirely sure of his own heart. He liked Jane very well, and enjoyed her company, but was that enough? Was that love? He could not say.

Jeremy and Jane returned to the attics, but there was no sign of the chair. The following day was spent in checking every room in the house methodically, and then the basement and finally, in desperation, Jane examined even the servants' rooms. But it was no use — the chair was nowhere to be found.

After this, Jeremy felt it expedient to return to Westerlea Hall, only to encounter Rosamund's knowing smiles again. "How was the piquet?" she said innocently.

"Very pleasant, although Mr Tyrrell is a far better player than I am," he said with an attempt at insouciance, but Rosamund only laughed the more.

The next day was Sunday, but on Monday morning Jeremy decided visit Woodside again, to see if Jane could come up with any more ideas for the numbers. Eleven coins might, perhaps, be enough to work out the pattern. It was too fine a day to be spent entirely indoors, however, so he sent for his horse and made a long circuit round High Frickham and back past Wood End, riding slowly back along the lane to Woodside, for although he was tolerably certain there would be no more attempts on his life, he could not quite bring himself to gallop along the very route where a rope had once been stretched between the trees.

When he reached the stables, Timpson was nowhere to be seen, so he took the horse into the stable himself and set about unsaddling and settling the beast. When he had finished, he set off for the scullery door into the house, a route which took him past Timpson's small cottage. There was the man himself, sitting on a chair in the sun, mending harness and enjoying a quiet smoke and a chat with his wife.

Sitting on a chair... one with an unusually high, carved back.

Jeremy executed an abrupt turn and made for the cottage. "Good day to you, Mrs Timpson. Timpson."

Mrs Timpson curtsied, and Timpson leapt to his feet, whisking his pipe from his mouth.

"Oh, you here, sir? And with your horse? Let me see to it—"

"No need, Timpson, he is safely stowed. I am intrigued by your chair, for it is a particularly fine one."

"Aye, so it is, sir. My predecessor, Mr McKinnon, was troubled with piles, sir, so Mrs Havelock very kindly gave him this chair, being as how it has such a soft cushion. She never did ask for it back, sir. Did I do wrong to keep it?"

"I told you it belonged to the 'ouse, Timpson," his wife said. "But would you listen to your better 'alf? No, you would not! 'e never does, sir. I told 'im, I did."

"Now, then, woman—" Timpson began, but Jeremy cut him short.

"No need to fall out over it. However, Miss Tyrrell was wondering where it had got to, so I believe she would like to see it. You will not mind if I borrow it, Timpson? I promise I shall return it to you, or one of equivalent comfort."

Timpson made no demur, and Mrs Timpson curtsied three more times, so Jeremy presumed he had her assent also and carried the chair in triumph into the house.

24: The Numbers

The final coin was a nine, just as Jane had predicted, with a two on the reverse. She was too generous to gloat over him, however.

"Now we have the full set," she said excitedly, her eyes afire. "What is the final sequence?"

He had carried the chair upstairs to his mama's bedroom, and placed it in front of the opened secretary, where it had always stood. It was the wrong secretary, and the chair was faded from sunshine, but that did not matter now. Only the numbers mattered. With a pencil, he added the last two numbers to the paper.

'1, 2, 2, 3, 4, 4, 5, 5, 6, 6, 7, 8, 8, 9, 10, 10, 11, 12, 13, 15, 20, 30, 43, 57'

"We have the nine, but now we have another duplicate, in the twos," he said. "How are we to make sense of it?"

"It is to do with the clock, that we are agreed upon," she said. "These high numbers — forty three, fifty seven — can only be minutes. There are twelve coins, and I believe that they are numbered from one to twelve, and only the numbers on the reverse are significant."

"Ah, so every coin with a high number on it, a number above twelve, that must be the reverse."

Deftly he sorted the coins and extracted the six high numbers — *'13, 15, 20, 30, 43, 57'*.

"So that gives us... let me see..." He flipped them over. "Oh."

"All the even numbers up to twelve," she said. "So now we have to guess where the rest fit in."

"But it is easy," he said, in rising excitement. "Look — five and four, but we already have coin number four, so this must be number five. And here is one... and seven... and five... three... nine, of course. And there... eleven fits in there. We have one to twelve, so all we need to do is to flip them again... Oh."

Now the numbers read — *'10, 20, 6, 15, 4, 43, 8, 13, 2, 30, 5, 57'*

Jeremy's mind exploded in exhilaration. "Oh yes!"

"You understand it?" she said, bewildered. "Ten past what? Twenty past what? I cannot make sense of it."

Without saying a word, he rearranged the line of coins into a column of pairs, and smiled at her, waiting for her to see it. She did not disappoint him. After no more than three seconds, her face lit up.

"Twenty past ten! Fifteen minutes past six! We have to set the hands on the clock!"

As one, they scrambled onto the bed, and Jeremy yanked open the doors that concealed the clock. The hands had stopped not long after the last time they had examined it, the time when they had watched the automaton and his lewd mannequins. The time when he had kissed her...

He had to take a deep breath, to shut out the memories. Now of all times was not the moment to be distracted by thoughts of kissing Jane, no matter how desirable she was, no matter how soft and warm her lips...

Concentrate. The clock, yes, that was it, focus on the clock.

"I have forgotten the numbers," he confessed.

Back to the secretary, to write them down in their pairs. Then to the clock once more, with no thought whatsoever of Jane's shapely ankles, and the feel of her in his arms, or—

Concentrate.

"It must be like an automaton, in some way," he said. "We have to set the clock to trigger… something."

"You do not know how?"

"No. But let me disconnect the hands first. Now, let me try the first time…" Twenty past ten. He wound the hands with the key, and set the time. "Hmm, now what?"

"Connect the hands again?" she suggested.

"Oh. Let me try." He did so, and deep within the clock, something made a deep clunking noise. "Oh. That is… interesting."

"Now disconnect, and set the next time… fifteen minutes past six."

Another clunk.

With trembling hands, Jeremy set the clock for each time in the sequence. Forty three minutes past four. Thirteen minutes after eight. Thirty minutes past two. And finally, fifty seven minutes after five.

And with a final clunk, the face of the clock opened an inch.

"Oh, a *safe!*" Jeremy breathed, gently opening the door to its fullest extent.

It was indeed a safe, with solid metal walls, and there within were four boxes. Nestled on top was a sheet of paper, written in Mama's spidery hand.

'Dear Jeremy, Well done! For I know it will be you, the cleverest, the most ingenious of all my children, who will solve my little puzzle. After my cousins both died there was no one who knew the secret, no one I could trust with it, but I was not worried, for I knew you would work it out. Did you enjoy it? I hope you did, and that my inheritance will now be used for its intended purpose, to dowry the girls and allow them to marry where they wish, with love and respect, as I did. Give my love to all your sisters, and especially to your papa. Tell him I hope he will be happy with Elizabeth, as he was happy with me, for a while. With all my heart, I wish you nothing but joy in your lives. Your loving mother, Anne Winterton.'

Jeremy could scarcely read the words for the tears in his eyes.

"What a wonderful woman she must have been," Jane said softly. "But look... they are all yours now."

They were his. Finally! He could hardly believe it. Reaching into the huge hollow behind the clock face, Jeremy pulled out the first box and opened it. Jane gasped. A parure of ten pieces, with mostly emeralds, set about with diamonds. The second box was another parure, this time of rubies. The third was nothing but diamonds, not set, but sparkling like fire in the low light from the window as Jane ran them through her fingers. And then the final box—

Jane uttered a little squeal.

"The Tilford Sapphires," Jeremy said, awed, picking up the necklace and moving it this way and that to admire it. In the centre, a single perfect stone of such magnificence that he could scarcely breathe. "Turn around," he said, with a grin.

"What? Oh no, no, no, Jeremy! I cannot wear them."

"They are meant to be worn. Turn around."

She did, bending her head forward so that he could fasten the clasp. Then she rushed to view her reflection in the looking glass.

His breath caught at the sight of her. Never had she looked more dignified. "They suit you," he said, and she burst out laughing.

"Really, Jeremy, they would suit a duchess, perhaps, but not Miss Jane Tyrrell of Woodside. Oh, but thank you a thousand times for letting me share this moment with you. I can hardly believe that you have done it at last."

"*We* have done it," he said, spinning her round to face him and catching hold of her hands. "We did this *together*, you and I, and it was as much your doing as mine."

"Yes! We did it!" she cried, her face alight with joy. "We solved the puzzle and found the jewels! *We* did it — you and I!"

Laughter bubbled up in him like champagne, overflowing into exuberance. "You are an extraordinary woman, Jane Tyrrell," he cried, picking her up by the waist, and spinning her round. "I cannot imagine why you never married before this…" Another spin. "…for any man would be proud to call you his wife."

Then, because he could not resist, he pulled her into his arms and kissed her long and passionately, and just as before, her ardour matched his own. He held her tight, allowing joy to fizz inside him, gradually spreading and filling him with warmth until his own self faded to nothing. All he was aware of was Jane held tight against him, so perfectly right in his arms, her lips giving him such sweetness that he felt his knees weaken. He wished they could stay thus for ever, in that strange place outside the everyday world where the only truth was this delicious love.

Love…

Was this what love was? Or were they just caught up in the excitement of the moment, and buoyed by their triumph? Did she still despise him, yet was woman enough to enjoy kissing him despite that? He did not care if she hated him, if she could not wait to be free again, so long as for this one glorious moment he could hold her and touch her and kiss her...

Her father's voice could be heard calling plaintively from the bottom of the stairs.

"Jane? Are you coming down for tea?"

They broke apart, but even then he could not quite release her. He laughed and kissed her forehead, and then, briefly, her lips again. Then, with a sigh, he let her go.

~~~~~

Jane dressed with unusual care that evening. The gown was an old one, but she had a pretty shawl to wear with it, and she allowed Lottie to take some trouble with her hair. Jane and her father were to entertain all Jeremy's sisters and their husbands at Woodside. The next morning they would begin their journeys home, Annabelle and Allan to Cheshire, Lucy and Leo, Margaret and Mel to Shropshire, and Fanny and Ferdy all the way to Yorkshire. Only Rosamund and Robin would remain in Brinshire.

And Jeremy. His home very soon now would be at Woodside. Once their betrothal was at an end, he would be able to buy it from her father and then it would be his, as it should be. Jane's share of the spoils would be ten percent of the total value of the jewels, an arrangement agreed privately between the two of them, for she felt no need to bother her father with such details.

Nothing had yet been said about the betrothal, but Jane knew what she had to do. All the happiness of finding the jewels and then that kiss — that glorious, unforgettable kiss — had drained away and now she felt sick. As she bathed ready for the evening, as she put on her best evening gown in honour of the celebratory nature of the occasion, as she sat restlessly while Lottie fiddled with her hair, she wished she could simply curl up in bed and never have to see Jeremy again.

A knock on the door made her jump. "Are you decent?" Jeremy's head appeared round the door. "Ah, good. I have something for you, Jane, if you will permit."

It was one of the twelve trumpery pieces that had been concealed with each coin. When he opened the box to reveal the necklace, beautiful in its simplicity, she laughed. "The chalcedony."

"It is such a good match for your eyes, and I thought... a gift to celebrate? You will not object?"

Lottie giggled, no doubt thinking it a charming gesture from a man to his betrothed. Jane's stomach lurched unhappily. "I do not think..."

"It is nothing... the merest trifle. The rest will go to my sisters, but this one is so perfect for you."

His sincerity was obvious, and she had not the heart to refuse, bending her head for the second time that day to allow him to place jewellery about her neck. The merest trifle... there was nothing in the gift to distress her. It was the touch of his fingers on her bare skin that made her shrivel inside, his gentleness, the slightest warmth of his breath on her neck, and the light in his eyes as he looked at her afterwards.

"There! Is she not beautiful, Lottie?"

"Oh yes, sir! Them stones is so pretty. Haven't I always said your neck is your best feature, Miss Jane? You should wear such necklaces more often."

"So she should," Jeremy said, and even Jane, whose experience of such things was limited, could see the admiration in his look.

When he and Lottie had gone, she sat for a moment to compose herself. What did it mean? Why did he look at her that way, and kiss her with such passion? What was it he had said? *'Any man would be proud to call you his wife.'* Did he mean it? Did he mean that *he* would be proud to call her his wife?

Was it possible?

She could not breathe. Perhaps everything she wanted was hers for the taking. All she had to do was to ask him if he meant what he said. Dare she put it to the test? If she could find the courage to do it, she would know the answer instantly from his face.

So, in spite of the horrid sick feeling in her stomach, she straightened her spine, raised her chin and went downstairs to face the evening.

They were all in high spirits — the Westerlea Park family and Jeremy and her father. All but Jane, who smiled and laughed and admired the glittering jewels laid out on a table in the drawing room, while inside her stomach churned. Before they went in to dinner, Jeremy hid the four sets of valuable jewels away in the clock safe again, although the lesser jewels were left out for the sisters to try on and choose from. For all that Jeremy described them as 'trumpery', they were of fine workmanship. Jane's chalcedony necklace felt comfortingly solid and heavy around her neck.

There was champagne served at dinner, and much merriment. Jane's father was as relaxed as she had seen him since Mama had died, and yet he would soon sell his home and have nowhere to live. If he was concerned at the prospect, no hint of it showed in his manner. Jane herself could not even begin to consider such practicalities until she knew precisely how matters stood with Jeremy. It may be that tomorrow they would walk down to the church to see about the banns, or… perhaps they would not. Her future was a blank page, for Jeremy to write upon. Would she be Mrs Jeremy Winterton, or would she dwindle into bitter spinsterhood?

She made a soft sound, somewhere between a gasp and a sob, unnoticed by most of the guests. But Jeremy noticed. He stretched his hand across to grasp hers where it lay in her lap.

"Poor Jane! It is always so — after a great excitement there is an equally great loss of energy. I once took part in a horse race up on the moors near Branton, and I was so agitated beforehand and yet calm of mind, if that makes sense. But after it was all over, I felt as exhausted as if I had done the galloping, and not the horse. You will be better in the morning."

He squeezed her hand and smiled at her. Although her rational mind told her that the touch of his hand could not heal her, nor could a mere smile settle her stomach, nevertheless she felt better after that, and managed to eat a little and take some wine. But he watched her for the rest of the meal, spoke to her with unusual gentleness, and went out of his way to pass interesting dishes to her and ensure her glass was topped up.

The gentlemen did not linger over their port, but neither did they re-join the ladies at once. Instead, many feet and male voices could be heard tramping up the stairs and along the corridor to Mrs Winterton's room. At intervals thereafter gales of laughter floated downstairs, as Jeremy demonstrated the fascinating action of the automaton figures around the clock. Jane was put to the blush trying to explain to the ladies just what it was that was so amusing. After some considerable time, the gentlemen made their way back to the drawing room, all of them with wide grins on their faces. Even Jane's father was laughing, a little pink about the cheeks.

Then there was tea and music and cards and more tea, and some of the guests were beginning to eye the clock and talk about sending for the carriages, and still Jane had not asked Jeremy her question. But eventually, as the last of the card tables began to break up, and the conversation became general, Jane found herself standing a little apart from the company, with Jeremy beside her, his gaze fixed on Leo and Ferdy, who were having a mock argument.

"Will you be here tomorrow?" she said, wondering if perhaps she might wait for a better time.

"Tomorrow? Hmm... well, I shall have to see off the family, you know, for who knows when we might meet again? And then I shall ride over to Brinchester, to talk to the bank and the solicitor... so much to organise. I should like to look in at the rectory, as well, to reassure Everton and Kit that I am still alive and will be back at work on the clock before too long. But I shall call on you later this week, if you like." He laughed at some jest of Leo's, then went on, still without looking at her, "Would that be acceptable to you? Friday, perhaps?"

Friday. She could not wait for Friday, she had to know at once or she would run mad.

"Did you mean what you said?" she blurted, knowing, even as she said the words, what the answer would be.

"Hmm? What did I say?"

"That any man would be proud to have me as his wife," she said quietly. "Would *you* be proud?"

His head spun round, eyes wide, and there in his face was the answer she had dreaded — there was no gladness, no surge of pleasure at her words, only shock. His words had been nothing but the excitement of the moment.

But he was a gentleman, and mastered his surprise at once. He even managed to instil his polite "Of course" with some enthusiasm. But she knew.

"I see," she said, without expression, as her world crashed about her ears. Then she fixed a false smile onto her face and walked across the room to join the others, trying to pretend that her heart was not breaking.

25: A Journey To Staffordshire

Jeremy could not sleep. Three times he climbed into bed, lay down and closed his eyes. Three times he gave it up, relit his candle and paced back and forth about the room. What did she mean by her words? Did she care what he thought of her? Did she now want to marry him? He could hardly believe it, and yet... those kisses... Lord, those kisses! Such unsuspected ardour beneath the prickly exterior, and yet he had never for one moment thought that there was more to it than momentary pleasure on her part.

Was it possible that she had grown to like him... or more than like, perhaps? He dared not hope, but joy flared in him every time the thought rose in his mind. Was it love, this flicker of hope? He had long since come to appreciate Jane as the woman whose company he most enjoyed. She was everything he could admire — her quick mind, her practicality, even her caustic words. And above all else, her honesty. There was no mealy-mouthed blandness with Jane. A man could never be bored with such a woman. She would always take him by surprise, as she had tonight.

She had asked him if he had meant what he had said, if he would be proud to call her his wife. For a moment he had been too stunned to answer her, too astonished at the glorious possibility her question put into his head. He had never dared to consider it, but now... Yet when he had given his answer, her face had closed up and she had walked away from him. What did *that* mean? Did she want him or not? He could not make her out at all.

As the first grey light of dawn began to creep into the room, he determined to put it to the test. First thing in the morning, before anything else — even before breakfast, if he managed to get up so early — he would go to Woodside and lay his heart open before her. He would explain, as he should have done long since, how he had grown to esteem her — no, to *love* her, how her prickly hedgehog had somehow crept into his heart. He would offer her a true betrothal and marriage, and she could accept him or reject him, as she pleased. At least then he would know the truth.

And then, finally, he got back into bed and slept.

The sun was well up before he woke, to find Hooper creeping round the room, replacing the washing water long since grown cold.

"What time is it, Hooper?"

"Ah, awake at last, sir? It is a little after eleven o'clock."

"Eleven... *eleven!* Good God, I had meant to be up hours ago."

"You should have left instructions if you wanted waking, sir," Hooper said huffily. "I would have woken you if—"

"Yes, yes, but never mind that. Not that coat, Hooper, the new one, and pantaloons today, not breeches."

"Oh. Something special occurring, sir?"

"No. Yes... maybe. Just... just get on with it, like a good fellow, and don't ask questions."

Jeremy was dressed in twenty minutes, start to finish, allowing Hooper to manage the neckcloth without any interference. Then he strode downstairs, where he discovered it had come on to rain. This caused an irritating delay while he tracked down first Robin and then Rosamund to request the use of their carriage, then waited for the horses to be put to.

Eventually he was on his way for the short journey to Woodside, trying to curb his impatience and failing miserably. How would she respond? With some acid comment, no doubt. He smiled at the thought of it. Yes, she would chaff him for his foolishness in not realising sooner how indispensable she was to his happiness. Or perhaps she would blush, as she did so charmingly whenever he paid her compliments. She was so little used to compliments, they always took her by surprise. If he were very unlucky, she might be out somewhere in the village, and then he would have to wait for her to return. Or he could go and meet her, perhaps... no, not in this rain, now lashing the carriage windows. And she would not be out in such weather either. She would be at home, apron on, no doubt. That made him smile again. Well, she need never wear an apron again.

The carriage stopped, and Jeremy leapt down and took the steps to the front door two at a time. He knocked, then rang the bell, then knocked again. He was just about to knock once more when the door creaked open. Jeremy smiled, but it was not Jane's face which peered out at him.

"Betsy?" he said. "Where is your mistress today?"

"Gone, sir."

"Gone where? Into the village? To Brinchester? Out visiting?"

"No, sir. Gone away in the carriage with Lottie, and their luggage on the back."

Jeremy could not take it in. Why would she go away, and without even a farewell?

"Left a letter for you, sir, with the master."

Tyrrell was painting, but he wiped his brush and took off his painting apron as Jeremy was shown in. "Winterton, my good fellow. Will you have some tea? Or something stronger, perhaps?"

"Do I need it?" Jeremy said, with a quick smile, puzzled but not alarmed, for Tyrrell's manner was not such as to give him cause for concern.

"That is not for me to say," Tyrrell said, handing him a neatly folded and sealed letter. "Read it, and then decide."

Jeremy broke the seal, and unfolded the letter.

'Mr Winterton, Pray forgive me for the formality of a letter, but as there is rain coming in from the west, I thought it best not to delay my departure. As your object is now achieved, our arrangement is at an end and I set you free to marry a wife better suited to you than I. If you go directly to London, you may not be too late to secure Miss Ridwell's affections once and for all, as you are very well qualified to do. It is my hope that she will love Woodside as much as I have done these past years. I am going to my sister's house for a little while, and shall take the opportunity to look about me for a suitable residence for Papa and myself near to my sisters. I trust that you will not object to Papa's presence for a while longer, but it will be most comfortable for him if he is not obliged to move until I have established a new home for us. Be assured that he will be gone from Woodside before you bring your bride there. As soon as I am settled, I shall send word. Yours in gratitude for your many kindnesses, Jane Tyrrell.'

Jeremy huffed in exasperation. "You know the substance of this, I take it? That she puts an end to our engagement?"

"That is not unexpected, surely?" Tyrrell said in his mild way. "Now that you have found the jewels—"

"Oh, she told you all that, did she?" Jeremy said, with some heat. Were there no secrets between father and daughter? What else might she have shared over the teacups?

"Not a word, I assure you, but it was not hard to guess, although I am not sure what Jane got from the arrangement."

"Ten per cent," Jeremy said, his anger dissipating. "Her little nest egg to ensure her independence after your death."

Tyrrell smiled and shook his head. "Ah, Jane! Foolish girl! Far better to marry than to be perpetually alone, no matter how rich. She always said that no one would ever want to marry her, except from pity, but it seems to me that she was wrong about that. What do you say, Winterton?"

Jeremy smiled ruefully. "I say that you see a great deal more than one might suppose, sir. Indeed I came here to try if I might transform our false betrothal into a real one, but I am forestalled. Now I shall have to find her at her sister's house. Which sister is she staying with?"

"She did not say."

"The Devil she did not! And you never thought to ask, I suppose?"

Tyrrell merely smiled again. "If Jane wishes me to know of a thing, then she tells me outright," he said gently. "If she does not, then no amount of questioning will reveal the answer. She will write when she has anything to tell me."

Jeremy could not deny the truth of it. "Then I must visit each sister in turn and make enquiries," he said, with a sigh. "Will you oblige me by furnishing their directions, if you would be so good?"

Tyrrell hesitated. "You do not feel, then, that Jane has already answered the question you intend to ask?"

That gave Jeremy pause. "I think… I have not yet asked her the *right* question, and so she cannot have given me an answer. Besides, this is no answer!" he said with sudden heat, waving his letter. "She cannot mean it! I do not accept it! When she understands how much my feelings have changed, she will think differently, I am certain of it."

Raising one eyebrow, Tyrrell murmured, "I wish you good fortune with that, Mr Winterton. I have always wanted her to marry, you know. Marriage to the right person is the greatest joy on earth, and I have always wanted my daughters — *all* my daughters — to experience that joy too, and have done whatever I could to lead them to that end. Jane has a mind of her own and will not be led, but perhaps she can yet be persuaded."

With quick steps, he went to his writing desk, and picked up a large sheet of paper, almost completely covered in his neat script. "I have anticipated your request, as you can see," he said gently. "I have given very precise directions, firstly to Charlotte's house, from there to Helena's, and finally, if needed, to Ruth's."

Jeremy scanned the paper. "Great Heavens, Stafford! I must get away. You will forgive me if—"

"Of course, of course! Go at once, and may God speed your journey and favour your endeavours. Go now!"

Jeremy went, but it was no trivial matter to set off for Staffordshire. He had to return the carriage to Westerlea Park, order his horse and Hooper's to be saddled, change into riding clothes and pack enough for a night or two away. This sent Hooper into a spin.

"Evening dress, sir? Or attire for morning calls? How many neckcloths shall you need? What if we run out?"

"Then I shall send you out to obtain more, Hooper. Jump to it, man, for we must be on the road within the hour."

"Within the hour?" Hooper gulped. "But—"

"No buts! I shall not turn you off if you forget anything, you have my word, but do get on with it and don't just stand there wringing your hands. I have a lady to win."

"Oh, a *romance!*" Hooper cried, clapping his hands delightedly. "I knew you was up to something, sir, when you asked for pantaloons and hessians, for you never— Yes, yes, sir! At once, sir!"

It was not quite within the hour, but eventually the horses were brought round, a couple of saddle bags strapped on, Rosamund and Robin waved them off, the two eldest children waved from an upper window and then at last they were away.

Mr Tyrrell's instructions were very precise, describing the most direct roads and tracks, and giving the names of the inns, and which were recommended for fresh horses, a decent meal or an overnight stay. They dined early, for Jeremy had missed breakfast, and then pressed on until the sky was reddening and dusk was almost upon them. They snatched a few hours of rest at another inn, where Jeremy slept not a wink, before leaving as soon as there was light enough to see by.

A view of the town of Stafford opened up before them in the distance, but their first destination was a few miles short of the town itself. In a small but pleasant village was situated the home of Mr and Mrs Henry Trimnell, a modest villa in a row of similar villas, each surrounded by a neat square containing lawns, a shrubbery and a kitchen garden. Much as Jeremy wished to ascertain at once whether Jane was within, politeness dictated that he wait at least until the occupants might be dressed before descending upon them unannounced. He passed by the house, therefore, and cooled his heels at the village's only inn for an hour, sipping indifferent coffee while Hooper polished off his own breakfast and Jeremy's too.

When he could wait no longer, they mounted their horses again and rode the short distance to the Trimnell's house. The door was answered by a very young housekeeper, or perhaps she was merely a parlour maid, it was hard to be sure, who showed him at once into the family's breakfast parlour. There sat husband and wife, with two small children, faces smeared with butter. The wife had a baby on her knee, and her swelling stomach suggested that she would soon be adding to the number of faces to be smeared with butter. The husband rose politely, frowning at the two older children until they did likewise.

Jeremy stopped on the threshold. "Oh... I beg your pardon... I do not mean to—"

"Oh, do come in!" the wife answered. Charlotte, according to Tyrrell's notes. "How exciting, to have a breakfast visitor! Please, sit down. Penny, lay another place for Mr—?"

"Winterton. Jeremy Winterton. Thank you but—"

"Oh, you are Jane's young man, are you not? Is there word? Has something happened? Oh, not Papa! Pray tell me that—"

"Everyone is well," Jeremy said hastily. "Mr Tyrrell was in perfect health when I left him at Woodside yesterday. As for Jane... is she here?"

"Here? Why, no! Were you expecting her to be? Oh, please, do sit down, Mr Winterton. You must have some chocolate. It is Henry's mother's recipe, and it is quite the finest chocolate ever made, I assure you. Henry adores it, do you not, my dear?"

Her husband ignored her. "Mr Winterton, is there something amiss? What makes you suspect Miss Tyrrell may be here?"

"She... she left me a note to that effect, that she would be staying with one of her sisters but she did not say which one."

Charlotte gurgled with laughter. "How like her! And so you have come galloping after her — how romantic! But she is not here, Mr Winterton. She must be with Helena or Ruth. Probably Helena, for she has the largest house, you know. Far more room for visitors. Yes, she will be at Helena's, although what she is doing gallivanting off and leaving you and Papa all alone I cannot imagine. But there, Jane was always perverse."

"Have you quarrelled, Winterton?" her husband said.

"Not at all," Jeremy said stiffly, not quite liking this interrogation. "But she left abruptly, and... I am concerned about her."

"No need to worry about Jane," Charlotte said gaily. "She always does what she wants to do, so you may as well get used to it, Mr Winterton. Timmy, stop that at once! No, I mean it, that is a very bad thing to do to your sister. Look what a mess you are making of— Timmy!"

"Obey your mama, Timothy," said his father in a tone that brooked no argument, and the child subsided at once, chastened. "Do you know where Helena lives, Winterton?"

"Mr Tyrrell gave me excellent directions, sir. If you will excuse me, madam..."

"Oh, are you leaving so soon? But you have not even tasted your chocolate... Timmy! You are a very bad boy. Do stop this instant."

Her voice receded as Trimnell escorted Jeremy back to the door, where Hooper waited stoically with the horses. "Straight on along this road, then turn left at the second mile stone. I hope you find her safe and well, Winterton."

"Thank you, Trimnell, but I have no reason to imagine otherwise."

"Perhaps not, but for all my wife's reassurances, I have never known Jane to go away before except with her father, and that rarely. They both like to stay close to home. I will not ask what may have driven her to take such a step, but I hope things can be patched up, for both your sakes. She can be thoughtless at times, and thinks nothing of the inconvenience and worry she may be causing others, not to mention the possible damage to her reputation."

"Her reputation is not at risk," Jeremy said with a smile. "She travelled in her own carriage, with her maid and her own coachman, to stay with her sister. What could be more proper?"

"She should have a man to protect her honour," he said brusquely. "I hope when you have her safely wed, Winterton, you will stamp out these odd starts of hers. Her father is as eccentric as she is, but it reflects badly on the rest of the family when she is allowed to run wild, and scamper here and there all alone, and you are obliged to chase after her in great haste. I hope you find her soon before there is much talk. Good day to you."

And with such cheery farewells ringing in his ears, Jeremy mounted his horse, and rode on, pondering the question of stamping out Jane's odd starts. Was that not precisely why she attracted him so, because he could never predict what she would do next? She might shock or alarm or infuriate him, but she would never for one moment bore him. He could not quite see the point of marrying a woman because of her eccentricity and then spending the rest of your life trying to make her conform.

Jeremy was in no danger of losing his way from one sister to another, for Helena Mayling lived in the very next village, a slightly larger version of Charlotte's place of residence. The house was, indeed, a much larger affair, very modern and plain, but with a pleasing symmetry about it. The grounds were not extensive enough to permit the sort of sweeping driveway affected by the great houses, such that every bend afforded a new vista, but the owners had done their best to emulate such a setting in a small way. So the drive wound back and forth, back and forth, edged with saplings no more than six feet tall. One day, perhaps in fifty years time, it would be an impressive approach to the house, giving tantalising glimpses between the trees of the glories of the landscaping — the ponds to one side of the house, and on the other, several artificial hills topped with newly-built ruined temples and towers, but Jeremy was in no mood to appreciate the whimsy of an artistically sinuous drive, not when he was in such a hurry.

A butler and footman emerged to receive them, and Jeremy was whisked into the house. The entrance hall was designed in the style of a medieval great hall, with wood panels, an arched roof and a massive stone fireplace large enough to burn a tree, with the family crest emblazoned on the lintel. Jeremy handed in his card, and then waited, examining the portraits lining the walls. He was not a connoisseur of art, but he suspected the paintings had less artistic merit than their ornately gold-decorated frames.

"Mr Winterton? It is not bad news, I hope?" A tall, elegantly-dressed woman approached, accompanied by a man already grey and a little stooped.

"Be assured that everyone is well," he said at once. "My mission is less distressing. I know that Jane is staying with one or other of her sisters, but she neglected to tell me which one. I have already called on Mrs Trimnell and—"

"No, she is not there, at least, if she is, she must have arrived at a very late hour, for we dined there last night. Nor is she here, so I must conclude that she is with Ruth, although why she would crowd in with *her* when we have far more room... That is very odd, but then Jane is the oddest creature, and she is getting more peculiar with every year that passes. One never knows what she will do next. This betrothal, for instance—"

Her husband coughed discreetly, and with a hint of pink in her cheeks she abandoned that train of thought.

"Well, she must be at Ruth's and that is all there is to it. Let me just get my bonnet and I will come with you."

"You are very good, but there is no need for you to overset all your plans for the day," Jeremy said, with a thin smile.

"Oh, it is not the least trouble in the world. Just give me a moment—"

"Mrs Mayling," her elderly husband said gently, "Mr Winterton's business with his betrothed is no concern of yours."

"But I should so like to see Jane."

"You shall do so, just as soon as she informs you of her visit to Mrs Featherstone. Until then, you must not intrude. We are to dine with the Featherstones tomorrow night, and we shall hear all the news then."

And with that she had to be satisfied.

Jeremy rode off again, sweltering now under the summer sun, but his spirits had lifted with each negative he encountered. There were only three sisters and if Jane were not to be found at the first two, then she must be at the third, and it would not now be long before he saw her again.

His spirits sank again as soon as he saw the house. It was not even as large as Lilac Cottage, and he could not imagine it had more than three bedrooms at most. There were chickens outside the front door, and the whole of one side of the garden was given over to the growing of vegetables. At the back was an orchard of elderly, misshapen fruit trees with a pony grazing beneath. The lines of small garments hung between the trees suggested the presence of a baby in the house.

However unpromising the house, his knock on the door was answered by a smartly dressed manservant, and he was shown into a neat little parlour with surprisingly fine furnishings. Mr and Mrs Featherstone, when they appeared, were dressed in the first stare of fashion, a very young couple who hardly looked old enough to be out in society, still less married with a child. Yes, perhaps Jane had felt more comfortable hiding away with her youngest sister, instead of the suffocating Helena or the chaos of Charlotte's family.

"Mr Winterton! How lovely! What a delightful surprise," they said, almost in unison, then laughed at themselves.

"Oh, let me speak first, Malcolm. Please sit down, Mr Winterton. Have you brought us news? A letter, perhaps, from Papa or Jane?"

Jeremy could feel his face fall. "No, I had hoped to find Jane here with you."

"Jane? Here? Oh no, she is not. Why we have not seen her since... oh, when you were first betrothed. No, she has not been here. Oh dear."

Jeremy's legs gave way and he collapsed into a chair.

Now what was he to do?

26: Hallow End

The Featherstones bustled about finding Madeira, and then, with a murmur of, "No, no, look how pale he is!", a glass of brandy. Jeremy drank it obediently, but he was not sure he felt much better.

"Have you had any breakfast?" Ruth said, bending over him to feel his forehead.

He shook his head, realising for the first time that he had eaten nothing since three o'clock the day before.

"Well then, that is the first matter to be attended to," she said, and her practical tone reminded him so forcibly of Jane that for a moment he was swept with grief. Wherever was she? Somewhere she did not wish to be found, that much was clear. Where she did not wish *him* to find her. Nothing could speak more clearly of her utter rejection of him.

Ruth and Malcolm led him, unprotesting, through the cottage to the kitchen at the back, sat him down at the kitchen table, and fed him ham and eggs and bread fresh from the oven, as the servants came and went around them. Then, scooping up a whole pound cake that was cooling on a windowsill, and an unopened bottle of Madeira, they repaired back to the parlour, where Ruth sat on the floor, knees up to her chin, eating the cake, while the two men shared the Madeira. The whole time, they asked no questions, and Jeremy was grateful for their forbearance.

He could not work out how he felt. Miserable, certainly. Hot, yes, and how bedraggled he must be after his long ride without bathing or much rest. He leaned his head against the chair back and closed his eyes. How comfortable to be out of the saddle, his stomach pleasantly full and a glass of Madeira in his hand. Dimly, he was aware of a carriage on the lane outside, and Ruth and Malcolm murmuring together. Then there was silence...

It was dark when he woke, the air heavy and stuffy. He shifted position, and at once a face appeared, bending over him. His heart leapt for a moment, then sagged again... it was not her, not his Jane.

"Are you feeling a little better?" Jane's sister. The young, practical one. Ruth, that was it. "There is water here for you, straight from the well. Will you drink a little?"

He drank, and it was cool against his dry throat. He drank again, deeply.

"Thank you. I beg your pardon... I just... nodded off."

"You must have been exhausted. We drew the curtains and left you to sleep it off, but I am afraid that Charlotte and Helena are here, and I shall not be able to keep them out for much longer."

He laughed and said, "By all means bring them in."

She whisked out of the room, and moments later they all trooped in, Charlotte, Helena and Ruth, with Ruth's husband behind them grimacing in silent sympathy at Jeremy. The ladies pulled up chairs and disposed themselves in a semi-circle around Jeremy, who felt even more dishevelled in the face of their dainty femininity. They were all ribbons and lace and artfully curled hair, and they made him ache for Jane's simple cotton gowns and aprons, with her hair pulled into a purposeful knot.

"Poor Mr Winterton," one of them said.

"How tired you must be, after so much travelling."

"Are you feeling a little more the thing now?"

It was true that he felt a lot better for some sleep and food, but there was still a great emptiness inside him that only one person could fill.

"I do not know how to find Jane," he said, wondering if he sounded too much like a petulant child whose toy has been taken away.

"She will have gone to Molly Inkerby," Charlotte said. "They were such good friends."

"That was years ago," Helena said. "I am sure Jane has not seen her since her marriage. What about Lucy... oh, what was her name?"

"Thomas," Ruth said. "She died two... no, three years ago."

"Oh!" the others said, in disappointed unison. "Then where—?"

"What did she actually say?" Ruth said. "Her exact words."

Jeremy pulled out the letter, and silently handed it over. The three sisters bent over it, reading portions to each other, commenting, asking no questions for what was there to ask? It was all laid out on the page in Jane's neat script. *'Our arrangement is at an end... I set you free... until I have established a new home for us... before you bring your bride there... I set you free... I set you free...'* The words buzzed in his head like angry bees.

"'*I am going to my sister's house*'," Helena said. "That is clear enough, yet she did not do so. Can something have happened to her, do you suppose? Some accident?"

"Oh no!" Charlotte said in distress. "Perhaps there was some mishap with the carriage."

Jeremy's insides lurched momentarily. Was it possible that—?

"There would have been word sent, if so," Ruth's husband said, and Jeremy was grateful for his calm good sense. "The roads are good, the weather has been benign, and there is sufficient traffic about that an overturned carriage would be noticed."

"Then where can she possibly be?" Ruth said. "Her words are clear enough, yet she did not come to any of her sisters."

For an instant, something tugged at Jeremy's memory, then drifted away like perfume on the breeze.

"Most likely she did not want anyone to follow her," Ruth's husband said, with a rueful glance at Jeremy. "She has given you false information, I fear, Mr Winterton."

"No..." Jeremy spoke slowly, trying to persuade his mind to rise out of the stupor of the summer heat and his own exhaustion. "Jane was never one to deceive. Her sister's house..." Abruptly the memory came into sharp focus. At night, in his old room at Woodside, his arm sore from the gunshot, and Jane watching over him. Her sister's house... "There is another sister—"

"No, no," they said together. "Only us. Just the three of us. No one else."

"A young sister who died," he said, surer now.

"Oh!" A chorus like a sigh. "Angela! She has gone to Angela's house."

"Angela! Yes!" Jeremy said eagerly. "She said... she said it made her feel better... a summer house in the garden, surrounded by roses. Angela's house. That is where she will be."

He jumped up, and would have left without a word, but Ruth's husband reached out a hand to stop him. "Hallow End is miles away, on the far side of Stafford, and it is already late in the day. You will not arrive before sunset, and Cousin Maudie will scarcely admit you if you arrive unannounced. Stay with Helena and Rufus for tonight, for they at least have a guest room, and you may enjoy a bath, a good dinner and a full night's sleep, then continue to Hallow End tomorrow. It is no matter of great urgency, for Jane will not be lost for the sake of a few hours."

"No, no, I must go," Jeremy said. "I need to see her, to be sure that... I hardly know what I want, except that I cannot wait even one night. Who is Cousin Maudie?"

"Great-aunt Theo's eldest. A widow now. My first cousin once removed, and also Ruth's first cousin once removed. Her grandfather is my Great-uncle Albert you see. Ruth and I are second cousins," he said with a smile.

Jeremy tried to work it out, and failed. Only one fact jumped out at him. "Jane is with a relation at Hallow End."

"Cousin Maudie, who is a first cousin—"

"—once removed, yes. I shall need to see that on paper before I understand it, but for now, it reassures me to believe that she is safe with family, albeit distant. I thank you all for your hospitality, but now I must go."

They tried to dissuade him, of course, bringing every argument they could think of to bear, but he could not, would not wait. He sent for the long-suffering Hooper and the horses and set off once more, with a neat list of directions from Ruth's husband,

and some bread and cheese and a flask of Madeira wrapped in cloths from Ruth.

"Just in case," she said, with a smile. "One never knows when one might find oneself in need of a little sustenance when travelling."

The afternoon heat was wearing, and Jeremy chose not ride through the centre of Stafford, but to skirt around the outside of it, where there were plenty of trees for shade and streams to water the horses. It was slow going, and although the route took them through picturesque villages, and past any number of small manufactories beside the waterways that would normally have drawn Jeremy's interest, he could think of nothing but reaching Hallow End before dark.

But eventually they came to a large, prosperous village at a place where two roads met and crossed a canal. Being thus of some importance for barges and road traffic alike, it was furnished with an inn of some size. Leaving Hooper to bespeak accommodation for them, Jeremy followed the directions of the ostler to the gates of Hallow End. They stood closed, with a neat cottage just inside for the gatekeeper. The house itself was out of sight behind trees, but the grounds were extensive, stretching away into the surrounding countryside. By riding around outside the walls for a little way, Jeremy could see the house itself, a substantial building of great elegance, its mellow golden stone just catching the last rays of the dying sun.

There were lights at a few windows, and the faint sounds of a pianoforte could be heard in the still air. Jane was somewhere in that house, perhaps watching Cousin Maudie at the instrument, or perhaps already dressing for dinner. Would she spare a thought for her former betrothed, or had she quite forgotten him already? Had she told Cousin Maudie about him? Did they laugh together about her abrupt departure, and imagine his shock at finding only a hastily scribbled note for her former betrothed? No... Jane would not laugh at him. She might be as prickly as a hedgehog, but she was not unkind.

Yet now that he was here, he was no further forward. He could not present himself so late in the day, so reluctantly Jeremy turned away and rode slowly back to the inn. There he discovered there was not enough hot water for a bath, and the dinner could only charitably be described as indifferent. Hooper ate it indiscriminatingly, but Jeremy retreated to his room with the bread, cheese and Madeira, as the raucous merriment of the bargemen in the taproom drifted up from below. He cast aside his coat, waistcoat, neckcloth and boots, and threw himself onto the bed, nibbling a little but mostly, it had to be said, drinking, until the flask was empty.

From his pocket, he pulled out one of his small puzzle boxes, and morosely made the movements to open it, then to close it again. Open, close. Open, close. It gave his hands something to do until he might be tired enough to sleep, but as a distraction from thoughts of Jane it was a failure. Inside the box he had concealed a ring, a small gift to mark the true start of their betrothal. Now he wondered if it would ever be given, or accepted.

Setting the box down beside his empty glass, he pondered the puzzle that was Jane Tyrrell. He had entered into the false betrothal with a very clear idea of its benefits. He would be free to buy Woodside and become a gentleman, and Jane would be free to live her life without the crushing burden of being the poor relation. They had succeeded in both objectives, magnificently, and Jane had released him from the betrothal, just as she had promised. Despite all that, he had never been so miserable in his life. He should be happy, but... he was empty inside.

Yet what could be done about it? Jane had made her own wishes quite clear. He could not even explain to his own satisfaction why he had chased after her in such a ridiculous way, except that he had set out the previous day to propose to her and somehow he could not let go of that objective. There were matters unsettled between them and things unsaid and business unfinished. He wanted — no, *needed* — to lay his heart at her feet, and express all his desire for her, all this strange, half-understood swirl of intense emotion... It was the intensity that frightened him most. He felt like an overheated boiler, and if he could not find Jane and talk to her and relieve the pressure, he was sure he would explode.

And if she would not have him— But he would not surrender to despair. How could she possibly refuse him once she saw the depth of his affection... of his love? For that must be what it was, this desperate longing to be near her, to hear her voice, to see those lovely eyes. He could not imagine life without her. For an instant, he had a vision of himself married to Ellen, with her perfect form and immaculate manners and her insipid conversation. The same banal remarks over breakfast and again at dinner. He had wanted men to envy him his beautiful wife, but what did that matter? There was more to a woman than surface beauty. He knew now exactly what he wanted, he had found the perfect wife for him, and no other would do. He would find her and explain it all to her so that she understood his feelings at last, and then she would be his. As soon as he found her and told her everything, this misery would be over and Jane would be his. Surely she would be his?

Ah, Jane! His delightful hedgehog. He picked up the puzzle box, then impatiently pushed it into the pocket of his breeches. He got up again, crossing the room to the open window, pushing it open even further to breathe deeply of the cooler, fresher night air.

Without his coat and waistcoat and the wretched neckcloth, he felt cooler and liberated, somehow. He need not play the gentleman when he wore no neckcloth.

The inn was quiet now, the merrymakers and servants all away to their beds, and no lamps shone into the yard. It was not dark, however, for the full moon was climbing majestically up the sky, bathing the countryside in silver. Jeremy leaned out of the window a little way, the night calling to him. Below him, the roof of a log store jutted out from the building. Impulsively he pulled on his boots again, and slithered out of the window onto the roof. From there it was no distance to the ground, his boots hitting the cobbles with a thump. He ran off before anyone came out to see what the noise was about.

He knew where he was going, and indeed it was doubtful his feet would have carried him in any other direction. The Hallow End gates loomed up before him, with no lights showing from the gatekeeper's cottage. He walked around the outside of the walls on the track he had ridden earlier until he got to the place where he could look across the park to the house. All was in darkness.

Now that he was on foot, the light of the moon showed him that the wall was uneven enough to be climbed, for it was built of rough slabs which gave easy holds for his hands and feet. It was the work of a moment to scramble over, and drop down on the other side. Here he found a well used track, smooth enough for a light carriage. He had a vision of Cousin Maudie and Jane driving sedately around the perimeter of the estate in a phaeton. Beyond it were shrubberies and small copses, with a number of single trees set into the lawn. It pleased him to amble about the grounds, finding as he went a sunken garden, a small stream, a grotto and a Chinese pagoda. He kept himself out of sight of the house, hiding behind bushes wherever he could, for in the moonlight his white shirt would be easily spotted.

Then he smelt roses. He knew at once what he would find if he followed the scent, and so it was — Angela's house, a small temple in the Greek style with pillars and a fine domed roof, in the same warm-coloured stone as the house. All around it — in flower borders, curling over the door and even scrambling up the walls as high as the dome — was a great profusion of roses, the perfume of many blooms filling the air with their heavy scent.

He smiled and walked all around it twice, and then settled on a curved marble bench built into the back wall. The roses nodded around his head, as if reaching out to greet him, and he felt at ease for the first time since he had read Jane's note. He closed his eyes and leaned back against the cool stone of the temple, and thought of the child for whom it was raised. Angela. The angel of the family, loved by everyone, yet she was gone. Sometimes one could not have everything one wanted, no matter how much one loved.

The thought hit him with the force of a hammer. What if he could not have Jane? How could he live without her? He was breathless with despair. But then the scent of the roses filled his nostrils and gradually, oh so slowly, he breathed again and was easy.

Perhaps that was how it was meant to be. His own happiness was bound up with Jane, but perhaps hers was not bound with him. It may even be that she would be happier alone and independent and free than married to him, or to anyone. Had she not always said so, and why should he suppose he knew her better than she knew herself?

He made his resolution on the spot — he would explain his admiration and the great affection he felt for her, he would offer her his name and then... he would accept her decision. Jane, his prickly Jane. Perhaps she would marry him and perhaps she would not, for she would not surrender her freedom lightly, but he would accept her answer either way. And if he had to live his life without her, he would do that as best he could.

This decision so energised him that he jumped up and walked all round the temple again. The doors were closed, but all the windows were open wide, and, by standing on the bench, he thought he could just reach one. Almost before the thought had settled in his mind, he had jumped onto the bench and scrambled onto the window sill. His boots scraped on the stone, and then he jumped down lightly inside the temple...

... and froze.

Jane.

There she was, curled up on a marble seat fast asleep, shrouded in blankets. Her face was pale in the dim light that crept into the temple.

His heart turned over in relief... she was safe, she was here and the misery inside him lifted and then drifted away to nothingness. He leaned his back against the cool stone wall and slowly slid downwards until he was sitting on the floor, gazing at her as she slept. He smiled. Finally, he had found her and the world was as it should be. He breathed a contented sigh.

Then she opened her eyes...

27: The Temple

Jane woke abruptly in the dark, with a spasm of fear. Someone was there, in the room with her. With a gasp, she shot upright.

"Hush, hush! No cause for alarm, Jane, it is only I."

The familiar voice reassured her, but she could not quite set aside her fright and her voice was sharp. "Jeremy? What on earth—?"

He was sitting cross-legged on the floor. When he leaned forward, the moonlight pouring in from the window lit his face, and she was shocked at his dishevelled, barely-dressed state, and the exhaustion written on his features. She had last seen him in full evening dress, happy and smiling at some joke of Leo Audley's, and now he looked as if the whole world had collapsed about his ears.

Her fear softened, but her heart still pounded. What was he doing here? Hope surged within her... was it possible that he wanted—? That he hoped—? No. She dared not follow that line of thought. Breathe deeply. Let him tell his own story. Breathe...

"You look terrible," she said, more softly. "Whatever has happened? How do you come to be here?"

"The window was open," he answered her seriously. "Nothing has happened, except that you went away and I could not understand—"

"Did you not get my letter?" she said eagerly, as hope flared up again. She determinedly tamped it down. "I should have thought it was clear enough."

"Oh, Jane!" he said, with a sound somewhere between a groan and a sob. "Nothing about you is clear. I have never known what is in your mind — in your *heart*. I thought I did, but then…" He took a rasping breath, and leaned back against the stone wall again, closing his eyes momentarily. "You are such a puzzle to me."

Breathe, Jane, breathe. She crossed her legs, just as he did, and wrapped one of the blankets around her. She had never been one to worry overmuch about the proprieties, but she was acutely aware of her exposed state. She wore only a flimsy nightgown, without the confining layers of chemise and tightly-laced stays and petticoat and gown. Even her legs were bare, and her hair was unbound. In the silence that fell, she could hear her own breathing, and his too.

Yet he was just as vulnerable as she was, for he wore only boots, breeches and shirt, the latter unfastened to expose his neck to the world. She had a wild urge to run her fingers down that exposed throat, to nuzzle it, to kiss it. What madness! Whatever was the matter with her? Think… answer him… What had he said? Ah, she was a puzzle.

"Well, I am very sorry for that." Her voice sounded odd. Was it the echoing stone of the mausoleum, or her own trembling desire? "Do I become less of a puzzle if you stare at me in the middle of the night?"

He gave a wan smile. "No. I think it would be a lifetime's study to understand you, Jane Tyrrell."

A lifetime! Did he know what he was saying? Did he mean it? She could not speak a word, as all her dearest hopes rose up to drown her in sweet anticipation. Such torment! His next words would surely be—

"It was such an amusing game, wasn't it?" Not what she had expected. "We played our parts to perfection, and the world was fooled, but it was all pretence, wasn't it?" The Lancashire accent was noticeable, suddenly. "It was just a lark, while we solved the mystery of the missing jewels. But somehow, without my noticing, it changed and it wasn't a game any more. How did you do that to me, my maddening hedgehog? I think you're not a hedgehog at all, you're a spider, weaving your web around me, binding me tighter and tighter until—"

"A spider!" she cried. "That... that sounds horrible! Am I going to eat you? That is what spiders do with their prey."

"Do they?" he said, sounding bewildered. "Am I your prey? Are you a spider... no, that sounds wrong. Lord, Jane, I hardly know what I'm saying." He rubbed his face tiredly.

Her heart ached for him, but she needed to *know*. "Why did you come here?" she cried. "What do you want of me?"

"Don't you understand?" He sighed, and closed his eyes again, resting his head against the wall of the temple. He fell silent again, and for such a long time that she wondered if he had fallen asleep. He looked so tired! He must have followed her here almost as soon as he discovered her gone, and not slept at all along the way, and surely that meant—

She would not presume to guess what it meant. Perhaps he truly did not understand her words and merely wanted his dismissal from her own lips. But if he did not understand her, no more did she understand him.

"I thought you wanted Ellen Ridwell," she said in bewilderment. "A demure wife, a *beautiful* wife, and a prosperous mill."

"Good God, no," he said, his eyes flying open. "Whatever gave you that idea?"

"Only that you said so, many times!"

"Oh. I suppose I did, but that was a long time ago. I thought you realised—? Maybe you didn't. Oh Jane, I don't know what's the matter with me. I've come haring after you, and now that you've been found, I can't find the right words. I can't explain... Maybe it doesn't matter... maybe it's too late... maybe it was always too late and—" His eyes opened wider and he sat up a little straighter. "Now I am rambling. Let me start again. I chased after you because there are things still unsaid between us... things that I want to say to you, at any event... that I *need* to say. I have to tell you all that is in my heart and mind or it will drive me entirely insane, but once I have said it all, then you can send me away if you want to and I will never trouble you again. Will you hear me? I will try very hard not to ramble, or call you a spider."

She was too full of emotion even to smile at his feeble joke. *All that is in my heart and mind.* Did that mean what she hoped it meant? Such torment, not knowing... He watched her expectantly, waiting for her answer, but her throat was too tight to speak. She nodded, and he gave a little smile, but for a while he said nothing, gathering his thoughts, perhaps. He was exhausted and barely coherent, but he was with her... he *wanted* to be with her, so she could wait in patience and hear what he had to say.

He took a deep, shuddering breath.

"Jane, I have been a deceiver for so many years, pretending… always pretending. Lying came so easily to me, and I was an expert at it. I lied to everyone, and fooled everyone, too, even myself, sometimes, and never cared about the consequences. I never cared about other people. I left my own father and sisters grieving for my death for fifteen years, until it suited me to reveal myself. As for Ellen — how arrogant I was! All I wanted was her mill, so that men would respect me. To be rich, to have a place in society, to be *somebody*. It tore me apart, knowing that I was born to be a gentleman but was shut out of that world, looked down on as if I were some kind of insect by people who were my equals by birth. I was prepared to trample on everyone to claw my way back there. Like our betrothal… I never thought about the *consequences* of it, the people who were excited and happy for us, and would be hurt later, and you… I never thought how difficult it would be for you. Or for me. I never… expected that."

There was a little catch in his voice that made her foolish heart skip and skip again. Then he leaned forward, and the intensity in his face was almost more than she could bear.

"I swear to you that I will never lie again. *Never!* I must be honest, to you of all people. You're the most honest person I've ever known, and you force me to be honest too. I came into Brinshire in all my prideful greed to claim my birth right, and you and your sharp tongue stripped away all my conceit, all my presumption and deceit. I want you to know that every word I say to you now is utter truth. I don't know how it happened or why, but these last few weeks have been the happiest of my life. You crept into my heart, and now I can't imagine life without you. I have everything I once thought I wanted — riches and a position in society and Woodside. I am finally *somebody*, and I find that none of it matters in the slightest without you. I don't know what else to say, except that I love you and if you ever feel that—"

She gave a little cry, hand to mouth, as jubilation exploded within her. Relief, too, but mostly blissful jubilation. It was all right! He truly loved her, he had come for her and he wanted her, and she would never be lonely again. *He loved her!* Oh, the joy of his words, to know that she was cherished, that he loved her as she loved him.

He murmured "Jane?", his voice bewildered, but she could only cry, rocking gently back and forth, too overwhelmed to be still.

"Jane?" he said again, but he made no move towards her.

Hastily she wiped her face on a corner of the blanket. "Sorry — It is only that—"

He was silent, watching her anxiously. He did not know, she realised. Although he had declared himself, he had no idea why she was crying. Then she laughed, and he looked, if anything, even more anxious. She had to speak, to tell him...

The words came out in a rush, for she was half sobbing, delirious with happiness.

"I love you too."

His face changed slowly, from concern to dawning realisation and then... joy, she decided. That was Jeremy's joyful face, an expression she had never seen before. But still he did not move.

"You can kiss me now," she said hopefully.

"I daren't!" he said, with a rueful laugh. "I haven't got a neckcloth on."

She was too dizzy with emotion to understand him. "Whatever do you mean?"

Another laugh. "When I have a neckcloth on, I am a gentleman and can be... restrained. But to kiss you here and now...

you in your nightgown with your hair tumbling down your back where I can run my hands through it…" She thought he sighed. "And… and I in nothing but a shirt— Lord, no! Have you any idea how… how beautiful, how *desirable* you are? Such temptation. It's difficult enough to let go of you when we're both fully dressed, but like this? No, I dare not."

"Oh." Beautiful. He had called her beautiful. It was only the heightened emotion of the moment, and he would probably never say such a thing again, but she would treasure it for ever. When he spoke of temptation, she had only the vaguest notion of what he meant, so she could hardly argue the point. She could not force him to kiss her, but it was unsatisfactory. She needed something from him to settle matters between them. "Then what shall we do?"

"I thought perhaps, given that it's the middle of the night, that you should go back to sleep and I should go back to the inn and do likewise. Tomorrow I shall present myself at the front door like a proper suitor, instead of sneaking through windows in the dark, and ask for the favour of a private interview with you. Then I shall offer you my hand and my heart and… and my entire life, and… well, the rest is up to you, but if you were so minded, it might involve kisses, which will be perfectly safe because I shall be suitably ensconced in a neckcloth by then."

"How absurd you are!" she said, trying not to laugh, or to cry either, for the thought of him going away again and leaving her alone was unbearable.

"Would that be acceptable to you, my darling?"

My darling. Her throat was too choked to formulate an answer, so she merely nodded. He jumped to his feet and set off at once for the window again, before turning and coming back to where she still sat, too overwhelmed by all that had happened to move. He loomed over her, his great height reassuring in its familiarity. Her great, tall, wonderful, *idiotic* Jeremy.

"I almost forgot," he said, pushing something into her hand. A small wooden box. "Something to amuse you… and a small gift, with my love." And then, to her infinite delight, he ran one finger very gently down her cheek, his face filled with affection. "Dear Jane," he whispered. "My adored hedgehog."

He leaned down and brushed his lips delicately against hers. Then, with a sigh, he turned and fled for the window, climbed swiftly out and was gone into the night.

She did not have the heart to tell him that the doors were unlocked.

~~~~~

The return journey to Woodside was a great deal more comfortable than the outgoing, and not merely from the advantage of driving. Jeremy sat at his ease beside Jane in the carriage, with Lottie opposite them and Hooper riding behind, leading Jeremy's horse. They had to leave Hallow End very early to avoid an overnight stop, and it rained almost the whole way, but nothing could dent Jeremy's happiness, not even Hooper's grumbles whenever they stopped to change horses. He could not repress his smiles, and every time he looked at Jane, she had a matching smile on her face. She had removed her gloves so that she could admire the delicate ring on her finger. As he had expected, she had opened the puzzle box long before he returned to Hallow End to claim her.

They stopped for a meal a little after noon, and Jeremy had no compunction in taking a private parlour for himself and Jane, and banishing Lottie to the common room with Hooper.

"May I ask…?" he said diffidently, when they had sated their hunger and were sitting cosily on a settle, hand in hand.

"Anything," she said. "I want to be honest, too. I will tell you anything."

"Why did you leave?" he said. "I thought we had reached an understanding, after you asked me if I would be proud to have you as my wife. Was my answer unclear?"

"You hesitated," she said at once. "I thought that if you really meant it, you would answer at once, but you hesitated, and then your answer was... polite."

"I was stunned," he said. "I thought you despised me thoroughly."

"How could I kiss you the way I did if I despised you? Whatever lies we tell with words and the mask of politeness, kisses do not lie."

He laughed at that, and felt compelled to test the veracity of the matter. But when he had satisfied himself on the point, he said, "I can see that you might have misunderstood my answer, but why did you run away at dawn, as if you could not wait to escape me?"

"Oh... was that what you thought?"

"I am not sure I had a rational thought in my head at that point. I had got myself all dressed up to propose to you formally, and somehow I could not tamely go home again with those words unsaid. It felt like unfinished business, somehow, and there is nothing the mill manager in me dislikes more than unfinished business."

She chuckled, resting her cheek on his broad shoulder. "So you wanted me to have the courage to refuse you to your face, did you? But I could not. I knew perfectly well that the *gentleman* in you would feel obliged to offer for me, and I could never, ever look you in the eye and refuse you, not when I want to marry you so badly. I am not so selfless. So the *coward* in me ran away, to somewhere you would not easily find me. But you *did* find me," she added. "How clever of you, and how romantic, climbing through windows at night."

"I think that was just the lack of rational thought again," he said ruefully. "No doubt it is due to the Lancastrian in me. Are you comfortable leaning against my shoulder, my darling? I would not disturb you for the world, but it does make it a trifle difficult to kiss you."

Obligingly, she adjusted her position a little and after that all conversation ceased. Hooper had to knock three times on the door before they could be induced to continue their journey.

Jeremy left Jane at Woodside and rode the short distance to Westerlea Park to tell Rosamund and Robin of his successful suit. To his surprise, Rosamund rushed out to meet him, heedless of the rain, as he approached the house.

"Oh, thank goodness you are here!" she cried, her face filled with distress.

"What is it? Not Robin? One of the children?"

"Oh... no, no, we are all well. No, it is— Come inside, quickly, and you will see."

Without even allowing him time to clean off the dirt of the journey, Rosamund whisked him into the library, where Robin and another man rose to greet him.

"Mr Ridwell?" Jeremy said, bemused. He was the last person he had expected to see. "Is anything amiss?" Foolish question, for he could see by the man's distraught face that something was terribly amiss.

"Then she is not with you?" Ridwell said, run a hand over his face. "I had hoped..."

It was left to Robin to explain. "It seems Miss Ridwell has disappeared from her aunt's house in London, leaving only a cryptic message—"

"She is gone to be happy, she says," Ridwell said. "What can that mean, Moreton? Nothing good, you may be sure. This Dallen fellow—"

"An elopement?" Jeremy said. "But why would they—?"

"Precisely," Rosamund said crisply. "He is his own master, with no family to disapprove of his marriage to whomever he chooses. If marriage is what he has in mind, then there is no obstacle."

"You think—? Good God!" Jeremy said. "That is appalling! But she can be recovered, surely. Even if he has turned her head with his blandishments, she may still be found and brought home."

"Robin has someone looking for Dallen," Rosamund said. "He knows all his friends, his haunts, everywhere he may be hiding. If Miss Ridwell is with him, she will be found, never fear."

"I wondered a little at him staying on in London," Robin said slowly. "Everyone of consequence has left for the country now, or Brighton perhaps, and Dallen was always a man to move with the *ton*. It seemed odd that he had not fixed his interest with Miss Ridwell long since, for he is a man of great charm, and very successful with ladies, in general."

"You mean he is a libertine," Ridwell said in shocked tones. "Yet every report spoke of him as a man held in the highest regard by society."

"So it is in London," Rosamund said gently. "Mr Dallen was received everywhere, and his manners and breeding of the very best. Yet he was... a flirt, shall we say."

Ridwell uttered a low groan. "My poor girl!"

"It is true that he always kept a mistress," Robin said, "but very discreetly, and never a woman he met in society. Miss Ridwell was under the patronage of my wife and my sisters-in-law, and was befriended by other ladies of the highest respectability. Lady Carrbridge took an interest in her, and Lady Ramsey. The Duchess of Dunmorton gave her a shawl, and took her driving in Hyde Park. She received vouchers for Almack's. Naturally everyone supposed that Dallen's intentions were honourable."

"Let us not assume the worst yet," Rosamund said. "Until we hear to the contrary, we will assume an elopement."

But the very next day set all to rest. An express rider arrived from Branton bearing a letter that Ellen had sent to her mother. Ridwell allowed them all to see it.

'Mama, I daresay you will be shocked to receive this but you have brought it on yourself. It is your example which decided me upon the step which I have now taken. I long ago decided that I will never live an insipid life like yours, sitting around waiting for something to happen. In particular, I shall never be owned by any man, and therefore will never marry. The arrangement I have entered into is a matter of business. Papa will understand that, I am sure. I will be paid handsomely for my services, and live a very comfortable life. When this current arrangement terminates, as it inevitably will, I shall keep all the jewels, gowns and gold, all the trinkets in my dressing room, and even the carriage and horses. I have no doubt there will be several such arrangements in future years. By the time I am your age, Mama, I shall be vastly wealthy in my own right, and able to live as I please. Most of all, I intend to have some fun, which I did not have at home, and would not have had married to that great lumbering idiot, John Moreton. What a dismal future you planned for me! But I have escaped you, and now I can do what makes me happy, without reference to you or Papa or

some stuffy husband. Goodbye, Mama. We will never meet again. Ellen.'

Ridwell wept quietly, and no one had any words to bring him comfort.

Epilogue

OCTOBER

Jeremy checked every part of the clock one last time. Even though he had gone over each rod and gear and spring the day before, he still methodically tested each part, as Kit called out its name.

"All done," Kit said happily, as the last angel was found to be in full working order. "All done. Everything will work now. All done, Jerry."

"Let us hope so," Jeremy said. "Miss Tyrrell will not be happy if I have to postpone tomorrow's wedding in order to fix something on the clock." Then, seeing Kit's horrified face, he added, "Just joking, Kit. Nothing on earth would cause me to postpone the wedding."

Kit's face lightened. "Got a new coat, Jerry. Got a new coat to go to the wedding. There'll be a wedding breakfast, too, won't there? New coat for the wedding. Wedding breakfast."

"There will be a very splendid wedding breakfast, Kit, and I too have a new coat, Mr Tyrrell has a new coat and Miss Tyrrell has a new gown, so I am told. We shall all look very splendid."

"Dudley doesn't have a new coat. I have a new coat. You have a new coat. Dudley doesn't have a new coat. He won't look splendid, will he?"

"Not as splendid as we shall look. There now, it wants only ten minutes to noon. Shall we go down and watch from the square?"

They descended slowly, as Jeremy went over it all in his mind. Had he forgotten anything? This would be the first time the automaton had been fully connected to the clock, the first test of all his work, and Kit's. He was sure he had forgotten something...

He shaded his eyes from the dazzling sunlight as he emerged from the clock tower door, then stopped dead as a huge cheer went up. Blinking, he gazed around. The square in front of St Mark's church was full. Several carriages were parked on the far side, and the rest of the space was filled with people, smiling, laughing, waving at him. He spotted Jane and her father near the front, next to Dudley Everton, and made his way towards them.

"What is all this?" he said, tucking Jane's arm into his. "Is everyone here to see the automaton? Let us hope you will not be disappointed. This is the very first test, so there is no knowing what will happen."

"That makes it all the more dramatic," Jane said. "Whether it works or whether it scatters angels all over the square, it will be talked about for years. Oh, here are your sisters. Just in time."

The crowd parted respectfully as Rosamund, Annabelle, Lucy, Margaret and Fanny and their husbands made their way to the front of the square.

"This is so exciting!" Lucy cried, from a hundred yards away. "We have been looking forward to this for such a long time. You are so clever, Jeremy, to be able to put this together, but then you always were so good with clocks. Such nimble fingers! I remember when you were quite small..."

The others smiled and let her chatter away, but not for long. The minute hand of the clock made its ponderous way to the top of the dial, and the crowd, even Lucy, fell silent in anticipation. The first bell sounded and then, to a low rumble of excitement amongst the watchers, the doors of the automaton slowly opened and figures appeared. First, several in servants' dress, carrying platters and barrels and flasks. Then the first of the disciples in their robes, as Kit muttered their names under his breath. Then finally, with a splendid gold halo, the Lord Jesus himself, one hand raised in a blessing to the crowd below. One by one, the figures moved smoothly out from one door, across the space below the dial and back into the other door. Above them, angels flew, trumpets in hand. As the notes of the last bell died away, the figures disappeared and the doors slowly closed.

The crowd cheered, and cheered again. Jeremy was thumped on the back so many times he thought he must be black and blue.

"It worked, Jerry!" Kit said happily. "Everything worked. All done now."

The assembled crowd began to drift away, chattering volubly. Jeremy and his family stood in a loose group, as Everton and Kit ushered them towards the rectory for a celebratory glass of something, and a cup of tea for Mr Tyrrell. As the square emptied, one man remained — a man with a very familiar face.

"Uncle Giles?" Jeremy said. "Is it really you? Whatever are you doing here?"

Giles Moreton laughed. "You did not imagine I should let you get married without being there to watch, did you? Is this the lady?"

"It is. Miss Tyrrell, may I present to you the man who raised me from the age of twelve, Mr Giles Moreton of Branton. Uncle Giles, this is Miss Tyrrell, who has been reckless enough to honour me with her hand in marriage."

He began to introduce the rest of his family, but Ferdy laughed and said, "Mr Moreton and I are already acquainted. We first met some ten years ago, although I have to say that he has aged remarkably well in that period, for he looks younger now than he did then. I congratulate you, Mr Moreton. Your acting skills were very effective."

Uncle Giles rubbed his nose. "I apologise for that, my lord. I didn't want you asking too many questions, and Johnny — Jeremy — was not then ready to face up to his situation. Pretending to be a doddery old man has always served me well in deterring too many enquiries, as it did with you. It pleases me now to acknowledge the truth. I can only hope that you will forgive me the deception."

"It is not for me to forgive you," Ferdy said softly. "It is Jeremy who was ill-served that day, for had I met him, as I had hoped, he would have learnt then that his father was dead, Woodside would never have been sold and a great deal of difficulty would have been avoided."

"Ah yes, but then I should never have met my dear Jane," Jeremy said. "You can hardly expect me to regret that."

"Oh, how romantic!" Fanny breathed.

~~~~~

The following day, the parish church at Frickham was as full as it could hold. The entire village had turned out to watch Mr Winterton, the new owner of Woodside, marry Miss Tyrrell, also of Woodside, and not a few people had driven or ridden or even walked from Brinchester for the occasion, too.

Jeremy arrived at church from Westerlea Park. Even though Woodside was now formally his, for Mr Tyrrell had honoured his promise to make it over to Jeremy as Jane's dowry, he had chosen not to take possession until his marriage.

"No point moving out for such a short time," he had said cheerfully, when Mr Tyrrell had proposed it. "Besides, where will you go? You are not planning to leave us, I hope?"

"I shall be very much in the way," Tyrrell had said. "You will not want your father-in-law underfoot."

"On the contrary, I should very much like to have my father-in-law underfoot. I could not reconcile it with my conscience to send you off to live alone, and this way you will have a choice of opponent for piquet or cribbage, or we may invite Mrs Plummer for whist. Of course, if you should decide to marry Mrs Plummer—"

Tyrrell hooted with laughter. "Mrs Plummer is an excellent whist player, but no one will ever replace my late wife, I assure you."

"Then I hope you will spend the rest of your life at Woodside, with your grandchildren about you," Jeremy said.

Tyrrell beamed at him and said all that was proper, but he did not seem surprised by the idea, and somehow Jeremy felt that this was exactly as he had planned all along. Tyrrell always seemed to be one step ahead.

The bride arrived, the ceremony took place and the newly married couple and the wedding guests repaired to Woodside to eat and drink and ponder the momentous matters of the day, such as Mrs Caddy's appalling hat, whether Dora from the inn was walking out with the handsome new ostler, and the extraordinary transformation Miss Grantley had worked on Percival Drake.

"The way he spoke out against Lady Elizabeth at the trial!" Rosamund said. "That was very brave, and they would not have convicted her without his testimony."

"But now she will be hanged," Fanny said.

"That is a mercy, surely," Robin said. "She would never survive transportation."

"But I still do not understand why she would do such a thing," Annabelle said. "I cannot believe that she was in love with Papa, for she has never loved anyone but herself."

"She was jealous," Margaret said. "She wanted everything Mama had — her clothes, her furniture, even Papa."

"But why?" Annabelle said. "Why would the daughter of an earl be jealous of the wife of a gentleman of very modest means? Mama was only one step away from trade, after all. Those jewels came from the family business."

"Whatever her origins, Mama was a lady through and through," Jeremy said. "Being a lady, or a gentleman for that matter, is not just about rank or wealth, it is also about manners, bearing, one's behaviour to others, one's conduct in every aspect of life. It is a question of character, and Mama was never other than ladylike, even when she was ill at the end. Everyone loved her and respected her, whereas Lady Elizabeth, for all her pedigree, was not liked at all. That ate away at her for years. So Drake said at the trial."

"It seems very harsh to speak against the person who has nurtured him," Fanny said. "But he wished to do the right thing, and now he is to turn Carrington Hall into an orphanage."

"It is high time Carrington Hall was used for a proper purpose," Rosamund said. "Lady Elizabeth held the most outrageous parties there, so it was said, with gambling for high stakes and women and all manner of improprieties going on. An orphanage is a far more respectable purpose."

"So generous of Mr Drake!" Fanny said. "But so romantic, the way Miss Grantley has brought him to a proper understanding. They are to be married in the spring, are they not?"

"And live in Lilac Cottage with Drake's two sisters," Rosamund said, with a huff of impatience. "I wonder how long that will last. It may seem spacious to Alice Grantley now after the squeeze at the vicarage, but when she has three or four children she may begin to wonder why the orphans are permitted to enjoy the delights of Carrington Hall and she, as the wife of the owner, is not."

Jeremy could not imagine that Frickham scandals were of any interest to Giles Moreton, so when an opportunity arose he said to him, "What news from Branton? Is all well there? What of the Ridwells?"

He grimaced. "Not good. Ellen is never mentioned, naturally. They have broken all contact with her, and try to pretend that she never existed, but it is very hard for them. They had hoped to marry her well so that they might hand over the business to a son-in-law, but that is impossible now."

"They should find a likely nephew or cousin, and train him up to take over," Jeremy said. "That is how these things are generally managed. I have written to Ridwell to suggest it."

"That might help him, but it will be no comfort to his wife. Mrs Ridwell is a broken woman. Have you heard news of Ellen? Your people know this man she is with, do they not?"

"They do, but we have heard nothing. Still, she has chosen her life and no one can help her now. It is a strange thing, but I suspect she will be happier outside good society than in it. She never seemed happy at home, playing the dutiful daughter and being shown off to every eligible man like a perfectly formed doll, with no mind of her own. Well, now she has discovered her own mind and is exercising her own will, even if it is not what her parents envisaged for her. She is beautiful enough and astute enough that she may well have a very successful career as a courtesan. But what of you? Have you found a replacement for me yet?"

"There will never be a replacement for you, Johnny — I mean Jeremy," Moreton said gloomily. "I had great hopes of handing over the whole of Hazlehead Mill to you after your marriage, so that I could live out my declining years in comfort by my own fire, waited on hand and foot. Now I must find another man even a tenth as competent as you, or else exert myself to manage the place myself. It is not what I had hoped for."

"Then sell the place, if it weighs on you," Jeremy said easily. "Sell up, and come and live here with us."

"Mrs Winterton will hardly want an old man like me living here," he said, but Jeremy saw the spark of hope in his eye.

"She will not mind a bit, and heaven knows, there is plenty of room. Besides, I know someone who will be very happy to have a fourth for whist every night."

"Oh... whist every night? That would be most agreeable," Moreton said. "I wonder if Ridwell would like to buy Hazlehead Mill?"

~~~~~

When breakfast was over, the guests settled themselves in the drawing room for a more detailed chat. Margaret and Mel took Kit out into the garden to visit the tree house. Kit could not easily be separated from Jeremy now, so although he would continue to live with his brother, it had been agreed that he would make regular visits to Woodside.

With everyone occupied, Jane drew Jeremy aside.

"Come and see the room I have prepared for you," she said. "You gave no instructions, except that it should not be your boyhood room or your father's bedroom, so I have had to guess what would suit you best."

"So long as it is near yours," he said, and she laughed.

It was, as he had expected, a perfectly ordinary room. It had once been one of the guest bedrooms, and still bore the original furniture, but Jane had redecorated and given it a pleasingly modern air.

"So where is your room?" he murmured, wrapping one arm around her waist.

"Right across the passage."

"Oh, but..."

He let her lead him there and open the door, and there was his mother's room, with all her original furniture, even the secretary with the clock built into it, but the room had been transformed with light draperies over the bed, pale panelling and a charmingly feminine wallpaper.

"This is truly your own choice?" he said, puzzled. "You did not settle on this room only because you thought it would please me? Or because it was close to mine?"

"Naturally I wanted to make it easy for you to find me, since you Lancashire men have no sense and are easily confused," she said, eyes twinkling. "But truly, I love this room... and the bed. It has good memories, but if you dislike it, then of course—"

"I do not dislike it," he said quickly. "It was... unexpected, that is all. But appropriate, for it is the best room in the house, and it pleases me that you like it as much as I do. Besides..." He pulled her into his arms. "This is where we first kissed."

He bent his head and pressed his lips to hers for a long, impassioned kiss, warmer than he had dared attempt before. But she responded with equal fervour.

"Goodness!" she said breathlessly, when they finally parted. "How ardent you are, Mr Winterton! Perhaps you have forgotten that you are still wearing your neckcloth, for I do not think it was exercising quite the restraint that you suggested on a previous occasion."

"Are you objecting?" he murmured, still holding her very close and patting little kisses all over her cheeks and forehead.

"If I *had* objected, you would not have had to ask me that question," she said tartly. "How strange to think that there was a fortune hidden in the bed. Is there anything in the safe now?"

He shook his head. "I put the remaining jewels in the bank, but if ever you want to look at them, we know we have a safe place to keep them."

"So now the clock is just a clock. Oh! I have realised why there is a clock in the secretary. It is to reset the clock in the bed after the safe has been opened... or the automaton activated." She blushed a little as she spoke. "I wonder... do you think we might watch the automaton in the bed clock? I should very much like to see it again, and I am a married woman now, after all.

"Tonight," he murmured. "Tonight we shall watch it together and you will understand all, Mrs Winterton."

"Very well, husband," she said demurely. "It shall be just as you wish."

"How very docile you are growing, wife," he said suspiciously. "I am not sure that I like it. What have you done with my adorably prickly Jane? I should not like Miss Hedgehog to become Mrs Mouse as soon as the wedding ring is on her finger."

She gurgled with laughter. "No fear of that, Mr Nonsense. Just for today, I shall be your obedient little mouse, but I daresay my prickles will have grown back in a day or two."

"Thank goodness for that!" he said. "I would not love you half so well if you were never to argue with me again. I want a wife who will stand up to me and tell me to my head that I am an idiot."

"I think I may safely promise you that I will abide by that requirement with great enthusiasm, but for today, may I be just the tiniest bit sentimental and tell you that I love you, Jeremy Winterton, with all my heart."

He gave her a little squeeze. "As I love you, Mrs Winterton."

"I am the most fortunate woman in the world to be your wife," she said with a soft sigh, "even if you are planning to fill my house with all the elderly gentlemen of two counties."

"Ah, the prickles are growing back already," he said. "Excellent. You had me concerned for a moment there."

THE END

This brings to an end the stories of the Winterton sisters (and brother!) of Woodside. I hope you enjoyed their various paths to happiness as much as I enjoyed writing them.

The next series from the pen of Mary Kingswood is called the *Silver Linings Mysteries*, which tells of the consequences for those affected when a small ship sinks off the Cornish coast. You can read a sneak preview of the first book, *The Widow,* after the acknowledgements.

For more information or to buy, go to:
http://marykingswood.co.uk.

Thanks for reading!

If you have enjoyed reading this book, please consider writing a short review on Amazon. You can find out the latest news and sign up for the mailing list at: http://marykingswood.co.uk.

This is the end of the *Sisters of Woodside Mysteries*, but there are plenty more traditional Regency romances to come. The next series is the *Silver Linings Mysteries*, which tells what happens after the *Brig Minerva* founders off the Cornish coast. In the midst of tragedy, several people's lives are unexpectedly improved. Book 1 is *The Widow*, and you can read a sneak preview of Chapter 1 after the acknowledgements.

The puzzle coins: Jeremy and Jane solved the puzzle of the clock by disentangling the meaning of the twelve coins found hidden in the furniture. The details of how they did it are described in the book, but for those who enjoy puzzles, you might like to work it out for yourself. You'll need twelve small squares of plain card, on which to write the numbers on the front and back of each card, thus:

- From the dressing table stool: 4/15
- From the washstand: 1/10 and 8/13
- From the armoire: 3/6 and 6/43
- From the dressing table: 10/30 and 12/57

- From the secretary: 2/20, 4/5, 7/8 and 5/11
- From the chair: 2/9

Knowing only that the coins are numbered from 1 to 12, you should be able to work out the exact settings for the clock hands to open the safe. If you want help, reread chapter 24, and you can follow exactly what Jeremy and Jane did to solve the puzzle.

Family trees: Hi-res version is available at the Mary Kingswood website: http://marykingswood.co.uk..

A note on historical accuracy: I have endeavoured to stay true to the spirit of Regency times, and have avoided taking too many liberties or imposing modern sensibilities on my characters. The book is not one of historical record, but I've tried to make it reasonably accurate. However, I'm not perfect! If you spot a historical error, I'd very much appreciate knowing about it so that I can correct it and learn from it. Thank you!

About the series: *When Mr Edmund Winterton of Woodside dies, his daughters find themselves penniless and homeless. What can they do? Unless they wish to live on charity, they will have to find genteel employment for themselves. This book is set in England during the Regency period of the early nineteenth century. Book 0 takes place 5 years before books 1-4, and book 5 ten years later.*

Book 0: The Betrothed (Rosamund) (a short novel, free to mailing list subscribers)

Book 1: The Governess (Annabelle)

Book 2: The Chaperon (Lucy)

Book 3: The Companion (Margaret)

Book 4: The Seamstress (Fanny)

Book 5: Woodside

Any questions about the series? You can email me at any time at mary@marykingswood.co.uk. I'd love to hear from you!

About the author

I write traditional Regency romances under the pen name Mary Kingswood, and epic fantasy as Pauline M Ross. I live in the beautiful Highlands of Scotland with my husband. I like chocolate, whisky, my Kindle, massed pipe bands, long leisurely lunches, chocolate, going places in my campervan, eating pizza in Italy, summer nights that never get dark, wood fires in winter, chocolate, the view from the study window looking out over the Moray Firth and the Black Isle to the mountains beyond. And chocolate. I dislike driving on motorways, cooking, shopping, hospitals.

Acknowledgements

Thanks go to:

Jane Austen and Georgette Heyer, who jointly inspired me to try my hand at writing a Regency romance.

Shayne Rutherford of Darkmoon Graphics for the cover design.

The Antiquarian Horological Society's Turret Clock Group, whose booklet *The Turret Clock Keeper's Handbook* was a delightful read and a wonderful resource, helping to keep me horologically straight. Any remaining clock-related errors are my own.

My beta readers: Barbara Daniels Dena, Amy DeWitt, Megan Jacobson, Melanie Savage

Last, but definitely not least, my first reader: Amy Ross.

Sneak preview of the Silver Linings Mysteries

Book 1: The Widow

Chapter 1: A Missing Captain

Nell examined her reflection in the cracked looking glass. The bruises had almost disappeared, and perhaps in another two days she could set aside the high, ruffed chemisette and the large cap with lappets in favour of more refined garments. By the time of the Sherrards' ball she would be completely healed, and need not fear to wear full evening dress. She sighed. Her velvet gown would do for one more outing, perhaps, but then... yes, this might be the last ball she would ever attend.

But she had made her choice, and would not repine. Her punishment was fitting, after all. She who had been the acclaimed beauty of the parish... of several parishes... of the county, even. Helen of Hampshire, she had been called, and it had been gratifying, even if the epithet did not resonate quite as strongly as Helen of Troy. Suitors had fluttered around her like butterflies in their brightly coloured coats. Would they even recognise her now, so thin and pinched as she had become? If only she could curl her hair properly and afford new slippers and stockings.

No, she must not regret. She had so much to be thankful for, after all. Her son, her home and a husband who loved her... sometimes. She slapped her cheeks to bring some colour to them, adjusted her ruff slightly, then turned away from the unflattering glass, head high, ready to face the day.

The two hours before breakfast were the most pleasurable of the day. With all the other occupants of the house busy elsewhere or still abed, she had her son to herself. Louis had been a sickly, undergrown child from the moment of his birth, and no amount of nourishing food had succeeded in giving him stature or the energy that came so naturally to most children. But when there is a deficit in one quarter, often there is an overabundance elsewhere, and so it was with Louis. He had such a quickness of mind and contemplative nature that he bid fair, at eight years of age, to leave his mama behind him before too long.

After morning prayers, he read aloud from the Bible, and Nell answered his questions on the passages covered as best she could. Then they moved on to Italian, which he had begun to learn after discovering a book of Nell's in that language on the shelf. Finally, Nell read three of Shakespeare's sonnets, which rested her own brain somewhat, for Louis had no time for poetry, regarding it as pointless, but he would listen quietly while she read it aloud. And finally Louis insisted that they pray again, this time solely for Papa, who was currently plying the Irish Sea as captain of the *Brig Minerva*, and therefore in constant danger, in Louis' mind, from storms and winds and powerful waves and tides and all the destructive majesty of the high seas.

"When will he be home, Mama?" he asked, as he did every day.

"In a few more days, or a week perhaps," she answered as she tidied away the books in the morning room, and laid out the slates for the ciphering lesson later.

A week perhaps, and then Jude would be home, smiling and holding her tight and calling her his dear love, and then her insides would tie themselves into knots until he went away again. But she would not repine. There was no point.

Breakfast was in the grandeur of the dining room, since the breakfast parlour was in the Lloyds' part of the house. All three families dined together, but at breakfast Nell and Louis were joined only by the widowed Maria Delanoy and her daughters, who had moved in after being swept up in the great disaster of five years ago. Since she could not afford to pay rent, Maria had taken upon herself the role of cook/housekeeper.

The two mothers discussed domestic matters while they ate, deciding on dinner, determining what needed to be bought that day and wondering whether they needed to order an extra quarter chaldron of coal to see them through to Lady Day.

"We have been rather lax about fires, I fear," Nell said. "Or rather, the Lloyds have been lax. Lydia is forever lighting fires in the bedrooms."

"Her boys have been greatly plagued by the grippe this winter, poor things," Maria said in her soft voice. "One cannot begrudge them the warmth while they recover."

"Those boys have been greatly plagued by mischief, more likely," Nell said robustly. "I do not think there is anything much amiss with them that a box around the ears would not cure. Lydia is too gentle with them."

"Oh, Nell!" Maria said. "She is hardly well herself just now, with another mouth to feed by summer, and she has been very unfortunate with her nursery maids. One must be sympathetic."

Nell paused and gazed at her friend. Maria was a gentle soul who thought well of the world, despite the world not seeming to smile upon her in return. It had not occurred to her that perhaps Lydia would retain her nursery maids more readily if she were to refrain from shouting at them.

"I suppose they pay good rent for their half of the house, and coal is included," Nell said in milder tones. "Well, if we run short of coal, we shall just have to eat our breakfast in the kitchen. That would save one fire a day, which would help."

"Aye, it would, and Jude will be home soon with money in his pocket. Perhaps he will not mind paying for a little extra coal this year, do you think?"

"Perhaps," Nell said colourlessly, but they both knew that she would never dare to ask him for such a thing.

At ten o'clock, Becky, the housemaid, came in to clear away, and Maria scurried away to the kitchen to begin her preparations for dinner. Nell took Louis and the two girls upstairs to the morning room for their lessons. The morning room was handsome, although small, since most of the frontage of the house on this floor was given over to the drawing room. Still, it was easy to keep warm, and it always felt pleasantly cosy on a cold winter's day. February was such a depressing time of year, but next month the weather might permit a day or two without the need for a fire. And the end of March brought Lady Day — the Lloyds' rent money and Jude's salary. Then it would not be long until summer.

After Louis' quickness at his lessons, Lucy and Jane were rather a trial. They were docile enough, sitting side by side in their matching aprons, with matching ribbons in their hair. Maria had an annuity of only twenty pounds a year, and contributed half for her keep, and sometimes Nell wondered if she spent every penny of the remainder on ribbons for the girls. They were pretty enough, with wide blue eyes, long lashes and the sort of dark, tumbled locks that would drive men wild in a few years, but they would need more than looks to get them through life unscathed.

Nell sighed, and handed out the slates. "Today we will practice money," she said. "Lucy, Jane — you will write down the amounts to be added together on your slates and work out the answer. Louis, you may write the answer directly, but do not say it aloud, if you please. First addition — if I buy three pounds of sugar at eight pence a pound, two pounds of meat at seven pence a pound and a quarter pound of tea at eight shillings a pound, how much will I need to pay for it?"

A quarter pound of tea... oh, if only she could afford tea! She closed her eyes for a moment, as the three children tapped away on their slates. Tea... and the best china cups, which were presently packed in sawdust and stowed in the cellar. And her drawing room back again. All the best rooms had been given over to the Lloyds, and although it had been her own idea to take in paying lodgers and it had saved them from having to sell the house, she could not help but resent it just a little.

"Are you quite well, Mama?" Her son's voice was sharp with anxiety. He worried about her, she knew that, but there was not much she could do about it. There was not much she could do about anything.

She opened her eyes to find all three of them staring at her. "Perfectly well, thank you, Louis. Lucy, do you have an answer?"

"Six shillings. I think."

"Jane?"

"Ten pounds."

Louis burst out laughing. "Ten pounds? You could buy half the shop with that much."

"No, I'd get change. Mrs Caldicott asked how much I'd need, and I couldn't work out the exact amount, so I decided I'd take more than enough. Is it a lot more?" she added, suddenly anxious.

"You would only need five and tuppence," he said. "I tell you what, Jane, if ever you have ten pounds, you may send me to do your shopping for you."

"May I?" she said. "That's very kind of you, Louis."

That set him laughing again.

"He did not mean it as a kindness, Jane," Nell said. "He meant that he would pay five and tuppence for the goods and keep the remaining amount, which is—"

"Nine pounds fourteen and tenpence," he said at once, before starting to laugh again.

"Another one," Nell said wearily. "Perhaps something a little easier. I need six yards of muslin to make a gown, and muslin costs one and six a yard. How much will it cost me altogether?"

Oh, for a new gown! If only—

The knocker sounded below. The girls at once scrambled from their chairs and raced to the window, peering down at the street below.

"It is a gentleman!"

"With a red coat!"

"And a great tall hat!"

"It will be for Mr Lloyd, I expect," Louis said.

Becky's quick steps were heard on the stairs, then the front door opening, followed by the murmur of a man's voice. Then silence. Becky's footsteps returning up the stairs, more slowly this time. There was a quick scratch on the door of the morning room, before she entered.

"Beg pardon, madam, but there's a gen'leman to see you. Askin' for you by name."

By name? Someone she knew? One of her brothers, it must be! "Did he give you his name?"

Silently Becky proffered a card. It had been so long since anyone had called with a card that the girl had forgotten to bring it on the silver salver that lay in the hall for the purpose.

'Mr Nathaniel Harbottle, Davygate, York', she read. No one she knew, then. Her excitement waned a little. But a gentleman visiting was still something, even if it was not anyone from her former life come to rescue her. No, she must stop expecting rescue. Such foolishness. Well, whoever Mr Harbottle was, she would see him, but not alone, and three children were not sufficient protection.

"Is Mrs Delanoy still in the house?"

"Yes, madam. She found some nutmeg left in the pantry, so she don't need no shopping today."

"Ask her to step up to the morning room, if you please — without her apron. Then show Mr Harbottle in." With a bob of a curtsy, Becky hurried off, leaving Nell to be thankful that she had not let her standards slip by a single iota. The servants got their uniform quota each year, so that Becky always had a clean gown to wear, and Nell and Louis looked respectable, if not exactly fashionable.

She and the children abandoned the slates on the worktable, and rearranged themselves according to Nell's hasty instructions. Again, she regretted the loss of her drawing room, purposely designed for just such eventualities. There were so few chairs in the morning room. However, there were enough to make a tolerable circle for conversation, and a window seat where the children could sit, rather squeezed together. "Not a word to be spoken, or you will have to leave," Nell told them sternly, and they nodded solemnly.

Maria hastened in, her cheeks rather flushed, and took the seat on the sofa next to Nell moments before the door opened.

"Mr Harbottle, madam," Becky said, in her very best announcing voice.

Nell rose smoothly to greet him. He was young, handsome and stylish, a man one might meet at a fashionable rout or ball. Well-shaped legs, broad shoulders needing no padding to enhance them, a warm smile and a pair of roguishly twinkling blue eyes... all of this Nell observed appreciatively as he entered the room.

He looked from Nell to Maria, and then settled his gaze firmly on Nell. "Mrs Caldicott? Wife of Captain Jude Caldicott?"

"I am, sir. This is my friend, Mrs Delanoy."

He bowed. "Madam." Another bow, fractionally less deep. "Mrs Delanoy." The two women curtsied in response. Then he spotted the children. "And these must be... no, no, let me guess, if you please. I think... the Miss Delanoys and... hmm, Master Caldicott?"

"That is so," Nell said, with a small smile. Lucy and Jane were clearly Maria's, for they had her dark curls, but Louis was more difficult to place. He had his father's blond hair, but his nose and mouth were all Nell and his eyes were his grandmother's. "Please sit down, Mr Harbottle."

She sat herself, and he then took the chair opposite.

"Thank you so much for agreeing to see me, Mrs Caldicott. Were your husband available, I should not have dreamt of troubling you, but I understand that he is at sea, and not expected home for some days yet."

"That is so. He commands the *Brig Minerva*, which is due to return in a few days, but with the vagaries of the weather and so forth…"

"Oh, quite, quite. Then perhaps I may be permitted to address my enquiries to you, in his absence?" She nodded her assent. "You are most gracious, madam."

He made her a small bow, and there was a brightness in his eye as he looked at her that she recognised. Such looks had once been very familiar to her. She had danced or moved about or talked or simply walked into a room, and men had looked at her with just such admiration. It startled her to realise that she still had that power. How gratifying that, at the age of six and twenty, she could arouse such a response in a passing stranger. She was aware of a little bloom of pleasure inside her, for who could not delight in having an admirer, even one so fleeting as Mr Harbottle?

He went on, "Let me not try your patience with useless chatter, but get straight to the point. I am searching for my cousin, one Felix Harbottle from Yorkshire, who was a naval officer at one time with the rank of captain. There was a breach with the family some twenty years ago when he married against the wishes of his family. We lost touch with him, although he wrote to his mother every year on her birthday — each time from a different port. So we know he is still alive, and still hearing the call of the sea, although no longer with the navy. Now his mother wishes to set aside the past and reconcile with her son, so she has charged me with the task of finding him. For two years, Mrs Caldicott, I have been searching diligently, but so far in vain. The navy has no trace of him, his former friends have had no word of him, and so I have moved from port to port, enquiring."

"From port to port? There are a great many ports in England, sir."

He laughed, and again Nell noticed those deep blue eyes, and his hair just that colour she so admired — like pale honey. But she had been driven astray by fair hair and amused blue eyes before, she reminded herself sternly.

"Indeed there are a great many ports, and sometimes I feel as if I have ventured into every one of them. However, most are fishing ports only, and I cannot feel that a former naval captain would be commanding a trawler, so I have restricted myself to the major ports only. I began with those from which a letter had arrived, and have now extended my reach to others, and here I am in your fair town, Mrs Caldicott. Southampton is a charming place and has... many attractions..." Here he paused and looked at Nell in a manner which there was no mistaking. "However, in one respect it differs not a whit from every other port in the country, in that no one has ever heard of Captain Felix Harbottle. May I hope for better tidings from you, Mrs Caldicott? Has your husband ever mentioned such a person?"

"My husband? I am very sorry, Mr Harbottle, but he has not."

"I am told that Captain Caldicott was also in His Majesty's Navy at one time, is that so?"

"He was, but it is a very large navy," she said with a smile. "I do not imagine Captain Caldicott knew more than a small number of its officers. Besides, he rarely speaks of his time in the navy. One or two of the battles, sometimes, with Louis, who has an interest in such things, but nothing of the people he knew."

It was a thing she had always thought odd, that he could talk impersonally of this battle or that, almost like an account in the newspaper, yet never mention the men involved. She had supposed it was his way of coping with the horrors of war, and had never pressed him.

"Do you know of any man, any officer on a ship and formerly in the navy, answering to my cousin's description? A man of three and forty, with fair hair and blue eyes?"

Nell considered that. "Captain Walker?" Mr Harbottle shook his head. "Captain Phillipson, then. Oh, but he was never in the navy, I believe."

"Neither of them has graced His Majesty's Navy."

"It is a common combination of features, but the navy... so few men leave the navy entirely. And then there is the age. My own husband would fit that description precisely, except for the age. He is not yet forty. Also, he married only nine years ago, not twenty, so his history is very different from that of your cousin. I am so sorry I cannot help."

"There is just one more chance. May I show you my cousin's likeness? Just in case you have ever encountered him under a different name, perhaps, or passed him by in the street." He produced a small framed miniature from a pocket, and handed it to her. "It was taken when he was but fifteen and only a midshipman, almost thirty years ago, but it is all we have of him."

She gazed at the boy's face, youthful and optimistic, and remembered the time when Jude had been just as hopeful of life, his eyes bright and lips curved into a perpetual smile, before disappointment had soured his disposition.

"I am very sorry," she said. "I do not recognise him. Maria, you go about the town more than I do — do you know anyone like this?"

Maria examined it, but then she shook her head. "He is a fine looking young man, but I don't know him."

"Ah." Mr Harbottle sat back in his chair, disappointment written on his countenance. "That is a pity. But perhaps you would be so good as to tell your husband of my enquiry, Mrs Caldicott? He may write to me if he has any information."

"I shall certainly tell him, sir. May I offer you some refreshment, Mr Harbottle? I am afraid that I have no tea or wine today, but there is ale and cake if—"

"You are too kind, madam," he said rising gracefully to his feet. "I have taken up too much of your time altogether, and will now leave you in peace. And you three," he added, looking at the children, "may return to your studies. What is the lesson today?"

They sat mutely, staring at him.

Nell laughed. "Do not imagine them to be ill-mannered, Mr Harbottle. They have been given the strictest instructions not to speak a word while you are here, on pain of— Well, I shall think of some dire penalty, I daresay."

"Then they are exceptionally dutiful, and I commend them," he said at once. "And their mamas, who have instilled such obedience into them. But may I examine your slates and see if I may guess the topic?"

Permission granted, he bounded across the room and picked up one of the slates. " 'Six yards of muffin at one and six the yard'. Muffin? Oh, *muslin*. That should be easy... let me see... that will be... four and fivepence three farthings... no, wait... twelve guineas... no, no, that cannot be right..."

The children giggled, and Nell smiled, too, and exchanged a glance with Maria, who was trying not to laugh.

"No, I cannot work it out," Mr Harbottle said. "You will have to tell me the answer."

"You are just funning, I can tell," Louis said. "You do know the answer. It is nine shillings."

"Is it?" Jane said. "Is that correct, Mr Harbottle?"

"It is indeed," he said, "and a very pretty gown it will make for one of the ladies. Let me see now... green, I think, if it be for Mrs Delanoy, and for Mrs Caldicott... blue, to match her eyes, do you not agree, Miss Delanoy? Or even white, if there be some blue upon it also, and a shawl of gold, with a gold chain about her neck, and sapphires on her fingers. Yes, that is what you should be wearing, Mrs Caldicott."

He smiled at her so charmingly that she could not possibly take offence. Nevertheless, she was very glad that Jude was not there to hear such flirtatious words.

END OF SAMPLE CHAPTER of *The Widow*

For more information or to buy, go to:
http://marykingswood.co.uk.

Made in the USA
San Bernardino, CA
02 January 2020

62575595R00227